AUG 1 5 2013

PRAISE FOR THE DARK AGE DAWNING NOVELS

MIDNIGHT

"The world in this s̲ _____ nse, and the setting is so _____ _ews

"I loved every secon_ _____ _th intriguing and solid _____ ___ to any fan of paranormal, fan̲tasy, or sci-fi romance, or for people looking to try something in that field." —*All About Romance*

"Ellen Connor's Dark Age Dawning series contains the best of the postapocalyptic genre with a strong paranormal twist . . . Her main characters and those who surround them are, out of a necessity, strong, yet their vulnerabilities are what draw the reader to them, and give the reader the ability to feel the shattered world through their eyes." —*Fresh Fiction*

"A dark tale of endurance that manages to hang on to a flame of hope. A bare-knuckle struggle for survival gives this intense story poignancy and a gritty realism."
—*RT Book Reviews* (Top Pick)

NIGHTFALL

"Dark, intense, and downright scary, this book is pretty full of awesome. The world they have created just might give you nightmares, but I also bet you won't be able to put this book down." —*Smexy Books*

"The absolute best thing about this book was the world. I have never read a romance like it, and it rocked my world. It felt so fresh and different from the usual paranormal romances."
—*Fiction Vixen Book Reviews*

continued . . .

"A chilling postapocalyptic series . . . Frighteningly intense in its depiction of the struggle to survive in a world run amok, there's edge-of-your-seat thrills mingled with supernatural forces, giving rise to a dangerous and passionate story."

—*RT Book Reviews* (Top Pick)

"A fascinating new series. *Nightfall* was an extraordinary introduction to a new postapocalyptic mythical world . . . This was a book that I just could *not* put down, and once it was over, all I could think was that I cannot wait to reenter the new Dark Ages!" —*Night Owl Reviews*

"One of my favorite aspects of *Nightfall* was its ability to be romantic, funny, and scary as hell—all in the same chapter. The story line was solid, the tension tense, and the twist both heart-wrenching and inspiring." —*Bitten By Books*

DAYBREAK

"An unforgettable tale packed with treachery, betrayal, and hope. A crisp storytelling style keeps the pace moving, and there's lots of emotional resonance. An outstanding capper to a terrific series." —*RT Book Reviews* (Top Pick)

"I've been looking forward to this book since I first met Tru back in *Nightfall* . . . If you haven't given this series a try, I recommend you get out there and rectify that. You're missing out." —*Fiction Vixen Book Reviews*

"A strong postapocalyptic thriller. Extremely fast-paced throughout, yet vividly descriptive of the dark landscape and starring two fascinating heroes." —*Genre Go Round Reviews*

"Ellen Connor maintains the same exciting, suspenseful undertone throughout the novel and the series. *Daybreak* is a masterful story based in an intriguing dystopian world."

—*Fresh Fiction*

Berkley Sensation titles by Ellen Connor

NIGHTFALL
MIDNIGHT
DAYBREAK

MIDNIGHT

Ellen Connor

3 9075 04837933 0

BERKLEY SENSATION, NEW YORK

THE BERKLEY PUBLISHING GROUP
Published by the Penguin Group
Penguin Group (USA) Inc.
375 Hudson Street, New York, New York 10014, USA

USA | Canada | UK | Ireland | Australia | New Zealand | India | South Africa | China

Penguin Books Ltd., Registered Offices: 80 Strand, London WC2R 0RL, England
For more information about the Penguin Group, visit penguin.com.

MIDNIGHT

A Berkley Sensation Book / published by arrangement with the authors

Copyright © 2011 by Ann Aguirre and Carrie Lofty.
All rights reserved. No part of this book may be reproduced, scanned, or distributed in any
printed or electronic form without permission. Please do not participate in or encourage piracy
of copyrighted materials in violation of the author's rights. Purchase only authorized editions.

Berkley Sensation Books are published by The Berkley Publishing Group.
BERKLEY SENSATION® is a registered trademark of Penguin Group (USA) Inc.
The "B" design is a trademark of Penguin Group (USA) Inc.

For information, address: The Berkley Publishing Group,
a division of Penguin Group (USA) Inc.,
375 Hudson Street, New York, New York 10014.

ISBN: 978-0-425-25440-0

PUBLISHING HISTORY
Berkley Sensation trade paperback edition / September 2011
Berkley Sensation mass-market paperback edition / August 2013

PRINTED IN THE UNITED STATES OF AMERICA

10 9 8 7 6 5 4 3 2 1

Cover art by Gene Mollica.

This is a work of fiction. Names, characters, places, and incidents either are the product
of the author's imagination or are used fictitiously, and any resemblance to actual persons,
living or dead, business establishments, events, or locales is entirely coincidental.
The publisher does not have any control over and does not assume any responsibility for
author or third-party websites or their content.

If you purchased this book without a cover, you should be aware that this book is
stolen property. It was reported as "unsold and destroyed" to the publisher, and neither
the author nor the publisher has received any payment for this "stripped book."

ALWAYS LEARNING   **PEARSON**

For our friends,
who stand by us in dark times and in light

ACKNOWLEDGMENTS

Once again we would like to acknowledge those individuals whose talent, affection, and support made this novel possible. Thank you to Laura Bradford, our first and most loyal advocate, and to Cindy Hwang for being the voice that guides and nurtures our ideas. The Penguin team remains incredible at all stages, and our heartfelt, astonished thanks to artist Gene Mollica for such gorgeous covers. We had no idea we could be so fortunate!

With love and appreciation, we thank our families for their encouragement and serenity in the face of our occasional bouts of crazy: Andres, Andrea, and Alek, as well as Keven, Juliette, Ilsa, and Dennis and Kathleen Stone.

Additional thanks to Larissa Ione, Sasha Knight, Jenn Bennett, Lauren Dane, Donna J. Herren, Carolyn Jewel, and Megan Hart, plus Cathleen DeLong, Zoe Archer, Patti Ann Colt, Kelly Schaub, and the Broken Writers. We hope you know how much your unfailing friendships mean to us and to the success of projects such as these. Thanks to Fedora Chen for her fantastic proofreading.

To our readers, we offer our sincere appreciation. *Mid-*

night is a tough and gritty journey, but as always, we promise the happy ending our toughened lovers deserve. Please let us know your thoughts! Contact us at author.ellen.connor@ gmail.com, and learn about upcoming books by visiting www.EllenConnor.com.

ONE

As time draws its unending circle in stone and bone, the pieces of the old world will be refashioned. Old skills will become new again. Through cooperation will new lives be forged, with bricks and mortar, loyalty and skill.

The monsters are not all raging beasts. Their dark, potent sickness will take many forms. Magic, however, will see into pure souls and provide extraordinary gifts. Logic must be set aside, even among those least prone to leaps of faith. Those who can leap will fly.

—Translated from the ancient Chinese prophet Xi'an Xi's personal writings

"We move in ten. Jameson, you run the count."

While Jameson was thin and quiet, he had a scary affinity for knives—and that meant nobody would question her choice. He was the child of a Filipina mother and an American GI, and when his dad died, leaving them destitute, he'd battled his way to some renown and joined an underground fight circuit. He earned enough money to bring his family to the New United States, but the Change meant no place was much better than another.

Rosa smiled. *Except Valle de Bravo.*

As deadly as any man in camp, Jameson held up his fingers, and everyone watched as he curled them down, one by one. Vibrations rocked the ground. Vehicles were few and far between these days. Only the old ones could be coaxed into running, if they didn't have computer chips or electronic components. It was also tough to find gas. But if things went well today, they'd be set for months.

Jameson completed the countdown. Rosa circled two fingers in the air, giving the signal to move out. The roar of bikes cut through the silence like a saw blade. Her driver, Falco, gunned the throttle. The motorcycle jerked into motion. Whooping, the rest of the bravos followed her lead.

In tight formation, they burst out of the scrubby undergrowth and onto the road, surrounding the truck. It was too big and bulky to gather any real speed. This shipping concern looked a little smarter than the rest. They'd done some custom bodywork, installing extra plating, iron bars, and barbed wire across the windshield.

It wouldn't do any good.

"Hold it steady!" Rosa shouted to Falco, who edged the bike closer.

He was her best driver—too bad he had delusions about what a great team they'd make in bed. So far she'd managed to keep him at arm's length, balancing the virgin/whore factor that kept her men both longing for her and afraid to touch her. But Falco was clever and more determined than most.

When the bike swung close enough, she levered into a crouch, using Falco's shoulders to steady herself. The enormous wheels spun at dizzying speed. With one misstep, she would wind up a pile of bloody meat. Pressing upright on the narrow seat, Rosa grinned.

The muscles in her thighs bunched as she pushed off. For a moment, there was only the air streaming against her face. Then she hit the side of the truck, splitting her lip against corrugated metal, but she found a handhold and pulled herself up. Gunfire cracked over the growl of the engines. One of her men swerved. Later she'd find out whether he'd been hit and how bad it was. Right now she had to focus on the job.

The sun beat down as she climbed, her arms burning with the effort of holding on. Sweat slicked her palms, making it tough, and she ignored the sound of her men returning fire. They knew their roles.

The driver tried slinging the truck, but he'd roll it if he wasn't careful. Surely he didn't want to kill himself just to keep the supplies out of their hands. Nobody was that devoted to his work.

With a pained huff, Rosa hauled herself on top of the vehicle and signaled her men to move on to phase two. The bike engines softened to a low purr as they dropped back. Now that she was in position, there was no point in them remaining as targets. They'd only waste gasoline.

Hot wind and stinging dust whipped her face while she crept along the roof of the truck, light as a cat. When she reached the cab, she slid her weapon from its thigh holster. A gun didn't need to be big to kill at close range, and anything heavier would make it hard for her to jump and climb.

Small magnets in her boots made her work a little easier. She'd often wondered if the drivers thought she had superpowers, since they could never seem to shake her off. Smiling at the thought, she dropped to her belly and set up her safety gear. Then she hooked her feet, dropped upside down beside the driver's door, and broke the glass between the iron bars—brass knuckles wrapped in cloth.

With her other hand she cocked the gun. "If you don't want to die right now, you'll stop the truck."

The driver gazed at her, wild-eyed, out of his peripheral vision. He was hardly more than a kid, but this was a brave new world. *You do what you have to.* Rosa could shoot him, disengage from the harness, and slide through the window fast enough to save the supplies. After all, she'd done it before.

From his expression, he guessed as much.

"Yes, ma'am," he said on a little moan of fear.

Maybe it wasn't nice, but given how powerless Rosa had been in her youth, his reaction was damn near an aphrodisiac. She bared her teeth in a fierce upside-down smile. "Good boy."

The truck gradually slowed. Doubtless the driver didn't want to risk having her finger slip on the trigger. Kill or be killed wasn't just a cliché. But she would always come out on top. People took advantage of the weak. She'd grown up with that knowledge burned into her brain.

When the truck stopped, her men roared back into play. She kept her weapon trained on the kid until Falco opened the passenger door and yanked him out. She could see he was pissing-scared, but the story would only enhance their rep, so she didn't rein Falco in. Instead Rosa levered back up, a feat made possible by rock hard abs. She stowed her safety gear before vaulting down with lithe grace.

Her second spoke to the driver in a low growl. "On the ground."

The kid complied, whimpering. He dropped facedown and put his hands behind his head without being asked. Word was getting around. Anyone passing through Valle lands would pay the toll or suffer reprisals. She didn't mind being considered a warlord. Fear was good for business.

Qué padre.

With teamwork and skill born of long years together, her men popped the trailer, making sure to protect against hidden guards. But no, it was a good clean haul: bottled water, toiletries, canned goods, and best of all—pre-Change liquor. Months had passed since they'd indulged in anything but *tiswin* or agave wine. The next Burning Night would be wild.

Once he secured the cargo, Jameson fastened the doors and added extra chains. It wouldn't do for anyone else to jack their stolen goods. Peltz in particular, the leader of a violent band of dust pirates, was getting too ambitious, treading on her territory as if he'd been nurturing and defending it for years.

The bravos ran back to their bikes.

"I'm leaving water and a smoke flare for you," Rosa told the kid. "Next time one of your people drives by, use it. Then tell them I own these roads. If they want to ship through my territory, they pay the toll. Otherwise I have this confiscation policy." She nudged him with a boot. *"Comprendes?"*

"Yeah," the kid squeaked.

"I've also set a sharpshooter on that ridge. If you move before he reaches a thousand, you get a bullet between the eyes. Count slow, just to be safe."

Apparently too afraid to speak, the boy nodded. Each settlement used professional wanderers who ensured the trade of necessary supplies—a dangerous task. She couldn't imagine why they had entrusted the delivery to him. A rite-of-passage thing? Or maybe this outfit was so poor and desperate that it used kids for drivers and risked the consequences of refusing her toll. Not a worry for her bravos. But an armed shipping concern like the O'Malley organization could pass through any day. Rosa needed to plan accordingly.

Falco grinned at her. "You ready to roll, *Jefa*?"

"Claro. Let's ride."

With an ease born of practice, she slid into the passenger side. One of the other bravos had his bike. Falco could drive anything with wheels, and Rosa functioned better as muscle, which confused a few bigoted *hijos de putas* at first. She only needed to beat them down once to teach that particular lesson. The bravos arrayed the bikes around the truck as a further deterrent to anyone who might mess with them. Still, she wouldn't let her guard down until they reached Valle de Bravo.

Falco glanced over at her, one hand on the wheel. "We lighting up the dance hall tonight?"

Burning Night was a tradition everybody enjoyed. But they knew better than to indulge on the same night as a successful raid. Such activity never failed to attract the attention of local nomads, who looked for any opportunity to catch the town unawares. Peltz, especially, seemed eager to exploit them. He was craftier than most. But Rosa was smarter; she'd had to be.

"We'll give it a night or two," she said. "Then we can cut loose. The bravos deserve it."

The liquor would make for a hell of a party, and the men

would have more fun if more women waited in town, but Rosa didn't mind the unique position of power. With the male-to-female ratio at such an imbalance, the bravos knew better than to demand monogamy—or they'd wind up with no tail at all. They'd had a little trouble at the start, but two executions had ensured that the rest of the Valle's males got the message.

No always means no.

"You and me, then?"

Rosa glanced over at her second, suppressing a sigh. Falco was tasty, if you went for the rugged, muscular, sun-toughened type—brown hair with lighter streaks, nice blue eyes. But she knew his game. He figured if he moved into her bed permanently, he'd take the de facto role of boss man. Not that he was a bad guy. He'd made his intentions clear.

She was having none of it.

Rosa flashed a smile to take the sting from her words. "You wish, Falco. You couldn't handle even half of me."

She pretended she wasn't tense, awaiting his response. Deliberately, she stretched her legs. Tightrope walking for fun and profit. She'd been careful not to sleep with anyone, refusing to be viewed as a sexual creature. Instead she was the militant Madonna for whom they'd die.

"One of these days, I'm gonna make you mine," he said lightly.

Yep. Right after hell freezes over, cabrón.

When the settlement came into view, she relaxed. She'd crawled to this place to die, but to her surprise, she hadn't. For months she'd hunted, gathered, and killed those mon-strous hellhounds all by herself, too tough to lie down and give up. And from there, she'd built. When survivors started to trickle in, Rosa had made it clear that the town was hers, a place where only the brave survived.

She didn't know what it had been called before, only what it was now. Valle de Bravo. The valley of the brave. The valley of her warriors.

The landscape was green in comparison with the dry

land that surrounded it. An underground river ran through, filling the wells. That was probably why folks had settled in this spot hundreds of years earlier, perhaps abandoning it when the mines played out. Rosa had first stumbled into a ghost town. From the dirty white adobe church to the abandoned clapboard general store, it had been like stepping into a different world.

Now she took in the scene with a practiced eye. Everything looked normal. Good. No raids while they'd been gone. The possibility always concerned her when she took a large number of able-bodied men on a supply run. Any number of enemy factions would love to get a foothold here, Peltz most of all. His filthy gang moved camp too often to be found outside supernatural means.

But the perimeter was secure. The young bravo at the gate stopped them, just as he ought to. Rio was hardly old enough to shave but had hard, savage eyes. He'd crawled into town from gods only knew where, all alone, much as Rosa had been. Some townsfolk bitched about her lax immigration policy, but after having suffered the boot of the New United States' ferocious anti-immigration measures on her neck, she couldn't refuse sanctuary to anyone. Newcomers only needed to prove willing to pull their weight and follow her rules.

As long as they were human.

She smiled at Rio, taking in his too-big khaki pants and the spiked leather wristbands Singer must have made for him. He looked fierce enough to tear someone's throat out with his bare hands—and, well, he was. Her bravos had kamikaze souls.

"All clear?"

"Quiet as the grave," Rio said with a wide white smile.

He motioned for the gatekeeper to let them in, and the convoy passed into the town proper. Half the population turned out to see what they'd brought back. A shout went up when they saw the cases of quality vodka.

Viv, the woman who ran the *taberna*, took charge of those bottles. She was a weathered little woman in her late forties, but hard work had kept her fit. Between her ageless Chinese features and the skewed gender ratio, she accepted help from the six men who offered. Attentive faces revealed anticipation, hoping for her company.

Rosa kept herself above that game. It wasn't hard. She'd spent enough hours pinned under grunting, sweating men to be glad of the Change. Apart from Falco, most of the bravos saw her as *la jefa*, not a woman to be banged in celebration of a successful raid.

They knelt to her before each job and kissed her finger-tips, having sworn blood loyalty to Valle de Bravo. Rosa insisted on the ritual because she knew such things strengthened spoken bonds. Now all her bravos bore tats, marking them as hers. She who took none as her own claimed them all.

Wicker, who ran the general store, assumed responsibility for the majority of items. The town ran on a barter system, and since the old man had once managed a business of his own, he was in charge of keeping the books. Too old to fight now, he had a calm temperament well suited to the task. Such a useful occupation salved his pride.

At the back of the truck, they found a rare cache of booty. Fabric. A soft "ahh" went up from the women. New clothes. Rosa couldn't remember the last time she'd worn anything new, made just for her. Sometimes they traded among themselves for variety, but it wasn't the same. This would be good for morale.

For a few moments Rosa watched the work, overwhelmed with a quiet sense of accomplishment. She'd done this, a woman who had never been able to get a decent job, no matter how smart she was. Pride swelled in her chest, making each breath hotter and sweeter.

I did this. These are my people.

And then the cry went up from Rio at the gate. "Raiders incoming!"

Rosa cocked her gun and ran.

TWO

ONE MONTH LATER

Chris jerked awake and sat half upright. A rock gouged the palm of one hand. The vivid spring dawn made him squint. He checked his weapon and found it primed nearby, but he heard no threat. The secluded crevice where he'd made his night camp served as a trusted partner at his back.

The last of his weariness gone, he eased out from the crevice and surveyed the surrounding gorge. Creosote bushes bloomed along the jagged upslope of striated limestone, their roots clinging to the smallest holds. A woodpecker made a racket, reminding him of those first few months after the Change hit the West Coast. They hadn't seen sign of any wildlife, not even insects, until the demon dogs had cleared out, starving and defeated. That so many natural creatures still thrived in the world should have given him some reason to smile, but Chris hardly remembered how.

He checked his Beretta in its holster and slumped against the cold, solid rock wall. A dream must have woken him. Closing his eyes, his skin already covered in goose bumps, he tried to recapture the last few moments of unconsciousness, fully expecting to find memories of blood. But the lingering images were not so violent. He saw a wisp of white, a flash of corn-silk hair.

Whenever he dreamed of Penny—the child he'd left behind after her mother died—he walked south . . . and always found something remarkable. Once he'd found water, just in time to keep his dehydrated body from shutting down. Another time he'd found a young girl. She'd been hiding in a tree, stranded after escaping a pack of demon dogs and too scared to climb down. In appreciation, her brother and mother had opened their meager stores to him.

Reluctant curiosity tugged him to his feet. After a quick piss, he packed his gear and stepped into the sharp daylight.

Climbing up the short bank of what might have once been a river, he allowed himself to think about Penny. It was for the best that she lived with his friends Jenna and Mason now. After Ange died, he had found it impossible to stick around beyond the spring thaw.

And Chris was alone. That too was for the best.

He reached the top of the rise and looked over the desert. Dawn still tinted the landscape, but the dry heat sizzling the back of his neck foretold the coming day. He scratched his jaw through his beard and searched for abnormalities. No voices. No prickling sensation of another human presence.

But then came an unexpected sound—an old sound that took a long minute to place.

Trucks.

What the hell?

He held as still as death, leaning nearer to the source as if that gesture might make the unbelievable more real.

Trucks.

He set off at an easy run. Across the length of the country, always heading south, he'd seen the occasional working vehicle and the trouble it could bring. Gasoline supplies had gone scarce, and owners developed twitchy trigger fingers when it came to protecting their valuables.

But he hadn't heard a big-throated, full-throttle rumble since Before—almost like rush hour and coffee shops and the White House. Old things. He gave up on pacing himself and hit a full run. The wonder of his legs responding to such an impulse no longer surprised him. After nearly four years of wandering, he wouldn't recognize himself in the mirror. Hard-won resilience waited in every muscle, with every strike of his boots against the flinty earth.

At the next rise he crept along on his belly and looked down. Glasses he'd relied on for years to correct a slight astigmatism had broken back near Colorado, but he didn't need them to see the distant remains of a two-lane highway. Long-ago engineers had blasted a canyon right through the middle of a wide granite plateau. The highway ran like a river down the middle. Without steady repairs from human custodians, baked asphalt had become striped with fissures. Despite the flowers and grass lining each crack, it reminded Chris of puckered scar tissue.

He burrowed his fingers into the cool, dry earth. Waiting. From along the western horizon rolled the trucks. Sunlight glinted off chrome, and dust swirled from beneath the tires.

Where had they come from? Who operated them? And where the hell had they found enough gas to speed along at a hundred kilometers an hour?

The sound of a gun being cocked turned his blood to ice.

"Don't move." A man's voice. Deep. Southern.

Chris lay still with his cheek pressed against the dirt. The Beretta at his hip might as well have been back in Oregon, but if he could get off his stomach, he might have a chance.

A heavy boot pressed between his shoulder blades. The man ground down and pressed cold gunmetal against the back of Chris's neck. "You armed?"

"Yes." His vocal cords felt fused together, and he tried

to remember the last time he'd spoken. Weeks. Maybe months. Not even to himself, that old mainstay of staying sane.

The man made a quiet grunt as he crouched and started a quick search, his motions rough and efficient.

"I was just passing through," he said as the man's hand neared the Beretta.

"Then no one will miss you."

"True enough."

"Then why are you smiling?"

Chris used that moment to strike. He swung his elbow back and up, connecting with his captor's inner wrist. The gun clattered to the rock. Turning sharply, Chris yanked the boot that had pinned his shoulder blades and twisted. The man fell heavily onto his back, clutching his wrist as his hand spasmed. A grimace warped his features, but he tried to kick with his free foot. They scuffled in the dirt, exchanging grunts and punches, until Chris scrambled to his knees.

He grabbed the Beretta off his hip, unhooked the safety, and pointed at his opponent's head. "Because I got nothing to lose."

Staring down his adversary, Chris realized what a lucky bastard he was. He'd thought Mason a big guy, but this man was *huge*—tall and muscular. Those trucks down on the highway could plow headlong into his chest and he wouldn't flinch.

Chris took aim at his bald head, where dark skin gleamed with sweat. Guns were pretty amazing when it came to leveling the odds.

"Don't kill me," the man said.

"Don't make me. What's your name?"

"Folks call me Brick."

Slowly Chris sidestepped until he could kneel and pick up Brick's discarded pistol—an ancient Colt .45. "All your weapons on the ground. Slowly."

A set of brass knuckles, a retractable truncheon, a palm-sized .22, and a wicked bowie knife hit the ground one by one. Chris loaded them into his satchel, never taking his attention from his prisoner. He didn't want those same weapons turned against him, should Brick get the upper hand again, but kicking them over the cliff would be an unthinkable waste.

"On your stomach," Chris said. "Arms and legs splayed."

Brick's snarling expression said that he didn't take orders well from strangers. But when Chris cocked his Beretta, the man obeyed. He lowered his body to the ground and went spread-eagled.

Chris shoved the Colt down the back of his waistband and frisked Brick, keeping his concentration on high alert. No sense in falling victim to the same ploy. He got the very strong sense that he'd only get lucky once against such a man.

Satisfied that he was drawing down on an unarmed opponent, Chris nudged Brick's ribs with the toe of his boot. "Up. On your knees. Hands behind your head."

Brick did as he was told, but only just. Yellow dust coated his damp T-shirt.

"I don't want to hurt you," Chris said. "Just passing through, like I said."

"Better pass through pretty damn quick once you turn your back on me."

"Won't turn my back, then. Thanks for the tip." The rumbling trucks were right down from them now. Chris climbed partway up an embankment. From that position he could see an entire east-west expanse of highway and keep the pistol leveled on his captive's chest.

"Can you fire a rifle?" Brick asked. For the first time, his voice didn't sound so murderous.

"I'm a fair shot. Why?"

"Because my people down there are expecting backup from me. High-vantage cover."

"Too bad."

"Man, I mean it. I need to be ready. They'll be sitting ducks otherwise."

"Should've done what you were told and left me alone."

Chris frowned. "How were you going to give cover without a rifle?"

Still kneeling, Brick kept his hands on his head, his elbows out wide. "In my bag, four meters to your left."

"Don't move."

Backing away from where Brick knelt, Chris located the satchel. By touch alone he identified the contents: a disassembled rifle. The man wasn't lying, but he couldn't very well hand him a weapon. Chris couldn't tell who he'd be helping if Brick's people were successful.

He could use some supplies. The food he'd had of late was scrounged from cactus and an occasional unlucky fox. And ammo. He needed ammo. If Brick knew the Beretta only contained three bullets, he'd probably risk a shoot-out. Even hoping that a favor could buy entrance into a community and replenish his stores, Chris resisted the urge to trust. Since the Change, people had become intensely tribal and reluctant to welcome strangers.

He'd be better off moving on. At least he could snag a new rifle and the other weapons. But instinct honed on his own told him that was the wrong move. Brick's pride had been damaged. If his people suffered, he'd track Chris down to hand over the blame—and any punishment. He knew this area better too. *Not a good idea to make this man my enemy.*

He looped the sack across his chest and returned to his position overlooking Brick and the highway.

The trucks had stopped just below, flanked by motorcycles. A dozen people roamed over the stalled vehicles. Soon the truckers had been yanked from their cabs, stripped of their clothes, and bound in a daisy chain by the side of the road. Chris couldn't make out facial details, but the attackers' body language seemed calm. A practiced operation.

Light glinted in a pattern.

"That's my signal," Brick said with his deep, deep voice. "They'll send backup if I don't respond."

"Nope. No way. Stay put. Better to let them think you

fell asleep, or that a rattlesnake took a bite out of your calf. Things happen." Chris stepped closer—but not within lunging distance. No way he could miss from that distance. The bunching muscle at Brick's jawline said he knew as much. "But don't even think about shouting for help. You'd be brainless before they even heard it."

"They could still need my help."

"Don't know," Chris said, flicking his gaze to the valley floor. "They seem to have everything pretty well in hand. How are you going to meet them? You have a vehicle too?"

"Yes. Two hundred meters to the east."

Chris circled his prisoner until they faced one another. "Look, I'm a doctor." Though technically a lie, his years spent learning animal anatomy put him light-years ahead of most people left in the world. "I propose a trade. If you take me to your camp, I'll offer my services for a week."

Brick scowled, his brain working hard behind his intense gaze. "In return for what?"

"Food, water, ammo. Nothing excessive. Just enough to get me on my way again."

"And if I don't?"

"I don't want to shoot you in the thigh, but I will. Your people will come for you, but they might not get here in time to stop the bleeding." Chris narrowed his eyes. The tension along his neck and shoulder blades sizzled. "I can't have you following me. Sorry."

"How do I know you're not lying?"

Chris side-shuffled over to his bag and used his left hand to unzip it. He angled the contents toward Brick. "Microscope. Scalpel set. Medical supplies. You see them?"

"Sure. But if you're a doc, you won't shoot me."

Cruel laughter bubbled out of Chris's mouth. He hadn't even felt it coming. "Try me. And then wonder where I got the clothes I'm wearing. I don't act unless provoked, but it would be a mistake to consider me defenseless."

Brick's eyes widened. What he saw on Chris's face and heard in his voice must have been enough.

"Sure," the other man said. "*La jefa* would probably like a doc passing through. A couple of ours could use a checkup."

La jefa? A female boss. Interesting.

Down below in the canyon, the trucks rumbled to life, their noisy engines growling at the sky. Echoes made them sound like a subterranean monster roaring to life.

"Good. Let's go." Chris grabbed his bag and gestured with the Beretta. "Keep your hands up."

A motorcycle waited just to the east, where Brick said it would be.

"Yours?" he asked, nodding toward the glossy machine.

Brick rubbed a big, wide palm over the leather seat. "Nice, isn't it?"

No flashy chopper or Japanese job, it looked welded together out of pipes and corrugated tin. Barely functional, certainly dangerous, but lovingly cared for. Transportation meant options. Options meant a greater chance at survival. And if Brick was the man who kept the contraption functional, that bike represented pride in his handiwork.

Once Chris had hidden away from people, focusing instead on the ways and patterns of mountain lions. Solitary creatures. Wide-ranging territories. But the last five years had cast his own species in a new, more flattering light—just as animal, but with a cleverness and ingenuity that seemed like a candle with a dwindling wick.

So few of us left.

Brick's tribe, whoever they were, seemed to have clung to a measure of technology and order. They had vehicles, organization, a settlement of some kind. Part of Chris's reason for wanting to meet them was pure curiosity. He'd encountered clusters of people barely clinging to life, cowed by the Change and the barbarism that had followed. Others didn't cower; they fought to the point of complete destruction. No society. No hint of humanity. What he hadn't seen was a fully functional group on a scale large enough to pull off that robbery on the highway.

He also wanted to know where those trucks had come from. Wandering down from the Pacific Northwest had offered no evidence to contradict the theory that civilization was finished. Supplies delivered en masse by semis suggested otherwise, and he wanted to know who was running the world after the Change. He'd learn what he could and move on.

Staying long enough to make friends and then watching them die was just too damn hard.

"Throw the keys at my feet," Chris said. "I'll give them back when we reach your camp. For now we're walking."

"They'll all jump you, you know. If not before, when we reach Valle de Bravo."

Valley of the brave? Nice. Chris liked the confidence of it—a big middle finger to the whole fucking mess.

"You'll just have to convince them that I mean business and that I'm worth keeping alive."

"Why would I do that?"

"Because you're closest to my pistol. And I meant what I said about having nothing to lose."

THREE

Rosa hated this part of her job.

Victory could make assholes out of otherwise perfectly good men, but when one went too far, she made an example of him. Thank God the idiot hadn't succeeded in raping Singer, or there would be no saving him. He'd gotten carried away after their return from the raid, forgotten his manners.

Regardless, it couldn't be allowed to stand. The bravo, Lem, stood lashed to the post in the center of town, blindfolded. Swift justice kept the reins in Rosa's hands. The minute she showed a hint of hesitation, Falco would try to take over, and running Valle required too much energy to devote to infighting, especially as Peltz's raids became more brazen.

She surveyed her audience. Most of the town had turned out after the trucks rolled in, and they stayed for the whipping. With an arc of her arm, she tested the leather, which gave a brisk snap. Tied to the post, Lem made a sound in his throat, half anger, half terror. Punishment was always worse when you couldn't see it coming. As if recognizing Rosa's readiness to begin, the crowd quieted.

"Lem didn't respect Singer's wishes when she asked him to leave her be." Rosa's voice carried well through the desert silence. "She has the bruises on her arms to prove it. Since this was his first offense, he gets ten lashes."

She didn't need to articulate what would happen if he offended twice. Valle de Bravo did not permit repeat offenders. When it came down to it, she performed the executions herself. Rosa had no taste for it, but sometimes a leader had to suck it up and deal.

Though the day was still young, the sun shone high overhead. Sweat trickled down her brow. Without another word, she laid into the young man. Her whip bit into Lem's back, but he didn't cry out. The leather sliced his skin, deep enough to leave marks but not so deep that he'd be disfigured.

Lem took his ten. When Rosa finished, Viv untied him and helped him to the *taberna* for a drink. She'd probably tend his wounds and make sure he didn't develop a lasting hatred of females. They'd perfected the routine over the last few years. Viv was better at doling out tenderness, whereas Rosa had nothing to give but steel and bone. The softness had been burned out of her beneath an unforgiving desert sun.

She fought off a wave of memory that would make her weak. How fucking sad—the end of the world had *improved* her life.

If only José were still with her to enjoy it . . .

The coppery tang of blood cloyed in her nostrils. She glanced down. The crimson flower of Lem's punishment had sprayed across her faded gray shirt. Though a man's garment at one point, Singer's cleverness with a needle had tailored a custom fit. Rosa wore it with a pair of khaki army pants, more because of the pockets than for any other reason. During her travels she'd hit an army navy surplus store, so her wardrobe contained a lot of military touches.

Still, appearances could be misleading. She'd even heard men say she looked sweet and harmless . . . until she smiled.

Brick was late coming back from his part in the raid, which was a blessing. Heading toward the gate, Rosa shaded her brow with her palm. She needed to head him off before someone else gave him the news. Usually he was a gentle giant, but when his sister came into play, he lost his mind. Singer was his last link to their old world. Shaken as she was, she could use a hug from her big brother. Lem was lucky Rosa had doled out the official punishment before Brick returned and broke his neck.

The sentry briefed her as she strode to the gate. "No sign."

"Strange," she said. "We should at least see a dust trail from his bike by now."

"You want me to send someone out?"

They'd driven off Peltz's men a few weeks before, but one could never be too careful. The sky was as blue as an angel's eyes and just as untouchable. Planes didn't roar overhead anymore, only the distant rush of wings from carrion birds. Nothing moved in the scrub apart from one old lizard that might have been one of Tilly's wild pets. Quiet was good.

"No," she said at last. "Brick's a big boy. We'll give him an hour."

A shout from another guard grabbed her attention. Rosa jogged over to where Manuel stood with a set of binoculars. He was older than Rio by three or four years. The two were close. Such bonds mattered in Valle, giving people a sense of community that made them willing to fight for its survival.

"There," he said, pointing.

Rosa took the binoculars and found her target. Targets, plural. *"¿Qué es eso?"*

Brick was walking his bike through the creosote and tumbleweeds. Not too surprising. He was forever battling that piece of shit to keep it running. And he seemed fine—

no limp and no visible injuries. The surprise was that he had company. Armed company.

"Be ready," she said to Manuel, handing back the binocs. "Brick's made a friend."

Rosa unfurled her whip and called all available bravos to man the front gate. By the time the two came into range, her crew had them pinned a dozen ways. Though she didn't like taking aim at Brick, she needed to make it clear that she didn't negotiate with hostiles.

Manuel called from his perch, "Throw down your weapon."

"No," the stranger said.

Brick propped his motorcycle on its kickstand and let his hands fall to his sides. "He's a doctor. He could've hurt me . . . but he didn't. That's all I can say."

There were no more doctors, any more than there were teachers, librarians, or bookstores. The youngest resident the town had ever sheltered had been five. Young Andre had been a baby when the shit hit the fan. When Rosa suggested that Andre might be ready to read, his mother had shrugged and asked, "Why?"

Not that it mattered now. They were both gone, like so many others.

"Let him come closer," she said.

Stepping out from behind her guards, Rosa approached the gate. Leaders made confident decisions. If the man had wanted trouble, he would have made some already. Distrust colored their world now, but so did quick action. Here, Valle promised sanctuary to all humans.

We're a dying breed now.

"What's your name?" she asked.

"Chris Welsh."

Rosa assessed him in a glance: everything about him told a story. Tawny hazel eyes set in a lean, sun-browned face, slightly irregular features, and wavy brown hair identified him as a white man. The full beard said he'd been away from what passed for civilization, which meant he possessed respectable survival skills. His battered boots spoke of a long walk. She surprised herself by noticing his mouth—and the lovely curve of his lower lip. He smelled of sage, sweat, and hot wind.

He'd also taken on Brick and won. A man like that could be useful, regardless of his claim that he was a doctor.

Her analysis took only a few seconds, but Chris didn't seem to notice. He was too busy staring at the whip. Rosa smiled. She tended to have that effect on men.

"Is that blood on your shirt?" Brick asked.

By Welsh's expression, it seemed he'd wondered the same thing.

She glanced down. No one could deliver ten solid lashes without a little spatter. "There was a little trouble after we got back."

"Is Singer all right?" Always, Brick's first concern was for his sister.

This wasn't going to be fun.

"She's fine, just a little shaken up." Rosa put a hand on the big man's chest. It wasn't her strength that stopped him, but her authority. "I took care of it."

"Who was it?"

"Lem. No further reprisals. Understand?"

Brick's jaw clenched at the same time his fingers curled into fists. "I respect the rules."

"Then feel free to go see Singer. She needs your affection right now."

"Did he—?"

"No," she said, shaking her head. "I swear to you, no. He wouldn't have gotten off with a whipping if he had."

The massive bravo responded with a fierce nod.

Rosa turned to the stranger, fingers still curled around the coiled leather of her whip. "Trouble or not? Your call."

"Not."

Although he didn't put his Beretta away, he dragged a set of keys out of his jeans pocket. He returned them to Brick, along with the man's Colt and rifle satchel. Again Rosa was impressed, despite herself.

"I made a promise," he said simply.

Brick set off down the dusty street with his motorcycle, leaving Rosa his desert stray. She cocked her head and waited. Silence revealed a lot about a man. Some cracked open and babbled. Some got pushy. This one, however, only looked her up and down. Not a challenge. Just . . . *awareness*.

"You're the boss here."

"I *am* Valle de Bravo," she told him. "Rosa Cortez."

She didn't extend a hand for him to shake. That would imply they were equals. If he proved worthy, he could kneel and pledge to her as a bravo. Otherwise he could move along.

"It's impressive what you've done here," he said. "I've come a hell of a long way and never seen anything like this."

That rang a bell for her. If he'd crossed a lot of territory, he might have news. It wasn't like they could turn on a radio and get an update, and the professional wanderers were only interested in trade. The potential for fresh facts was worth the risk of letting him stay a few days. Information was gold, and he might know more than he thought he did—maybe about rumors of General O'Malley consolidating power in the east. She could use such info to defend Valle and plan successful raids.

While the bravos loved Rosa now, their regard might wane if times grew lean. She'd stay on top, no matter what she needed to do.

"We'll get you geared up, assuming you have anything we want. The town operates on the barter system. There's just one thing we need from you first."

"Why do I have the feeling that's the catch?"

"Because you seem like a smart man," Rosa said. "You just need to pass a little test before we can let you roam free among our own."

Almost casually, although Rosa knew otherwise, he played with the safety on his pistol. "What test?"

"Valle is human territory. Skinwalkers aren't welcome

here. If they have brains enough to heed a warning, we advise them to move along. If they're the other kind, we kill them."

"You want me to prove I'm human. How am I supposed to do that?"

Rosa grinned, knowing she was scarier when she did. "Leave that to us."

But her smile didn't shift him. He grinned right back, raising the hairs on her nape. "Will it hurt?"

"Is that a dare?"

"Just a question."

"You'll live through it, unless you show claw and can't understand us after the shift."

His eyes remained inscrutable behind his bland expression. He shrugged as if whatever she offered couldn't be worse than what lay behind him. That made her curious.

"Bring it on," he said, his voice a sexy rasp.

"Glutton for punishment?"

A weight of secrets hid in his moss-gold gaze. For a dizzying moment she had the awful feeling that he could see right through her, as if the sunlight had made her a window, transparent except for all the dirty streaks. Rosa held his gaze with effort and widened her smile.

"Not particularly," he said. "It'll be worth it to sleep in a bed, eat hot food."

"You assume we have hot food."

"Yes, I do."

Rosa tongued her lower lip. "How many rounds you have left in that shooter?"

"Three."

"Show me."

Chris opened the chamber and gave it a spin. His honesty and calm replies should have reassured her that he was on the level, but Rosa fought a shiver. No man had dared confront her with a direct gaze in months. His acquiescence held an undercurrent of rebellion that didn't suit her at all. *You're in command because I'm letting you,* his demeanor said.

But he had it wrong.

"Keep it holstered or it's mine. Use it against my people and you're dead. This way."

She covered the ground in long strides, reaching an outcrop of buildings. The extra sentries at the gates flanked into two sets of two. She'd trained them well. Among them was Rio, young and quick on his feet; he hadn't lost his eagerness to please. Their history meant he looked to her as sister and mother in one, and his admiration soothed a small portion of her loss.

But she would always mourn José.

"Trouble?" the kid asked.

"Not exactly. We need to do a stress test before we can grant hospitality."

The bravos nodded. Unlike punishments, which took place where everyone could see, this would be conducted quietly. That way if the newcomer shifted and went full-on hungry monster, he could be contained. Collateral damage had prompted them to learn from their mistakes.

"Are you going to tell me what to expect?" he asked as Rio led the way around the *taberna*.

There was a small building behind, generally used for storage, but they performed the tests in the old root cellar beneath it.

"No," she said. "You might change your mind."

Inside was dark and cool. No windows let in light. Stacks of salvage leaned against the walls, mystery items they'd stolen in raids. Some of it was more technical than they could handle. Maybe Chris could help determine what it was good for. But if he was a medical doctor, he probably wouldn't be good at patching shit together. The old world had specialized to the point of stupidity. Now it paid to be a jack-of-all-trades.

Chris peered at the dirt floor while Rio popped open the wood doors that covered the pit. Quicklime and wooden supports kept the packed dirt in place. The root cellar smelled of clean clay. She climbed down the rope ladder, leading the way. Like the kid he was, showing off, Rio leaped. He found and lit a candle, which cast a snapping dragon of a shadow. The other three bravos forced Chris down. When he hit bottom, he didn't look frightened as many men did. Not in the least. Rosa's stomach did a flip.

"Are you going to torture me?" He sounded remarkably composed about the whole thing, more than anyone she'd ever encountered. His tone was almost academic curiosity, and maybe a quirk of amusement.

"We're not monsters."

"And this?" he asked, gesturing to his weapon.

Rosa closed the shadowy distance between them. They locked gazes for far too long. "Hand it over."

A cat's grin shaped the masculine lips she'd admired. "If I'm gonna get rolled, I expect to get laid first."

"Excuse me?"

"If it's true that I'm just here for a test, then you can leave them with me. I don't want them stolen—no offense. They won't give me any advantage if I'm a skinwalker, and I'd have used them already if I wanted to cause trouble."

"You seem to think you're the boss of Valle. Funny." She snapped her fingers.

Rio and Manuel grabbed his arms, but again he offered no resistance as they bound him with rope. That took the satisfaction out of claiming his satchel and his Beretta.

"I've never run across a skinwalker that could keep from shifting when he's tied up in the dark," Rosa said. "Something about the stress brings the change."

"How long?"

"Eight hours will do it. Not long enough to cause you any harm. If you need to piss, Rio will help you before he leaves."

The kid shot her a look that said he'd rather die, but she already knew what Chris would say. "I'm fine. Water's been scarce."

She nodded. "For a human, this is uncomfortable. For a skinwalker, it's pure hell. We have to know the truth, and this is the easiest way. See you on the other side."

He shrugged again, with a carelessness that was fast getting under her skin. "Lights out, then."

"Yep. Lights out." Rosa scaled the rope ladder, not looking back. She already knew that whether he proved human or skinwalker, Chris Welsh was dangerous.

FOUR

The darkness in the root cellar was complete. Chris lay on a lumpy mattress, weary beyond all bearing, but hunger wouldn't let him sleep. He had given up on looking for shadows and shapes, but noises came to him in choppy bursts, keeping him company: an impatient shout, chains being dragged along concrete, laughter, distant music.

To think these people had Rosa Cortez to thank for such a miracle of humanity made Chris a little nauseous. What, exactly, had he managed? When all the columns were tabulated, he'd caused more harm than good—the opposite of the doctor he'd claimed to be.

His stomach grumbled, so he closed his eyes and allowed a moment of pure indulgence. He considered Rosa. A deceptively small woman built for battle, but she also offered intriguing hints of softness. Something about her turned his mind to sin.

Rather than think about her all at once, which was like ripping open every Christmas present as fast as possible, he picked her lips. For now, just her lips. Sneers and smirks were not the stuff of poetry, but Shakespeare had never seen a smile like hers. The upper curve had been rimmed with sweat, while the full flesh of the lower lip was chapped—or gently gnawed. Did she get nervous? Was that her release?

He couldn't wait to see more. She was succulent fruit in the midst of a wasteland.

Literally.

Of course he was hard. Eight months was a long time to go without. The last woman had been anonymous, someone he'd fucked for the release and a night's shelter. She hadn't told him her name and he hadn't asked. Such encounters had marked his years alone. His last loving touch had come from Ange—who was dead because he'd failed her. He exhaled heavily. His burgeoning arousal withered. Eyes open, he found only more darkness, but it was better than memories of blood.

How many hours had passed? Chris wondered how long Jenna would have been able to stomach being bound and abandoned in the dark before going wolf. A hell of a lot longer than eight hours. No matter how successful Rosa had made her small desert community, it wasn't safe—not if they were working on superstition and incorrect data. Part of him, the Before part, wanted to set them to rights. But working against entrenched prejudice tested his patience and would get him skinned. Scared, angry villagers didn't like hearing that Frankenstein's monster was just like them.

That hard-eyed kid opened the hatch and threw something down, then disappeared again. Despite hands bound before him, Chris groped in the dark until he found a sack that contained a skin of water and some flat bread. They didn't intend to spoil him, it seemed, until they knew his nature. Such a primitive waste of time, but he didn't let that deter him. He devoured his meal, then rolled onto his side and went to sleep.

"You're napping?" The light of purple desert dusk flooded the cellar, which meant he'd passed their absurd test.

It hadn't been bad, actually. The cool cellar was far from

the worst place he'd slept since leaving Mason and Jenna's home. At least it had been dark, safe, and out of the sun's heat. Having food in his belly helped too.

Still groggy, Chris rolled to face Rosa. He wasn't surprised to see her checking on him personally. The possibility of facing a feral, thoroughly pissed-off shifter? No problem. *La jefa* was the first down the rope ladder.

Two sets of male hands grabbed his upper arms. Rio and Brick forced him to his knees, but he didn't resist. Their trust would be hard-won.

Rosa stood before him. Later he'd dwell on how she smelled, like caramelized sugar and pure sex.

Instead Chris squinted up at the gun she held against his forehead. "Time's up?"

One look at Rosa's face should have sobered him, but he liked how fast she breathed when she was pissed. "Get him up," she said. "I can see he doesn't take this seriously."

"What? I was tired."

Rio and the other man yanked him up. Blood rushed to Chris's head and spots blinked as rapidly as he did—lack of food, lack of water. What they'd given him hadn't been enough to stave off the effects of long months of deprivation. But he couldn't give in to the dizziness. He had too much to prove, though he had no idea why he wanted to impress this woman.

Rosa stood toe-to-toe with him. She barely reached his chin, but confidence made her seem divine. She'd bring the whoop-ass no matter her stature. Chris found himself wanting to grin again.

"You'll have to take the test again. There's no stress in sleep, therefore, there's no telling what the hell you are."

"Don't be dense." He shrugged out of his guards' hands. "If you're using this to determine citizenship for your town, then I guarantee your population is roughly ten percent shifter."

Those ripe, full lips fell open. She nodded toward her guards and said, "Get out."

"Jefa—" Brick started.

"Wait for us outside."

Brick and Rio climbed out of the cellar. A match flared and Rosa lit a candle. Chris resumed his seat, fingers laced in his lap.

She leveled the gun at his chest—a big fucking gun, one more suited to Mason than her small hands. He felt sure he couldn't rush her without Rosa ventilating his chest.

"Talk."

"I've been wearing the same clothes for a long damn time. A wash, a shave, some food—I'd appreciate it."

"I bet you would." Her words were deadly sweet.

"I'll tell you anything you want to know." He chanced another look up and down her compact body. "Not that it'll matter."

Her fingers tightened on the grip of the gun. "What the hell is that supposed to mean?"

"You're throwing people into a basement in the hopes they'll shift. It's like dunking a woman to see if she's a witch. You're working off hearsay. It's not worth my time trying to correct so much bad information." He stretched his legs. "So maybe I'll just trade for a few things and move on."

"You're mistaken if you think you're in charge here."

"No mistake, *Jefa*. You are."

He could see her mind working, testing his words for the sarcasm or disrespect she wouldn't find. *Chew on that one, boss lady.* Frustration replaced anger on her face, and she readjusted her grip—practically fidgeting from someone so cool and calm.

"You have some nerve, *pendejo*."

"I thought a woman like you would appreciate candor." She scowled. "A woman like me?"

Chris spread his hands, palms up, submissive. But he didn't feel that way. He was charged up. Sparring with Rosa felt . . . *vital*. A reason to wake up in the morning—and that was something he hadn't known in a long time.

"Your decisions affect everyone in town. I don't intend to make that job any harder."

"Jefa!" came Brick's voice. Then a tolling bell rang out. "An alarm?" Chris asked.

Rosa hesitated. In one quick sweep, her gaze crossed from Chris to the door above. "We call them hellhounds. *Dios*, we haven't seen them in six months at least. I don't know exactly what they are."

I know what they used to be. The hellhounds had once been human beings, driven to shift into monsters by the magic of the Change. But worse than that, they'd once been people of a criminal mindset—humanity's worst given a feral form to match their bestial natures.

But she might not be ready to hear that, and maybe it was better if she didn't know. God knew he wished he didn't.

"Let me fight. If I turn on you, plug me with that cannon you're holding. I'll deserve it. But that's not going to happen."

She didn't respond, simply spun toward the promise of battle. Seconds later she was up the ladder and gone. Chris snuffed the candle and scrambled up the ropes. He took her silence as acceptance.

Goddamn dogs.

Adrenaline boiled in his veins, and his muscles prepared for a fight.

Outside the cellar, Chris witnessed a miracle of defensive organization. People holding shotguns and pistols ringed each building, six meters between each primed body—no more, no less. From teenagers to old men, they stood stone-faced like sentinels. Determination outweighed even the most obvious expressions of fear.

"Hold your positions!" Rosa commanded.

She strode down the middle of the dusty street, her body swathed in twilight. A sniper rifle she hadn't been wearing in the basement hung between her shoulder blades. Chris fell into step behind her. If she didn't like it, she could shoot him. But the sight of her alone on that deserted street set him off.

"Team One, report," she called.

"No hellhounds," came a shout from the southernmost building.

"Team Two."

The call-and-response continued as she traversed the town. Chris eyed every shadow as if it might spring to life. Not too far from the truth. With every negative call-and-response, the tense muscles of his neck and upper back eased.

But at the pop-pop sound of small-caliber shots, he sprang into a full run.

"Hold positions!" Rosa shouted to the others. "Hold until the all-clear!"

Chris rounded the corner of what looked like an old-time tavern, something out of a John Wayne movie. He snagged a handmade broom and snapped off the bristles. The stout handle would make a passable weapon. Nobody was paying him any attention.

A trio of two men and a woman ringed the rear of the building, still in formation. An injured monster writhed in the dirt some two hundred meters away. By its side, another two lay dead.

Rosa strode to the fore, her weapon leveled. Chris grabbed her arm. She looked ready to spit, but he held fast. "Don't move," he whispered. "Only three out there."

"What—?"

"They hunt in pairs." He scanned the area, senses screaming.

"They're animals," she hissed.

"And animals follow set behaviors. Cougars hunt on their own, lions in packs. With these . . . hellhounds, it's pairs."

"There it is," a man on the left said under his breath. He squinted through his rifle's sight. "One hundred meters out. Ten o'clock."

Rosa's face seemed carved out of marble, but Chris read the understanding and appreciation in her eyes.

"Take the shot," she said softly.

One crack later and the dog yelped, fell.

Chris hoisted his makeshift club and strode out into the scrub.

"You idiot," Rosa shouted. "You don't even have a gun."

"Then cover me."

"Hector and Manuel, on me. Everyone else, hold."

Chris stepped around a rattlesnake den and wove through the tangle of tumbleweeds. He would have liked to have his solar-powered lantern, a comforting human artificiality in the midst of enveloping dusk. But he continued, propelled by the chance to brain another one of the fuckers that had killed Ange. He hadn't seen one in a couple of months, as if their disease had run its course. But for people like Chris, they'd left a hideous scar.

Once he would have held back. The truth about those disgusting, fetid creatures had appealed to him for mercy. Not anymore.

The injured beast yelped and whined. Its back leg had been shattered. Blood poured out of a cavernous gut wound. That sick, unnatural shimmer of dark magic swirled around its body even as it lay dying. A stench of decay fogged out of its slack, panting mouth—what brimstone would smell like. Appropriate for creatures that had made the world a living hell.

His muscles cold and stiff, Chris slammed the staff into its skull. One shot. Good-bye.

A new monster at his back gurgled. Chris spun and slammed the toe of his boot into the thing's gut, again, again. Harder. An old rage wove into each strike. His chest felt wrapped in flame. He kicked until its insides slipped onto the desert floor and filled the waffle pattern of his worn hiking boots.

Sweat dripped in his eyes as he dropped to all fours.

"Shit," Rosa breathed.

Even the desert seemed to hold its breath. Chris shuddered. The ends of his fingers and the backs of his thighs had gone numb. Slowly, as if coming out of a deep trance, he stood and wiped the slime off his hands.

The closer he got to them when they died, the more satisfying it was. Or maybe he just liked tempting fate. But no matter how grim the fight, Ange was still gone.

"Back to town," Rosa said, her voice low. "Five more minutes and then sound the all-clear."

Chris had committed their names to memory—Hector and Manuel. They strode back to town with Rosa's purpose giving authority to their steps.

"You said you're a doctor." She lifted her chin. "You serious?"

"Yeah," he said, still wiping his palms along his jeans. His voice was far steadier than it should have been, considering what he'd just done. "I'm not an M.D., but I have a Ph.D. in research zoology. In this day and age, that's the best most people have. And when it comes to skinwalkers, knowing a little something about animals is a plus. I've treated patients all over the West."

"Did they run you out of the territory for malpractice?"

"No." His throat felt like he'd swallowed a shattered bottle. "I just never stayed."

Gory memories crept into view. He'd been fascinated with Ange's red-gold hair. Strands wet with blood had stuck to her forehead just as she died. Later, after all the fighting had concluded, he'd made himself take a hard look at what remained of her body. They'd stripped her, made her into a shredded, lifeless thing. He would remember that moment always.

Guilt gathered in his muscles like lactic acid following a hard run.

"You didn't seem much like a doctor just now," Rosa said.

"Did you want me to say a little prayer first?"

"Why?"

Chris scrutinized the woman. The lines on either side of her nose were deeper, pulled taut. The strain of living on the defensive was taking its toll on their leader. She'd gouge his eyes out with her thumbs before admitting as much. Her silent, stoic determination tightened a band around his chest; he couldn't inhale deeply enough.

Maybe he could make a difference here before moving on. She deserved that much help.

"So . . . do I stay? Long enough to trade, *Jefa*?"

"You say my title so mockingly."

"No disrespect."

Again she searched his face, looking for reason to dispatch him as dispassionately as one of those beasts. But he meant it. She held a corner of society together by the strength of her will. For that, she had his admiration. So he endured her scrutiny, as stone-faced as one of her bravos.

Rosa slung the sharpshooter's rifle over her shoulder, securing it with one hand on the strap. The message was clear. Her trust only stretched so far.

"Tonight you can bunk in with the smallest company of bravos, above the *taberna*. You cause any trouble, they get to shoot you. *Comprendes*?"

"Yup. And tomorrow?"

"Tomorrow you swear allegiance to me."

FIVE

Rosa had seen the look in Chris Welsh's eyes before, in a dying wolf that had chewed off its own leg to escape a trap. It was a sick combination of desperate and feral, compounded by complete lack of hope. Recognizing that, she should have made him move on right away. Such a man didn't add to a community; he only soaked it in his own bitterness and set it on fire.

"I'm not swearing anything," he said. "I don't want to join your elite few."

There had been travelers over the years. Not many. If the desert didn't get them, then skinwalkers, hellhounds, dust pirates, snakes, or scorpions did. Most chose to stay, but committed wanderers preferred to go on in search of some far-off El Dorado. Traders came and went, rarely to be seen again. She had no problem letting them fill up their bottles and canteens, barter if Wicker was interested, and then head out.

Mostly she had just been baiting him to see how he'd respond—and predictably, his hackles went up, like the wounded animal she'd compared him to. His reaction provided insight into his otherwise opaque character.

She flashed her teeth in a smile that was anything but friendly. "We don't look for crazy in our bravos anyway." That was the only way to describe how he'd charged beyond the safety of the town perimeter to kill hellhounds hand to hand. "As I said, Wicker in the general store handles all our goods. Not now, though. Everyone will be on high alert tonight."

"Old time general store, eh? Looks ancient."

"No shit." Rosa laughed. "We weren't the first ones here."

It had been a miracle to find structures in place in a defensible valley, nourished by underground rivers. Even in the dry season, they could survive here—most of their citizens, anyway. Rosa had long ago accepted that people died, and sometimes you couldn't do a damn thing to stop it. Though she was suspicious of him, she wouldn't deny Valle any potential for medical care, even if he had not been trained for people. She didn't like doctors anyway. They never wanted to give it to you straight, so they wrapped the ugly truth up in tests and treatments, offered chances, and refused to deliver on what they promised. Unless you could pay more.

"I won't bother you long," he said.

"No, you won't. But later I'll want to talk to you about what you said underground."

"About the ineffective nature of your test?"

"Not so loud, *estúpido*." She stepped away from the gate without looking back. He'd follow her, because all men did, because they feared her or they liked watching the sway of her hips. Either way, she got the same result.

To Rosa's surprise, he stood where she'd left him, a frown pulling his brows together. "I'm not used to being called that."

"Then quit acting like it. Come on."

His sigh carried in the silence, but he did follow. She didn't speak again until they reached the privacy of her casita. The walls were cool and white, thanks to the nearby limestone and salt flats. A while back, they'd loaded the trucks with enough supplies to make whitewash for ten more years. The rugs on the adobe floor, she'd woven with her own hands. Each one told a story, not that she expected him to notice that. Or care.

Her furnishings were simple: a hand-carved rocking chair, a table with two dining chairs. She'd made the place comfortable with patchwork cushions Singer created out of old clothing and buckwheat hulls for stuffing. Doubtless Dr. Welsh would be surprised to learn they had a garden of edible desert plants, filled with barrel cactus for the yellow fruit, beans from mesquites, paloverde trees, yuccas, and agaves. Most times they cooked communally to ensure no one went hungry.

Rosa wondered what he thought of her simple home, with one room for living and one for sleeping. Like everyone else, she used the latrine and the public showers. In all honesty, it was nicer than where her family had lived in Guatemala. There, after each storm season, they'd needed to rebuild the *palapa*.

Jaw clenching, she told herself to forget those days, since they were lost and gone. She unstrapped her rifle and propped it against the wall, still within easy reach.

"It's very nice," he said, as if surprised.

"We live well here. Or as well as any since the Change."

"I'm beginning to see that. You wanted to talk to me about—"

"Yes." She indicated he should take a seat at the table, and then, being a good hostess, she set it with a ceramic plate of sliced prickly pears drizzled with honey. Then she poured two cups of agave wine and joined him.

"Down there, you said we're probably ten percent skin-walker." The very idea sent a shiver of horror through her, but she hid it. "Explain."

That couldn't be right. But to defend her people properly, she needed to hear him out. Listen to the crazy man, so she could dismiss his claims. Their system worked. No nonhumans made it past their defenses. Rosa was almost sure of that. *Almost.* Tension shriveled her belly.

He stared at the plate as if it held writhing maggots instead of pretty rounds of peeled fruit. "You don't use a scientific method. There are two kinds of . . . skinwalkers, as you put it. The bad ones, like the hellhounds we just fought, have no self-control. You can tell them on sight because they attack instinctively. The good ones—"

"The only good skinwalker is a dead one," she said flatly.

"Do you want to hear this or not? If you're going to waste my time, then I'd rather get a good night's rest, finish my business, and be on my way."

"Sorry." But she wasn't. Not really.

By the sharpness of his look, he knew that. She wasn't used to men who met her eyes without glancing away. It made her feel bristly.

"The good ones," he continued, "retain their humanity. They control the change. Just putting them in the dark won't tell you if they're wholly human."

No. That couldn't be true. Her hands curled into fists. "How do you know this?"

"A long time ago, a lifetime ago, I had a friend named Jenna who was also a wolf. You'd need to torture someone she loved to make her change if she didn't want to."

So they weren't safe. No matter what they did. Anybody could be hiding an animal in his skin. Rosa met Chris's gaze. *Including you.*

She ought not let him out of her sight, since he called skinwalkers his friends. Instinct told her to kill him before he caused further trouble, but violence gave lie to the promise of sanctuary—a pledge she didn't take lightly. If the men believed her word was worthless, even to an outsider, she would lose their support. If she lied to one man, what would stop her from doing it again? That was the first spill down a long, slippery slope.

"You don't tell anyone else," she ordered.

He shrugged. "It's not my business what folklore you disseminate. I'm just passing through."

We need a new system . . . the old one is flawed.

While Rosa worried the problem, he took a slice of fruit as if he expected her to poison him. Rosa swallowed a sigh and chose a piece for herself. She ate pointedly to prove it was untainted, and then downed her wine. Viv was improving; this latest batch was light and sweet, with no sour maguey taste.

"Eat as much as you want," she said. "I imagine it's been a long time since you had fresh fruit." Yet he didn't show any signs of deprivation: no swollen joints or black, bleeding gums. Maybe he had found plants along the way. That hinted at more resourcefulness in the face of hardship.

The man didn't reply, instead taking her at her word. He finished half the plate and swallowed from the cup. "What *is* that?"

"Agave wine. We also have *tiswin*, saguaro beer. And honey mead." That was it in the way of drinks, except for the vodka they'd salvaged. But no one could count on such windfalls. The heartiest learned to fend for themselves.

From the look of him, Chris was still hungry. At that late hour, the communal meal would be finished. She rose and drew a wrapped basket from her cupboard. The dark sourdough bread made from buckwheat flour still smelled rich and good, even a couple of days later. Because it was near the beginning of the week, she had fresh cheese as well. Wicker had arrived with three malnourished goats, including a buck. The animals had since bred into a small herd that he tended with great affection, which provided milk for the settlement. The old man hadn't traveled from far away, unlike everyone else, and he'd brought all he could fit in his ancient pickup truck, including the goats. Rosa always assumed that, coupled with his skill at trade and keeping the books, he had once been a farmer.

Rosa placed the bread and cheese before Chris, along with a knife she'd carved out of deadfall saguaro branches.

After studying her for a moment, he dipped the knife in the clay pot and covered the bread with the creamy cheese. He ate as if he hadn't had a decent meal in years. She didn't want to feel sorry for him, even though she knew how it felt to be alone in the wilderness.

"Thanks."

"I'd do the same for anyone. Why do you think people stay?"

"Your natural charm."

The quick answer surprised a laugh out of her. Around the bravos she always kept up her intensity, never wanting them to forget who she was. From morning to night she never relaxed, never let down her guard. Never laughed. Yeah, this *güero* was bad news.

"Let me know when you've had enough to eat. I'll walk you over to your room above the *taberna*."

He raised a brow. "You think I need an escort?"

"I don't trust you. You confessed to consorting with skinwalkers." She lifted her shoulders, resolute. "That makes you a sympathizer, at least, if not something worse."

"They're not all evil," he said softly. "Like people, it depends on their natures. If they don't attack you on sight—"

Rosa slammed her palm on the table. "They can spread their disease. If you hadn't noticed, *pendejo*, the monsters are winning. Humans are the minority now."

He fell quiet and finished his food. "This place is amazing. I haven't had bread in years."

"We're proud of it," she said, slightly mollified. "You ready to go?"

Chris nodded and pushed back from the table. Stepping out into the heat shocked the system, after the shady interior of her little house. She'd chosen it because it had the best vantage of all points in town, as well as excellent airflow for cooling. Rosa lifted a hand in greeting as they strode down the main thoroughfare. It gave her a sense of achievement to see everyone turning in for the night or preparing for evening patrols. Another day well lived.

"There aren't many women here," he observed.

"It's a problem, but we're working on population. And we have our first pregnancy." She couldn't help the pride that flavored her voice.

It had been Tilly's decision, above all, but her baby offered Valle de Bravo something they hadn't known before: hope for the future instead of mere survival. If they could increase their numbers, they might make it. Their sons and daughters might prosper in this dangerous place.

Welsh shook his head. "You must be nuts, bringing a kid into a world like this."

SIX

Chris awoke with a start. Fading images of violence and the sound of distant trucks still clouded his mind. His surroundings were unfamiliar, enough to cause a momentary panic. He wasn't used to this much comfort.

Slowly his respiration returned to normal. He was in a communal room above the tavern. Sunlight tipped in through the windows at an extreme angle, still early in the day. His body felt pummeled and sore, as if sleeping indoors had already broken down the resilience he'd forged in the desert.

Low, masculine voices sounded, throughout the room and from below the floorboards. Instantly he tensed. He reached for his Beretta. Voices meant people, and he could never be sure around people. Some would skin a man and steal hard-won possessions as easily as breathing. Chris hadn't gone that far, but he knew enough to be wary of those who had.

Again he forced his body to accept what his mind knew. He was in a haven—the largest he'd seen in the days since the Change.

And her. *La jefa*. She was here too.

"Sleep well, Doc?"

He identified the speaker as Manuel, one of Rosa's young guards. "Sure."

"I'll say you did," Manuel said with a chuckle. "We were about to check your breathing and claim your goods. You've been asleep for over twenty-four hours."

Chris blinked. He'd assumed it was the next day. Maybe that explained the soreness of his body. He'd simply unplugged. Perhaps his unconscious mind had been satisfied with the safety of this place, permitting him the bliss of a long crash. He'd been sleeping in hour-long bursts for so long that he was almost relieved to know such survival skills weren't a curse.

Still, knowing he had an audience, he forced his weariness aside. He wanted to trade, and he sure as hell wanted more food. Scrounging in the desert was no way to live. It was survival, nothing more. The few hours he'd already spent in Valle represented more true luxury than he would've imagined possible. He wasn't too proud to say that having another taste held huge appeal.

So that meant doing what he could for the town, at least for a few days. He would eat his fill, gear up, and return to the road a stronger man. Chris couldn't see the sense in setting down roots when they had become so impossible to defend. Hardscrabble living was a much easier prospect on one's own.

Mindful of the wary expressions worn by the young bravos who shared those quarters, he dressed in his spare set of clothes. The threadbare material and two missing buttons were almost embarrassing to wear in human company, but he'd avoided that concern for months. Maybe he possessed enough in his satchel to trade for a few new pieces. And damn, he needed a razor. His last straight razor had been worn down to bluntness after a boar took off with his hunting knife stuck in its side. Since then, he could either use the straight razor for cooking or gnaw on hides. The choice had been simple.

After combing his hair with water from a communal wash stand, he packed his belongings. Without a word, he nodded a good-bye to Manuel and headed to the ground floor of the tavern. Those in charge of meals were already hard at work, providing breakfast for the town. Chris's stomach clenched with a powerful hunger. The food Rosa served had been enough to remind him that variety and nutrition were precious.

Out the tavern doors, he strode through the desert morning sunshine to the general store. Everyone was busy, and they eyed him with a combination of curiosity and wariness as he passed. He didn't mind that score, because he was just as busy trying to figure them out.

A community. A real, thriving community. *Amazing.*

He pushed into the general store where an old man haggled with another young bravo.

"I don't care what you think it's worth," the shopkeeper said. "I am not trading a bottle of vodka for that mirror. First of all, it's cracked. And second, you know the rules on rationing alcohol."

"Come off it, Wicker. *La jefa* expects us to do the work of six men and be content with homemade mash."

"She expects us to pull our weight, *hombre*. Nothing more." Wicker pointed with the handle of the broom he held. "And you better watch yourself, if you don't want to wind up with worse than marks on your back."

Making a note to himself, Chris matched a name to a history. This must be Lem, the one who had pushed himself on Brick's sister. Already, talk of Lem's punishment of ten lashes had come around to Chris's ears. Knowing an environment as soon as possible was essential—not just the leadership, but potential troublemakers too.

"You don't scare me, old man," Lem said with a sneer.

"I'm not the one you need to be afraid of, and you know it."

Chris cleared his throat. The pair turned to watch as he pushed into the main room of the shop.

Twenty days north, a pair of grizzled sisters in their fifties, each sporting a semiautomatic rifle, had allowed him to trade his supply of dried rabbit. They'd kept their ammo and treasures in a hollowed-out tree stump. This trading post was a lot more elaborate. He hadn't seen its like since leaving the little place Mason and Jenna had been carving out of a mountainside. But even they hadn't possessed lantern oil, vodka, bolts of cloth, spare tires, shoes, and enough seeds to populate a greenhouse. Each species was stored in a separate Tupperware container, neatly labeled. The containers alone were probably worth a fortune in goods and services, let alone the potential harvests they contained.

The excess—because that was what it seemed to be— was staggering.

"Morning," Wicker said with a nod. Tall and lean, with salt-and-pepper hair, he wore boots, jeans, a faded shirt, and a straw cowboy hat. In his midsixties, he was a tall and lanky Texan if ever there was one. "You must be the traveling doc."

He nodded. "Rosa mentioned something about trading."

"Yes, but she wants to be here when you do." Wicker winked. "What a man trades says a lot about him. Be here tomorrow after the noon meal."

"Fine," Chris said with a shrug. "Then, can you tell me how to find the pregnant woman? I'm supposed to check on her."

"Make a left out on the street. They live in the little house with lizards painted on the front door."

"Lizards?"

Wicker only grinned. "Ask Tilly. That's her name. And feel free to leave your gear. No one will touch it again until you do. You have my word."

Chris offered his hand, which Wicker shook—the first to do so within Valle's boundaries. He could put his faith in nothing more. "Much obliged."

"As for you," Wicker said to Lem, "back to work. You'll have to wait till the next Burning Night to drink the hard stuff. Rules are rules."

Lem stomped off with a trail of curses under his breath.

Wicker only shrugged, then went back to his work with the broom. His stooped shoulders made him seem shorter than he actually was, which was probably pushing two meters.

Chris found himself almost staring at the man. Such a curiosity. He hadn't seen many people outside of a certain age range. Fifteen to roughly fifty—that seemed to be the sweet spot. Too young and too old meant almost impossible odds for survival.

With one last covetous glance toward the supply shelves, he turned and stepped back out into the daylight. He'd see what he could do for this woman, Tilly, and earn his right to eat and rest up in a safe place. That was the goal. Learning names and histories meant nothing. Not anymore.

The townspeople watched him no matter where he walked. He hadn't felt so conspicuous in ages, usually keeping to the shadows and lonely trails. Carrying only a small stash of medical supplies, he kept his head up and his expression friendly. Neutral.

Sure enough, he found a door painted with lizards. It stood half open, encouraging air flow. He knocked on the wood trim. A woman's melodic voice beckoned him in. Chris got as far as touching the door handle when she came into view.

"Oh!"

The woman, Tilly, stood in the entryway, so obviously with child that Chris stared. He hadn't seen a pregnant woman in five years—since the Change finished its slow crawl across North America. She might have been an extinct species come back to life.

"Sorry," he said. "I'm Chris Welsh. Maybe Rosa told you to expect me?"

"Oh, you're the new doctor. Come in."

She ushered him inside, leading him to a tiny kitchenette that contained a table with two chairs.

"We just don't get many new faces around here," she said. "Please sit. I'd heard rumors that you were in town, and Rosa came by yesterday to confirm. I can't tell you how relieved Jameson and I are to have you here."

"Jameson? The baby's father?"

"That's right. He's out on patrol now, but he knows you were planning to stop by once you rested. I can't imagine how hard it's been for you out on your own all this time. I tell you, if I didn't have Jameson, I would've died a long time ago."

Chris gripped the end of the battered wooden table. His brain was almost spinning, trying to keep up with her quick chatter. Her accent was strange too, like Cape Cod blue blood. Hearing her speak was hearing ghosts from another lifetime.

"Can I get you something to drink?"

"Sure. Anything."

Tilly brushed a strand of blond hair back from her cheek, tucking it behind her ear. She was elfin, petite, sunny. Maybe she wasn't exaggerating in saying that the baby's father had helped her survive. She didn't look strong enough to carry the weight of her child, let alone fight off hellhounds and hostile skinwalkers.

She brought him a glass of cool water, which tasted faintly of copper. But he'd had far worse. "I'm not really a doctor," he felt compelled to say.

Tilly waved her hand. "Oh, I know. Rosa explained it all. But believe me, I'm not picky. These days, anyone who's had an anatomy class is tantamount to a master surgeon."

"Have you had a baby before?" For his own sake, he dearly wanted that answer to be yes. She would know what to do, have more experience to draw from. But for that to be true, she would have lost the child too.

None of that melancholy could be found in her expression. She smiled broadly, her hands curled over her stomach. A sundress that would've hung loose on Rosa Cortez stretched tight over Tilly's ripe bulge. "No, this is my first. Jameson's too. Can you imagine, being so happy at a time like this? It almost doesn't seem right."

Chris shrugged. "Maybe you're due."

"It's because of Jameson and the baby, of course, but it's also because of Rosa. We came here about two years ago, stumbling into town with nothing. She took us in like she does everyone." A wistfulness touched her bright smile. "I know she has a lot riding on me coming through this birth in good shape. All of Valle could do with some good news."

"Good news?"

"Well, a baby means new beginnings, right?"

Cringing, Chris wondered what the hell he'd gotten himself into. The weight of a whole town's hope seemed to ride on this sunny blonde, her unborn baby, and him. All he'd wanted to do was trade and move on. This felt . . . entangling. Personal. Parts of him that had been on the move for years were none too happy about the prospect. After two divorces and more time spent avoiding human company than seeking it out, he had no success with long-term commitments.

"Like I said," he murmured, "I can't make a promise other than to do my best. I need you to rest, but also keep a regular routine of exercise. Walk as much as you can to keep your muscles fit. You'll need them."

And frankly, that was all he could do. An ob-gyn from years past would have checked her urine, her blood pressure, her dilation. He had neither the equipment nor the expertise for any of that.

Some doctor.

But this eager woman didn't need the burden of his doubts.

"I'll do that, Chris. Do you mind if I call you Chris?"

He smiled, overcome. She had a personality like champagne bubbles. "Not at all."

"And if you need anything, just let me know. Jameson is a really good hunter. He kills all the lizards I call."

Chris blinked. "Excuse me?"

She rubbed her stomach again. "Isn't it weird? All the inexplicable things. One morning I woke up and found a lizard sitting next to me on a rock. Jameson and I hadn't eaten in days. He bagged it. We were desperate and ate it. After that . . . I could just think of a lizard and one would come running."

"You're serious."

"Sure. I try not to anymore because we don't need the meat and I don't want to abuse the gift." She shrugged as Chris tried to reconcile the weirdness of this sunny woman and her frank talk about calling lizards. And eating them.

But that was the Change. Chris could either accept the irrationality of it or go mad. He'd chosen the former a long time ago.

SEVEN

That afternoon Rosa worked in the garden. As with all chores, the townsfolk traded off the responsibility. That meant the men had their turns as well, but today Mica, Abigail, and Ingrid labored beside her, pulling weeds and harvesting produce. The needs of the community meant they didn't have much opportunity to store food, instead eating fruits and vegetables as soon as they came ripe.

"What do you think of the new guy?" Mica asked, leaning on her hoe. She wasn't pretty, but she had a bright, friendly personality. That made her good company by any definition.

Rosa didn't answer, figuring the woman must be talking to Ingrid. But the rest of them stopped working and gazed at her, brows raised. For a moment Rosa pictured Chris Welsh. Her stomach muscles tightened. As a rule she didn't rate men's attractiveness, not even playfully, but if she did? He'd win.

"It's too soon to say, but we could use some medical help, that's for sure."

Abigail nodded. "Especially with Tilly being near her time."

"That's not what I meant." Mica went back to work, but her eyes glinted with mischief. "He's pretty damn fine, even with that beard and a year's worth of trail dust. Don't you think?"

Somehow Rosa kept her expression noncommittal to avoid being teased. "He's okay. More important, he looks strong enough to fight."

"Is that all you ever think about?" Thankfully Mica let the subject rest and turned her attention to Ingrid. "So what's the deal with you and Ex?"

The tall blonde shrugged. She'd hacked her hair down to a fingertip's length from her skull. The resultant wild spikes suited her. She had a strong face rather than a beautiful one, and her arms were ropy with muscle. "I like him fine."

"But you're not looking at him to get you in the family way," Abigail guessed.

Ingrid laughed. "God, no. And I can't, even if I wanted to."

The other women expressed sympathy, but Rosa remained silent. Her experience whispered that being barren might not be a bad thing. At least if the worst occurred, it was impossible to be stuck with your rapist's child. Of course it also meant Ingrid would never hold a baby given to her in love, but maybe it was a safe trade.

Rosa let the familiar gossip wash over her: who was sleeping with whom, who wanted to, and who had been eating more than his share at dinner. Abigail excused herself to prepare enough buckwheat flour for the evening meal, and Mica went with her to help. Since the grinding was done by hand—a slow and time-consuming process—it was impossible to make more than necessary for one recipe, given that the bread supplied the whole community. Rosa sometimes worried that Abigail was too old to work so hard, but she knew how to bake and claimed to appreciate being useful. At least Mica showed some willingness to apprentice to her, so there would still be bread even after Abigail was gone.

Ingrid and Rosa finished in the garden and went to clean their shovels and tools. Though Ex could repair them and make more, they'd learned to be careful with their possessions. Sometimes a sturdy tool made the difference between life and death.

"Something eating you?" Rosa asked, sliding a rag up and down the metal.

Ingrid glanced at her in surprise, her mind returning from wherever it had gone. "Nothing I can put my finger on, but that new leader, Peltz, is bothering me."

"In what way?"

"I feel like his strikes are more feints than a fully committed assault."

"Like he's testing our weaknesses?"

"Exactly."

From Ingrid, Rosa took such words seriously. The tall, lean blonde had a martial bearing and knew krav maga, one of the most efficient, dangerous hand-to-hand fighting styles. Once, after having a bit to drink, Ingrid had confessed that her style had been practiced by the military of various provisional governments—particularly after the East Coast Fuel Wars that followed the Change. Rather than probe for salacious details, Rosa had merely asked for additional training to supplement the dirty street fighting she'd learned growing up. So if Ingrid felt that greater battles loomed on the horizon, Rosa would do well to listen to her warning.

She stacked their gardening implements in the storage shed. "Your recommendation?"

Ingrid shrugged. "We've already got patrols out, trying to locate their camp. But so far we've only found the remnants. Cold ashes. Garbage. For now, they're staying one step ahead of us."

"I'd love to know how," Rosa muttered. "It's not like they're so well organized."

"They weren't before."

"You think Peltz is that smart?" *Dios*, she hoped not.

"Hard to say, but he's doing something right with the constant relocating. They're always within striking distance, though, and that makes me nervous."

"Agreed."

She walked with Ingrid toward the *taberna*, mulling the problem. "Can you think of a way we could lay a trap?"

"Like how? Tie a naked woman to a rock?"

Rosa laughed despite herself. "*Cabrona*. Not what I had in mind."

"Then no, not off the top of my head. I'll keep thinking and let you know if I come up with anything."

"*Gracias.*" As Ingrid was about to go into the *taberna*, Rosa touched her arm. "*Oye*, I wanted to say something."

"Can you tell me over a drink?"

"*Claro.*"

Inside was dim and cool. Between meals, only a few townsfolk lingered. *Qué bueno.* This wasn't for anyone else's ears, as Falco would shit kittens if he got wind of it. Rosa picked a table as Ingrid retrieved a couple of mugs of *tiswin*. No ice, but even lukewarm beer tasted good after working in the hot morning sun.

"What's up, Rosa?"

Ingrid was the closest thing she had to a female friend. Though Rosa cared for the other girls, they had a softness she couldn't understand. Ingrid was forged of familiar steel. This woman would fight tooth and nail until her last breath. Pale blue eyes shone with strength and courage.

"Falco's been putting the pressure on lately. With the raider attacks getting worse and supplies running low . . ." She shrugged. "I don't know what the future holds. If anything *did* happen to me, I want you to step up. Don't let him run Valle unchallenged."

"You're asking me to be your successor? Are you having premonitions or something?" It wasn't a sarcastic question. Since the Change, Rosa had seen proof of weird powers cropping up. Tilly and Bee were the most prominent examples in town, while others claimed glimpses of the future. Learning of stronger magic wouldn't surprise Rosa.

"I'm just trying to be prepared," she said.

"I understand. And I promise I won't let him go unchecked."

"*Gracias.*" Rosa tossed back her beer and rose. "I'm off to check with Bee on the status of the hives."

"She's still not talking, huh?"

"Not really. I don't know if she can't or if she just refuses to."

"As long as she keeps us in honey, I guess we can't complain."

Rosa had long suspected that there was something supernatural about Bee's ability to control her pets—and that she could send a horde of angry, stinging insects after anyone who pissed her off. That was part of why she didn't insist on the woman taking a larger social role.

But once a week Rosa visited and brought supplies to exchange. Though Bee formally lived in the town limits, she was also the closest thing Valle had to an eccentric hermit. Most of the bravos whispered that the magic flowing through her veins had driven her mad.

She swung by the general store and with Wicker's help put together a basket. The old man had mentioned Chris's visit to the store that morning, making her all the more curious about what he had to trade. But that could wait until tomorrow. The walk toward the far edge of town gave her time to think about Ingrid's concerns regarding the dust pirates. Rosa shared them, but other than constant patrols, she didn't know how to find the bastards.

Peltz's raids were starting to interfere with her ability to profit from the shipments that passed through Valle. That had to stop. Rosa's men only preyed on those who refused to pay the toll for safe passage through her territory— territory Peltz often violated, not to mention attacks on the town itself. His disrespect made her livid.

Before she knew it, she stood outside Bee's adobe house.

The drone of insects was thick out here, buzzing all around until it became a throb in Rosa's ears. That was, to be frank, a little unnerving.

Still she called, "I'm here with your trade goods."

It took a while for the old woman to show herself. She presented an eccentric picture in her long coat, heavy glasses, and wild gray hair, knotted in an unlikely fashion atop her head. Rosa wasn't sure just how old the woman was, anywhere from forty-five to sixty. And, as ever, bees crawled on her hands and arms, alit on her thin cheeks, and swarmed around her head. Rosa visited because nobody else wanted to, but also because each refusal to yield to her private urge to run away screaming made her a little stronger.

"Here you go," she said, offering the basket.

The other woman peered over Rosa's shoulder with blurry eyes, as if she saw something behind her. Rosa fought the urge to whirl and stare. She *had* during her first few visits, before figuring out that Bee didn't live in the world she knew. At least, not exactly. Not wholly.

Bee claimed the supplies with long, dirty fingers and shuffled into her home. Where she kept the hives. The idea of them swarming around her food and drink, nesting in her hair, made Rosa a little light-headed.

Calm down. We need the honey.

At last the exchange was made—silently, like it always was. Rosa accepted the basket full of honey jars and stepped back so Bee could close the door. But she didn't. Instead she hovered a moment, her gaze still fixed on the horizon. Rosa couldn't resist the second urge to turn. When she did, she saw just what she'd expected. Nothing.

This time, though, Bee pointed. A hundred yellow-and-black-striped insects coated her thin arm. Then she spoke for the first time in all the years Rosa had known her, with a voice like rusty nails ground beneath a heavy file. "The shadow falls. Valle burns. Everything changes. The world is born again in fire."

A chill rolled through Rosa. "What does that mean?"

But, try as she might, she couldn't pry anything more

out of Bee. Amid a swarm like a dark cloud, it took the full extent of Rosa's self-control not to panic and slap at them. With the slow motions of a sleepwalker, the old woman returned to her home. All that remained of her eerie words was the buzzing of the bees.

EIGHT

The next day at the general store, Chris glanced at Rosa. She stood beside him with her arms crossed as they waited for Wicker to appear. Her nose angled sharply down, possibly indicating native blood. Such a strong profile. Nothing about her was weak. She'd set her sights on creating a petty kingship out of the old ashes. Chris admired her resolve, but she was nuts if she believed it would last.

But Valle was an easy place to grow comfortable. He could see why people settled here: good food, a strong community, a sense of purpose, and order out of chaos. The few patients he had already treated voiced nothing but respect and gratitude for *la jefa*'s strong hand.

"How long have you been here?" he asked. Call it intellectual curiosity. He couldn't help but wonder how she and her people had succeeded.

"Five years. Since just after the Change hit this area." She aimed an inquiring look at him. "You're impressed."

"Yeah."

"Is there . . . ?" Rosa frowned and shook her head. "Never mind."

She seemed to pull away, although her body remained still. Chris reached out. The temptation to touch overwhelmed good sense and her distinct boundaries. Wrapped in the cotton sleeve of a faded T-shirt, her biceps tightened beneath his fingers. She flicked a lethal gaze toward that point of contact. He could have predicted as much. Touching her was like grabbing a rattlesnake. What did surprise him was the flicker of fear across her expression. She glanced around the empty store, almost reflexively checking whether anyone had seen them.

Chris let go. While the old world slowly, inexorably fell to dust, he had studied wildcats for nearly two decades. A scarcity of females always caused trouble. Fighting followed. And death. Sure, some would survive, but that wasn't much of an option for humans when so few remained. Rosa, as a leader and a woman, must have realized early the tenuous nature of her position.

But touching her. Touching *anyone*. Some things were even more primal than good food and a safe place to sleep.

He fisted his hands behind his back. "What were you going to ask me?"

He could see it behind her mahogany eyes, how she worked, probing him for sincerity. But she took her duties as leader seriously. With information as valuable as supplies, he might as well be the morning edition. Too bad. She would be disappointed by how often he'd eschewed human contact, even before the worst of the Change. Other wayfarers undoubtedly knew more.

"Is there any place out there like ours?" she asked.

Again with the hope. How the hell did she wrangle that fickle bitch every day?

"No. Not even close."

She offered her toothy smile again—the scary one. "No wonder you stare like a kid at the base of a skyscraper."

"I stare when I like what I see."

"Save it." She pounded on the counter with her fist. *"Oye*, Wicker. *¿Dónde estás, mano?"*

The old shopkeeper finally ambled out of the back room, his face slack as if he'd just been awakened from a nap. "So, we finally get to see what you have. Eh, Doc?"

Chris swiped the sweat from the back of his neck, surprised to find himself grinning. But he needed to get his mind off Rosa and back on negotiations that would determine his immediate future. "Medicine, mostly. Antibiotics. Some asthma inhalers. Painkillers. Electrolyte powders. Hell, even lice shampoo and athlete's foot cream."

Wicker and Rosa wore matching expressions of surprise. "What'd you do," she said, "knock over a drugstore?"

"Near enough. I met a guy who did. He was a walking pharmacy."

"Did you kill him?" Wicker asked.

"Didn't need to. He could hardly breathe when I found him under a tree. In exchange for his stash, I let him use my Beretta."

Wicker shrugged as if he'd seen or done worse. Chris wouldn't be surprised. He had too. But Rosa was wearing that peculiar look again, the one that said *he* was the one to be feared.

Mason had been a scary character. Jenna too. And even the teenage delinquent, Tru, when he manned up. Somewhere in the last few years, Chris must have crossed over to where he deserved suspicious scowls and a wide berth. Funny. It took being around relatively normal folk to hold up that mirror. Out there, he hadn't noticed it happening.

"Well, with that stockpile you can have your run of the place." Wicker stepped behind a counter and spread his hands. "The best mankind has left to offer."

Chris parsed out a few of his less vital medicines and traded for a pile of small luxuries: a bar of homemade soap, two pairs of socks and plain cotton boxer shorts, a handmade toothbrush and a few sachets of powder, a face towel, and a mini sewing kit with safety pins—the stuff of royalty. Negotiating for a pair of homemade jeans, a new shirt, and a pair of sturdy cowboy boots took longer. That cost Chris his stockpile of six hairbrushes and a working pocket watch he'd found outside of the parched, tumbledown remains of Las Vegas.

"No razors?" he asked.

"Nope. Those go quick. Gonna have to ask among the bravos."

Damn. He wanted a shave. Walking around like a mountain man hadn't bothered him when he lived alone. But back in the company of people, he felt the need to clean up properly.

"And ammo?"

"None to spare," Wicker said, wearing an expression made for gambling. "Sorry."

Chris noticed how quiet Rosa remained during the whole exchange. Her interest in his choices was obvious. Would he hand over lifesaving antibiotics in exchange for two liters of premium vodka? Not likely. Chris had become a different man since the Change, but he had yet to consider himself reckless or self-indulgent.

"What do you have by way of real luxuries?" he asked.

Wicker cocked his head. "Like what?"

"More than basic hygiene and vice. What about books?"

A look as quick as a lizard over noontime rocks passed between Wicker and Rosa. "No books," the man said curtly.

Whatever.

He'd forgotten how opaque human politics could become. If they wanted to keep their secrets, fine. But that didn't mean he had to like being shut out.

"And what about women?" he asked.

Standing to his full height, Wicker was almost as tall as Chris. Nearly. His age should've rendered him low on the potential threat scale, but arms crossed, scowl in place, he conveyed deadly intent in a damn convincing way.

"How do you mean?"

"I mean sex," Chris said. "Surely the women here have a price."

"No." Rosa's lips hardly moved as she spoke, and her hands curled into telltale fists where those cargo pants hugged muscled thighs. "Sex is a consensual exchange here. None of our women can be bought."

Chris grinned. "We'll see."

"Push me on this and you're gone, Welsh."

"I'm gone anyway, remember? No books, no sex—a guy has to find entertainment where he can." He stared her down for a long moment, waiting for her to back off.

She didn't. And her quick, angry breaths lifted her breasts for his perusal.

"That's more like it. Damn entertaining." He took a long, slow, thorough trip down her body—and found eyes throwing flame when he returned to her face. "Seems you're all out of what might interest me, Wicker. I think I'll keep the rest of my stash."

Cool metal pressed flat behind his right ear.

The raspy voice of a young man was deadly quiet. "You'll hand over those meds."

"Like hell."

"Jameson, put the knife down." Rosa's command was as sharp as barbed wire.

Tilly's husband? She'd mentioned he was a tough guy, but Chris hadn't expected a sneak attack.

"You know the rules," Rosa said. "We granted sanctuary. He stays. *Unharmed.*" She looked Chris up and down with the same thoroughness but with a great deal more contempt.

"He's got medicine," Jameson said quietly, pressing the knife against Chris's scalp. "Tilly might need it. So I don't think I'm letting him go."

"She might. But we're not tearing down the rules because you're worried."

Rosa nodded toward where Wicker had pulled a rifle out from under the counter. Not that Chris felt reassured. Jameson's breath said he stood close—very close. At such a range, rifles hardly distinguished between targets and bystanders. Besides, they all had reason to off him, despite what Rosa claimed.

This wasn't like taking on Brick, one-on-one in the desert. This was a close-quarters standoff. Under such conditions, most people checked their brains at the door. He had to hope that wasn't the case for Jameson, no matter how worried he might be about his wife.

"So you know phenobarbital from azithromycin? Dextromethorphan from sulfamethazine?" Chris shrugged his bag onto the ground. "Have at it. Then you can ask Manuel how I treated an infected cut on his heel, or Abigail about the antiseptic wash I gave her for her swollen gums. Today I mostly traded hygiene products. Luxuries, not the important medicines I've been giving away since I arrived."

Rosa walked over to the counter and angled Wicker's rifle barrel down. "Put the knife away, Jameson, and we'll make this work."

The man hesitated. Then his knife no longer chilled Chris's neck.

"That wasn't a request," she said. "You want me to cast you out?"

"You'd send us away? *Now?*"

"I didn't say anything about Tilly." Rosa offered her scary smile—and Chris relaxed. She had this, though the idea of letting her handle his problems rubbed him wrong. "What do you think, Jameson? You think she'd give up this life and trek out into the wilderness with you? Risk the baby? Does she love you that much?"

Checkmate.

She went on, "I've made it clear to the ladies that they don't need to do anything they don't want to. We take care of our women."

Jameson withdrew and Chris spun, scooping his satchel off the ground. He took a place beside Rosa, his shoulder brushing hers. Only then did he get a good look at his would-be killer, the husband of Valle's only unborn child.

Jameson was one scary mofo.

Thin and wiry, he wore the sleeves of his white T-shirt rolled up like a street tough. His cheeks were hollowed out, his eyes deep set. The bowie knife that had just pressed against Chris's neck dangled loosely from the man's fingers. Another six knives of varying size hung from a low-slung belt.

"Here's the deal," Rosa said. "The *only* deal, because I'm not haggling. The doc will do what he can for Tilly, including the provision of any medicine she might need—just as he's been doing. He's already met her, checked her out yesterday when you were on patrol. You're freaked over nothing, *mano*. And he'll stay until the baby is delivered safely."

Chris made a noncommittal noise. Jameson showed visible relief.

"In return, he receives room and board as long as he's here."

"I'm not one of those dogs, Rosa. If you want my professional expertise, you have to do better than a few scraps."

"I see what our food means to you. Bread with honey. Wine. And you tasted Viv's stew. Even that much is worth your time."

Crossing his arms against the clench of his stomach, he knew she had him. But he refused to give in without a little show of resistance. "It could be weeks before she delivers."

"True." Rosa's expression remained neutral, watching him. "Wicker, do you still have that spare room available upstairs?"

"Yup."

"There you go, Doc. Even *private* room and board."

Nice. He wondered how many other bravos were permitted the liberty of haggling with *la jefa*, even to such a small degree.

"Why do you care so much?" About Jameson and Wicker, about . . . everyone. It was clear she poured her heart and soul into this place—into everyone else's troubles.

"I want Tilly and Jameson's baby born healthy. I want her strong afterward." She pinned him with a hard look just this side of imploring. "It's important for our future. They all need to see it's possible to do more than just survive."

What she left unsaid was easy enough to figure. A drop in morale could mean an end to her leadership.

Damn complicated animals, humans.

"Ask me," he said.

Rosa's softness died away. But unlike Jameson, who stood to lose all he'd gained since the Change, Chris had no ties. No weak spots.

So he waited.

"Fine," she bit out. "Will you stay until the baby's born?"

"May as well. Sure."

"You're a real son of a bitch, aren't you?" She banged her way out of the store and stomped down the porch, muttering in Spanish about roasting men over a spit.

NINE

Rosa was pleased. Ten days had passed since her successful run against those last trespassing truckers—ten days since Chris Welsh came to town. But with no further signs of aggression or intrigue, it was time to celebrate. Tonight they would finally let off some steam. A proper Burning Night.

The fiddle sang out, its bright, infectious notes driving the bravos to dance in the plaza that blazed with the orange of a bonfire's flames. Since there weren't enough women to go around, the men formed up en masse. Rosa couldn't remember who had started this tradition, perhaps as a mockery of the old country line dances—given the tunes Wicker could play. But the diversion had taken on a life of its own. This too was a test of their manhood, each vying to execute more intricate steps, ever faster movement, and quicker footwork.

She watched from the sidelines, stifling a smile. They each wanted to impress a woman enough to get her to take him home for the night, but most of them had long since given up dancing for Rosa's benefit. She no longer received significant glances from anyone but Falco. Firelight danced on their sun-burnished skin, rippling in mysterious patterns. All of them bore her mark—the tattoo each received after initiation—which gave her a secret smile.

There was something beautiful and primitive about men dancing for the pleasure of women. The bravos took pride in their grace. It was every bit as much of a battle as any other part of their lives, only with a more desirable reward.

Wicker was too old to play the game, so it was just as well he could fiddle. She admired his skill with the instrument; it was the only time he ever looked truly happy. Rosa knew a couple of the songs he played, such as "Turkey in the Straw" and "Cotton-Eyed Joe." Not for the first time, she wondered about the loved ones Wicker had lost, but they didn't ask such questions. Coming to Valle de Bravo was like being reborn.

Falco stepped out of the line and jigged his way toward her, his feet a blur. The other men hooted and clapped in time. Not for the first time, he beckoned. But for the hundredth time, she laughed and shook her head. Anger flashed in his handsome face. Whatever life had been for him before the Change, it hadn't taught him much about rejection.

Which was too damn bad.

Jolene had been giving him the come-hither eye for the last four months. A brown-haired woman in her midthirties, she had probably been overweight before, but hard work in the communal garden and the obligatory omission of junk food and processed sugar had firmed her up. With her bone structure, Jolene would never have Singer's sylph slenderness, or even Rosa's own compact, lean muscles, but some men—Brick in particular—liked a woman thick. Falco wasn't one of them. God, how Rosa wished he'd notice Jolene's interest and leave her the fuck alone.

Jo gave him one last look and then grinned at Brick, who was dancing for *her* benefit. She seemed capable of wising up, at least. When the big guy approached her, she took his hand and swung into a turn: heel out, right cross, twirl. Shit, it looked like so much fun. With a faint sigh, Rosa wished she could dance in her own right, like one of the men.

She tipped her head back, the music washing over her, and stared at the stars. Their torches and lamps didn't compete with the spectacular light show overhead. So strange to realize grandchildren wouldn't believe them about a time of man-made lights so bright they fogged the stars. That world seemed like a distant dream to her now. But nothing was more real than the desert sky, where black swirled with diamond dust.

"Why aren't you dancing?"

Of course the doc would interrupt her stargazing. Rosa refocused, surprised at what she saw—Chris Welsh, as if for the first time.

He must've traded for a razor. Shaving revealed a lean, hard masculine beauty and sun-weathered skin. A mane of rich chocolate-dark hair tumbled toward his collar in ragged waves, softening a face that had seen tragedy. His golden hazel eyes held a familiar sorrow, as if he carried a weight too heavy for bearing but too personal to put down. She shared that burden, knowing her brother's death would haunt her always.

Run, Rosa!

José's voice rang in her head, drowning out the music. For a moment she heard only screaming, and it took effort to clear her thoughts.

Belatedly, she addressed his question. "If a woman accepts a man's invitation on Burning Night, it's as good as saying she intends to spend the night with him."

"Helpful," Chris said. "Straightforward. No chance for mixed signals."

"Exactly."

"Why do you call it Burning Night?"

"Because they're all blowing off steam."

Well, most of them, anyway.

She watched Lem, the young man she'd whipped, with an edge of concern. He wasn't much more than twenty-one, homely and socially awkward. The kid had a huge crush on

Singer, but she wasn't interested. Still he watched her, even as he danced. Rosa's danger sense kicked in. She had hoped that punishment, combined with Viv's maternal comfort, would discourage further bad behavior, but given Lem's expression, she couldn't imagine this ending well. Wicker's report that he continued to try and trade for liquor did not settle her misgivings. Yet she couldn't exile him for what he *might* do.

"But not you, *Jefa*." Chris's tone held an odd note, one she couldn't place.

For an instant she felt tempted to tell him how hard it was sometimes, but she knew better than to let her guard down in front of a man, even one who insisted he was just passing through.

"You could," she said. "Maybe convince one of our ladies to welcome you officially." The teasing words left her feeling sour, but she pretended not to care, pointing the others out to him one by one. "That's Jolene, but I don't think you could pry Brick away from her tonight. Although maybe his younger sister, Singer . . ." She tilted her head toward the slender young woman with silky black hair and caramel skin. "But she's too young for you."

"Agreed."

Huh. In Rosa's experience, men's attitudes toward having sex with younger women could be summed up in a few disgusting words: if there's grass on the field, play ball. It was to his credit if he wasn't just saying what he thought she wanted to hear.

"That's Mica." Poor dental care and a weak chin made her downright homely, but she had a fit body, and a number of the men didn't seem to mind. She was popular enough that two bravos vied for her attention. The torchlight was kind, highlighting her strong legs and pretty hair.

"And Abigail." She indicated the plump, grandmotherly woman with the white hair, tapping her foot merrily. "She bakes all our bread."

"Maybe I ought to get to know *her* better."

Rosa skimmed him up and down. "*Sí*, she may be willing. She's been known to get down after a few drinks."

The doc seemed startled. "Seriously?"

"She's a woman, isn't she?"

"Would it mean cake for breakfast?"

"I guess that would depend on you, cowboy. Are you *worth* cake for breakfast?"

¿Qué haces, estúpida? That tone could almost be construed as flirtatious, and Rosa didn't play. The men had to take her seriously.

Fortunately, he focused on the question. "Hell, I don't know."

She went on as if she hadn't stumbled. "Viv, she's the small Chinese woman. She might give you a tumble."

"Good to know."

That left Bee, who never came to town, and Ingrid, who seldom danced. Tonight she must've decided to disprove Falco's claim that she was a lesbian by hooking up with Ex, the quiet ex-con who did all their ceremonial ink.

Tall and lean, with gunmetal gray eyes and dark hair starting to silver at the temples, Ex didn't talk much, but his movements gave him away. To Rosa's mind, the tattooist was more dangerous than Jameson because he didn't advertise his dangerous potential. His skills were not limited to smithing. He'd been part of some society that liked to pretend they lived in the Middle Ages. Imagine such a weird hobby being useful after the Change. It didn't track with what she knew of his having been incarcerated. Often she wondered what he'd done to be arrested, but she would never ask. Prison had only refined his skills in the metal shop.

"Where's Tilly?" Chris asked at length.

He likes pregnant women? Pervertido. *Or maybe he just likes Tilly.* She was a very sweet person, after all—sunny and pure, and Rosa couldn't relate to her at all.

"She doesn't feel up to dancing. And Jameson would put a knife in your eye for looking at her. They're our only monogamous couple."

Thank God. If the other women paired up, that would leave too many disappointed, sexually frustrated men. Rosa would be unable to keep a lid on the situation then. As it was, the daily balancing act was almost impossible to manage, and she hoped more women would make their way to Valle from other, less-sought-after settlements. In the meantime, Falco had been demanding a halt on male immigration for the last six months.

Chris chuckled. "I wondered if she might be strong enough to join in, but maybe not. I'm not . . . *interested.*" Pausing, he studied the festivities with a melancholy air. "Never thought I'd see anything like this again."

"What's it like out there?" In this area, she admitted the superiority of his experience. He bore the unmistakable stamp of a man who had hard years behind him, running from something.

Once Rosa had found the valley, she hadn't ventured very far. They patrolled and raided the stretch of road leading into and away from their territory, quite strategically located. From drivers they'd hit and traders who came and went, she learned of settlements to the north and east. If anyone survived to the south, they hadn't come through to talk about it.

"It's empty," he said. "And quiet. I don't think I realized how quiet until right now."

She nodded, familiar with the weight of silence. Before Rio joined her, she had spent her days listening to the birds, the insects, and the rattle of snakes. Sometimes she sang or talked to herself; it didn't help all that much. But once she had someone to look out for, things mattered more. Having nobody was the worst feeling of all.

The doc shared more of his travels, which Rosa intently absorbed. "I even came through Vegas on the way," he said. "You know how some places are just stamped in your memory? Timeless. That was Vegas for me. Hard to see it in ruins."

Her *abuela*'s house in Juárez was like that. Always smelling of fresh corn tortillas and the pot of beans on the fire, that casita remained unchanging in her mind's eye, with its cool adobe walls and a shrine to the sacred Virgin Mary.

"It's never good if you try to go back," she said quietly.

His mouth twisted. "Yeah. I didn't mean to." His gaze went distant, over the dancers and into the darkness beyond. "Tabitha and I got married there, one night at Paris Las Vegas. Did you know the Eiffel Tower replica's built on a two-to-one ratio to the original? We learned that on the tour. One hundred and sixty-four meters."

Rosa eyed him with bemusement. "I had no idea."

"Imagine just . . . taking a tour. Staying in a hotel. It seems ridiculous now, even wasteful. But the New United States had succeeded and its borders were sturdy. The Change was a problem for the east to cope with, as if it would never touch us out here." A sick laugh chugged out of his chest. "I told Tab we'd just have to make do with Sin City's version of Paris, because who knew if the original still stood. I'd said it as a joke."

"Did she die in the Change?" It was a personal question, but he'd brought up the past first. That gave her the opening.

"I don't know. We divorced a year before."

Though she had no idea how anyone else kept time, they used the abbreviations BC and AC. Before and after. So this happy honeymoon belonged to the BC world. Those memories were often painful, especially if he didn't know what had become of this woman. Sometimes closure offered more comfort, even if the news was grim.

"Are you looking for her?" Maybe that was why he wandered. Sweet, if so. She had a secret softness for men on impossible quests. It probably sprang from reading too many Arthurian myths.

"No. I think I travel just to get away from myself."

"What was Vegas like, the second time?" Rosa could tell he needed the question because he carried the haunted echoes. They trailed him like ragged feathers on the edges of his shadow, drifting darkness.

"The Luxor collapsed. The Bellagio fountains have

cvaporated. And the Eiffel Tower's toppled, half buried in the sand. There are a few packs holed up—skinwalkers, you call them—and a few humans. But most have gone crazy with the isolation. At least there were no bodies in the streets. The sands and the hellhounds had taken them."

Packs? That distracted Rosa beyond much hope of concentrating on whatever else he said. The idea that the monsters were social and cooperative with each other made her feel sick. Falco strode over before she could question Chris. The party was breaking up, and he didn't seem to like how long she'd been talking to the new guy.

"Introduce me," he said, eyes narrowed.

Rosa smoothed her braid back over one shoulder, staring the man down. "You don't get to make demands, Falco."

TEN

Rosa didn't back down so much as walk away with the win. Quite a trick. Back turned, pace achingly calm, she owned her exit like she owned the loyalty of everyone in town.

Except maybe for Falco. The jury was still out on him.

Chris wasn't riveted because of mere intellectual curiosity. Years spent studying animal behavior made the signs easy to read: tight shoulders, unblinking stares, intimidating postures. But he watched Rosa and Falco with a deep gut interest. This wasn't just a sexual showdown; it was a battle for control of Valle de Bravo.

Back with the dancers and their female admirers, Wicker wrapped up his speedy jig. A dry desert evening breeze scooped against Chris's cheeks and neck. The air was cool compared to the hot flush of awareness soaking his skin. This wasn't what he needed. Rosa was more off-limits than the dead zones. And Chris . . . he should've moved on. He would. Soon. No one needed a thorn like him in her side.

But he'd promised Rosa to stay. And in spite of his reservations about bringing a new life into this world, he had to admit that Tilly's optimism and happiness were as potent as a drug. He would do what he could for the woman.

At the moment, however, he wanted more than permission to eat and recover. He was far more interested in Rosa herself.

Chemistry. Libido. Dangerous things.

"Going to follow her?" Chris asked, keeping his voice even.

"And get a face full of saguaro needles? Hell, no." Falco muttered something that sounded like "uptight bitch."

"Well, then," Chris said, mostly to see what the guy would do, "I think I'll give it a try."

Falco smoothed his hair back. "I wouldn't if I were you."

"Why's that?"

"Best case, you get somewhere with her that doesn't involve losing a nut. But then you'd have to face me."

Chris nodded. "Seems I'd have already taken on the scarier opponent." He clapped Falco on the shoulder. "Sleep tight."

"Eh, *pendejo*?"

"That seems to be my new name here. Is 'Chris' too plain?"

"You won't last long here if you keep up that bullshit."

"Sorry, friend, but again—I've survived worse. We all have."

He stalked into the night, away from the party, loosely following Rosa. The evening breathed a quiet vigor. The sounds of the desert urged him to open his senses. He'd gotten into the habit of walking during the late, dark hours. Not out of any need to conserve resources or avoid trouble. Water only required the patience to find it, and the creatures were more active at night.

No, Chris just liked it. Always had. Maybe that was why he'd started sleeping out in the desert once again, no matter his small, private accommodations above Wicker's store. It didn't make sense, he knew, to abandon the safety of the town. But the people, the activity—he hadn't felt this hemmed in for years. The caves along a ridge outside town were where he went to get away from the busyness of Valle.

He strode across the baked dirt. Its dusty warmth held a comforting smell, but also one that made him restless. Sage and juniper added a spicy perfume.

"*Jefa?*"

Moonlit, she sat cross-legged on a flat, tall rock. Her forearms draped loosely over her knees. Her back was straight but not rigid. Loose wisps of hair softened the strong line of her jaw. She looked like a yoga teacher in the midst of guided meditation.

He'd set out after her in part to provoke Falco. But again it came back to the simple things. Here was a beautiful, interesting woman. Chris had a terrible track record at caring for others, for keeping them safe, but he was still a man. And he was just passing through. Maybe they could have some fun before he moved along, since he wouldn't tip the balance of power. Nobody needed to know.

"What do you want?" she asked with a weariness he hadn't expected.

"Does he always give you trouble?"

"Not generally. I think you bring it out in him. *Gracias.*"

"*De nada.* May I sit?"

She broke the serene balance of her pose and scooted to one side of the rock. Chris hoisted himself up. "Wow," he said. "Some view."

"Good lookout."

The sloping valley lay beneath a blanket of silver light. Cacti stretched angular arms toward the moon. Bounded by sharp peaks in the distance, it was truly the perfect location for a settlement.

"Good lookout, my ass," he said. "You sit here because it's worth appreciating."

Rosa jerked her head around, staring at him. "Why would you say that?"

"It's true, isn't it? Nothing wrong with small pleasures." He stared out across the saguaro and scrub. "Hell, you don't allow yourself any others."

"Think you're smart, don't you?"

"I was once. Damn, what I wouldn't give for something to read. My brain feels like mush." He rubbed his jaw, enjoying how it felt freshly shaved. "But I do know one thing."

She bent her neck low, as if the burden of taking another breath had suddenly become too great. Chris knew that feeling. Knew it. Ignored it.

"What do you know?"

"That you've backed yourself into a tidy little corner here. *La jefa.* A general doesn't consort with her officers."

"So I should consort with you? Because if that's where this conversation is going, I'd rather be silent."

"Nope."

He picked a bone-dry thistle where it had caught on his pant leg. He held it up and silhouetted it against the moon. Once, he'd had great stores of patience. The majestic mountain lions he tracked for weeks had demanded such discipline. Quiet. Watching. He had waited for them to make the first move.

Rosa was no different—her wariness and strength.

"So why are you here, then?" she asked.

Chris stifled a smile. A disinterested cat would walk away. An angry one would attack. The curious ones stayed in plain view, finding excuses to keep an eye on him. He glanced toward her, noticing the glint off her smooth black hair. A sweet scent clung to her skin, along with the salty musk of dried sweat.

"If I could have sex with you, I would."

"Oh, I bet," she said.

Few women were as naturally seductive as Rosa. Sexual encounters since the Change were ones he'd rather not recall—mercenary swaps, bodies at work, the mind as distant as possible. In the ten seconds it took for a passable orgasm to fade, he was back to lying with a woman for whom he cared nothing, feeling unclean.

Rosa was different. Perhaps it was because she didn't need a damn thing from the likes of him. That wasn't cause for shame. It was reason to pursue.

"Just wanted to get that out there," he said. "You're sexy as hell. Maybe you don't know that, but I think you do."

"So let's do it right here, *sí*? There's a moon out tonight."

"No, you have a town to lead. I get that. I'm not here to destabilize your regime."

She abruptly stood and dusted her cargoes. "Get lost, Welsh."

Instinctively he reached up and took her hand. She stilled, her body snapping rigid. He was ready to get cold-cocked at any moment, but the surprise of contact seemed to paralyze her—like it did him. Her skin was a little chilly from the night air. Underneath was blood and flesh, all warm, all vital. Pulsing.

He'd been alone and wandering for more than three years. So much space, almost all of it deserted. The number of times he'd touched and held another living being was so small. Rock was rock. The air was the air. He felt more in common with the elements than with these people. The draw of coming back into their fold was undeniable. And terrifying.

Chris gave her a little squeeze and let go. He fisted his fingers and wrapped his other hand around them, as if capturing a butterfly.

"I wanted you to know something else," he said. "The other day at the store—there's no way I would use trade goods to bargain a woman into bed."

Rosa cleared her throat. The curve of her thigh was right at Chris's eye level. That closeness urged him to cup the back of her leg, right where it met her ass. Turn her body toward his. Nuzzle her stomach.

"Then why did you say those things?"

"Honestly? To goad you. You're a hard woman."

Her laugh spilled out.

"But I also wanted to know what sort of place this is. What kind of people you've become." He stretched out and extended his legs. The rock bit at his elbows where he rested his weight. "You asked what's out there."

"I did."

"Some really dire shit."

"Shit where women have to use sex to get medicine?"

"Yes," he said. "But I'm not that."

"Neither is Valle de Bravo. I won't let that happen. Ever."

The starkness in her voice told him so much, but left all the mysteries in place. Chris closed his eyes and tipped his face toward the sky. He could almost feel the starlight. Every sense had opened, reading in high def. He tongued the top of his mouth, pressing it there to keep his mouth shut.

"How did *you* survive the Change?" she whispered.

Chris indulged in a soft smile and a little bit of nostalgia. "Got lucky. The right people pounded on my door. You?"

"I'm too stubborn to die, I guess."

His smile broadened. "I like the sound of that. You must make life interesting."

"What can I say? Pure talent."

She shifted her weight. Chris wanted to look up and watch her. Was she smiling? He heard the levity in her voice but didn't dare move for fear of scaring her off.

"Chris?"

"Hmm?"

"I have books."

He didn't know which kept him silent—the glorious possibility of finding new reading material or the fact that she'd admitted as much. He knew a leap of faith when he saw one.

A wash of déjà vu slid across his line of sight. *That dream.*

He'd had a dream a few nights earlier, in which that moment's pieces lined up exactly. Rosa standing, her hip at eye level. The night air. The rock overlooking the valley. And she'd mentioned having books. Then they'd fast-forwarded in that disjointed way dreams worked, with moments flooded by cloud. He'd seen himself jumping down from the rock, knowing stealthy violence had come to Valle— filthy men on foot.

Chris had awoken believing it a ridiculous farce, if only because no one had books. They'd all been used for kindling years ago. That one mistake had been enough for him to let the dream go.

But this . . . this was too strange. Looking out over the same desert, adrenaline surged like floodgates flinging open. He clambered to his feet. Rosa made a little yelp sound in her mouth and skittered back. Afraid she might fall off the rock, Chris grabbed her for the second time.

"What the hell—"

"Quiet."

She twisted his thumb backward. "Let me—"

"Quiet," he cautioned. "Do you hear anything? Out there?" He thrust his chin toward the empty night desert.

"Welsh, if this is some kind of game . . ."

He let go of her hand and stepped to the edge of the granite slab. The spiking dread beneath his sternum said they were in danger, just as he'd felt in that uncanny dream. But from where?

"Wait, you're not joking." Rosa joined him at the precipice. "Talk to me."

So many sounds, when broken down one by one. Fiddle music that sounded like a lullaby. Breezes. His own galloping heart. Chris breathed through his nose to try to focus.

"Quit talking and let me listen."

"Fuck off."

"There. I hear it." Chris froze, dead still, and Rosa took his cue. "Do you?"

"Hear what?"

"Engines."

Had she been a woman prone to panic, she would've staggered. That was what he saw in the way her eyes flared wider than usual, the way her lips parted. Instead she seemed to gather into herself, concentrating as he did. Chris counted three of his own heartbeats for each second that passed.

"I don't hear anything."

"Engines," he said again. "There, over that ridge. More than one. Diesel. Trucks, not motorcycles."

Her nostrils flared on a sharp inhale. "Dust pirates?"

"Who?"

"Men who live in the desert. No families. No community. They venture into our territory to strike shipping trucks, but they don't leave survivors. Lately they've been looking hard at Valle. Little strikes to gauge our defenses. Maybe they're tired of roving."

The engine noises cut off. Chris shivered. It wasn't a relief that he could no longer hear them.

"Have they ever attacked here?"

"*Sí*. But we make them pay for every step."

"But you just grabbed a big haul, out there on the highway. Tempting."

"The valley gives us the perfect position to see anyone coming—especially trucks."

Chris vaulted down from the rock and turned to look up at her. "How many bravos do you think are sober and ready to fight? Right now?"

She flicked her chin toward town, then back to that southwest ridge. "We ration alcohol. Some men are always posted on sentry duty, and the rest would be ready in a minute. We always keep the Burning Night random, well away from a raid. That way no one can see our pattern to learn when we're vulnerable."

"And these pirates have always attacked from their vehicles?"

"That's right."

All he could hear now was the desert quiet. But something else was out there. Chris could practically hear them creeping in, all shadowy echoes of that blasted dream. The future of Valle de Bravo depended on Rosa putting her trust in him. No easy task, considering he barely trusted himself.

"But what if they didn't have a minute?" He held up his hand, offering it to her, silently urging her to come with him. "No trucks, Rosa. Not this time. What if they were coming in on foot?"

ELEVEN

"You sure of this?"

Chris's silence wasn't reassuring, but she couldn't afford to take chances. Peltz had demonstrated a little more intelligence than other roving bands. Just a little, mind, or else the raiders would've changed their lifestyle. But from his patient strategy, he must be ruthless and cunning. Maybe he envisioned taking over Valle de Bravo, with his men in place of Rosa's. A leader that arrogant would figure women wouldn't care who protected them.

Rosa smiled and shook her head. *Shows what he knows.*

Bouncing on the balls of his feet, Chris's impatience demanded her attention. He wanted her to call the bravos in from Burning Night on the idea he could hear something she didn't. The old adage "better safe than sorry" made her pull the pistol out of her gun belt and fire two warning shots into the air. Then she scampered down the hill at a run. The men were already forming up, most cussing and half dressed. If Chris was wrong, she'd let them beat him senseless for interrupting one of the few nights they got to drink and carouse.

"What the hell?" Brick demanded.

Ingrid didn't look any happier at having her night with Ex interrupted. Neither of them hooked up often, so this meant a rare break from their taciturn natures.

"We got incoming," Rosa said. "I want all able-bodied men at their posts."

"We'd see them," Falco said. "Hear their trucks."

She narrowed her eyes. "Who's giving the orders here?"

The answer was obvious when they all grabbed weapons and prepared to fight. Ex was one of their best shooters; he scaled up a lookout post. Falco did too, as he was damn fine with a rifle. Other gunmen did likewise. Jameson waited in the middle of town, knives at the ready, and Brick fell in beside him, fists upraised. He fought barehanded better than most men could with any number of weapons. Ingrid, too, preferred to fight in a melee. Opponents nearly always pegged her as a soft target. It was fun to watch them underestimate her as she ripped them up with krav maga.

Rosa cocked her head. Now she could hear it in the silence too—the telltale crunch of footsteps over loose rock, the occasional muffled curse drifting on the night wind. She smelled them as well. Living as they did, dust pirates stank of what they ate and drank: half-rancid meat and poorly fermented sour mash. The stench carried on the night wind.

Chris had been right. She'd deal with that uncomfortable fact later.

Now it was a matter of determining how many approached.

Thanks to early warning, the bravos had time to get into position and defend the perimeter. Rosa shouldered a rifle and ran into what had been a church. She jogged up the steps to the tower, wiping sweaty palms on her pants. But the flash of nerves went in a blink. This was her life.

Rough, unkempt men in makeshift armor edged over the ridge. If not for Chris, Valle would have been caught flat-footed. When the first man came into range, she sighted and took the shot—a clean kill right through the neck. It wasn't the clean shot of a sniper, but one intended as a deterrent. So fucking messy. He gurgled as he died, blood spurting from the wound in his throat.

"Think twice!" she called to the rest. "I can drop five more of you before you take ten steps. All my men are in position. You can't do anything but die here."

A raider screamed, "Mexican bitch! I'm gonna tear your head off and—"

She shot him before he finished the sentence. "I'm from Guatemala, you *hijo de puta*."

They didn't listen, of course. They charged toward town. Rosa dropped three of them as fast as she'd claimed. The other two were smarter, using cover to block her shots. More crept in from all sides, slinking between buildings. For the first time since she'd settled in the valley, Peltz's dust pirates reached the center of town. But her bravos were ready, sweeping out of shadowy hiding places. Even half drunk, they were more than a match for this desert trash. Such men didn't train or build; they only scavenged and stole. They were human hyenas, as bad as those damned hellhounds.

Ingrid grinned as two men ran for her. With her slim build and gleaming pale hair, she looked almost ethereal in the moonlight. She greeted the first with a block, a blow to his windpipe, and a smashing blow to the back of his neck. He went down before the second one reached her. Lightly, Ingrid leaped away from his clumsy attack. She kneed him in the groin and followed with a punishing kick to his knee.

Rosa took a shot when she had one, but with the close fighting below, she feared hitting one of her own men. Close combat hamstrung her other sharpshooters too, but they maintained a wary eye. Falco and Ex laid down cover fire, preventing more raiders from cresting the hill.

"West, Falco," she called. He turned to drop a couple of late stragglers.

She studied the battle in the street below, looking for

tactical advantage. Brick laid a raider out with one punch and whirled for another. Death came from above, as Ex shot the one Brick had knocked out. *Efficient, playing to our strength.* Rosa nodded her approval. They would do this. They would keep doing it until no one remained to offer challenge.

To her surprise, Chris waded in. He had a lean build that didn't seem suited for hand-to-hand. But he appeared to enjoy brawling. Satisfaction showed in every well-struck swing. He fought as if he'd learned the hard way. No fancy moves. Just anger and wiry strength. Good intuitive technique, though—flurry to the kidney, slam to the eardrums, hook, uppercut. The last blow sent his opponent's head snapping back. Rosa heard the crunch even from her position.

Damn. Broke his neck. Chris was stronger than he looked.

Another ran at his back. She shouted a warning. The raider managed to get a knife in Chris, but she couldn't tell how bad it was. He threw the bastard to the ground. Rosa sighted and shot, slugging a bullet into a meaty shoulder. Chris took advantage of the wound and dug his fingers in. The other man screamed and screamed . . . until he didn't anymore. The doc showed no hint he had trouble taking lives.

Jameson preferred to fight alone. He was so fast that he could take on three or four men at once. His blades gleamed as he twirled, part Filipino knife style, part gutter survival. With his free hand he broke a man's arm. The raider screamed while Jameson cut his throat. Dead in five seconds. She'd never seen anyone stand up with him longer than that. Lightning speed combined with his utter focus.

Echoes of gunfire came from other parts of town. Rifles sparked from rocky outcroppings, dropping any attackers who still crawled. She identified Mica and Viv as the shooters. None of the women but Ingrid would fight in close combat, but the rest were fair shots. They did their part in defending Valle.

Rosa took aim at those who tried to run, except for one. She called to him, "Tell your leader we'll hit back if he doesn't stop testing our defenses. I promise we won't be as kind as we were this time."

"I'll tell him," came the terrified reply.

Shit, he sounds young.

A knock of guilt always stirred in her chest when that happened. Maybe if they'd had a chance somewhere better, they wouldn't turn into mean, dishonorable drunks like the rest. But in the midst of an attack, she was never in the position to invite such kids to stay. This one had to carry her message. He turned and limped out of town, but Jameson watched his back with complete intensity. It wasn't until he'd vanished from sight that Jameson turned toward the house he shared with Tilly. Sometimes Rosa envied her that devotion.

Footsteps warned she had a visitor incoming, so she wiped away the longing. She wasn't surprised to find Falco. He was nothing if not persistent.

"All clear," he said. "You want me to tell the men—"

"I give the orders." Rosa kept her tone polite, but firm. "Thanks anyway."

This struggle wasn't going to stay civil for long, but hopefully it wouldn't catch fire tonight. She was too tired to stake a proper claim. She brushed past him before he could decide to make more of her refusal.

Rosa ran lightly down the stairs, rifle slung over one shoulder. They still needed more ammo; it was an ongoing concern. Their supplies were low, and she was loath to tap into the emergency stores. Eventually it would mean hand-to-hand combat for the rest of their days.

"Good work," she called. Everyone hooted in response. "I need a couple of extra volunteers to stand watch in case they double back."

They always had at least one man on duty, but it seemed wise to play it safe tonight. Rosa scanned the crowd, seeing whose hands went up. Rio, of course. It seemed like the muchacho never slept. Eventually Lem put his arm in the air too. Made sense. He might feel the need to earn back the respect he'd lost by trying to force himself on Singer.

With the town safe, the bravos dispersed—already trading good-natured stories about their part in the defense. Rosa smiled as she turned for home, hoping to make it there before someone confided a problem that she needed to handle. The adrenaline kick of the fight was seeping out of her pores. It had been a fucking long day. She needed to sleep.

She had just closed the door and lit a lamp when a knock sounded. Biting off a particularly foul curse, she went to answer it. With the door open only a crack, Rosa glared at whoever opposed her getting some rest.

It was their new doctor, of course.

"Go to bed," she snarled.

He grinned at her. "If you insist, but I really came by because you mentioned books."

Right. Men always want books in the middle of the night.

In her experience, men used all kinds of excuses to get their foot in the door.

She didn't budge. "Not tonight. Besides, if you want to see them, you got to earn it."

"Earn it, how?"

"Deliver the baby. Then you'll deserve a look at my library."

"I'll do everything I can," he said gravely.

"I—" She curled her fingernails into the wood of the door. "Thank you. For what you did tonight. You probably saved us some wounded, at least."

He nodded once. Dark shadows filled his eye sockets, making it hard to read his expression. After a half dozen heartbeats, standing there quietly, he turned to go.

Rosa saw the tear in his shirt and the gash down his back. From that raider he'd battled. The slash wasn't deep, and only about ten centimeters long, but Chris wouldn't be able to clean it. Infection set in fast in the hot weather, and they couldn't spare the medicine. In fact, he had brought more drugs with him than they'd seen in two years. They had learned to get by without, sometimes with heartbreaking consequences.

She sighed faintly. "Go to the *taberna* and wait for me. I'll be there shortly."

"Why?"

"You're injured. Somebody has to patch you up."

"Why you?" Something in his tone said he wanted a specific response, a hint of softness.

Hell if she would admit to such inclinations. She hadn't gotten where she was by revealing her weak places. So she offered, "Who else would bother?"

"Grim fucking point. I could come in, if that would be easier." That didn't sound like a line. Too tentative, like her concern struck a strange note with him.

But it wasn't personal. They needed him for Tilly and Jameson's sake. Otherwise Rosa had no stake in whether his back healed.

"Not in my house. Not after dark. There would be talk."

But as she watched the tall, lovely line of him walking away, she knew her initial assessment was on the mark. He would bring trouble, even as he'd brought medicine and a glimmer of hope.

TWELVE

Chris couldn't remember the last time he'd been so satisfied. Tired. Fucking exhausted, actually. But satisfied. The chill shiver of dread that had walked up his spine disappeared as soon as he'd first set eyes on Peltz's dust pirates. They were intruders. He had no claim to Valle, no place here with these people, but they had stepped onto his turf.

That was how it had felt, anyway. He strolled to the tavern, enjoying the sweet soreness in his muscles. Stronger than he'd ever been, he was also more attuned to the nuances around him. Maybe it was because he'd spent so long on his own, just him and the wilderness. How else could he explain being able to hear silent footsteps across a desert valley, or the rumble of engines out of Rosa's earshot?

But it was either believe his senses or in the odd déjà vu of his dream. He didn't know which was the least disturbing. A thought jabbed like lightning into his brain.

Jenna's senses had been remarkable after her first shift.

He caught the toe of one boot against the heel of the other, then stopped in the middle of the dark, dusty street.

Could the Change be affecting him too? Not once, ever, had he come close to feeling like some wolf was ready to bust out of him, not even in those furious few minutes after Ange had been slaughtered. His mind was always there. His body stayed human.

With a soft chuckle, he continued his walk. For all his familiarity with the possibilities, he still couldn't fathom what it was to shift from a person into an animal. The mechanics, the internal wiring—none of it was quantifiable, and he'd thought himself long past trying to measure anything. That was for the best, or else he'd have to face the sort of man he was now—the kind who did murder and walked away content.

"Hey, Doc," Brick called.

He sat on the porch outside the *taberna* with his striking young sister, Singer. They shared a cigar—one puff each, passing it back and forth, probably a rare treasure savored in honor of defending their homes. "Nice work today, *mano*."

"Tú también."

"You want a drag?" Singer asked.

She flashed a brilliant smile, which Chris took as a dare rather than a come-on. Let the hazing begin. He might be game if he thought he would stay past the birth of Tilly's child.

He wiped a hand across his brow. God, he felt like a butcher after a twelve-hour shift. "No, thanks. I need sleep. Soon."

"Hey, *güero*, that's a nasty cut." Singer pushed away from the post toward him. They met halfway on the steps of the cantina. She was the loveliest blend of Hispanic and African American, with a smile that had turned decidedly more inviting than challenging. But she was also sixteen. Although Chris was hard up, he wasn't a bastard. "Want me to stitch it up for you?"

"I've got it, Singer," came Rosa's sleek voice. "Get some sleep."

She didn't stop as she passed them on the steps. Chris watched her go. Shit, he was already getting used to that privilege.

He shrugged to Singer and tipped an imaginary hat. "Maybe next time I'm wounded."

"Next week, then." She winked and rejoined her brother.

The two of them snickered about something. Chris didn't want to know what. The muscles and skin around that slice on his back were really beginning to burn. And he felt so fatigued, he was damn close to punch-drunk.

He'd thought the tavern would be full of bravos celebrating their victory, but perhaps the exhaustion of Burning Night and the raid had used up their stores. The place was dark and deserted. They were probably all in bed. Sensible people.

Across the room, Rosa lit a match from behind the bar. Soon an oil lamp filled the open room with gold. She had a let's-get-this-over-with attitude about her. He had the perverse need to know if it was genuine.

"Singer offered. You should go back to bed."

"No good," she said, shaking her head. "If Singer starts making a play for you and you accept, then I'll have hell to pay with Brick and Rio."

"You're not making the prospect of staying all that appealing."

"I didn't intend to." She patted the bar. "C'mon, then."

"This won't hold, *Jefa*. If you don't get more women in here soon, this place will eat itself up."

Rosa stilled. A leather tie tried to hold all her hair back, but the battle had left her fierce, wild, ragged around the edges. Dark silken strands slipped down to frame her face. She looked younger, suddenly, and even more petite. Maybe it was because, regardless of the responsibilities she shouldered, she was a mortal who had limits.

"I know," she said tightly. "But haven't you noticed that fewer women survived?"

"Are you asking for my wisdom and input?"

"I'm serious."

"So am I."

He stripped off his shirt. He used the material to rub the grime from his face, then tossed it aside. Hardly a few days in his care and it already needed mending. Typical.

Rosa stared at him. Holy hell, she lit him on fire.

Self-conscious, aroused, he rubbed the back of his neck. Her gaze followed the movement, then slid down the length of his torso. She actually took a step back from the bar as he approached.

"It's hard for you to ask for help, isn't it?" he asked. "You only ask because you'd die before missing the chance to help your town."

"Shut up."

"Nope." He reached the end of the bar and turned his back. Rosa was either going to do this or she'd back down. Both possibilities had his fatigued mind alert once more— almost as alert as his body. "I knew a man once who acted like you do. Mason was a hard-ass. Held the whole world on his shoulders. He didn't imagine anyone else was up to the task."

She dipped a cloth in a basin of water and touched it to his skin. Chris hissed softly, then eased into the pain. He forced his muscles to relax as she cleaned his wound.

"What happened to him?"

"He fell for a woman who gave as good as she got. Now they have each other's backs."

"Good for them."

Silently he agreed with her. He liked testing Rosa, but he knew his own limits. Chris had let Ange down when she needed him—the last in a long line of injuries he'd done to the women who loved him.

"Ow," he snapped.

"Poor baby." She worked in silence as he soaked up the stinging pain. An antiseptic of some kind. "I don't think you'll need stitches. Just try not to aggravate it."

Rosa's fingers were nimble and surprisingly cool. He closed his eyes and absorbed the simple, miraculous pleasure of being touched. She didn't hurry. Neither did she linger. Every brush of skin against skin fired up Chris from the inside out. Starved for attention, his body interpreted efficient care as downright primal.

She bandaged him, and already he was crumbling. Soon it would be over. He'd cram back into himself and seal it up tight. But with Rosa's hands on him, he couldn't remember why.

The lightest brush of her fingertips trailed down the right side of his spine—nowhere near the slice. She brushed up his side and laid her hand on his shoulder. Palm flat. Nails curling slightly, testing. Teasing.

Chris made fists at his sides. Blood boiled all the way down to his capillaries, screaming for more. Whatever breath he'd been ready to exhale stayed trapped in his lungs.

She swallowed so loudly that he heard it. Two quick steps back and she was herself once more. He could practically feel an icy wall shoot up between them.

"All right, then. You're good."

"Shit," he muttered.

Fun's over.

He was a sorry-ass mofo if that had become his definition of a good time. But no one had touched him voluntarily—nothing to gain by it—since Ange. No guilt would follow these moments. No shame. Only a pounding greed for more.

Intent on accepting the touch for what it was and moving on, he rolled his shoulder. The dressing tugged, but the pain was a triviality compared to the ache in his cock. A quick glance toward Rosa revealed her head bent low as she boxed up the first-aid kit.

"That has been my experience," he said into the thick silence. His throat was as dry as the desert outside the tavern door. "About the women, I mean. For most of the clumps of people I've come across, the ratio was about two to one in favor of men. I don't know why. Maybe something with the Change, or just how piss hard it's been to survive the aftermath."

"You got that right."

She shoved a wad of bandages back in the kit, but they were a fat tangle. Ends popped out as she closed the lid. With a huff, she started again. Her fingertips were trembling.

"Rosa?"

"Leave it."

Yet speaking Russian would've been easier than turning away from her. He edged around the bar and took her hands. She slapped him away, but he tried again.

"So my turn to ask you again," he said. "And maybe you'll give me a better answer than, 'I'm too stubborn to die.' How did you survive the Change?"

"By fighting."

"Hellhounds?" He remembered that was her name for them—and a fitting one, it was.

"People."

He held still, facing her, willing her to continue. Something told him this was important—a key part of her character. Why she intrigued him so greatly was a mystery. Maybe because she was the first person who felt like a *person* since he'd left the Northwest. She had depth and flaws and strength. Grit. Most of what he'd seen between here and there was cowering. It got old, downright suicidal, to think that was all humanity had left to give.

"Will you tell me?"

"By fighting," she repeated, her face gone distant with dark memories. "You fight and fight—with rocks, sticks, your bare hands if you have to. And you never stop. Never. You never lie down. If they keep coming, so do you. That's the only way you survive this." She studied him then, dark eyes intense. "As you already know. See, everybody who makes it to Valle has passed his or her own trial by fire. Isn't that right, Doc?"

"Yeah. It is."

"You have so many questions, like you've earned my secrets. Why don't you tell me about yours?" She stepped closer in challenge, and his body responded to her proximity on a wholly different scale.

"What makes you think I have any?"

"Everyone does. So tell me about her."

"Who?"

"The woman who broke your heart."

The lance-accurate assessment stabbed him in a sore spot. Okay, maybe he wasn't ready to have this conversation. He cleared his throat and turned away. "I'll make the rounds again tomorrow and check up on everyone who needs medical attention. I patched up what I could of the injured bravos, but their wounds will need attention as they heal."

"Good." Her smile said she knew he was backing off.

"Thank you. For trusting me tonight."

"*De nada.* It was a good call. And you fought like a bravo."

"Don't get any ideas," Chris said with a quiet laugh. "I'm not staying long enough for some swearing-in ceremony."

"You're probably just scared of needles."

He had seen the town's distinctive tattoo that evening during the Burning Night celebrations, when bravos had stripped their shirts near the bonfire's searing flames. Hector had inadvertently provided a close-up view. The young man had taken a bullet to the meat of his upper arm. He'd been relieved that the tattoo remained intact.

"I'm surprised you didn't name the town after yourself."

Rosa's expression sobered. "I'm nothing without my bravos."

Something in the way she said it made Chris want to be a part of her society. To belong. More than that, he wanted to claim part of that possessive pride in her voice.

Only then did he realize he was still bare chested. If she moved forward, Rosa wouldn't even reach his chin with the top of her head. She was much shorter than she appeared among her people. Her mouth would brush his chest. He'd only just managed to calm his erection, but that mental image had it jerking back to life.

"Rest now," she said.

"Sure. You too."

She dimmed the lamp until darkness swallowed the tavern. Her footsteps echoed across the empty room, toward the door. Chris closed the distance between them with a few quick strides. "Those books," he said, feeling as green as a junior high kid at his first dance. *Idiot.*

"Yeah?"

"What kind are they?"

Rosa leaned in, her face a mere breath from his chest. His skin felt stretched tight. She inhaled—*oh, God, she's breathing me in.* The primitive heat nearly incinerated him. Full-on fellatio wouldn't have been as erotic.

She straightened and tucked a lock of hair behind her ear. "Wouldn't you like to know?"

Lamplight from one of the nearby buildings illuminated her ass as she stepped out on the porch. "Go ahead, *Jefa.* Keep walking away from me. I like the view."

THIRTEEN

"You are so beautiful," the dream-Rosa said.

She *had* to be dreaming because she didn't speak to men like that, certainly not ones she barely knew. But it was one of those dreams, where she could only watch while her other self did whatever the hell she wanted. And apparently, she wanted Chris Welsh.

But this was fine. Better than fine, actually. She could indulge curiosity here without worrying about how it would affect the balance of power. Falco couldn't see inside her head and bitch about the fact that he didn't factor into her wet ones.

So she drank him in. Like a golden cat, Chris sprawled on her sisal mattress, her handwoven blanket covering one lean hip. His belly made her want to trace each ripped muscle with her tongue. God, he was gorgeous. He had the scruffy wildness of a man who knew how to take care of himself. It couldn't be otherwise if he'd really been out there alone for years.

She felt for him something like tenderness. Perhaps it was the ageless allure of the cowboy, riding the plains alone, so that when he rolled into town with a barely leashed air of violence and blood spilling in his wake, a woman's pulse quickened. Chris only needed a horse and a battered hat, because he already had the broken-down boots. They lay on her bedroom floor.

"You think I'm beautiful?" he asked with endearing skepticism.

A guy like him must've had women crawling all over him before the Change. Even dream-Rosa shook her head in disbelief. An ease existed between them. According to the dream, then, they had been lovers for some time.

"Does that modesty thing really work for you?" she asked.

"Come over here, and I'll show you how confident I can be." His low rasp sent shivers through her.

She eased into his arms and was astonished to find how perfectly she fit. Arousal curled into her stomach. Such an unfamiliar response, but it wasn't their first time together. He wouldn't be so comfortable in her bed otherwise.

Maybe I've been drinking. That notion matched her blurry feeling as she sank into the moment. It was impossible to remain unmoved when he sat up, muscles rippling in his chest and shoulders. Some men grew weathered and ugly through trial and hardship, but it had molded Chris into a god. The heat of his skin seared hers.

She wished for more than lamplight to study him by. In the morning she would kiss every bit of him as the sunlight spilled through the open archway. Lick the rays of light patterning his body, all laid out for her pleasure. She would make him come again and again, until he was too weak to move, let alone work.

She whispered, *"Mi corazón, mi vida. 'Te amo como se aman ciertas cosas oscuras, / secretamente, entre la sombra y el alma.'"*

Grinning softly, he offered his translation. "'I love you as certain dark things are loved, / secretly, between the shadow and the soul.' Where's it from?"

"Pablo Neruda."

"Never heard of him."

"I'd be surprised if you had."

But even if he had never read Neruda, he loved books as much as she did. That was more than any other man could offer these days.

"You kill me with poetry in a world like this," he said. "You're like a desert flower, all hidden sweetness. The rain brings you to bloom."

"Are you the rain, then?"

"Maybe. When did you get this one?" He pressed a kiss to her shoulder.

"Before the Change."

She'd never told anyone that before. Too many bad memories made up the past, ones of impotence and failure. It did no good to look backward—a direction that would only break her into pieces. So she resolved to enjoy this respite.

"I hate knowing you've been hurt . . . but I admire you for being so strong."

"You're strong too," she said, testing his biceps, then working lower. Slowly.

No reason not to go for what she wanted. She liked taking charge because of the times she'd taken no pleasure in sex, pinned down and hurting. Now she felt most comfortable on top, and he showed no sign of minding her preferences.

"Not the sort of strength I meant. *Oh.*"

Rosa leaned in, watching his face as she touched him. She knew exactly how he wanted it, how much pressure, how much friction. Lovely cock, smooth and hard, a glimmer of fluid at the tip that said he was hers. With her other hand, she cupped his balls, thumbing the underside. He tensed his thighs, lifting up.

"You like that, Cristián?" She gave it the Spanish pronunciation, which made him growl. He was hers, right down to what she called him.

"God, I love the way you say my name."

"*Lo sé.* That's why I do it."

He pulled her on top and she lay down to kiss him, her

dark hair falling in a silky curtain around them. Rosa seldom let it down, but it was her one vanity in a world where the sensible course would have been to hack it off. Instead she wore it to the middle of her back, using braids and tails to keep it tidy. Right now she was fervently glad she'd never cut it. She was like Salome dropping her seven veils, one by one.

His mouth tasted of agave wine and fierce desire. Chris buried his fingers in her hair and she moaned softly, his tongue stroking hers. The kiss went on forever, sweetness and lust commingled. He already knew she liked little bites on her lower lip and gentle suction.

"Sí. Perfecto. Más, mi amor."

Unlike most men, he knew the importance of those long, languid kisses and the caresses that set her whole body alight. Rosa let her thighs spill to either side of his hips and rocked against him. Bare skin, hot and smooth. He traced his fingers down her spine, stroking. Tingles spiraled through her, her nipples pebbling against his chest. She shifted to nudge his erection against her wetness and rose a little, teasing him. He groaned long and low.

"Mmm." With a smooth motion, he sat up so she was straddling his lap. He bent his head to her breasts. "So pretty."

It wasn't fair how well he knew her body, how quickly he could bring her to boiling. Rosa held his head and floated on the hot, buoyant tide that surged through her each time he licked or bit or nuzzled. She trembled as he sipped at her nipples, perfect delicacy interspersed with the barest edge of teeth. A moan escaped her.

In retaliation she took his earlobe between her teeth and bit gently, then licked. She knew how he felt about hot breath, right there. She whispered, "You want to fuck?"

He jerked in reaction. *Sí*, he liked the dirty talk, and she loved teasing him.

"What do you think?" He eased back in invitation.

"I think you can't wait to get inside me again. I'm the

hottest piece of ass you ever had." She laughed down at him as he grinned, delighted by his responsiveness and his need.

But it only matched her own. For some reason it felt like forever since she'd touched him. Her memory had fogged, but it didn't matter. He was here and he wasn't going anywhere.

Suddenly she couldn't wait another second.

Rosa reached between their bodies and curled her fingers around his cock. Splendid. She lifted up and his expression of open adoration nearly killed her. Nobody ever looked at her like that. Not at Rosa Cortez. She glided down slowly, taking him so slowly, savoring his delicious skin.

"Ay, sí," she whispered.

She loved this angle, when he was so deep inside her. For a moment she held still, just feeling him—the heat and hardness. His heartbeat sounded in her body, the throb unmistakable and sublime. His breath quickened, though they were just joined. No movement yet.

"Ride me." His hands framed her hips, a slight tremor revealing his urgency.

Another low growl slid out of him as she started the smooth up-and-down glide. The pleasure built in her belly, a heat she'd never known. Not from sex. It sank barbed hooks into her, a passion that ravaged and shook.

She moved faster, nearly overwhelmed by the intensity. Surely they should be slow and easy, playful this time. They'd already slaked the urge once today. Hadn't they? Rosa wrestled with the sense that she didn't understand everything, but lost the thread when he shifted and found a sweeter spot. Leaning forward, she blew out a breath and rocked harder.

"You like it fast," he teased, wrapping his arms about her. "It's a race, love. Let's see who can get there first."

Me, she thought, arching and stilling on him. The climax surprised her with its long, luxuriant waves, nothing quick or furtive, but endless beauty unfurling like a single perfect rose in a field of thorns. Overwhelmed by a storm of wildness, she bent and took his mouth, savaging him with a teeth-and-tongue claim that drove his orgasm. At the right time, she knew it was possible to make him come with a kiss and a whisper of "Cristián" against his lips. He went with a roar, bowing beneath her, and she savored each pulse.

She lay down on him, in no hurry to disrupt the closeness. Chris held her and stroked her back, soothing away the occasional shiver. Lightly, he dusted kisses on her brow and temples, all sated male beauty. What a gorgeous face, such strong bones and slightly imperfect symmetry. Looking at a man like him made a woman think of babies, simply because he was so fucking lovely. She touched her fingertips to his chest, testing the muscle, and he gave a pleased purr.

A feeling swelled in her, so deep and profound that she had to say the words. It was no longer enough to quote someone else's lines of adoration.

"Love—"

Sweaty and disoriented, Rosa awoke alone in the predawn light. She panicked, thinking she wasn't alone. Scrambling to her feet like a scalded cat, she stumbled to the wall, in need of its cool solidity at her back. She traced the whitewashed adobe with a shaking fingertip. *I know this crack. And that one. This is the real world. I'm not crazy.*

In the silence she listened for any sign she wasn't alone, that someone had come in and . . . done things to her in her sleep.

But no, she was fully dressed—though somewhat sticky.

No sounds came from outside, apart from a distant woodpecker and the quiet hum of insects. At times like this she missed music.

It took a long time for her heartbeat to settle. *Means nothing. Just a dream, some echo of how I felt patching him up the other night.*

Sí, she'd enjoyed the feel of his skin more than she expected. Rosa was a sucker for a taut, lean, muscled back, and Chris had one of the finest she'd ever seen—a back made for fingernails. And to be honest, she didn't think he'd mind some scratch marks. He radiated wildness in the same way as the mountain lions that sometimes came down from the hills. She could never bring herself to shoot them, so the bravos just ran them off.

Eventually, as her heartbeat slowed, she convinced herself it was nothing. Not a big deal. She was a normal woman with normal needs, even if she lived like a nun. So what if a hot guy got her a little worked up in her sleep? Hell, at least she was pretty relaxed.

It was a damn fine dream.

Smiling, she gathered her things so she could head to the communal bath—just a jury-rigged gravity shower, but it served the purpose. She needed to wash away the memory. Indulging in such fantasies at night was one thing, but during the day she had to be in charge. Falco was a good man, but he didn't see the sense in her carrying the burden alone, and he wanted like hell to take his place beside her. She'd worked too hard to share.

God only knew what the doc would see in her when they met next. As she walked, she tried to perfect her poker face. The memories still wouldn't let go. That hadn't been just a sex dream, but something deeper and more profound. That scene had filled her with soft, troubling emotions, and right now, she kind of wanted to shoot him for messing up her head.

Why him?

The question plagued her as she carried her basket of shower things—homemade soap, rough cloth for washing, and a dry towel—toward the bath. At that early hour, she wouldn't find anyone else around, which was why she preferred to get clean before the rest of the town stirred. Some of the bravos liked to watch, and the women didn't mind, she guessed, or she would've heard about it. But Rosa valued her privacy—the one thing that hadn't been taken from her. She refused to explain where she had gotten her scars, or that she'd collected many of them before the world went to hell and monsters prowled the dark.

Rosa rounded the corner and stopped short. Chris was already in the shower, eyes closed, his hair sleek and dark. Diamond droplets of water glistened over his tanned skin, and her mouth went dry.

FOURTEEN

Chris couldn't shake that damn dream.

He scrubbed his scalp, eyes pinched shut, as the image of Rosa riding him sent shock waves down his spine. Lukewarm water skated over his skin, but it was just a tease. Her fingernails had dug deeper, giving him a jolt with each caress. That was what he wanted. A shudder rippled across his shoulders.

Tipping his head back, he rinsed the soap from his hair. Such a luxury. He took his time, soaking in the feel and letting the dream claim him. His cock stirred. He'd woken up sticky and already satisfied—hence the early shower—but a fantasy that potent wasn't meant for just one use. It was a gift from his subconscious that would keep on giving. He could survive any sexual dry spell on the memory of Rosa's expression as she came. Unlike any he'd ever seen on her lovely face.

But, God, if her face was beautiful, her body was hot enough to end all brain function. High breasts with dusky brown nipples. A tight waist. Hips that flared wide—all athletic curves. He'd loved sliding his fingers down her ribs, taking in each little ridge until he could grab her hips and hold on tight. And the way she'd stared down at him, as if he were a feast for her alone. No woman had ever looked at him with such possessive intensity.

The idea of belonging to Rosa wove heat into his chest. It was more than just being horny, more than lust. But it was also a hell of a lot scarier.

He shoved that thought aside. Turning toward the wall, he fumbled for the nozzle and turned off the water, conserving the scant supply. Then he grabbed his cock with one hand and braced his weight with the other. The whole damn village would be awake soon. He wanted to enjoy himself just a little longer, before the day dried up his fantasies.

What had she whispered to him? Dirty talk, he remembered. He'd liked that too much. But the actual words they'd shared were more elusive than the blunt-force images of Rosa thumbing her own nipples. As he hardened, he sank into the memory. His hand moved faster along his dick, from balls to tip and back. Finding his rhythm, he pictured Rosa rocking on his lap. Her hair had hugged the outer curves of her breasts as she bucked.

"It's a race, love," he'd said. "Let's see who can get there first."

She'd used him and he'd adored it.

He was breathless now. His strokes became shorter, truncated, just flicking quick pulses over his swollen head. So hard. So close. His orgasm gathered and built like a blaze over kindling. A moan started low in his chest as he remembered that last kiss—the one that had sent him over the edge. Sharp teeth. Rough. She'd grabbed his hair, fingers tunneling to the scalp. She'd fucking savaged him with her sweet little mouth.

God, what had she said?

"Cristián."

Release hit him like a sledgehammer to the back of the head. With a hard grunt, he shot against the wall. He used his free hand, fisted tight, to bang the slippery stucco. Pleasure washed over his skin.

Chris came back to the world with the sudden feeling of being watched. *Shit*. With as much confidence as he could muster, he turned.

Rosa was leaning against the opposite wall. A small bundle of bath supplies waited at her feet. She wasn't standing in the doorway as if she'd just walked in. No, she had settled in. To watch him.

"All done?"

"Yeah," he gritted out.

He was still stark naked, holding his flaccid cock. *Shit. Shit. Shit.* He grabbed his washcloth off a nearby hook and wiped his hands, then ran a little water to rinse the wall. As calmly as he could manage, he found his towel and began to dry off.

Rosa didn't budge. She followed his every movement with a dark, unreadable gaze. "Don't do that again unless you want a hard-up bravo to help you out. There are one or two."

"Lay off, all right?"

She looked perfectly relaxed, her hands tucked behind her back. That pose thrust her breasts against a plain white button-down, one long enough to just cover her ass. Did she use it as a nightgown? It looked rumpled as if she'd slept in it. Beneath the clinging cotton her nipples were rock hard.

In the dream he'd been arrogant. He'd known what it was to be wanted. Maybe that was because she'd looked at him the way she was doing just then. Stark appreciation shone from her luminous brown eyes. He could knock down trees with his bare hands when she ate him up with her stare.

Chris wrapped the towel loosely around his waist and eased nearer. Any minute she'd pull a gun on him, but he didn't care. She was the inspiration behind two of the most satisfying orgasms he'd had in years. And he felt like paying homage to his muse.

"Thank you," he said.

"For what?"

"Letting me finish."

She licked her lower lip and smiled. "I won't lie, Cristián. I enjoyed the show."

Only then did he realize that the name he'd heard wasn't a fantasy. She'd been there the whole time. She'd stolen the name from his dream and tossed him over the edge with it.

What the hell?

He believed in possessed dogs and people who could shift into animals a damn sight more than that much coincidence.

"What did you call me?"

That got her. She scooped up her toiletries and slipped away from the wall. "Forget it."

"No, Rosa. I mean it. What did you call me?"

With her back toward him, she said, "Cristián."

A cold shiver warred with the lust that name sparked off inside him. But he kept pushing.

"Why?"

"It's the Spanish way."

He stood beside her and breathed. The dream hadn't gotten her scent quite right. More salt. Less sweet. "But how did you know it was Christian, not Christopher? And don't say 'lucky guess' or some bullshit. You said it like you knew."

But dream-Rosa and voyeur-Rosa were gone. She was *la jefa* again, all prickly thorns and sharp edges. "Drop it."

She tensed when he settled his hand on her shoulder. "You said it and I came," he whispered against her temple. Her body hummed a quiet tension that made him think of live wires and lightning strikes. "*You* did that to me."

As if the effort took all the strength she had, she met his gaze. The panicking tension in his bones was reflected in her dark gaze. Chris grazed his thumb over her lower lip. She didn't move, didn't blink. Just slowly sank her teeth into his flesh. He hissed softly, then absorbed the pain, wanting more. Shit, even now—wanting more.

"Entre la sombra y el alma," he whispered.

Rosa blinked. She spit him out and shoved hard against his chest. Taken aback, Chris stumbled away. His feet slipped on the wet tile so that he nearly fell.

"What the fuck did you say to me?" she snarled.

"Sure, it's fine when you crawl into *my* head."

"It was just a dream!"

Chris froze. His head felt hot, heavy enough to fall off his neck.

No way. Too weird.

They stared at one another like opponents across a ring. If he pulled down the collar of her shirt, would he find a gunshot scar on her shoulder?

An alarm sounded outside. Rosa kicked the wall and spewed a few choice Spanish curses. "All I wanted was a goddamn shower!"

"What the hell is that? That's not the hellhound alarm."

"No. Trucks. It's time to mount up for a raiding party."

"How long do we have?"

"About five minutes."

She tore out of the shower, with Chris following right behind. "I'm coming with you," he called.

"You're not a bravo. So you're staying here."

"Like hell."

He raced to his room above the store and dressed in a blink. He kept just enough of his possessions in the room to keep any curious snoops from discovering that he spent every night out in the caves.

Out on the main street the bravos had already started to assemble, like Minutemen of old. Bikes, guns, bleary but determined faces—all ready to roll. Brick strapped what looked like a small cannon to his back. A bandana covered his bald head. He straddled his bike, then leaned over to accept a hot, open-mouthed kiss from Jolene. She wore only a threadbare robe that flapped open at her knees when the hot morning wind kicked up.

"Be careful," she said simply, and then turned back toward the nearest building. A woman seeing her husband off to a day at the office might do so with more drama.

Ex grinned into the low red sun edging over the horizon. "Shit, it's early," he said. "This had better be good. Like, Cubans and cocaine good."

"As your doctor," Chris drawled, "I'd advise against both."

"Okay, tools, then. I can always use new tools."

Rosa strode down the street. She'd thrown on cargoes and was fastening a black leather vest over the white button-down. Not enough time to have donned a bra. Chris was high on adrenaline, but that fused so easily with thoughts of sex.

But something else nagged at him. That feeling of déjà vu had returned. Not a sense. Not really. More like a warning, like the flicker of a dream he had already forgotten.

"Where do you want me, *Jefa*?"

She checked the chamber of her pistol. "Here."

"Bullshit."

"Bullshit is you arguing with me," she hissed. "You don't see Jameson arguing with me when I told him to stay behind with Tilly. I won't have her alone this close to her due date. And if he can agree to stay behind, you sure as hell can."

"Rosa, think about it. You said it could take months between shipments. Now you get another rolling through so soon?"

"My patrol said it's the O'Malley organization. They're based out east and truck quality supplies—ammo, gasoline. We've warned them before about our tolls. Now their goods are ours to claim."

"It's not that cut-and-dried." Daring what he wouldn't have tried even a few hours ago, he grabbed her biceps. "It isn't right—just like the raid the other night."

She shrugged out from his grip and holstered her weapon. Next came the wicked bowie knife she strapped to her hip. But her frown said she was thinking. "A trap?"

"I can't say."

"All the more reason for you to stay. Help protect those who stay behind."

Falco tore down the street on his stripped-down bike. He wore goggles and a nasty grin. A shotgun rested at an angle between his shoulder blades. He slid the bike's rear tire as he skidded to a stop, spraying an arc of dust toward the end of town.

"Ready, *Jefa*?"

Rosa didn't hesitate. She climbed aboard. Chris tasted bile and blinked through a haze of red. What the hell was wrong with him? She was the same fearless bitch she'd been two weeks ago, but seeing her astride Falco's bike ripped away part of his brain. The rational part.

"*Mis bravos* have been doing this for years," she said. "I trust them."

"But you don't trust me."

Her grin was as heart-stopping as the one she'd flashed in the shower room. "No. Not you. But if you're bothered, remind me when I get back—we can talk about your initiation. I like the idea of you kneeling at my feet."

"Fuck that."

She winked. "*Adiós*."

With a fierce cry, she signaled to the cyclists. Her bravos echoed the call up and down the street, no matter whether they sat astride a bike or cheered from a second-story window. Falco gunned his engine, then flipped Chris his middle finger. The motorcycle bolted out of town in a shower of grit and exhaust. Brick, Ex, and the others fell in sync behind Falco in a loose triangular formation. They reached the edge of town within seconds and tore off into the desert.

Chris watched the fan of their dust trails with a sick, hard knot in his gut. This wasn't lust and it wasn't some misplaced jealousy. As messed up as the last few days had been, he still trusted his instincts. As a scientist, that had been a hard lesson to learn. The Change had beaten it into him.

In his mind he saw flickering images: dirty faces, a bike without a rider. It was the touch of another dream, but he had no idea what it meant. All he knew was that he needed to act—just as he had with the raiders on foot.

It was happening all over again.

FIFTEEN

Rosa put the crazy shit out of her mind for the time being. Right now, she couldn't afford to think about Chris Welsh. *Cristián*. Not when they were about to hit an O'Malley delivery. Part of her suspected he might be right—that it wasn't normal to see more supplies so quickly—but they needed the provisions. Being *la jefa* meant weighing the risks against the possible benefits and deciding which side of the scale weighed more. She'd done all right so far.

Still, it didn't hurt to keep it tight.

"Let's be careful," she called to Falco as they crested the hill.

Thanks to the signal from the settlement, they had time to catch up with the trucks along the straightaway. That was her favorite place to strike. Oh, they didn't hit every shipment that passed through her territory. Rosa always offered them the chance to ally with Valle and pay the toll first, but she didn't give second chances. Once the olive branch was rejected, she considered their goods fair game. These trucks bore the stamp of the O'Malley organization, who ran the eastern seaboard. Rosa would be surprised if word of her small-potatoes operation had reached the big man's, but she had taken cargo from him a time or two.

Three vehicles, big for a convoy. Most shipments consisted of one single, desperate trucker looking to trade hurricane lamps for something his town needed more. The wanderers were the bread and butter of their respective settlements. If the bravos didn't patrol the wilderness and keep the trade routes free of pirates, there would be no chance of legitimate commerce at all. Alliances, along with leaders who kept their word, made all the difference in the world. Rosa had a rep for doing exactly as she said she would, which served everyone well.

As Falco pulled alongside the back truck, Rosa checked her gear. Lem and Rio would have to take her role on the other two rolling semis. They were light and fast, so they should get the job done. Brick had ridden on ahead to provide cover when they brought the trucks to a stop.

Timing was crucial. Mentally, she warned them to be careful. *Check for guards inside before you commit to the drop.* But the time for saying it aloud had passed. She could only hope they'd trained enough.

"Ready?" Falco asked.

"Claro."

In response, he maneuvered the bike into position as Manuel did the same for Rio and Ex did for Lem. As they had practiced, she counted backward from ten, hoping that her fliers were doing the same. On one, she pulled up using Falco's shoulders. Her bravos came up as well. Relief surged through her, permitting her to let go. Deftly Rosa made the leap and pulled herself up to the top of the truck. Setting up her gear was second nature by this point. It took no time at all to strap into the harness and secure her boots.

She crept toward the front, a task complicated by the speed at which they moved and the ruts in the road. There was no highway department, no more road crews to fill in potholes. Eventually the asphalt would become impassable, further dividing the land. Rosa balanced with her hands, creeping toward her goal. She came to the final downward slide, where the trailer met the rusty red cab. The magnets in her boots helped with the landing, but she still needed a few seconds to make sure she was set. She signaled the drivers to fall back.

Daring a peek, she saw only one man, so she prepared to drop and make her play. As she drew her pistol and flipped, a noise slammed from the back of the truck. *Mierda.* The trailer doors. Shots sprayed out, pitting the pavement, right at Falco, Manuel, and Ex.

Chris was right. It's a trap.

She couldn't tell how bad it was, but her bravos returned fire. Over the thump of the tires on the road and the roar of the engines, she heard the shots. Thuds and cries.

"Call your men off," she ordered. "Or you die."

"You first." The driver brought his gun up. Rosa twisted, taking the bullet as a flesh wound in the side instead of a gut shot.

This is gonna suck.

Before the driver could get a bead on her, she swung back into position and plugged him above the ear. Kill shot. Now she only had a few seconds. Using her stomach muscles, she pulled herself up, slid out of the foot straps, and flipped down into the cab. She kicked the dead man out of the way, grabbing the wheel just as the truck started to tip toward the steep drainage ditch. The trailer rocked like a terrifying pendulum; it took all her strength to wrestle the great beast back into the center of the road. She slowed it, her breath coming in great gulps, steadying as she parked.

Pain blazed in her side, but she couldn't let anyone see her weakened. She forced herself to bound out of the truck and drop firmly onto the pavement. Rosa rounded the semi to take stock. Up ahead, both Rio and Lem had captured their trucks—not without a beating, though. Lem had split his face open somehow, and Rio sported a slice down his thigh.

None of the vehicles contained cargo. They had been full of armed men, who opened fire when her team fell back. That implied they understood her tactics and her strategies. She guessed the O'Malley knew about Valle after all.

"Status?" she asked, taking inventory with a quick glance.

And came up one man short.

Hand pressed to her side, she jogged back a hundred meters and found Manuel beside his bike. Four rounds in the chest. At Rosa's approach, his eyes opened and his fingers flexed as if seeking comfort. Throat thick, she knelt beside him, conscious of the bravos coming up behind her. They had never seen her on her knees before. But she had never led one of them into a trap before, either.

"Make it . . . mean something," Manuel whispered.

"I will. The bastards will pay, I promise you."

Blood trickled from his parted lips, his fathomless eyes wide with anguish. A strong man with a heart like his—he could live for longer than he deserved to, suffering all the while. They didn't have the means to repair damage from four bullets in his chest and belly. By Manuel's expression, he knew this.

"Pray . . . with me . . . *patrona*."

The hurt swelled to unbearable proportions. Rosa did not deserve that title. A *patrona* was a combination of great lady and munificent benefactor, one who protected her people, making sure they were safe and prosperous. That he should speak the word in his final moments cut her to the bone. Tears pricked behind her lids, but she did not let them fall. Overhead, the sun beat down, picking out crystals in the pavement. High up, the vultures circled. Rosa bowed her head and took Manuel's hand in hers, a blood-slicked tangle that made her skin coppery dark. The sweet stink of it mingled with their sweat.

No priest. No holy oils to anoint his brow. He only had Rosa Cortez—and she had never felt more inadequate. For a terrible moment, she feared she had forgotten all her prayers. But then one came to her. The bravos stood ominously silent.

"Receive him with gladness and grace, and give him a

hero's welcome, for he is the bravest of men. Holy Mary, Mother of grace, Mother of mercy, defend him from the Enemy and receive him at the hour of his death. Make a place for him among the halls of the blessed. Into your hands, Father, I commit his spirit. Amen."

As if he'd been waiting for that moment, Manuel heaved a last, labored breath. His fingers slid from hers. She had seen people die before and had always thought it should be more dramatic. She had learned from television that, after death, the body immediately weighed twenty-one grams less. Her *abuela* had said that was the departing soul, its absence leaving the physical shell lighter.

"Is he going to be okay?" Rio asked.

Mierda. Sometimes she forgot how young he was. She didn't want to tell him the truth. Didn't want to deal with the terrible fucking mess, but it was her job.

Rosa pushed to standing and turned, willing herself to speak the right words.

"No," she said quietly. "He's gone. Put his bike in back. I'll drive him to town, so we can have a proper service."

"You got him killed." Had Rio been loud or disrespectful, she could have chastened him. Instead his voice only held raw grief. "He was like a brother to me, and you got him killed."

Twice the wound there, because Rio had always idolized her—thought she could do no wrong. But now he saw too clearly that she had feet of clay. She couldn't show weakness, though. That would only give Falco the opening he needed.

"I'm sad too. But it's a risk we take each time we mount up. Manuel was a good man, and he will not be forgotten, but if we don't take these chances, then Valle dies."

"That new guy told you it was a trap." This from Lem.

Rosa became conscious of her isolation. She couldn't fight them all off if they had a coup in mind. Even with four rounds in her gun, she didn't know if she could kill a bravo. The shock of betrayal would make her hesitate.

Despite hating that weakness, she kept her face impassive. "I said we should be careful. But if we don't find more ammo, we'll be fighting dust pirates with rocks and sticks. Or General O'Malley will keep sweeping westward until small settlements like Valle are his to control."

"It's true," Falco said. "Fears of his influence in the east grow every day. We've heard it from traders. And another attack like we survived on Burning Night will exhaust our ammunition."

Odd. She would've expected him to pounce on this opportunity to undermine her leadership. But Falco wasn't a complete bastard, nor was he underhanded. If he took the town from her, he would do so through honest means. And he'd make sure she saw it coming a mile away. She need not fear a knife in the back, only a loss of power that meant crawling into his bed.

"I wish we'd found some," Rio said, shoulders hunched.

"Me too." But wishing didn't make it so. "We got whatever's left in their guns at least."

"It wasn't your fault." Ex didn't talk a lot, but when he did, people listened. "And I say that with a bullet in my shoulder."

"Can you drive?"

Ex nodded. "I'll be fine until that doc can take a look."

Before they left, Brick zoomed up. "Trouble, I take it?"

"Yeah. Escort us back?"

Brick nodded.

Everyone was injured in some form or another, except for the big man. Falco's blood was seeping from under his shirt, and Rosa's soaked her top. Time to get the fuck out before the O'Malley sent more men. Falco swung Manuel into his arms. Unable to watch, she rounded the truck and got into the cab. It was fitting that her fallen bravo would ride beside her on the way home. All the way there, she would look at him and see her own failure. Falco belted him in on the passenger side and shut the door without speaking.

Mustering her strength, she called to Lem and Rio. "You each take one of the other trucks."

Once home, they would strip the vehicles of gasoline and metal, which could be used for crafting. The salvage wasn't worth a man's life, but out here, they needed to use every resource they found. Ex and Falco escorted them back to Valle on the bikes, keeping an eye out for trouble. Rosa didn't expect any, didn't want any. Surely the day had already offered up its worst.

SIXTEEN

Chris paced for all of three minutes after the sound of motorcycle engines faded along the northern horizon. He knew that violating Rosa's order would be a blatant disregard of her leadership and an insult to her personally. After what they'd shared that morning—whatever the hell that was—he was less inclined to insult her and much more inclined to get close to her.

But the glimpses of another dream were coming clearer now. Rosa was riding into trouble. He knew it like he knew how she tasted, although both were equally impossible.

He gave up on being rational. Years of living after the Change made that way too easy.

While there were no more assault bikes to be had, he had a vehicle in mind. Brick had refurbished a sleek Japanese motorcycle for Singer. The girl could no longer take it on joyrides in the desert, not with gasoline rationed. She kept the bike now like a pony she could never ride, washing it, admiring it.

He didn't have to look hard to find her. She stood on the porch of the building she shared with Brick. A white peasant top edged with a fringe of light blue lace looked almost too pretty for their world.

"I'd like to borrow your bike," he said bluntly.

Singer shook her head with a laugh. "I don't think so."

"It's important."

"Why?"

"Because I think *la jefa* and her boys are riding into a trap."

She'd been twirling a strand of hair in that way she had of flirting without flirting. She suddenly stopped. "Brick too?"

"He's with them, isn't he?"

"What kind of trap?"

"Look, I don't know, okay? Just let me borrow the bike. You know I won't be able to get far before they return. If I'm full of shit and just stealing your property, Rosa will sic someone on me right quick when she gets back."

"You bet she will."

Chris was ready to scratch out his eyeballs. The memory of his dream was more powerful now—a firefight, a small truck fleeing. The strength of it itched like being walked over by needle-footed bugs. "I did good by warning the town, right? This isn't bullshit, Singer. Please."

Maybe it was the "please" that convinced her. Maybe she was just an easier sell than most of Valle de Bravo's residents—although he doubted that one. She nodded once and took him around back. Within minutes she had the gas tank filled, ready to ride—all efficient, practiced movements.

Singer stroked a bit of chrome, her face surprisingly emotional. "If you hurt it . . ."

"I'll bring it back safe," Chris said, swinging his leg over the seat. "And Singer?"

"Yeah?"

"Gracias."

The young woman brushed at her eyes. She had her brother, her sewing, and her prized possession. That was it. The weight of her trust was a heavy thing.

"De nada, Doc. Get going, then."

Chris wasted no more time. He sped off to the north, loosely following the clean scars left by motorcycle tires in the dry, dry ground. In the distance he caught the sound of gunfire. *Shit.*

He kicked the engine to life. The bike took off like a champion thoroughbred at the races. Chris grimaced, but adrenaline made him daring. The expanse of the desert seemed entirely endless. Flatness stretched out past more flatness, creating an illusion of watery waves, not solid ground. He felt the sun against his right cheek. So that was east. The highway should be straight ahead.

But something . . . that dream told him to turn left. He knew it wasn't Rosa. Rosa was exactly where she should be, riding along the east-west highway that cut through her territory. Gunshots or no, she and her boys would hold their own. In that she'd been right. Chris would only get in the way.

Frustration burst over him like shotgun pellets. He'd been nailed that way once, when a scared homesteader opened fire on him—like being hit with a blowtorch in two dozen places. He felt that way now, overwhelmed by the struggle between what his mind wanted and what his dream dictated. The dream needed him to turn toward the west.

Away from Rosa.

And that felt just plain wrong.

He revved the engine and turned, putting the rising sun to his back. Two shallow rises later and he stopped atop a gully no wider than two grown men laid out head to toe. Down the middle of it ran a beat-up old pickup truck. Covered in so much dust that it nearly blended with the gully floor, it traveled slowly, quietly. The muffler was in good shape, and the driver must've been willing to sacrifice speed for stealth.

Maybe the raid on the highway was a diversion. Maybe this was one big coincidence. But for the first time since the alarm had sounded that morning, his logical mind and the dream aligned. He was supposed to be here.

Chris checked the ammunition in his rifle. Then he set about picking a slow, careful path down into the gully, walking the bike toward the ravine floor. Whoever drove the truck might not even be on the lookout for trouble, especially if the highway raid was, in truth, a diversion. But if Chris were discovered, he could pass for a lone drifter rather than one of Rosa's bravos.

Then the rock beneath his heel gave way, and he slid flat onto his back. Only holding on to the bike's handle grips kept him from sliding all the way to the bottom of the incline. Chris nearly lost his grip but managed to regain his balance. The truck was almost out of sight now, traveling at that slow, furtive pace.

Sweat made his hands into oil slicks. He wiped them on his shirt when he finally reached level ground. The back of his throat was parched.

With the empty gully stretching out before him, its floor almost entirely coated by shadows, he remounted and took off flat out. It was a good bike, responsive and damn fast.

Minutes passed, with the cool shaded breezes making the best use of his body's sweat. He inhaled deeply as he raced after the truck. At least now he knew he was doing the right thing. Whatever his overactive imagination wanted him to discover was inside that truck.

He wondered after Rosa. God, he hoped she proved as tough as she acted. Even as he kept his eye trained on the horizon, he ached to see her again.

The truck was visible now. Chris was loath to waste something as valuable as a tire, but he might not have a choice. He'd rather take them by surprise than try to play one-man army. He got as close as he dared with the bike, then dismounted quickly. He'd become quite a shot over the years—out of necessity rather than desire. The stock of the rifle fit easily along his shoulder. He lowered onto one knee and braced himself. Two slow breaths later, with the truck crawling onward, he fired.

Rubber erupted from the right rear tire. Another shot

and the left matched it—completely flat. The truck skidded to a stop. Chris was already back on the motorcycle, his heart pumping blood faster than he would have thought possible.

He had just declared war. But he was feeling territorial. This was Valle land, damn it. The driver and passenger doors opened. Shotguns emerged before bodies did.

"Drop them," he shouted. "I have you sighted." His voice echoed off the gully's bowl-like walls.

Two shotguns hit the ground with metallic thuds.

"Out and on your knees," Chris said.

As gingerly as he'd handled his initial encounter with Brick, shotgun primed, he circled the vehicle on foot toward the driver's side. After a smooth grab, he had *two* shotguns. A quick check revealed the man's weapon loaded and ready.

"I'll take this," Chris said. "In lieu of payment."

The driver was surprisingly short, entirely bald, and wearing a one-piece mechanic's overalls. The fabric may have once been blue but now reflected only hard wear and lots of dirt. Chris quickly shuffled over to the passenger side. He kicked the other man's shotgun out of reach. If the driver was the talent of the pair, his partner was the muscle. Fully as tall as Chris, he was built like a pro wrestler who sprinkled his breakfast with steroids.

"Start walking," Chris ordered. "Same direction you were going."

"Hell, no."

Chris leveled his shotgun. "Try again."

"You won't shoot me." He reached behind his back as he said it.

Chris didn't need the invitation but he appreciated it. One pull of his index finger and the man lay on the ground clutching his foot.

"Now walking out of here will be trickier, but you have your orders."

"Our orders are to deliver this truck to L.A.," the driver

said. He'd edged around the hood, his hands behind his head. "If we don't, we might as well be dead."

The sound of fists banging on the inside of the truck bed caught Chris's attention. "What the hell?"

A bowie knife hurtled past him, just missing his right arm. The driver's hand was still extended. The wounded passenger lunged forward. Chris jumped back, shouldered one weapon, took aim with the other, and ended the man's life. Perhaps preferring to take his chances with the desert, the driver took off running.

The times had not changed so much that shooting a man in the back held any appeal. Chris was too stunned, and the banging resumed. He rounded to the rear of the truck.

"You better not be armed," he muttered, knowing his decency had hit low ebb three minutes ago.

Still cursing, Chris dropped the tailgate. The stench of sweaty, unwashed bodies hit him like a punch to the nose. He staggered back.

"Holy Christ."

Inside were eight young women, all crammed together, barely dressed. One looked no older than Penny would have been now. Maybe fourteen? His stomach constricted into a ball.

Pain forgotten—or at least pushed aside—he made a snap decision. "Back in. Now!"

Rather than protest as Chris thought they would, the girls merely shrank from his raised voice. Any fight they might have once had was long gone. His heart ached for them, which was as unexpected as it was unpleasant. "God damn it," he muttered as he locked the hatch once again.

They didn't know he was one of the good guys—or what passed as good these days. But he didn't want them scattering off into the desert. Fear would keep them quiet until he turned them over to people who could comfort them better.

He hid Singer's bike behind a patch of scrub; someone could come back for it later. The engine rumbled to life with a single turn of the key. A shame to ruin such a well-maintained old bucket of bolts, but Chris saw no other way.

"Let's see how well this piece of shit drives on two rims."

And how Valle de Bravo would adjust to eight new female residents.

SEVENTEEN

Singer met Rosa at the front gate, and Jameson took the truck from her to park it with the others in the scrap yard. The girl looked worried and uncertain—not a good sign. In general she was remarkably composed, considering how rough life was, and she wasn't easily disturbed. Something bad had happened.

How surprising.

Blood loss was starting to make Rosa dizzy, but she forced herself to remain upright. "What's wrong?"

"The doc—Chris—he asked to borrow my bike . . . but he's been gone awhile, and—"

"And you don't know if you did the right thing. If he's coming back. In your place, I'd be wondering the same thing."

Singer seemed relieved she wasn't angry, but honestly Rosa had no energy to spare. The loss of the bike, while heartbreaking for Singer, wouldn't kill the rest of Valle.

"I'm sorry if I made a bad call," Singer said.

"Don't worry about it right now. I promise you, if he

doesn't come back in twenty-four, we'll assume he's a thief. Then he becomes shoot on sight."

The girl focused on the red staining Rosa's shirt. "You're hurt."

"*Sí*, many are. Find Viv and tell her to prepare the *taberna*. I'll herd the bravos."

Dios knew, none of them liked medical attention, but to neglect a wound was simple stupidity. More light-headed by the second, she met the rest of the men. At least they'd gotten gas and metal, if nothing else. It wasn't what she'd hoped, but better than nothing. Otherwise her shame would be insupportable.

The other bravos fell in behind her, but Falco came up to walk beside her. *So that's how it's going to be. First I let you walk next to me. Soon you'll be giving orders. Then you're in my bed, and finally I'm just the woman who sleeps with Falco.*

For the first time in years, her position felt shaky.

In the *taberna* Viv had cleaned several tables. This doubled as a hospital, as Wicker didn't want blood to spoil irreplaceable goods. The bar had been built to clean up easily, even in the Old West days before the Change. It was still stucco and adobe, with whitewashed walls and a clay floor. The furnishings were made of saguaro wood, and some of Singer's fabric creations hung for decoration. Rosa grimaced past the pain, imagining bullets being dug out of cowboys who got wailing drunk on a bottle of something raw. Life hadn't changed so much after all.

Apart from the magic and the monsters.

Viv treated Ex first. The bullet was lodged in his shoulder, and she had to do some digging. Rosa sat beside him and held his hand, letting him squeeze until she thought he would crush her fingers. He had great strength from working the forge, but she took it without protest. She was tough, impossibly tough, and that was why people didn't mess with her. It was a point of pride that all her men be treated first, even if she had sprung a slow leak.

It will clot soon. I won't bleed out. Not a major artery.

Singer pitched in, likely wanting to make up for her foolishness in trusting a drifter with her prized possession. She bandaged Rio, who remained stoic. He had been trying to get with the seamstress for months, but Singer thought he was too young, too inexperienced. His expression was proof that age didn't make a bravo; courage did.

Viv was experienced with injuries. She didn't talk much about her life before, but Rosa had the impression she'd patched up people for a living—probably not in any official capacity, despite her skills. Or maybe she just had a lot of kids. Either way, Rosa didn't ask; that went against Valle's code. Here, no one's past mattered.

La jefa needed that guarantee of absolution most of all.

By the time the others had all been tended, Rosa was seeing spots. She didn't dare stand when she heard the rumble of an unfamiliar engine. The vehicle was obviously disabled. She could tell that from the thumping as it went. But no way could she investigate what was happening, not without falling on her face. Time for some delegation.

"Rio, go check it out. Lem, lock and load behind him." She only hoped their anger and grief over Manuel would make them compliant. A few heartbeats passed before Rio nodded and left. Lem followed, his expression conflicted but his stride purposeful.

She sat there, rigid with tension, while Viv finished up with Falco. Rosa didn't relax until Rio called, "It's the doc. He hijacked a truck . . ." His tone gained wonder. "A truck full of *girls.*"

Madre de Dios.

"Of course he did," she muttered. "Why would he stay put when there's a whole desert full of trouble to get into? *Cabrón.*"

"What're we gonna do with them all?" Rio came to the doorway of the *taberna* to aim an inquiring look at her. "They look starved and scared to death."

"They were probably intended as slaves and whores," she said softly.

No wonder they're scared. But she'd never say that

aloud. It would give away too much of her past—and that she was determined to share with no one. She needed to act, not dwell on old failures.

"Viv, Singer, get the women to the town hall. Reassure them. Take food and drink. They won't trust men right now. And find Ingrid if any of the bravos hassle you."

Viv frowned. "You're still bleeding."

"I know. The doc can tend me now that he's back. Those women need you more."

And she had a few choice words for Cristián, the rotten, couldn't-follow-orders bastard. A small part of her, though, a very small part, was glad he would be the one treating her wound. An even tinier fragment admitted relief that he hadn't stolen Singer's bike and disappeared from their lives.

Even if it would be best.

A few minutes later the *taberna* had cleared out, as neither Ex nor Falco could resist the chance to go stare at new women. She had faith in Viv's ability to play mother hen, should the need arise, and Singer could be surprisingly fierce, especially with Ingrid as her role model.

Rosa arranged herself in her chair to mask the fact that she was about ready to fall out of it and waited for Chris. He arrived with none of the chastened quality a bravo should have, especially one who had proved less than diligent about obedience.

But he doesn't wear my mark. I can't hold him to those standards. Not yet, anyway.

There would be consequences for Manuel's death. She had not avoided those. The women's arrival might delay them. Maybe it would give her time to devise a strategy to consolidate her leadership and reassure people that one mistake didn't make her incompetent. It remained to be seen how Falco would handle things, what with the perfect moment to foment rebellion.

"You wanted to see me?"

Rosa resisted the urge to relax and absorb his voice, just drink it into her skin. It was not relief. And it was not desire. Couldn't be.

"I may need stitches," she said tersely.

Surprise sent his eyebrows shooting toward the lock of chocolate brown hair that tumbled over his brow. "What happened?"

"Gunshot wound. A graze, but it needs to be closed."

"I'll be right back."

Don't let me faint. Not in front of him.

She leaned her head back, eyes closed, hoping that would help the dizziness. But he caught her at it, returning much faster than she'd expected. A low flush of shame surged through her at being exposed, but Chris didn't react. Instead he focused on the blood staining her shirt. With gentle hands, he raised the fabric, tucked it under her arm, and cleaned the surrounding area with the soap and clean water Viv had left behind.

"Six stitches should do it," he said. "And you were right. It's a graze."

She laughed softly. "I think I'd know if I had a bullet in me."

"You've been shot before?" he asked, threading the needle.

"Five times."

His gaze was keener than she liked. "How many since the Change?"

"Three."

"So you were shot twice before?"

She shook her head, and then regretted it when the room spun. "That isn't something you need to know about me."

Cristián—*Dios*, why did her mind insist on calling him that?—took the rebuff without protest and fell quiet, sewing her up with capable hands. He had tended such injuries before. Maybe he hadn't been a real medical doctor in the world before, but he was the closest thing they had now. With a faint sigh, she realized she needed to keep him here. Whether he felt like trouble was irrelevant. He would be good for the town, and that made up her mind.

After he finished bandaging her wound, he asked, "Do you want something for the pain?"

"No. Let's save it for people who hurt more."

"Or who aren't as strong as you?"

How could he know that? The pain was a test of her mettle. If she gritted her teeth and tolerated it without aid, she proclaimed her power. She ignored the sense that he could see inside her and examine all the dark places not even she could touch.

"I intended to bitch at you," she said then.

"But you're not going to?"

"No. I don't think it would do any good. And I'm not sorry you saved those women. So I guess I'm wondering how you knew where to find them."

And whether it has anything to do with that hot dream.

Dios, it was so hard to look at him now without seeing him beneath her. A trickle of sweat rolled down her temple. She'd had far too much bad sex to want a man touching her ever again. And yet she did. Just him. Not Falco or anyone else. *Cristián.*

A flicker came and went across his expression—not the usual blank confidence she assumed was a front for something else. Rosa was a master at hiding her true self too, so she had to respect a fellow magician of the soul. But she wasn't backing off either. His inexplicable behavior had to make some kind of sense, somehow, or she couldn't strategize. Or sleep at night.

"I saw them," he murmured, an edge in his voice, as if he too thought that sounded crazy. "No, that's not exactly right. It was more of a . . . dream?"

That single word shot fire beneath her sternum.

"Like when Peltz's men came in on foot?"

"Like that, yes." Chris paused, gazing at her with an inscrutable expression. "But neither was clear. They came in bits and pieces. The closer we got to the moment, the more distinct the two images lined up—dream and reality."

Things since the Change had been chaotic and strange. Rosa didn't discount the possibility that he'd developed some kind of gift as part of the magical tide washing the world. Others in Valle could do marvelous things, like Tilly and Bee calling to their animals.

"Do you dream, Rosa?"

Mierda. He was going to bring it up. Best not to seem timid. "*Sí.* Last night."

He leaned in, just a little. Rosa caught the scents of sweat, dry dust, gasoline, and sweet sage. His lovely, sculpted mouth was very, very close, and she watched him frame the words. "I've never . . . I've never known anything like that."

Her breath caught. "Me either."

EIGHTEEN

Chris was going to kiss Rosa. No two ways about it. Truck-loads of starving women, gunshot wounds—none of it mattered.

He leaned closer, his fingers gripping the armrests. Deliberately, needing a coconspirator, he nudged her legs apart. Rosa sat trapped between him and the chair, but she didn't stop him. Didn't blink or flinch or offer that sarcastic smile. Instead, her nostrils flared on a ragged inhale. Her dark brown eyes were wide and fixed on his. Memories of the heat they'd shared that morning burned away the distance until his mouth hovered so near to hers.

So near now to the flesh he wanted to taste, he whispered, "Say my name."

"Cristián."

That one word, soft as a sigh, was a starter pistol firing. Game on.

Chris touched his lips to hers. Just a hello. Electricity arced between them at that gentle introduction. She was as tough as a woman could be, but there, beneath his mouth, she was softness. Dizziness that had nothing to do with the real world slunk into his brain like opium smoke. He could get drunk on her—Rosa and the knowledge that here, now, impossibly, she was giving in.

The pull of more sweetness to come called to him, tempting a more forceful connection. Chris eased into her space with his body and nudged into her mouth with his tongue. He slipped just the tip along the seam of her lips. Another jolt of pleasure and primal conquest when she opened to him. She tasted as she had in his dream, all sugar and salt, but this was like a rainbow after years of monochrome.

As he deepened the kiss, his muscles hardened. He angled his head and did what he'd wanted to do for days: he plundered. With tongue and teeth, hard, demanding, he kissed her the way they'd dueled in his dream. *Their* dream. Because, just like he knew the sound of pleasure in the back of her throat, he knew they'd shared that same erotic encounter.

That impossible knowledge intensified the privileges he demanded. He cupped her nape, then curled his fingers into her hair. She met him with ferocious energy. His invasion was repelled—not entirely, but to establish the terms of their duel. Rosa pushed up from the chair, her arms wrapped low around his back. A quick tug later, his shirt hiked up and her fingernails scored his skin.

Chris knelt on the floor in front of the chair and pulled her up, out, onto his lap. She straddled him as if she'd done so a hundred times, knowing just how to snuggle her breasts against his chest. Her ass filled his hands. All blood fled his brain, concentrating into a fierce erection. Rosa worked her hands up to his shoulders, teasing, testing.

They should stop. This was crazy. *Dangerous.*

But she'd figure that out soon enough. He abandoned her mouth for the taste of her throat. She tasted of dust and sweat and sweet woman beneath. Chris sucked the thin, soft skin in the hollow behind her earlobe. Rosa moaned against his temple. She bucked her hips against his, a most excruciating rhythm.

Something changed then. The urge to lay her back and continue plundering was as driving as hunger, but Rosa . . . swayed.

Chris knew enough about the woman in his arms to know she never swayed. Not even, he suspected, in the midst of some fantastic foreplay.

He pulled back just enough to see her, catching her face between his palms. Her pupils had dilated. Her eyelids fluttered.

"Rosa?" He shoved the hair back from her temples, then more roughly, trying to rouse her. "Hey, now. Stay with me, Rosita."

When the fainting spell continued, Chris eased from beneath her body and up from the floor. He lifted Rosa with relative ease, again struck by how such a resilient woman could be so small. Though nearly limp from exhaustion, she was not a burden to carry. He nudged open a rear door and found a little break room with a shabby couch. The couch was a bonus, as he'd only had privacy in mind. No one could see *la jefa* this way.

He stretched her out on the couch, her head angled against a flattened, dingy throw pillow. No satin for her. No finery. Not ever. At the moment a little respite was all he could offer—away from curious eyes who would harshly judge her momentary lapse.

"Rosita, c'mon, now."

She roused back to full consciousness with a start, then a grimace. "*¿Qué—*"

Chris caught her upper arms and eased her back onto the pillow. "Relax. Relax. We're in the little room in back of the tavern. No one here but us."

"So that means you can continue now, does it? Don't think so, *cabrón*."

"It means you can catch your breath without wondering who's watching."

He slumped cross-legged onto the floor, his back to the couch. He couldn't look at her, not and regain some minuscule control over his body. The dream, the shower, and then the truck in the desert—he was a man wound goddamn tight. But it wasn't enough just to have permission, however tacit, to kiss Rosa. He was the same greedy fool he'd always been, wanting more than he deserved. He wanted all or nothing. That impulse had landed him into two marriages before he was ready.

Right then, however, she simply didn't have it in her to finish what they'd started, even if she was willing. Now that the rush had passed, he didn't think so. So he breathed deeply and tried not to think about the taut pressure of her firm, small breasts against his chest.

"Gracias," she whispered.

"De nada." Chris dropped his head back against the couch cushion and stared at the ceiling. "I told you, I have no intention of messing with your position here. But I want you to consider something."

"What?"

"Us. Consider indulging, just a bit."

"I don't think I can," she said, her voice pinched.

But she touched his hair, smoothing it back from his forehead. Chris closed his eyes. Such a wonder—being touched. The soft pattern of her caress continued long past when he thought she'd stop. *Any second now.*

He offered a stunted little laugh. "Are you sure?"

She surprised him with a soft sound; it wasn't much of a laugh, as malformed as his, but it *was* one. "I'm sure."

She exhaled, then pushed into a sitting position. Chris turned to face her. Her dark gaze wasn't entirely focused, but she was back in control. He respected the wall she rebuilt between them. At least, he told himself he did.

"I have this urge to take a nap," he said with a half smile. "And you should do the same."

"What are you talking about?"

Chris shrugged. "Maybe we'll get lucky there instead. No one else would know."

"I'd know."

He tongued his lower lip, still tasting her there. "It's a wicked turn-on. I like being what you think about, Rosita."

"You don't get to call me that."

"Yes, I do." He stood and took her hands, brooking no protest as he helped her to her feet. "But not in front of anyone else."

"You say that like I'm going to give you the chance to get me alone again."

"Don't see why not. Isn't that what Valle de Bravo is all about?"

"How do you mean?"

He swiftly, gently kissed her on the forehead, although the self-discipline of that chaste move required fat stores of restraint. "I live in hope. Just like the rest of you."

Before he could learn how that particular sentiment was received, Chris exited the little room. He left because he'd already pushed them further than either could stand. She had her town to run, and Chris had the memories of what happened to women unlucky enough to catch his eye.

The sunshine outside the tavern was a lot harsher than he wanted. He wanted a dark, close, intimate room and Rosa, no matter how dingy the couch. But distance was good. Too bad she followed him out into the sun, making distance an impossible wish. They passed Abigail on her way back inside.

Chris asked, "How do they fare?"

"Not sure, myself. Viv wants extra grain ground up for their meals. Quick as possible."

Rosa nodded, then gingerly tested her sutures as she and Chris walked toward what might have once been a town hall. Viv and Singer had coaxed the scared girls inside. The building was squat and consisted of only a single room, but that room was big and open. Only two windows and one door offered entrance. How long had Chris been kissing Rosa? Surely not that long. But the modest open space was now equipped with eight separate sleeping areas—a rug, quilt, and pillow for each new woman. Viv and Singer were a wonder of industrious efficiency. Ingrid stood guard with a wicked semiautomatic pistol and a cat-o-nine-tails.

"Viv, status?" Rosa asked.

The petite woman, even smaller than *la jefa*, wiped her hands on a pale blue apron. "Mica and Jolene plundered every house in search of the spare bedding. Singer has water on the boil so we can find them under all the grime. And she's raiding her supplies to see about new clothes, too."

Chris peered inside. "How are they, medically?"

"Don't know yet. We can't feed them too much. Half look starved to me. Need to start them on small doses of bland food, a little at a time. Right?" She glanced at Chris for confirmation.

"That's right. And when they're stronger, I can check for disease or parasites. Maybe we'll get lucky and I'll have the right meds to treat them. Who else has had contact with them so far?"

"Me and Singer."

He considered. "Good. Let's keep it limited to the four of us until we know if they have any medical problems. Even if the other women want to help out, keep it as you have been: collecting supplies and preparing food."

Rosa frowned. "A quarantine?"

"Nothing so strict. But lice, TB, venereal disease—no need to take chances."

"Good." She still looked fatigued, but the dizziness was long gone. Not to mention the vulnerability—in its place was a hard determination that, for some reason, seemed to have little to do with her regular duties. Looking over the room full of eight debased young women, she was as unreachable as he'd ever seen her.

Was it about her? And her past?

"Now, about the test," Viv began

Rosa flinched. "The test . . . ?"

"For skinwalkers."

An almost comical expression flickered across Rosa's drawn features. She hadn't even considered the possibility. These girls, frightened and battered, had slipped past her defenses.

"I suppose when they're stronger," she said without conviction.

"Look," Chris said, "they would've changed by now. There isn't anything you can do to them that's worse than being locked in that truck. No guarantees, but I'd be shocked if any of these women were skinwalkers."

Rosa's shoulders bowed, just slightly. *Relief.* Damn, he hated seeing her so keyed in to their plight. It made her someone he wanted to protect, when she'd never let him.

He resisted the impulse to put an arm around her shoulders. Instead he focused on what she'd want and need: protecting the town. "And Ingrid will be fine by herself, standing guard?"

"To start. Ex will respect any boundaries without question. Jameson too, because of Tilly. Then maybe Brick. He's not monogamous with Jolene, but he's honorable and will want to keep an eye on Singer with all the bravos sniffing about."

"Good. You're going to need them."

He nudged her surreptitiously. Rosa took the hint and turned, facing six bravos as they crossed the street toward the town hall. Rio and Lem were among them. Chris didn't have a bone to pick with either, but Rio was young and Lem was too eager with the women. That Falco took up the rear of the small cadre, however, set Chris on edge.

"We want to see them," Lem said. He was still armed from the raid. "We *deserve* to see them."

"Not a chance." Rosa shored up her stance. "They're weak and in need of medical care. And then the rules remain. Their choice. No exceptions."

But Lem protested. "We deserve something. Manuel is dead because of that raid. We could've died too. What do you say to that?"

Chris flinched internally. No wonder everyone had been so strained and shaken since the return. Having lost a bravo would shake them up under the best, most successful circumstances. To lose one during a nearly useless raid would only push the limits of Rosa's control. The mood was turning ugly, but he held his tongue and stayed put. Rosa's fight, he kept telling himself. But that didn't make their posturing and threats any easier to stand.

"I say Manuel took the same risks we all did," Rosa said. "He paid a dear price for our bad luck."

"Bad call, more like." Lem jabbed a finger toward her. "*Your* bad call."

"Watch it," she said, her voice dark and low. "You're way out of line."

Lem took another step, which was about three too many for Chris's liking. Damn it. Whaling on the guy wouldn't help Rosa maintain her footing as their leader. Nor would it prevent six very hard-up bravos, if given the chance, from taking advantage of the new women.

Chris wracked his brain for the right solution.

Leadership.

Strength.

Loyalty—

A show of loyalty.

"So you like my find, Lem?" he asked.

The younger man blinked, as if seeing Chris there for the first time. "Sure thing, Doc. Best raid we've had in years."

"We?" Chris leaned against the side of the town hall, posture negligent, arms over his chest. "I don't remember offering them to anyone else. What's that old expression? Finders keepers."

"Bullshit!"

"Here in *el valle*," Rio said, his eyes narrowed, "we share everything we grab on raids."

"Ah, but that's the catch, isn't it? I'm not a part of Valle de Bravo." He lolled his gaze toward Rosa, willing her to trust him. She did the best she could, perhaps, by simply staying quiet. And waiting. She watched him with equal parts curiosity, resentment, and hope. "What does it take, *Jefa*, to become a part of this town?"

"You swear an oath."

"To whom?" He knew full well, but he liked flirting

with her—liked it when everyone else could assume it was still antagonism.

"To me," she said.

"Swear that you're the uncontested leader of Valle de Bravo? Then I turn over all my ill-gotten gains?" At Rosa's nod, he asked, "And what do I get in return?"

"The full loyalty and protection of the town."

"Let's do it." He pushed away from the wall, then stared at each of the six bravos in turn. Lem was easy to intimidate, as was Rio. No surprise that Falco didn't budge—a fight for another day. "But I won't turn these women over to just anyone. They deserve the respect Rosa promises to everyone who lives here. So there's no way in hell I'm signing on if folks want to mess with the way things are run."

"Just what are you saying?" Falco demanded.

"I'll swear allegiance to Rosa and free these women. They'll have the choice of staying." He paused, letting cold menace flavor his words. "But only if every other man swears again too."

NINETEEN

Damn him.

His plan was brilliant, and he had to know it. *Pendejo.*
In one maneuver he would join Valle, establish his place,
and tie the men's loyalty back to her. Rosa needed the support, no question, but hereafter she'd owe him a debt. He
had to see that as well.

Everything was quiet while Falco and his cohorts considered the terms. She gave no sign of her inner turmoil; this
was the closest she'd ever come to losing power. The circumstances of her salvation didn't sit well with her, particularly not with her mouth still tingling from his kisses. Chris
didn't approach like other men, with clumsy innuendoes or
cocky assumptions. He had a deeper confidence, probably
gained during those long years on his own. And their sexual
chemistry was undeniable. But she had no intention of succumbing, even if he'd surprised her with his lips.

Not that he'd want me if he knew the truth.

Predictably, Lem broke first. He was the weakest link in
Valle, and the prospect of more women, one of whom might

choose him for protection proved too much temptation. Of course, that indicated his word didn't mean much.

But once he said, "I'll swear," the others followed, Falco last of all. He watched her with a steely, speculative look, glancing between Chris and her as if trying to puzzle out the connection. There would be hell to pay if he ever discovered those heated dreams and stolen kisses. This arrangement only worked so long as she was celibate and had no excuse for refusing him. Falco wouldn't take kindly to another male supplanting what he felt was his rightful place.

Once all the men agreed to Chris's terms, she said to Singer, "Prepare a gift package and tell Ex to ready his needles."

She could tell by his expression that Chris hadn't expected pageantry, but, like all sovereign nations, they had their own pomp and circumstance. The promise held meaning and served to make the citizens of Valle feel as if they belonged to something important. Such tricks might not work with Chris Welsh, but she had to try to turn him into one of her bravos in truth, or all of this would become an empty charade.

"Now?" he asked.

"Why not?"

Chris mashed his lips together. "And the funeral?"

"Dawn," she said tightly. "We bury the dead at dawn. Now go with Rio to prepare."

He was mouthing *gift package* when the boy took him off to bathe. Rosa grinned at his confusion. But one couldn't be solemn while covered in blood and dirt, so she went to make herself ready as well. She took a quick shower—the one she hadn't gotten that morning—and headed to her house to don the proper vestments. Singer had outdone herself with the costume. It was a long pristine white robe with red embroidery. Rosa wore it for this occasion and for consecrations.

She styled her hair with a touch of oil to make the braids sleek and smooth, then coiled them in a complex coronet to lend height and authority. Rosa had no mirror to check her reflection, merely working on muscle memory. She tucked one item into the sleeve of her robe before hurrying back to the plaza, intent on arriving there first.

With some relief, she saw she was the first on the scene. Rosa ignored her misgivings and faint resentment that her position had become so precarious—and so quickly—that she needed bolstering from a stranger. Only he wasn't. Not really. Not in her head and not in her dreams. Two weeks had taken the edge of unfamiliar off him, even without their bond. She held to the inexplicable conviction that they knew each other, and that her dark places would not faze him at all.

Ruthlessly, she stifled those feelings and waited for the action to begin. When Singer arrived with the basket, Rosa slipped her secret gift beneath everything else.

Soon enough the bravos returned in their customary garb. As Rosa wore white, they had donned black and red to symbolize the violence they stood ready to do on her behalf. Chris caught her gaze across the crowd, his expression pure puzzlement. But he didn't laugh at their posturing, which was most important. Smart boy. He needed to appear to take it seriously. Despite the ostentatious trappings, Rosa did. Sometimes she felt this was the only thing in her life that had meaning.

For most people, the Change meant the end of all bright, beautiful things. But it had saved her.

She stood at the end of the plaza, waiting with silent patience. The bravos moved toward her as one. Since Chris was taking his oath for the first time, he led them. That clearly left a sour taste in Falco's mouth, but he had no grounds for complaint. They stopped one meter away, and she accepted a censer of herbed oil from Singer, who played the part of the maiden. Rosa had cobbled this ritual together from old movies and memories of the shadowy Catholic church where she'd attended Mass with her *abuela*, so long ago.

"Kneel," she intoned.

The men obeyed. Even Chris, though he didn't look delighted. But he knew how important this was for her. Something hot twisted in her chest when he didn't resist. It hurt, but in a good way. An unfamiliar way. No man had ever humbled himself before her—against his will—just because she needed him to. It made her think that her Cristián wasn't like other men she'd known, that it might be good to learn more about him.

When did I start thinking of him as mine?

She put that mental confusion aside to focus on the service. Stepping forward, she used her oil to trace a *V* on each man's brow. From her fingertips wafted the sweet scents of sage and lavender—plants that, with care, tolerated the climate here.

Then Rosa stepped back, her demeanor grave.

"Christian Welsh, you come before me as a wanderer. I have the power to grant you solace and shelter, as long as we both shall live. Valle de Bravo takes all those with willing hearts and hands, committed to the protection of our town and to my service. Do you so swear?"

"I do," he said somberly.

For the first time it occurred to her that she had written the vows to sound in some ways like marriage. Perhaps she had even done so subconsciously. Each man who made his pledge would feel bound to her in a personal way. But never sexually—not on her part, anyway. Chris's hazel eyes were dark and knowing, as if he took her words for their deepest meaning, as if she had promised him something in turn.

A home. That's all.

The other men renewed their vows as well. She traced their tattoos with the scented oil to remind them where their loyalty ought to lie. With each soft, silent touch, she wanted them to think about how poorly internal conflict served when there were so many foes to fight outside the valley. But she didn't know if Falco cared about that. He was steaming by the time she finished, his face flushed and contorted. He hated to be made a fool, and Chris had outmaneuvered him.

"I accept you as mine," she said to Chris.

It was the accepted verbiage. She had spoken those words to every man willing to fight for her town. They bore her ink on their skin. But this time she knew a shiver of pleasure, quite outside any prior experience. By the flicker across Chris's expression, he sensed it too. His lips parted and she remembered—without wanting to—the sweetness of his kiss.

"So sworn, you are entitled to bear arms for Valle de Bravo. I offer you a gift in return for your loyalty."

Chris cocked his head, still kneeling but not at all humbled. The truth showed in the way he met her gaze. Directly. Challenging her despite his supplicated posture. At Rosa's gesture, he took to his feet, as did the other men.

"This blade, forged in our fires, symbolizes the strength and commitment of your bond to your new home. Use it only to defend the valley and to drive away our enemies." Rosa handed Chris a beautiful dagger, keen edged and graceful—some of Ex's best work.

The guns she presented with less ceremony. They hadn't been forged in town, obviously, but they too served a purpose. Chris now carried Valle arms. He belonged.

But that wasn't all. He wore the uncertain look of a child on Christmas morning, one whom poverty had taught to expect nothing. He knotted his fingers, as if uncertain what to do with his hands. Maybe the service was touching him more than he'd imagined it would. Rosa liked to think that. Beyond a calculated move, maybe, just maybe, it meant something to him too. That gave her hope he wasn't as broken as she'd first thought—that maybe he had more inside him than salt and bitterness.

"One final gift," she said. "In turn we pledge to care for you, Christian Welsh. Nourish your body and soul. As a token of that promise, I offer you the bread of life." She handed him a basket full of brown buckwheat bread, half a wedge of goat cheese, and agave wine. With her eyes she told him there was more too, something she had never given another bravo.

Rosa didn't know if he understood her silent message, but his voice was husky when he said, "Thank you."

The rest of the bravos were too interested in the new women to care much about Falco's injured pride at the moment, so after the ritual ended, they went to pester Ingrid and Viv, who more than held her own. The shotgun she held was not for show. If Rosa symbolized both maiden and whore, then Viv was a younger representation of the crone. The men instinctively respected her. Falco growled as he stalked off, with no excuse to linger. He was not required to bear witness to the marks.

"It's almost done," she told Chris, when everyone else had gone.

"What now?"

"The tattoo." She led the way toward Ex's workshop, careful to keep the hem of her white robe out of the dust.

"Can I pick where I want it?"

She nodded. "I don't dictate where. It's your body."

His expression gained layers of intensity. "But if it *was* yours, where would you put it?"

The question had other meanings, and the heat in his gaze sent answering shocks through her. "Your back."

"Why?"

There was no one around, no one but him, to hear this unprecedented admission. "Because it's beautiful. I'd like to see my mark on it."

Just imagining that made her a little flushed. He had beautiful skin, tanned and smooth, his muscles lean. They pulled when he moved in a graceful display of predatory strength. She'd never wanted that in a man because, in her experience, strong men victimized those physically weaker. Now she wondered if it was possible—whether a man could use his power to protect a woman rather than subjugate her.

No thinking like that. You didn't build Valle with a man's backing, and you don't need him now.

Yet the hunger didn't diminish, a hunger no food could quench.

He held her look for two beats, his expression inscrutable, before pushing through the doorway. The forge was quiet, cooler than usual because the dawn raid had occupied Ex all day. He'd sterilized his equipment in accordance with her prior request. He greeted them with a nod. Quiet on the best of days, with a bullet just excavated from his shoulder he was hardly in the mood for chat.

"Where?" he asked, lofting a needle.

Chris glanced at her, his lovely mouth curved into a delicious smile. He pulled the black ceremonial shirt over his head and turned away from Rosa. Her mouth went dry.

"On my back."

TWENTY

Chris forced his clenched muscles to unfurl. The first pinch of metal biting into his skin was like being doused in scalding water, but soon he sank into the steady pain. He breathed through his nose, journeying away from the discomfort.

Funny, he hadn't even asked what the design was, but probably the abstract pattern worn by the other bravos. Since it was Rosa's mark, he didn't bother with any other concern.

Men came and went at first. Brick and Rio arrived to speak with Rosa in hushed voices about preparations for Manuel's dawn funeral. The rest just came to check whether Chris was the kind to squirm. He might have been once, back when the idea of getting a tattoo would have made him cringe. This was different—important. He remembered tales of Maori warriors, so fiercely decorated. If they could endure pain for the sake of appearance, imagine the agony they could withstand to protect what they valued.

But soon the visitors stopped coming. It was just Ex, Rosa, Chris, and the steady stab of the needle.

Ex took a break to fetch more ink. He cocked an eyebrow and asked Rosa, "You're staying?"

Chris broke open a wide grin. Just two words to reveal that she wasn't in the habit of observing the whole process. Two words to prove that the chemistry between them was extraordinary.

"Yeah, I'm staying. I want to make sure he goes through with it."

After mouthing *liar* at her, Chris eased back into his meditation. The sting continued between his shoulder blades, but he was beyond thinking of it as pain. This was too damn entertaining.

For the next hour, maybe more, Rosa stayed rooted to a place along the wall of the forge—all the time watching. She barely moved except to occasionally shift her weight from foot to foot. Her stitched wound must be aching, but still she stayed. Chris wondered if she could feel the intimacy of what was happening. Ex was just a human tool, the means to do Rosa's bidding. Every stab of the needle into Chris's skin was her command, her claim over him.

He should have been scared shitless.

Instead a strange sort of peace infused his blood and his muscles, just as it had during the initiation ceremony. Years ago—hell, even a few weeks ago—he would have found the whole farce laughable. But it had meant a great deal, far more than he'd expected.

"All set," Ex said in that efficient way of his. He wiped Chris's skin with a cloth, then applied an ointment of some kind. It cooled after the continuous burn of the needle.

"Thanks."

Ex only nodded. "Rosa can bandage it when your skin's dry. I'm gonna lie down."

Only then did Chris notice the drawn, slightly ashen pallor to the man's face. He'd been shot that morning too. All Chris could do was thank him again and shake his hand. Then he and Rosa were alone.

"How does it look?" he asked in the silence.

Rosa pushed away from the wall. "I'll get you a mirror."

She returned a few moments later with two polished pieces of steel. Not exactly mirrors, but functional. Only, Chris wasn't exactly interested in the tattoo. His brain and his body were still firmly in her keeping. So when Rosa offered the steel, he didn't peek. Not yet. He only held her gaze.

"How does it look?" he asked again.

She licked her lower lip. Appearing apprehensive in a way that didn't become her, she appraised the forge. But they were still alone. "Nice," she said at last. "It looks . . . right."

"Good."

"You know, you don't look like you'd be arrogant, but you are."

"You make me want to be. Among other things."

She tipped her head. "Such as?"

"Strong. Worthy." Feeling too exposed by the sudden flush of honesty, Chris stood from the bench and stretched. "But I also want someone to share that wine with, so maybe I should stop wishing."

He took one of the makeshift mirrors. Rosa circled around behind him, her movements stiff. If they managed to keep from tearing each other a few new holes, he would need to check her bandages before retiring for the night. She must be hurting—physically and mentally—after such a turbulent day, but not even her expression complained.

She stood behind him with the other mirror, angling it until he could see the mark he'd carry for the rest of his life.

Chris inhaled sharply. Yes, it was the mark of Valle de Bravo. But on his own body, so personal, he was struck by its unexpected vitality and beauty. The symmetrical black symbol stretched between his shoulder blades. Organic. Wholly primitive. Wide and narrow, the base was flat like a horizon. But at the top it licked up toward his shoulders and nape—black flames, maybe, or shadowy waves of heat off the desert. He'd never imagined something so primal engraved on his skin. The scar where Rosa had tended his

Burning Night wound would fade relative to the tattoo's permanence.

A memory tugged at him until he frowned.

"You don't like it?" Rosa asked. He was too intrigued by the design to tease about the hint of disappointment in her voice.

"No, that's not it. I recognize it. And not just from on the other men."

"Oh?"

He pushed a hand against his forehead and fought to remember. Someplace intimate. Someplace cool. He'd seen that design—

"The rugs in your house," he said.

Rosa dropped her piece of steel. She snatched it up again and turned away, but not before Chris caught a glimpse of her startled expression.

He wasn't letting *that* go.

As nonchalantly as he could manage, he met her against the far wall where she'd retreated. "Tell me," he said quietly.

"I didn't think you'd notice."

"You have a habit of thinking the worst of me. I don't like it."

"Bite me."

"Best invitation I've had in years."

She pushed away from him.

"Oh, c'mon, Rosa. All I asked was what the goddamn symbol meant." He cocked his hands on his hips. "Jesus, it gets *old*."

"Fine." With more dignity than a princess, she stared him down. "I saw those shadows on the desert floor when I first came to *el valle*. It was dawn. The sun had only just started to push back the night. And I . . . I wasn't scared. For the first time, maybe ever. I wasn't scared." She shrugged. "I knew I'd come home."

Chris swallowed thickly. He couldn't breathe. A deep, instinctual part of him knew what choking out those words had cost her. Likely she'd never admitted anything close to it. He didn't know whether to congratulate her or apologize for dragging it out of her.

Instead he crossed the close, dark forge and took her hands. She flinched, but she didn't pull away.

"It's beautiful," he whispered. "Thank you."

"I should be thanking you and you know it."

"That's all the admission I needed to hear." He rubbed the back of his neck, feeling the echo of the needle's burn. "Viv and Rio are preparing Manuel's body?"

"That's right. We'll bury him at first light."

"May I make a suggestion?"

"I get the feeling you will anyway." She smashed her lips together.

"Make me a visible part of the ceremony."

"You really know how to push a woman."

"Not pushing. You know it makes sense. Integrate me quickly, for the sake of symbolism. A unified front."

Rosa swiped a lock of hair back and tucked it behind her ear. Her smile was hard and rueful. "Shit, if Falco was half as smart as you . . ."

But Chris was not in the mood. The last few hours had been too intimate, too meaningful, to keep dealing with her reflexive coldness. "This isn't about Falco. Hell, this isn't even about us."

"Us."

"Yes, us. And the vow I just made. Hell, Rosa, it's about your home branded on my body."

He took hold of her upper arms and pulled her closer, not to kiss, not to hold. Just to get into her stubborn skull. He felt like throwing his weight around. She tilted her head back to stare him in the eye.

"You've made something good here," he said, as soberly as she had spoken the words of the initiation ceremony. "I'm sure as hell not gonna let it be destroyed. Falco is an opportunist, not a planner. He's interested in what he can grab. That's not me. I've made some pitiful vows over the years, but this isn't one of them. Put your ego aside and let me help."

The war was plain to see on her face, more like a wounded animal than a woman.

"But then I'll lie low for a few days," he continued. "I'll stay out of sight, just checking on Tilly and the new girls."

"Good," she said with a halfhearted sneer. "Wait a few weeks and maybe one of them will take a shine to their benevolent doctor. You might get lucky."

Chris smiled slowly. "We both know why I won't let that happen. Besides, I'd rather read the book you stuffed into that basket of food."

Rosa's eyes widened. "How . . . ?"

"Don't worry, I don't know which title it is. At least that'll be a surprise."

"But you knew it was there."

"Yup."

"How?"

"How the hell should I know?" He slid his hands behind her back, tugging her near. Tension pushed between them like magnets flipped the wrong way around, but Chris didn't back down. "How do I know anything about us, hm? How do I know the sounds you make in the back of your throat just before you come? Or that you have a scar from a bullet wound right here."

As if to confirm how crazy it was, Chris eased open the collar of her white ceremonial gown. There on the inside of her left shoulder, in front of the joint, a round scar marred her caramel skin.

"You tell me how," he said, his voice gaining strength. "How did I dream that?"

"I don't know, okay? Just keep your voice down."

"Ah, even now. We can't make a little noise without you worrying whether the town thinks we're fighting or fucking."

"You don't have the right to do either."

"Horseshit," he spat. "Rosa, knowing you but not having you is ripping me up."

"You've changed the rules on me. I can't keep you at arm's length like everyone else. You want to tell me why that is?"

He heard an invitation she would never put into words. And so Chris pulled her close. They were both injured and weary, needing to lean a little. It was twilight now, the sky darkening outside the workshop. A single lamp near the workbench filled the center of the room with light, but that only made the space more intimate. Shadows swallowed the walls and windows.

"You think I wanted this to happen?" he asked against her temple. "I've been divorced. *Twice.* Twice I've woken up beside a woman I once loved and just . . . stared at her, wondering when I stopped caring. That sort of failure doesn't leave a guy, believe me."

"What were their names?"

He hadn't expected that. He cleared his throat before saying, "Tabitha and Mary Jane."

"What were they like?"

Closing his eyes, he felt their memories inside his heart like ghosts drifting around a graveyard. But they were so long ago. So far gone, as was everything before the Change. "I met MJ when we were freshmen at the new Cornell campus in San Diego. She was blond." Right now, he couldn't even picture her face, which seemed wrong. "Vivacious, always in the mood for a party. She had the loveliest Australian accent. Her student visa was expiring, and we feared immigration crackdowns, so—"

She traced a fingertip down his jaw, distracting him from her question. "So you married her because she was beautiful and needed a protector?"

"No, I loved her. Or thought I did. But we were different in our means of coping with imminent disaster. Her diversion of choice was people. Parties. Mine was work, studying zoology. We lasted only a little over a year."

"What about Tabitha?"

"Brown hair, always concerned about her weight, even when food went scarce. We were better suited, more mature. She studied economics with a government internship in Fresno, the new capital. I spent months at a stretch in the wilderness of British Columbia, finishing my Ph.D. The timing between us was always wrong. I'd come home for these fantastic weekends, but we spent weeks hardly speaking." He shrugged. "Eventually even the weekends petered out. We didn't know each other anymore. Tab found another man, and I didn't blame her. I was almost . . . relieved."

"But you talked about your honeymoon. Seeing the Eiffel Tower in Las Vegas. You must have been happy. What happened?"

Surprised, he pulled back enough to study her face. He couldn't believe she'd remembered. That meant something, surely—that they were more than this volatile chemistry.

"It's a bad feeling to realize it's your fault," he said. "I mean, I wanted them both to be happy. I wanted Tab and MJ to laugh again. Just not with me."

Rosa pulled away in response to his honesty.

What did I say?

Maybe it was the idea that he could just stop caring. He sounded capricious even to his own ears. But when forced to choose between work and love—well, it had never been much of a choice. Afflicted by the uncertainties of the Change, they needed stability he had never been able to provide. He'd hidden from reality as best he could, until one day it had banged on his door at that Oregon nature station. Walking south from the only friends he had left— from Mason and Jenna, from young Tru and Penny—he'd simply slipped back into hiding.

If Ange had lived, would he have stayed? He liked to think so. But it bothered him a great deal that he couldn't say for sure.

"Then how was this afternoon any different?" she asked. "If you make a habit of vows you can't keep."

"Those things we know? The things we shouldn't know?"

"Yeah?"

"That's how I'm sure this time. I'm not going anywhere,

Rosita. I'm . . . I'm a different man now." He shook his head at the inadequacy of that statement. He was practically a whole different animal.

"But you admit the divorces were your fault?"

"Yeah. I was a terrible husband. Work came first, always." He tried to make light with a wry smile. "You know how that is."

But Rosa wouldn't be budged. She wore an expression that said she was going to keep flaying at him until he bled. Chris steeled himself. If he was in this, he was in it for good. Valle de Bravo was an amazing place, but it was *her* place. He didn't see himself sticking around for just food and shelter, no matter how nice. Unlike Falco, who seemed able to wait around for her change of heart, Chris wanted Rosa or nothing.

So he braced for it, whatever she needed to hear— whatever she needed to make her believe he was on her side.

"Then who broke your heart?"

Chris flinched. Images of blood coated his vision. He'd let Tab and MJ down, but not like . . .

Here we go.

He released Rosa and reached for his shirt. She stopped him, just her hand on his.

"Cristián, who was she?"

He exhaled slowly, finally meeting her imploring gaze. *Idiot.* To think he could do any better with Rosa and the people in this town. He shouldn't be here. And yet, how could he not? She'd marked him with more than his tattoo.

"Her name was Angela, and I watched her die."

When additional words died unspoken, he swallowed around a thick lump. Rosa gave his hand a little squeeze. Silently, she was his companion through the horror of those long-ago moments.

"We only knew each other for a few weeks. She was a mother. Penny, her little girl, was only about nine. They'd come through those first days of change in the west like I did—by sheer luck. By falling in with the right people. Stronger people."

He stared into the dark shadows of the forge. Enduring the sharp pulse of Ex's tattoo needle would be preferable to revisiting this horror. "Ange and I—we had a lot in common, both quiet and unsure in a world gone to shit. There were a couple of seriously intense days where we just held each other. I'd never been like that with a woman, just needing someone to hold. Nothing more. We connected."

Rosa stroked the hair at the nape of his neck, softly with a lulling rhythm. "She died?"

"Saving her daughter, yes. We both tried. She ran out of ammo and . . . I saw the resignation in her eyes before they took her down." Chris pulled away from Rosa and stood, pacing the forge. It was a large room but filled with all of Ex's machines and tools. "I should have been faster. I thought so for years. Or I should have locked her up to keep her safe."

"You'd try to keep a woman from saving her child?"

"She might still be alive."

"Cristián, I cannot imagine she'd want to live if her safety meant her daughter's death." Rosa watched him with more calm and sympathy than he had ever seen from her wide, dark eyes. "Where's the girl now?"

"With my friends, Jenna and Mason. I . . . I had to go. After I buried what was left of her mother, I just couldn't stay."

TWENTY-ONE

That explained everything.

Rosa wished she hadn't asked, or that he hadn't answered. It was easier to call him just another *pendejo* before she realized he had the capacity to care . . . and to suffer. She stood in silence in the shadowy workshop, trying to decide how to proceed. Did he seek forgiveness or comfort? Perhaps neither from her, but she felt compelled to speak.

"People die," she said softly. "Sometimes there is no saving them."

From the slight shifting of his expression, she knew he hadn't wanted that response. Nothing she offered had yet to ease his pain. *Mierda*, she didn't know anything about men. Not like this. Not one-on-one. She only knew how to please them sexually or how to manage them en masse, but nothing about soothing wounded souls. It wasn't the sort of thing bravos asked of *la jefa*.

But then, Cristián wasn't just another bravo, and she suspected he wanted her to admit that. Her brother was the only man she'd ever loved wholeheartedly. Their father had been a brutal *hijo de puta*, and only their *abuela* had saved them from his fists, more times than she could count. Though she had been a small woman, Rosa's maternal grandmother had been able to force her father from her house with only a dark stare.

That had been Rosa's introduction to the power women could wield over men. As she grew up, she had lost that sense of power. But she had it back now. She'd wrested it from the desert, from the Change. She wasn't sure she could give it up, even for a man with whom she shared intimate dreams and an inexplicable yearning.

His dark gaze compelled her—and she didn't like it. Yet the words came anyway as he stared, demanding . . . something.

"I couldn't save my brother," she said. "José. He was two years younger, and I promised my grandmother I would always look after him. But when the Change overwhelmed Mexico and she died, it was so hard."

She had never spoken of this to anyone. Valle de Bravo offered a fresh start, away from the pain of the past, although she would carry the scars to her grave. He seemed to know that instinctively. Had Chris moved or spoken or touched her with kind intent, she could not have finished. He only stood in shadows and silence, listening to her heartbreak. That made it possible for her to go on. It seemed right she should show him her gravest wound. There had been other anguishes, awful indignities, but nothing had scalded her spirit as deeply as this failure.

They had been in Juárez looking for a coyote, a human trafficker, to take them across the border to the New United States. Because it had seceded from the rest of the country, heavy border patrols excluded everyone. Everyone was terrified of hellhounds and skinwalkers and the unstoppable change. She'd saved money for that expense by selling her body—not that José ever knew the truth. It was to fight for their survival. Rosa had been determined to forge a better life.

That part of her story she would not tell. But the Change . . . he would understand the hardship and loss of surviving it.

"When the monsters came, everyone said it was *el fin del mundo*, that we would see plagues of locusts and blood from the heavens. No traffickers were willing to risk being shot on sight by the New U.S. military. So we looked for help. Somewhere safe." Rosa fell into the hole of her memories. "We were near starvation when we met our first skin-walkers. They were human at first. We thought we'd found some measure of sanctuary. When they turned on us, I tried to fight. I told José to run . . . and he did. They chased him down. Tore him to shreds while I—"

A long, shuddering breath escaped her.

Enough. He's seen your pain. It's a fair trade. You pushed to see his scars, so you deserve this.

She didn't wait to see what he would say in response. "It's late. The funeral will begin early tomorrow. In lieu of a priest, I speak the words."

Rosa hurried out of the workshop toward her house, praying to silent, uncaring gods that he wouldn't follow. She couldn't take any more of Chris Welsh right now. Already she felt as though she would die if she didn't have time to shore up her walls. Otherwise he would edge closer than any man ever had.

Many had known her body; none had ever touched her soul.

"Wake up." José had a cup of weak coffee in his hand. They couldn't afford much of it, so they brewed it sparingly, sometimes reusing the grounds.

Rosa didn't know their legal status, living in their grandmother's house. Death had taken her months earlier. Abuela had not left any papers saying the casita *belonged to them. Not that the collapsing governments respected property laws from before the Change. If a person wanted something badly enough, he found a way to take it. Rosa only had one thing of value to fend off starvation. What men wanted, no matter the world's chaos. So she peddled her body with determined desperation, though there were a thousand other girls just like her in Juárez.*

But when she saw José, only fifteen years old and dependent on her for survival, she put aside her aversion. It was only a job, like any other. Better that he believed her lies about working in the factory. He was a friendly boy, if a little slow—and that was why she did not send him out into the world to look for work. She worried that he would be hurt or someone would take advantage of his innocence.

She took the coffee and drank it, eating some cold corn tortillas for breakfast. It was all they had. As she had no protector, she sometimes had to run from men who wanted to take but not pay. Juárez was a rough town, and she dreamed of escaping. Rumor had it that even the New United States was slowly succumbing to the ravages of the Change. Maybe the border patrols would relent. Maybe they could still find somewhere safe.

The scene shifted and Rosa realized, stirring uneasily, that this was wrong. Not real. But she couldn't shake herself awake. With growing horror, she watched as the scene settled into the arroyo where they'd encountered the skinwalkers. She did not want to see this played out again. Not ever again.

She was sweating furiously when she willed herself awake. Thinking about him always brought dreams of her brother, as if his spirit could not rest.

With no way to sleep again, she got up, lit a candle, and took down one of her books. She read the words she must speak in the morning for the sake of Manuel's soul, committing them to memory. Officiating at funerals was her least favorite part of the town leadership, but she would never shirk her responsibility.

By the time morning dawned, she was ready. The same robe she wore for the consecration service also served as funereal vestments. She donned them once more. This was the first time she could recall wearing them two days in a row. She hoped it was not a sign of things to come.

With great gravity, she stepped out the door and found Chris waiting for her. He'd assimilated enough to be wearing the black armband, although he couldn't mourn someone he had not known long. Yet it was a sign of respect.

"We need to talk," he said without preamble.

She shook her head. "I need someone to stand watch this morning. And I'm choosing you."

"The watchtower's on the other side of the valley." A muscle bunched along his jaw. "Away from the funeral. Away from *you*. Am I being punished?"

She sighed. There was no time to explain that she needed someone she could trust up on that tower. Right now, not knowing how deeply Falco had swayed the other bravos, she only trusted Chris, because he was new. And he was *hers*. In a deeper way than the others.

"Just go. Please." She attempted to soften the order with the last, gentle word. By the angry sound of his boots as he turned, it hadn't worked.

I can't deal with this now.

Rosa hurried toward the plaza. Everyone was already assembled in their best, with black armbands tied in respect for Manuel's passing. This was the only time they all gathered without weapons. She'd often worried it would be the perfect time to strike, but no outsiders understood that much about their customs. If the dust pirates ever found out, she'd know they had a traitor in their midst.

The idea sent a cold chill through her.

She focused on the congregation, the grieving and the sorrowful. How odd for a former whore to become a leader and a part-time spiritual counselor. The Change had brought with it many strange and wondrous things. In some ways, for all its brutality, the new world was cleaner and simpler.

"We have lost one who was dear to us," she began. "But time will take that pain, until we remember only the sweetness of his life. And there is always the possibility of return. It is nature's way to reuse what goes back to the earth.

Why would it be different with the soul? Perhaps we can look for Manuel in a new baby's smile."

She glanced at Tilly when she said that, hoping the other woman wouldn't mind her child being used in such a fashion. Tilly merely nodded.

Reassured, she went on. "We will begin the honor of memories with Manuel's closest friend, Rio."

Rosa stood aside so that he could take the center focus.

The boy bowed his head. "I remember when Manny first arrived in Valle. He was only a little older than me, and we got to be such good friends. We drank together, had our first woman together." A soft rumble of laughter went through the crowd, and Rio colored up. "Well, not exactly. I mean, we grew up together, I guess, and life will be shit without him." His voice broke. "I'm going to miss you, *mano*."

She caught Singer gazing at him with liquid sympathy. Rio had been trying to interest her for months, and it looked like she had a soft spot for him after all. Poor kids. To grow up in a world like this. But the pre-Change world had been no paradise either.

Brick took his turn next, speaking of Manuel's valor. Ex talked about his willingness to pitch in, and Jolene wept as she admitted to being his first bed partner. That was more information than anyone needed, but people grieved as they would. It wasn't up to Rosa to find it fitting or not. Once everyone who wanted to had spoken, she closed the service with a brief prayer, the same one she'd offered for his soul as he lay dying. She didn't know very many of them, after all. It would have to serve.

Rio led the procession out of town toward the rocky ground where they built the bonfire for their dead. Since the Change, they had adopted rules about disposing of human remains, aware of new diseases to guard against. With such limited medical care available, they could not afford to invite pestilence with careless hygiene.

Everyone except Rio would remove the black armbands before bed. As chief mourner, Rio had the right to wear his for a full month. Then the town would move on. Here in Valle, they tried not to let the dead linger. The border between life and death was dangerously thin, and no one wanted to invite trespass between the two realms.

Just because the dead haven't risen doesn't mean they won't. Once she would've considered skinwalkers a monstrous fiction created by moviemakers. But she'd seen differently, firsthand.

Manuel had been arrayed on his pyre with as much reverence as they could summon, surrounded by dry leaves, fragrant herbs, saguaro wood, and dried flower petals. That was Viv's doing. In her way she always tried to make such events easier and more respectful. Rosa was always thankful for the older woman's presence.

Brick led the town in singing a farewell hymn, something deep and moving. Rosa let her mind wander right up until Rio lit the fire and the smoke curled skyward, supposedly bearing Manuel's soul toward his rebirth. She didn't know if she believed that; she only said she did because it comforted the others. Rituals mattered. And so did self-awareness.

That's all, then. Manuel is gone. And it's my fault.

TWENTY-TWO

Chris climbed up the rusted iron ladder to the watchtower on the outskirts of town. From up in its crow's nest he would be able to see the entire lay of the valley. But at the moment he saw nothing but red. She'd banished him.

He pulled to the top and flopped down to sit. His feet dangled over the edge. With an automatic rifle lying between his shoulder blades, he felt the scrape of metal and fabric over the bandages covering his new tattoo. Marked for life. And not a damn thing to show for it.

What was worse? That he'd opened up to Rosa about his ex-wives—and, more painfully, about watching Angela dic? That Rosa had found the courage to reveal a few dark corners of her past? Or that she'd completely shut him down afterward?

The wind ferried away his curse. One step forward, five steps back.

Down below, at the north edge of town, the procession began the slow walk toward where Manuel's body was laid out on a pyre. From that vantage Chris could only make out the dead man's form wrapped in pale cloth. He hadn't known Manuel well; the armband he wore was out of respect, not mourning. But Rosa had excluded him. Purposefully. The crow's nest might as well have been an emotional Siberia.

For such a strong woman, she was behaving like a damn coward.

Chris stretched and felt the strain of the last two weeks in his muscles. He'd had another dream of Rosa—only in this dream she'd been younger, wide-eyed and hardened at the same time. Tears looked wrong on her face, but so did a girl's bright smile. It had been like watching a grainy home movie of her life Before. But no matter how realistic, that dream hadn't held the aura of magic and strangeness that the ones bearing premonitions did.

He was beginning to tell the two apart.

After what he'd witnessed since the Change, and after what he'd recently experienced firsthand, he wouldn't put it past the ways of this new world. The science he once trusted and explored and, hell, even loved—it no longer mattered. He had needed to grieve for that passing too. It was not the gut-wrenching pain of losing a human being, but the quiet loss of part of one's soul.

He stood and surveyed the valley, making a circle to appraise each horizon. Sunlight had just crawled over the distant eastern slopes. Long, long shadows licked across the desert floor, reminding him of the tattoo still healing on his back. But then he was back to Rosa again.

Damn.

Fatigue made him tight and sluggish, as did a tension he hadn't known in years. When walking the wasteland, he had been his own person. His solitary years spent studying mountain lions had been equally liberating. The whole continent had fallen into chaos, but he had been at peace with the silence and the wild. It was lonely. It was grueling and violent. But anything that bothered him too much became a memory come morning. He just kept walking. No wonder even calm, studious Tabitha had eventually demanded a divorce.

This . . .

Staying was much harder.

With his track record, he shouldn't have been surprised. Itchy feet had been his life's opus. She gave him reason to stick around and try for something better, but what if Rosa wasn't an option? Could he stay in Valle if its leader kept stealing into his dreams but turning her back on him in reality?

It bothered him a great deal that the answer was no. The vow he'd taken during the initiation had been, in truth, a commitment to the settlement as a whole. But he knew better. And if she was being honest with herself, so did Rosa. He had spoken those words to *her*.

With nothing better to do, Chris checked the sights of his weapon and its ammunition. The clip was only half full, maybe less. One day even this basic means of survival would change. "Kill or be killed" would revert to clubs and rocks.

The scent of burning wood teased into his nostrils. He looked north. Flames and heavy tendrils of smoke danced up from the pyre. *God bless, Manuel.*

Soon he could give up this exile and go to work. The new girls needed a full medical appraisal, the bravos injured during the raid required his care, and he should look in on Tilly. Then, that evening, he'd settle in and read the book Rosa had given him. *The Collected Tales and Poems of Edgar Allan Poe.* That morning he'd meant to ask about her reason behind it. Had she just pulled the fattest one off the shelf? Had she given it any thought at all?

But nope. Hadn't happened.

That didn't mean he wouldn't relish reading it. He literally couldn't remember the last thing he'd read. The prospect made the hollow in his chest a little fuller, a little warmer, as if he still had enough pieces of soul to keep functioning.

A glimmer of light in the west caught his attention. His finger tightened reflexively on the trigger. He narrowed his eyes, staring, staring, until blinking became something other people did. The glimmer had been right between two sharp peaks, perhaps kilometers off, where he camped at night. It didn't return. None of the preternatural alarm bells went off in his brain, but neither could he relax.

Metal, maybe? Or a reflection off glass?

The procession was filing back into town, breaking up now that the bonfire had calmed.

"Hey, Doc," called Ingrid. She looked up at him from the base of the ladder. "My shift. Go get some breakfast."

"Thanks."

As he climbed down, he made a decision. He would check out the area between those peaks. But not now. He didn't want to get the town in a tizzy if his suspicions were wrong, and he didn't want Rosa to think she couldn't trust his gut feelings. No, he decided to check it out that night, when he returned to the caves to sleep.

"Keep an eye on the western horizon, between those two peaks," he said to Ingrid.

Discretion was one thing, but failing to pass along a possible threat was another. Ingrid had keen senses and a quiet temperament. He felt right in trusting that she wouldn't make more of it than it was.

She took the watchman's rifle he handed over. "Trouble?"

"Nah, just thought I saw something. It's probably nothing."

The town was quiet when he walked back. The funeral had cast a contemplative blanket over the whole place. Chris returned to his room above the store. It was more like a bus station locker, just a place to stow his gear. He rummaged through his satchel, throwing together a complement of general medical provisions. A wide variety. Then he steeled himself for dealing with these new women. Some might suffer from ailments he couldn't cure.

Shifting his shoulders back, nodding once to himself, he headed downstairs. Wicker was sweeping and humming tunelessly in his rough baritone. He looked up. "Oh, hey, Doc."

Falco and his closest allies might resent Chris's initiation, but no one else gave off that vibe. They just . . . welcomed him.

"I'm heading over to check up on our new guests," Chris said. "I'm assuming we have free run of supplies here if we need to get them cleaned up?"

"Sure thing," Wicker said, grinning. "I'd love to see those gals spiffed up and healthy."

"You and twenty other bravos."

Wicker shrugged his lanky shoulders. "And the odds improve."

"Amen," Chris said, his enthusiasm feigned.

His desire would find no outlet among starved, terrified girls. Rosa was the woman he wanted.

He shoved out of the store and into the street. Again he was struck by the overall change in mood when other townspeople greeted him warmly. But unwilling to analyze it too closely, his mind on the task he faced, Chris kept his replies brief and his strides long.

Brick stood outside the town hall with a shotgun cradled in his arms. "Morning, Doc." Without hesitation, he stepped aside and opened the door for Chris.

Rosa was already inside. Of course she was.

Their gazes met over the head of a thin brunette. Chris looked away first.

The women had made little nests of their floor space. Some were still asleep at that hour, their blankets pulled tightly around thin bodies or flung away by restless feet. The intimacy of seeing how each woman slept—there on the floor, without much privacy—added to Chris's tension. No matter who they were, they deserved better. His job was to get them well enough to make that happen.

He walked over to where one woman was sitting up. She wrestled with the task of feeding herself some sort of paste. Viv must have made it to help ease their stomachs back onto solid food. The woman's posture was defensive, hunched over her ration, legs drawn up near her chest. Chris's years-long study of wild animals came back like instinct.

"Good morning," he said.

She flinched.

He set the medical bag against the wall. Slowly, giving

her plenty of room and time to get used to his presence, he knelt. "Good morning," he said again. "My name's Chris. I'm the doctor here."

The woman showed no sign of comprehension. Skin like coffee with cream. Dark eyes. Black hair.

He tried again. *"Buenos días. Me llamo Cristián."*

Her eyebrows lifted, ever so subtly.

"Soy el médico aquí. Estás en el Valle de Bravo."

Maybe it was the news that he was a doctor or that their settlement had a name, but her posture sank toward abject relief. Her hands began to tremble. Two tears slid down cheeks that still bore the desert's filmy dust.

Chris eased closer and wrapped his hands around hers, steadying her grip. She tensed but did not pull away. "I'll help you," he continued in Spanish.

After a try or two she let him guide her hand, bringing the spoon to her mouth. His chest was hot and crushed by a vise of emotions he couldn't sort out. Pride, maybe—in himself and in her trust. Rage toward those who'd abused her. And the knowledge that he couldn't leave the valley while these women needed his care.

Strength eased back into her with every swallow of paste. It smelled of buckwheat and maybe even the agave wine. She ate with more and more enthusiasm. Soon the bowl was empty, and she pushed out a heavy sigh. Although the process probably exhausted her, she looked rejuvenated by the meal.

"Bueno," he said. *"Bueno. ¿Cómo te llamas?"*

"Sara," she whispered.

He asked her age. Nineteen. He asked where she'd been born. Guadalajara. He asked if she knew the names of the other women. She looked around, her expression bleak, then shook her head.

"I saw them for the first time in the truck," she said in Spanish, her voice cracking.

"Who did this?"

Again she shook her head.

Chris didn't want to push her any harder. He offered an

encouraging smile. Then he made another decision: in no way were these women ready to be examined by a man, doctor or not. They had endured hell. Living rough had been a test of his mettle. What these women had needed to do to survive since the Change . . . He didn't feel hearty enough to go there.

With one last smile, he stood and left Sara. Rosa had moved on to another woman, a thick-boned blonde who should have seemed robust and stout. Instead she looked wasted, her eyes like those of a soldier with PTSD.

"Can I talk to you a minute, *Jefa*?"

Rosa may have noticed the distance in his tone. He hoped she did. But she wore her poker face too. She nodded and followed him to the back of the hall.

"These women aren't ready for me," he said quietly.

She blinked as if surprised by his appraisal. "No, they're not."

"The one I was talking to is Sara. She said she hadn't met any of the others until they wound up in the truck together."

"The dishwater blonde there, she's Allison. She said the same thing. Traded along until she wound up here with this lot." Rosa seamed her lips together, then seemed to force herself to relax. "I've heard of it happening. Wandering traders say the O'Malley is notorious for trafficking women."

"Bastard," he said tightly. "Doctor's advice? Food. The gruel seems to be working. Water as they want it." He rubbed the back of his neck. "Maybe if Viv and Singer could help, they can get them cleaned up and into new clothes. Good for morale."

"Right."

"We'll give it a week, see if they respond. Then maybe they'll be mentally strong enough to endure a physical, especially if they bond with you three."

"We could be there during the exam. I think that would . . ." She cleared her throat, her attention on Allison. "That would help them."

Rosa's slide back toward emotion only highlighted how she had been behaving. Curt, professional, but amenable. She hadn't balked at his suggestions out of reflexive pride. He liked that she was at least to the point of considering his advice for what it was: well-intentioned.

"I'll introduce myself to the rest, if they seem willing," he said. "Then I'll leave it to you and Viv."

Without waiting for a reply, he returned to tending the women. One draining, heartbreaking hour later, Chris had done all he could. For now. Three more hours of rounds meant cleaning gunshot wounds and checking for signs of infection. None of the bravos qualified as a model patient. Ex insisted on working the forge despite his shoulder wound, and Rio was back on guard duty. Their machismo left Chris with a headache. At least the women seemed grateful for the help he offered.

A shower followed. Then a nap, riddled with erotic fantasies—no glimmer of premonition, just his body being desperate. He woke up, cursed, paced, and waited.

When evening finally arrived, he felt like a free man as he walked into the desert.

TWENTY-THREE

Rosa didn't need anything from the store, but she lingered in the hope that she would catch Chris either heading up to his room or coming downstairs. The impulse was alien, but she wanted to explain her motive for sending him to stand guard during the funeral. In her way, she had trusted him as much as she was capable of doing. He hadn't seemed to appreciate that. For all they'd already shared that was extraordinary, they still misfired.

Wicker glanced up as she made her second pass. "Looking for something in particular?"

"Just seeing what new goods have come in."

"Not much." He continued sorting fabrics before adding in a conspiratorial tone, "Did you know the new doc's already got someplace better to sleep? He's quick, I'll give him that."

Rosa's blood chilled and then heated, a wave of inexplicable emotion going tsunami in her skull. Before the Change, she'd seen the aftermath of such disasters on television. That devastation was inside her now.

Somehow she managed a casual response. "Oh?"

"Yeah. He don't bunk up in here anymore. Keeps some stuff upstairs, but that's about it." Wicker twisted his lip in concentration. "I can't figure who he's with, though. Brick and Jolene spend a lot of time together these days, now that she's given up on Falco. Singer's too young. Viv seems a mite too old for him, though could be he don't mind. Maybe Mica? Ingrid?" He shook his head. "But I've never known her to take up with anybody besides Ex now and then."

"Well, it's not one of the new girls," she said, her throat tight.

The memory of how he tended to the abused women had stayed with her all day. His patience. His quiet care. The sound of Rosa's first language on his tongue affected her—so out of proportion with whatever he said. But his diligence and concern for the plight of those girls had burrowed into her soul.

Wicker shrugged. "It's a puzzle, all right."

But what if she'd gotten Chris wrong? She knew so little about him. He'd love to stick his dick in her. So? That wasn't enough to call what they had something real. She stalked out of the store, brows drawn down.

"'Knowing you but not having you is ripping me up,'" she growled.

Sí, claro.

She climbed the watchtower, her heart tight, muttering curses all the while. To think she'd been *waiting* for him. How he must be laughing. Christian ought to be castrated, the way he wielded his wounded eyes and his smooth, practiced ways. *Dios*, it had been years since a man had fooled her about his sincerity.

"Everything all right?" Ex asked.

Of all her bravos, Rosa liked him best because he minded his business. Most likely he shouldn't be on watch up here so soon after being shot, but just try to stop him from doing exactly as he pleased. *Necio*, this one. Stubborn as hell.

"*Claro*. Mind if I sit for a little while?" Rosa settled in cross-legged, knowing he wouldn't read her presence wrong. No point in going home when she was too wound up to read or sleep.

"Suit yourself. It's a quiet night. Mostly."

Really, she should take a deep breath and let this go. *Don't think about Chris anymore. Don't think about him working between someone else's thighs, gazing down at her face. Don't think about the sweat on his skin or the sounds he makes—*

She ground her teeth, maddened because she knew too many things about the shape of his desire. It was wrong and frightening, but irresistible too. The urge to see if that shared dream had any basis in reality teased at the edges of her mind.

Instead she gazed out over her territory, which always filled her with pride and tranquility. The sky was darkening, a gorgeous sunset in vivid hues, all stark beauty in the slashes of red and violet, with dark hulks of mountain in the distance. This was all that mattered. Not faithless men and their ability to cause such hurt.

Ex's final word registered at last. "What do you mean *mostly*? Did you see something?"

"Nothing unusual. The new bravo walks out of the valley fairly often. Not every night, but always after lights-out."

Fear and betrayal slammed through her and stole her breath. What if he was meeting someone? For the first time since she'd left the store, she hoped it was for sex. If she caught Chris giving information to their enemies, she'd have to execute him.

And I don't want to.

Dios, no. Not Cristián.

But with a hot, sick feeling in her gut, she remembered the first time Brick had come across him. Chris had been watching their raid on the highway. Since then, the regular activity of their rivals had been changed up. The attack on the town. More trucks luring them beyond the town's defenses. The dummy shipment. The girls he'd somehow found.

What if he'd done everything to gain her trust, only to use it against the whole town now that he was a bravo?

"How long has this been going on?"

"The last week or so." Ex fiddled with a closed switchblade like a smoker who missed holding a cigarette. "I thought you knew."

She bit off a low, virulent curse. "What route does he take?"

Ex succinctly laid out the course, which led out to the west. She remembered a hidden trail out that way. Her heart lifted a little. Maybe it was just for sex, a partner who didn't want anyone to find out what she was doing.

Like Singer.

The girl had trusted him with her bike, which she loved better than most humans. She'd flirted with him too, in that sweet, casual way of hers. If it *was* Singer, at least that made Chris a filthy old bastard, not a traitor. But Brick would make a testicle necklace out of the first man to touch his little sister. Rosa had to find out before he did.

With a wave for Ex, she made her way back down and out of camp, following the worn goat track behind the tall rocks. At night it was very dark in the valley; she felt swallowed up by shadows. Slipping away was like shedding her skin. She was on an errand that would affect her people, but being out of their sight for just a few moments was oddly freeing.

Rosa picked along the rocks with cautious but rhythmic steps. The ancient path was only for the surefooted. It led nowhere except to a bluff honeycombed with caverns where native tribes once made their homes. All the way she wrestled with disturbing possibilities, but she couldn't be sure unless she verified it personally. Her leadership couldn't withstand another mistake so soon, not when she had used Chris's initiation to firm up allegiances. Unexpectedly and unpleasantly, her position depended on him.

On him being the man she'd hoped he was.

Rosa crept quietly up to the caves, just shallow cuts into the mountainside. Although she heard no human sounds, she knew he was there. Taking a breath, her hand on the hilt of her knife in case he kept hostile company, she peeked inside.

The scene within made her go still.

Chris sat alone inside a small, close cave. He had created a livable camp with a few essential belongings—not his satchel full of medicines, but his initiation basket, a solar-powered lantern, and blankets.

Rosa watched him, the line of his neck bowed low, as he shifted against the cave wall.

He was *reading*.

He'd retreated, but he'd taken her gift with him.

She meant to slip away silently, but some sound gave her away. Or maybe he just *knew* with that awful link between them.

Without looking up, he said, "Done spying on me?"

Rosa stepped into the mouth of the cave with a casual shrug. "I had to be sure your behavior didn't pose a threat to Valle."

"Makes sense." His tone was casual, but his eyes snapped sparks in the soft light. "It's what you care about, your town. But I bet it doesn't keep you warm at night." He marked his page and set the book aside. Every movement was slow, controlled, edged with friction. "You're too afraid of getting close. You might get hurt again, and you fear they'll see that you're not an alabaster Madonna—that you need and want and *feel*. I tell you, it was a hard thing to realize you're a coward."

She swallowed hard, her accent thickening. "*Basta*. You don't know nothing about me."

"That's because you're scared to death of what might happen if I did."

"Fuck you."

"Anytime, Rosita. I'm open for business."

That last word struck a nerve. Did he know? She took two steps back, quick anger warring with hurt and fear. Sex had only ever been a transaction. Nothing more. She'd learned what men wanted as a means of survival. It had never been something she wanted for herself, except in dreams, when he looked at her with haunted hazel eyes, asking for something she might not be able to give.

The tautness of his features softened, as if he glimpsed her pain in the dim light. Damn him, he saw too much.

"Don't be like this. I had to check. It's my job."

"Or you could *trust* me."

"I do," she said softly. "As much as I can anyone. But I thought . . ."

"What?"

"That you were meeting someone."

His mouth tightened. He pulled his knees up and rested his forearms there. "On my watch earlier, I thought I saw something out this way. But I checked all over and didn't find anything."

He'd been acting to protect Valle. His vow mattered to him. Those revelations sent relief streaming through her, as cool and welcome as a wind blowing down from the mountains. She didn't want him to be the man who walked away when things got tough. To her dismay, she wanted to believe him when he said he'd changed. But she didn't know if she could withstand the disappointment of being wrong.

"Thank you."

He went on as if she hadn't spoken. "And sometimes I don't want to be in town."

"But why stay out here?"

"Too many people. I'm not used to it."

She enjoyed the company of her bravos, but after long years alone, he probably found it hard to be surrounded by voices and movement all the time. Another piece of him clicked into place, ringing true. In silence, Rosa watched the play of light and shadow across his face, and in her head, she confessed the truth. *I wanted to see you. I hate that I was jealous. Why, why do you matter, Cristián?*

"I have something to tell you about this morning," she said.

"Oh?"

Tentatively she eased to the ground and sat at the edge

of his blankets. The rock felt cool beneath her fingertips. She'd never shared such an intimate space with a man, and it didn't feel natural. Yet for Chris's sake, maybe for them both, she'd try. On a soft puff of breath, she explained her reasons for sending him to the watchtower.

Chris was still frowning, but the tension around his mouth eased. "So you wanted me up there. *Me*. Nobody else." He sounded hopeful, as if being needed was his drug of choice.

"I believed you wouldn't permit a threat to pass under any circumstances." And there it was, a blind and naked thing, the nascent trust. "You wouldn't sabotage me or want me to appear weak."

"I never would," he said with a bashful grin. "I like your strength."

A ripple of energy flickered between them, almost visible to the naked eye. It robbed her of breath, like a sudden fall into deep water. Terrifying, but also exhilarating. His troubled hazel gaze locked on hers, as mysterious as a desert night but without the same chill. Instead she saw only his warmth.

"Do you feel that?" she asked unsteadily.

Chris nodded. Her explanations seemed to have leached his anger, but the intensity remained. He trained his considerable powers of concentration on her, making her restless. With unspeakable daring, she reached out a hand and touched his biceps, wondering whether the contact would conjure a raging beast. He merely studied her fingers on his skin as if they held the key to a puzzle he was determined to solve.

"I think that's the first time you've touched me on purpose. While I'm actually awake."

"Why are we dreaming about each other?"

"The Change is probably behind it." The resignation in his posture didn't seem natural. The scientist in him must have taken years to make even that much peace with the unexplained. "I can't pretend to understand half the things I've seen."

I shouldn't know how it feels to make love with him.

But her body did, remembering things that hadn't yet come to pass. She went slick and hot, aching for him. Rosa shifted on the blanket. Need rose in her in an undeniable madness, so that she curled her hands into fists and tightened her thighs.

"I don't like this," she whispered. "It feels like I can't control my body."

"Because you want me?"

"Sí."

The air in the cave was sultry, as if their presence generated more heat than the stone could absorb. By lamplight she saw the rapid rise and fall of his chest. Her simple admission of desire had unwoven his steady focus. She'd gotten to him. His reaction made her feel so . . . *powerful.* As did the relief that he hadn't gone looking for some other soft body to slake his longing.

"I want to kiss you again," he said, the words quiet but strong. "I can't promise I'll stop there, but I won't make love to you unless you want it as much as I do. Will you come to me, Rosita? Will you let me touch you?"

The icy dagger in her chest melted. No man had ever asked to give her pleasure. Before Chris, she wouldn't have thought it possible. The curve of his upper lip called to her, inciting a craving she no longer wanted to control. Making up her mind, she knee-walked to him. She didn't tense when he drew her onto his lap.

His hard cock pressed against her bottom as she settled against him, but his conscious movements remained smooth, slow, patient. He wound his arms about her loosely and lowered his head to hers, lips seeking a delicate caress. She gasped a little at the soft heat. Who knew it could be so gentle and slow? *Ay, Dios.*

Chris brushed his tongue against hers—a tease and a promise. His hands didn't wander; they remained tender and light at her shoulder and waist.

Rosa hummed a sound against his mouth, relaxing into the kiss. This was different from the last one they'd shared.

Less crazed. More deliberate. And she loved it. He teased his tongue past her lips, but she didn't know what to do.

He whispered against her mouth, "Suck. Softly."

Such a command should have been embarrassing, but the moment gained intimacy. He didn't laugh at her lack of expertise or ask why she couldn't kiss. Lazy spirals of desire made her want to straddle him and slowly rub against him like a cat. He nipped her lower lip, then drew his mouth down the side of her throat. His caress was absolutely delicious. Tingles sprang up in places she hadn't known could feel so good.

"I like this," she breathed against the bristles of his jaw.

"A little more?"

That was the difference between this man and every other. Cristián asked; he didn't take. He was someone she could enjoy without fear. Someone worthy.

Her slow smile felt like a sunrise of the soul. "*Sí, por favor.* A little more."

TWENTY-FOUR

Beyond obvious reasons, Chris was thankful for the erotic dream he'd shared with Rosa. It gave him incentive to take it slow. He would stay strong and re-create that pleasure— making it real for the first time.

Because holding her, truly holding her, pulled apart his control.

He settled his mouth over hers again, more forcefully this time, but with a slowness that made inhuman demands. She tentatively flicked her tongue against his lower lip. Chris rewarded her by opening to her curious exploration. He made every escalation hers to determine.

As if sensing that encouragement, her body melted against his chest. She was finally giving in. Finally giving him permission.

Chris closed his eyes. Her touch was light, her kisses shy, but she unraveled him. He settled in for a long battle, his mind against his body. For Rosa's sake, for the sake of their tentative trust, his mind needed to win.

Only when she made a little sound of frustration in the

back of her throat did Chris bring a hand up to her nape.
The heaviness of her skull nestled in his palm. He extended
his fingers up into her hair. She pulled back just enough to
rip the tie off the end of her braid. Then she found his
mouth again, renewing an exploration that grew bolder by
the moment.

Using both hands, Chris loosened her braid. Dark hair
spilled over her shoulders. His touch gentle, he pushed at
her shoulders, holding her at a little less than arm's length.

Questions twisted her brow.

"Relax," he said with a soft laugh. "Okay? Try? I just
want to look at you."

Like a bashful girl, she twisted away until her face was
in three-quarter profile, draped in dark hair. Chris cupped
her cheek and urged her back to center. Her deep brown
eyes were wide, luminous, filled to capacity with doubt.
The curtain of her unbound hair softened each feature until
he could nearly imagine her carefree and happy. The pressure gone. The fears banished.

With his vow of patience and control renewed, he
brushed the hair back to bare her throat. He eased nearer,
muscles trembling. She tasted of the desert and a sheen
of salt. But beneath lay sweet woman. He kissed, licked,
suckled softly at that sensitive skin. Rosa tipped her head
back with a moan. Her fingers found the caps of his shoulders and dug deep. The taut ache in his cock kicked up a
notch.

But still he took it slow. If Chris had a plan at all, other
than keeping from embarrassing himself like a teenager
with his first girl, it was to leave her wanting. He would
tease. She would demand more. And then she wouldn't be
so afraid.

It was a good plan, in theory. The way her nails gouged
his flesh, however, made it maddeningly difficult.

Needing a moment to breathe, he whispered in her ear,
"Will you answer something for me?"

Her fingers went still. *"¿Qué?"*

"Shall I undress first, or you?"

The look on her face was comical, but Chris didn't laugh. He was too busy appreciating how seriously she considered his question.

"You," she said at last.

"Will you do the honors or me?"

Now she smiled. The vixen inside the hesitant, wounded woman was coming out to play. God, he hoped so.

She leaned back along the blanket, all athletic curves and gorgeous midnight hair. "You. I think I'll watch."

"Determined to make me work for this, aren't you?"

"All good things require effort."

Grinning, breathing as evenly as he could, Chris stood. The cave was no bigger than a king-size bed at its base, but a conical roof meant he could stand without having to stoop. He started with his shirt. Inside he was laughing at himself as he undid each button. Chris Welsh, male stripper. But the look in her eyes made him feel like the most potent, desired man on the planet. Hell, maybe he was.

He shrugged out of the shirt, glorying in her gasp. Her gaze was a prairie fire, heating all of his exposed flesh. He balled the shirt and tossed it toward her. Rosa brought the fabric to her nose and inhaled—an intimacy that stole the strength from his knees.

She smiled at him and licked her upper lip. "Turn around. I want to see your back."

Chris shivered. The bandage covering his fresh tattoo had itched like hell that evening, so he'd removed it before settling in for the night—smiling as he did when thinking about stubborn bravos. The mark would still be slightly reddened, but it was still hers. She had claimed him.

He clenched his jaw and swallowed. Patience. Strength. He needed both now to give her the satisfaction of making demands. There would be no taking on his part, not with a woman who had endured so much. Only giving. He had never been so selfless—could only hope he was up to the task.

"Go on," she whispered.

To say he was as unhurried with his boots and jeans would be a lie. He was losing it. His stiff cock was a compass needle pointing due north.

He was just about to pull off his shorts when Rosa edged forward and grabbed his hands. "Let me," she said.

"Damn."

Her laughter was as much a gift as her trust. "Got that right."

Clenching his molars, Chris braced for her caress. She hooked her fingers inside the waistband. A gentle tug. Then a rougher one. She never touched his skin, just the underwear, but her agitated breath fanned over his upper thighs—then across his freed cock.

He grabbed her wrists and knelt, pushing her back. "Enough," he ground out.

The smile shaping her dusky lips was more confident now. Maybe he wouldn't have to be a saint. Maybe he wouldn't have to hold back—just hold on. With a little more time, she would join him. His Rosita would not break.

"*Ay*, you're beautiful," she whispered up from the blanket.

Chris looked down at himself. He was just a man on his knees, but Rosa's passionate intensity made him feel like a god. And he couldn't ever remember being so hard, so ready for a woman.

"Your turn." Cupping the backs of her calves, he pulled until her legs, spread-eagled, bounded his. "Shall I undress you?"

"*Sí*."

No hesitation. He could've shouted his relief.

Instead he turned to the serious task of removing her clothes while maintaining his control. He started with her cargo pants, mostly because he didn't trust his dexterity to last. He worked at the belt, two buttons, and zipper until he bared her flat, taut stomach to the lamplight. He couldn't resist bending close enough to dip his tongue into the shallow well of her belly button. She jackknifed, giggling.

Chris pulled back, his face slack with wonder. "You're ticklish?"

"Shut up, *cabrón*."

"You are."

He tugged her cargoes down past the gorgeous slope of her hips, then all the way off. But he did so just to return to her stomach. Rosa pushed at his head. He caught her wrists and held them clear. Starting with the elastic edge of her plain panties, he licked up to her navel. Again. Then again. She fought him, her laughter a whirlwind in their cave, until she gasped for mercy and cursed in Spanish. Only his fear of doing further harm to her recent injury kept him relatively gentle.

She was breathless by the time he stopped, and too dazed to see that he'd undone half her shirt. He nuzzled upward from her stomach, kissing, licking, tasting his way toward her breasts.

"You play dirty," she said against the top of his head.

"I like that you sound pleased."

"I don't know what I am right now."

He looked up from where he'd opened the last button. "You're breathtaking."

"I'm just Rosa Cortez."

Chris stilled. "Do I need to spell this out to you?"

He sat back, still stark naked and fully aroused, and pulled her up to a seated position. His hands more edgy now than when fighting off beasts and raiders, he smoothed her shirt from one shoulder. The skin he revealed to the light was smooth and light brown, like caramels or coffee with cream—a decadent pleasure made real again, here in the time of change. He kissed it, just lip against skin. Then again, again, down her lithe arm as he stripped her bare.

"You're breathtaking," he repeated against the sensitive crook of her elbow. "You play at being the untouchable Madonna, but I know the truth. You really are. You have more experience with sex than a woman should be forced to know. But at my touch and my kiss, you tremble."

He smoothed the other sleeve off her arm. She shivered. Her nipples were hard points against her functional white tank top.

She was staring at him now, as if trying to dig inside his head. "Cristián?"

"Yeah?"

"Thank you for this."

"Don't thank me yet," he said, grinning. "I'm trying to hold on here."

She flicked her gaze to his throbbing erection. "You look like it. Shouldn't we do something about that?"

"Oh, I plan to. But not yet."

"Chris, you don't—"

"Shh," he whispered, slipping the tank top up over her head. "Let me take care of you. Trust me, okay? I got this."

She was smiling again when she lay back against the blanket. But Chris had lied. The sight of her naked torso—marred only by the bandage he had applied—nearly undid him. *Go slow. Be careful. Make it good.*

Shit, he hadn't ever asked so much of himself.

And it had been years since he'd seen a woman so beautifully exposed. Sex since the Change had been furtive and base—always ashamed, mostly clothed or done in the dark. Rosa was . . . *glorious.* Her breasts were small and proud, with pale brown areolas surrounding hard, tempting nipples. Her skin was luminous.

Had she ever willingly displayed herself like this to a man? If so, it had been a rare event. The toned, athletic cut of her abdominal muscles and graceful arms were a delicious contrast to such feminine softness.

So were the bullet scars that marred her shoulder, her lower left hip, her upper thigh.

Chris had to shut them out. He couldn't think about the pain she'd endured—not and curtail an impotent rage. The past was the past. And the longer he waited, reveling in the sight of her, the more fidgety she became. He wanted to indulge his senses, but the delay gave her time to think. To reconsider.

So he gave them both the pleasure they wanted. His mouth watered as he leaned nearer and suckled one pert nipple. She arched from the blankets with a surprised cry.

Her hands cupped the back of his head, fingers tunneling, before sliding down his nape to his shoulders. There her fingers became reverent. Blood hammered in his ears. He couldn't breathe—didn't want to. Just feel.

He moved to her other breast and paid homage, palming that slight weight. Rosa wiggled beneath him. She panted, making furious little noises in her throat. Chris smiled against her nipple and licked, nibbled, sucked deep. Again she reared off the blanket, sending a jolt of fire down to his cock.

He could smell her arousal now, which dragged him down, down to where her panties remained a scant barrier. She seemed beyond noticing when he stripped them off. Her hands kept working at his shoulders, scraping and tightening. Each spike of sweet pain lanced at his control. But he held on, if only for the promise of tasting her.

He could tell the moment she knew his destination. Tension returned. Her breathing quieted. "Chris . . . I—"

"I said, I got this."

Her inner thigh was impossibly soft. He kissed her again and again until her tension dissolved.

With infinite care, he spread her thighs. She fought him for every moment—not physically, but in her mind. He could practically feel the war between desire and fear. Why he needed to push her like this was probably something too sadistic to analyze. But when she was spread to him, open, vulnerable, her body humming with an electric intensity, the answer was so clear. Her trust was for him alone. A heady aphrodisiac.

He knelt between her legs and tasted. Rosa groaned. She writhed so much that Chris spread his hands wide on her inner thighs and pressed her into the blanket. The implacable cave floor and his tense, splayed fingers held her lower body still. He feasted. He teased and explored. He dipped his tongue inside, senses flooded by the scent and taste of her need. Fierce, breathless cries filled their retreat, ratcheting his desire to an unbearable peak.

Concentrating on the knot of tight nerves, Chris dedicated his mouth to her first orgasm of the night. He circled his tongue, nipped with his teeth, sucked hard. Rosa was lost to a babbling rush of Spanish. He found the rhythm she liked and kept at it, circling, circling, until her spine went taut and she unleashed a stark cry. He held his mouth against her quivering center until the storm receded.

"Come to me, Cristián," she gasped.

It was more than he could take.

"Tell me I can fuck you," he grated out. "God, Rosa. I need—"

"*Sí*. Do it."

TWENTY-FIVE

Chris crawled up Rosa's body, kissing, tasting. One plunge and he was inside her.

After such phenomenal pleasure, she thought she could stand his body on hers. The warm glow still permeated every muscle. She should've been relaxed and blissful, but the moment he slid up and pushed inside, everything went cold. She detached, as she always had. If she closed her eyes, she could almost float up to the ceiling and watch him ride her.

Maybe he won't know, if I move and moan. No one else ever cared.

The practiced sound escaped her lips before she could stop it, and he froze above her, his body locked. "What's wrong? Am I hurting you?"

No. The men who had come before did that. But they had stolen the pleasure from her, leaving too many bad memories. Much as she wished it could be otherwise, much as she hated it, she tried to smile because it wasn't his fault. She was broken.

She almost lied, but the passionate honesty written

plainly across his beautiful features called the same from her. "It's . . . it doesn't feel good."

"Me?" He was already pulling back, even though tremors shook him from head to toe. He should have been driving on, heedless of her desires. That lifted some of the tight band across her chest. "I'm doing something wrong?"

"No." Each word felt torn from her, so difficult to speak through a throat gone thick with old dread. "Maybe I just can't—"

"Shhh." Though the move obviously cost him, he withdrew completely, easing beside her on the nest of blankets. "We'll figure out the problem. I'll fix it."

"I don't know if I can be fixed."

"I've got all night." He settled, drawing her back against him.

At first she tensed, sure he was going to pounce on her, but despite the insistent throb of his erection, he only held her. His breathing was a little ragged, but otherwise he seemed calm. Any other man would be furious, slapping her for the annoyance and bother. Well, the ones she'd known, anyway.

Rosa let out a slow breath.

"I'm sorry," she whispered.

"The point is for us both to have a good time. Otherwise it's not worth doing."

That sure hadn't been her experience, but she eased even more, relaxing into his arms. This felt good. Safe. Spooning, she'd heard it called once—though she had never understood why a woman would want to linger once the act was done. She always wanted them to stop touching her as soon as possible so she could wash.

Careful of the bandages he had applied, Chris stroked her ribs just below her breasts. Her breath hitched. Her nipples tingled. He kissed the nape of her neck softly, though his body felt hard and tight against her. This patience had to be hurting him. *Mierda*, she wished she could be normal. Like Jolene. The way she laughed and carried on with Brick, she must really enjoy it.

"You like when I touch you," he said to himself, as if thinking it through.

But she answered him anyway. *"Sí."*

"And I wasn't hurting you?"

"No." She had no idea why he hadn't lost patience with her. *Dios* knew, sex couldn't be worth so much time and trouble. Maybe she should offer to do him with her mouth, and they could call it a night.

"Can we try it another way, Rosita?" His voice went husky and he cupped her breast in one hand, gently plucking at the nipple.

Sometimes men liked to push her facedown and take her from behind, but she wasn't sure that would be any better. Still, she mustered her courage and said, *"Claro."*

So gently, he lifted her leg and eased between her lips, but he didn't penetrate. She'd never done this, on the side with the man behind. It felt strange but good, with no bad memories to assail her. Chris stroked a hand down her belly, caressing until he came to her clitoris. His touch lightened further, rekindling her need with delicate strokes. Without meaning to, she moved her hips, increasing the friction between her thighs. There were no bad reminders when freed from that pressing weight. She fell a little further into the spiraling heat.

After endless, incredible moments, he whispered into her ear, "I'm coming inside."

She would've agreed to anything just to keep his hands where they were. A sharp surge of pleasure surprised her when he pushed in. With each stroke, the feeling built. She rocked back to meet him. His clever fingers teased and touched in counterpoint to this easy, fantastic rhythm. Her breath went staccato. With his face pressed against her back, he pumped his hips in deliberate motions and groaned with each long, deep thrust.

He was shaking but kept caressing her, not letting her feel anything but this fierce pleasure. It wasn't anything like what she'd had before. This was considerate, so careful and measured, devoted to driving her wild with fingers and shaft. And it was working. She loved the feel of him, the heat and the pressure in conjunction with the cadence on her clit.

"If you hold still," she whispered, "if you come all the way in, then stop and just—"

He did as she pleaded. He pressed down, just as she needed, and she came *so* hard. Her whole body arched as she contracted on his cock. But before she could learn what it was like to have a lover she wanted, a lover who gave her pleasure, his orgasm inside of her, he pulled free. His slick length slid against her bottom. Rosa felt his fingers moving, urgent tugs, as his breath became more frantic, and she wished she could see what he was doing.

"Say it," he gasped. "My name."

"Cristián. Come for me."

With two more swift pumps of his fist, he tensed and gasped. His seed spilled over the curve of her hip. Shuddering, he fell back, and she rolled as he released her, wanting to see his face. She wasn't sure whether she had done what she was supposed to for him, but it was enough that she'd managed to get off with his cock inside her. She'd never imagined that was possible—at least for her.

Tentatively, Rosa draped her thigh over his, tracing the muscles of his stomach. She had no experience with what happened afterward. But *Dios*, he was fucking beautiful. Dark lashes tipped in gold fanned on his cheeks, and his lips parted slightly as he sought to steady his breath. He opened his forest-dark eyes. He was smiling, but she had no idea why. Most men would've asked for their money back after her performance.

"Thank you," he said.

She eyed him, wondering if he was fucking with her. "For what?"

"For giving that much of yourself."

That wasn't a lie. She'd yielded him something, maybe something she hadn't even meant to. She studied him for a moment in silence. "You didn't mind."

"What?"

"How bad I was at it."

"I loved discovering what you enjoy, Rosita. If you let me, I'll continue my research." The words held a teasing tone that disconcerted her, as if finding out how she wanted him to fill her *concha* mattered in the grand scheme. Sometimes she thought he was a little *loco*.

"So I'm your science project now?"

"No. You're an incredibly beautiful, complicated woman."

He ran his fingers through her tousled hair, as if marveling at its softness. She felt oddly naked, even more than she had in the beginning, because he saw how much she valued that secret femininity. Chris recognized her hair as her crowning glory, and he appreciated the time and effort that went into its keeping. Rosa curved her body against his and snuggled in.

Maybe there were no rules. Maybe she didn't have to worry about getting it just right.

"I like looking at you, too," she admitted softly.

That was a pretty big break from the persona she adopted with other men. By his widening smile, she could see he understood as much. He stroked the line of her shoulder in response.

"I think I get why this is hard for you," he said. "But it would mean a lot if you told me, like you told me about your brother . . . Only don't run away afterward this time. Stay."

She froze. There was another demand. *Talk more. Give more. Tell me everything.* He wouldn't be happy until he scooped her out and examined all her hidden spaces. Reflexively, she pulled back, unwilling to share the past she was still trying to forget. He let her go, but now his face held sorrow instead of contentment.

On a gust of angry breath, she decided to stay, as he'd asked. And *talk*. *Dios*, he would make her crazed with his endless words. It served no purpose that she could see, only raising old ghosts, but she did not like that look on him. When he first came to Valle, he'd been haunted. But her company and her confidences gave him an easier smile.

That made no sense either, as most bravos found her a right bitch, but Cristián just wasn't normal.

"Fine," she bit out. "For a bedtime story, you can learn all about my life, *sí*? *No hay problema.* I *love* the sharing."

He laughed softly, his expression easing. And that she *did* like. So she went on, "For most of my life I lived in Guatemala. We were poor. My mother died when we were small." *Short sentences, stick to the facts, and don't let the memories drag you down.* "My father was a bastard. He drank and he hit us, my brother and me. My *abuelita* protected us. She made pottery. My father, he didn't like that she denied him his children, so he went to *la policía.* They were going to give us to him. So she took us in the night, and we went to Mexico. We got as far as Juárez. From there we were going to the New United States, but the Change made crossing the border impossible. Army men everywhere."

"How old were you?"

"When we first got to Juárez? Fifteen. It is a terrible place."

"I remember hearing stories."

She turned her cheek against his chest, hoping that would help. It didn't. "When we could not pass the border, we used what money she had been able to save from her business in Guatemala. She bought a little house. It had been meant to found her shop once we emigrated."

"You don't have to go on."

He stroked her back lightly, though, holding her as though she mattered. And that made her want to finish, so she would never have to speak of it again.

"It was a long time ago. While my *abuela* was well, it was not unbearable in Mexico. But she got sick. We had little money for treatments, so I cared for her until she died. After that we had no income at all, and I had a brother depending on me. The Change panicked everyone. No money. No way to work." She lifted one shoulder in a half shrug. "I had only one thing left to sell. I'm sure you know the rest."

Secretly she waited in heartbroken stillness for his judgment. An educated man like him would be revolted to hear his suspicions confirmed. There was only one reason a woman could be so familiar with sex but not know the niceties of kissing or the pleasure of orgasm. She had no idea why he'd insisted she confess everything to him, like he was some priest to forgive her transgressions. Certainly she didn't feel better or cleaner, just sad and afraid.

He pulled away, confirming her silent fear. But what he did next surprised her. He cupped her face in his hands and gazed into her eyes, his own brimming with anger.

"I would like to kill everyone who's ever hurt you," he said softly, conversationally. "Starting with your father. I wish I could change everything because it pains me to think of it, but then you wouldn't be the woman I know. I don't see how you've become so strong instead of breaking into tiny pieces." He paused. "I've never wanted anyone this much in my whole life."

Her chest felt odd and tight, and her eyes burned with unshed tears. She touched his face, tracing each feature with reverent fingertips. "Maybe I *do* like the sharing. But can we play some more now, Cristián?"

He kissed her then with such passion that her whole body went white-hot. And they spent the remainder of the night learning other paths to pleasure.

TWENTY-SIX

Chris had known he would wake up alone. That much was a given. However, the reality of waking to the chilly morn, his arms wrapped around a wadded blanket rather than his lover, took the shine from what he and Rosa had shared. Disappointment washed over him like cold water. He'd been a piss-poor husband before the Change, but he'd never gotten off on one-night stands.

And morning sex was one of life's simple pleasures.

That wasn't an option, in spite of the hard-on he tried to calm. His mind helped his body turn traitor, revisiting the night's intimacies. He lay on his back in that small, lonely cave, reliving every touch, every kiss, every brave concession she'd made.

But he was no longer content with dreams and memories. He needed to see her.

Chris pushed off the ground with a frustrated growl. He kicked into his clothes as if punching hard enough might relieve his thrumming pulse. After packing his possessions, leaving the blankets and putting the lantern in the sun to recharge, he stepped into the desert. Daylight mocked his groggy brain. The last pair of sunglasses he'd owned were in pieces somewhere in Utah, crushed during an adrenaline-soaked fight with a gang of thieves.

He walked back to town, using long strides to shake the stiffness out of his limbs. Sleeping on the rocky cave floor was never exactly comfortable, but he made the trade-off for privacy. And holding Rosa, alone together, had made the experience one to be relished.

Wicker was in the store, as always, and nodded as he came in. Then he stared a little longer than normal. Chris ignored the man and kept walking. He dropped his possessions on the floor of his tiny speck of a room. A half hour later, after a quick shower, he was on his way to the town hall to check on the new girls.

Singer ran up to meet him.

"Doc, it's Tilly!"

The jump from slow, bleary morning to full-on alertness hit him right in the chest. His heart rate kicked up to race car speeds. "Where's Rosa? Find her and Viv. Meet me there."

"Got it."

Singer sprinted off toward the watchtower. Chris followed her flight, briefly, realizing that Rosa was indeed up there. Made sense. How better to obscure the stark facts of the previous night than to be the one on watch when Chris sauntered out of the desert?

But he didn't have time to dwell on it. He chugged toward Tilly and Jameson's little house, psyching himself up for what might lie ahead. Childbirth. Damn. He was no expert—not by a long shot. This fake-it-till-you-make-it routine was giving him a complex. One day it wouldn't be good enough.

He knocked on Tilly's door, then strode in when he heard her scream.

"Doc," Jameson said, meeting him in the entryway. The man was as pale as milk. "God, I—what do we do?"

"Breathe, first. C'mon."

Jameson led him back toward the bedroom he shared

with Tilly. The dark curtains were closed, making the space as much a cave as the one Chris had slept in. The stink of sweat hung heavy in the still air. He threw his medical satchel on a nearby chair, then went to wash his hands in the nearby kitchenette.

"How long?" he called over his shoulder to Jameson.

"Since about four this morning. She was good until just a few minutes ago. Then she lost it."

Chris nodded, returning to the bedroom. Tilly lay sprawled on a coverlet that had been wrinkled and knotted by her fists. She looked relatively fresh for a woman in early labor, but a second scream in two minutes hinted this would go quickly.

"Hey, Tilly," he said, kneeling by the side of the bed. He smoothed the matted blond hair back from her face. She mauled his other hand with a killer squeeze. Only after the contraction had passed did he try to talk to her again. "I guess it's going to be somebody's birthday."

"Guess so." She offered a wobbly smile. "Got an epidural on you, Doc?"

"Afraid not. You're gonna have to do this the cavewoman way."

"Ugh. I don't think I can."

"Of course you can. You're built for it. Every woman is."

That had been true, once. But the evolution of modern woman in the age of C-sections left the human race with no way to cope with the reinforced trait. He'd seen the same thing in animals bred in captivity, as they became less and less able to give birth without human intervention. The Change would require a quick reversal of that trend or the hellhounds, skinwalkers, and deprivation wouldn't be the only threats to mankind's survival.

Here and now, there was no surgical solution—at least not one both mother and child would survive. Chris put a good face on it, knowing fear would do Tilly in.

"Just stick with me here, okay?"

She nodded, but she didn't look convinced.

"Here's the thing," Chris said. "When you're scared at

night, when you're feeling overwhelmed by the Change, where do you go? In your head? What do you think about?"

Tilly leaned her head back onto the pillow, her chin tipped toward the ceiling. She swallowed. "I think about being at the beach at Cape Cod. We used to go there in the summers, spend months with my grandma. We left when the Change hit the East Coast. I never saw it again. But God, it was beautiful. I still think about how clear the water was."

Chris grinned to himself. Only in the world after the Change could a blue blood like Tilly wind up with a tatted thug like Jameson. He liked the contrast, even if the shadows over her favorite memory were difficult to ignore.

"Good," he said, keeping his tone light. "That's good. Next time you feel the pain coming on, I want you to breathe as slowly as you can through your nose and go back to Cape Cod. Got that? And I'm going to give you Jameson's hand. You break it if you need to."

That got a laugh out of her.

"No, wait. Jameson, you got a comb? Sort of palm-sized? Anything like that?"

The man rummaged amid their possessions, then returned with a small black plastic comb.

Chris nestled it into Tilly's hand so that the tines poked into her palm. "When the pain comes, you squeeze the ever-lovin' shit out of this, got it?"

"What the hell is that gonna do?" Jameson asked.

"Think about the last time you needed a bullet gouged out of you." Chris didn't question his assumption that Jameson had, at some point, required such a procedure. It seemed a standard-issue wound among bravos. "Did you bite down on something?"

"Sure."

"Took your mind off it a little? The pain in your teeth?"

"Yeah."

"The body can only process information from so many nerve endings at a time. If she can focus on the pain in her hand—a pain she can control—it'll distract her from the contractions." He smiled down at Tilly. "Worth a shot anyway."

"Sure, Doc," she whispered.

After weathering another minute of Tilly's agony, her fist clenched around that little black comb, Chris dragged her partner to the kitchenette.

"I need to know something, Jameson," he said, his voice low. "Are you ready to listen to me? Because needing to explain every little decision will waste time. And debating will only worry her. Unified front, got it? I need to have you on my side."

The wiry man hesitated, which was probably only fair. Chris wondered if he'd trust himself in Jameson's place.

"Yeah, Doc. I'm on it." Jameson didn't seem nearly so intimidating without his usual complement of knives—and with a healthy dose of fear shining from his eyes. He obviously didn't respond well to feeling helpless.

"Now, you will wash your hands before you touch her, no matter what. Go. Stay with her."

Viv and Rosa came in shortly thereafter, faces lit with expressions of excitement and concern. Chris let his gaze linger on Rosa for two extra heartbeats. She'd gotten cleaned up—new cargoes, new shirt. Her hair was pulled back, braided as tightly as he'd ever seen.

She wouldn't look at him.

That's not good.

But he saved his disappointment for another time.

"I need water that's been boiled—at least a couple of liters," he said.

"I'm on it," Viv replied, hurrying out.

"Rosa, wash up. You're going to check her dilation."

"What? Why me?"

"Smaller hands. It'll hurt her less."

"Madre de Dios," she muttered, crossing herself. Then she blinked, as if the reflexive gesture surprised her. "Fine."

Tilly moaned. Chris and Rosa returned to the bedroom to find Tilly's eyes rolled back, her body as stiff as iron. Jameson cringed under her fierce grip. But no screams this time. Maybe those little tricks were working. Chris desperately needed them to work.

"Oh!" Tilly gasped.

Her water broke.

"Well, shit," Chris said. "Maybe you won't need to check her after all."

"Jameson, more blankets?" Rosa asked.

"Here, under the bed."

While Rosa and Jameson wriggled fresh blankets under Tilly's rear, Chris returned to the side of the bed. He leaned close to the laboring woman's face and kept his voice calm— no matter how crazy-fast his heart beat. "You tell me when you're ready to push, okay? We're all going to trust your body to know what it needs to do."

"Okay." She grabbed his forearm. "Doc?"

"Yeah?"

Whatever she was going to say died on her lips. She simply stared up at him, her expression filled with more trust than any man deserved. Chris fought the compulsion to look away. This wasn't his job, wasn't his life. This was some strange dream where a pain-stricken mother-to-be and her terrified lover depended on him for the survival of their baby.

But there was no one else.

Chris nodded once, soberly, as if to acknowledge the promises she wanted—the promises he couldn't make. Instead he said, "You're doing great."

Viv had recruited Ingrid for the muscle required to haul in liters of boiled water. The women set up a receiving area for the new baby, complete with washcloths, towels, a sterilized needle and scissors, thread, and an array of tiny clothes Singer had crafted. Tilly endured each pain as it came, her ability to focus and ride out the contractions much better now.

The air in the room was stifling, stuffed with five bodies that generated a healthy dose of anxious heat. Chris stepped out to the kitchenette and mopped his forehead with a cloth, then popped open a window. A breeze eased over his face. It was warm but it was better than nothing.

Rosa met him there. She didn't say anything, just stood,

her worry like a mask over her features. Jameson wasn't the only one unaccustomed to feeling helpless.

"What do I do?" she asked.

"Wait."

"I hate waiting."

"Amen."

He walked over to her, drawn to her, needing a moment of comfort in her arms. They could do that for each other. They could make the worry and hurt go away.

But Rosa stepped back. Her expression closed off. No worry. No uncertainty. Just a clear-cut warning. "No," she said simply.

Chris watched her go, feeling mule-kicked. He braced his hands on the countertop and bowed his head. "God damn it, Rosa," he muttered.

The worst, he realized, would be if nothing changed. He would know her body and her taste, and he would know her rejection. All at once. Her trust would be a fleeting thing, never to be relied on. Roasting on a spit sounded more appealing.

Tilly cried out. Shoving his personal problems to a distant corner of his mind—at least he had experience with that—Chris hurried back to the bedroom.

"I need to push!" Tilly gasped. Her nightgown was soaked through with sweat. She gripped both Jameson and Viv, using their hands like a rock climber used pitons, holding on for dear life.

Chris moved to the foot of the bed. "Everybody get ready. Jameson, come down here with me. Rosa, take his place, *por favor.*"

Shoulder to shoulder with the baby's father, Chris lifted the hem of Tilly's nightgown. Jameson's face turned an even more sickly ashen shade. "She's bleeding," he whispered.

"Just a tear," Chris replied under his breath. "A few sutures and she's good as new."

Jameson swallowed and nodded, as if to reassure himself.

Chris used one of the washcloths to wipe away the blood. "Grab that clean swaddling. You'll be holding your baby in no time. Tilly? Honey? You're crowning, girl. Gimme all you got."

It might have been ten minutes later. It might have been ten hours. All Chris knew was that watching that dark head emerge into the world was among the more stressful, amazing, terrifying experiences of his life. Jameson murmured prayers under his breath, clutching the baby blankets. Viv's and Rosa's hushed words blended into a feminine white noise of encouragement, while Tilly huffed and cursed, moaned and shrieked.

"Hold up," Chris said. "Don't push!" He fumbled with the umbilical cord, slipping it from around the baby's neck, over its soft, slippery skull. He double-checked until he was satisfied. "All right, go for it."

One shoulder on the next push. The second on the one after that. And with a final grunt, the tiny new life slid free of its mother. Chris caught it in his trembling hands.

"Holy shit," he breathed, suddenly light-headed. "It's a girl."

Tilly burst into exhausted tears, while Viv offered her thanks to God. Jameson rocked back onto his heels, an expression of rapture molding his harsh features. Then he blinked, like an actor remembering his line. He handed the swaddling to Chris, then cut the cord with a hand nowhere near steady. Together they awkwardly wrapped the new baby girl in the strip of plain cloth.

Chris had to swallow past the hard, heavy lump in his throat. He placed the whimpering infant on her mother's stomach. "Congratulations, Tilly. You have a daughter."

Feeling triumphant, larger than life, Chris looked up at Rosa, and the tears glittering in her dark eyes humbled him.

TWENTY-SEVEN

"Thank you," Rosa said later.

She marveled at how Chris had handled the crisis, stitching Tilly afterward. Jameson thought the doc was a genius, no two ways about it. Now she sat with Chris in the *taberna*, together but not alone. Falco and his friends sat at another table, watching. Conscious of the attention on her, she tried to behave as she did with every other bravo, but her success was impossible to gauge.

"I've never done that before," he admitted. "At least not for a human."

"You've delivered litters before? I guess that's what comes of hanging out with skinwalkers."

"No, my first experience was helping endangered wild-cats bear their young." He frowned, his knuckles whitening as he clutched his glass. "The skinwalkers aren't all like that, you know. Like monsters."

Ignoring his comment, she signaled Viv for another drink. "More wine, please."

Viv brought the bottle and left it. One bravo got out his musical pipe and another set up his drums. It seemed they wanted to celebrate the new life. Tilly hadn't decided yet what to name her daughter, but Rosa privately thought Hope would be a good choice, maybe the *perfect* choice, because that was what she represented for their town.

"Don't change the subject, Rosita." He said it softly enough that she didn't think anyone heard, but she glanced around to be sure.

Really, she shouldn't be sitting with him. It would arouse comment. Falco was seething, trying to figure out why she could tolerate Chris's company and not his. She'd say it was because the doc had saved their asses by delivering the baby safely. God knew, Jameson would be uncontrollable if anything had happened to Tilly or his baby girl. She'd feared he would need to be put down like a rabid dog, and they'd lose the whole family.

"Why? I already told you—I'm not changing my mind on this. I know what I know."

"You're a stubborn pain in the ass." He downed his wine and listened to the music for a while, watching Jolene and Brick open the dancing.

"So I've been told." But her tone held no rancor. Between the joy of the newborn and the mellow feeling from the wine, the world didn't seem half bad today.

This wasn't a festival like Burning Night, just a simple dance. Celebrations mattered because they brought a community together. Singer came in with bread and honey, carrying trays to the men. Rio tried to hold her in conversation, but the girl grinned at him and slipped away. Rosa wasn't sure if she was playing hard to get or she wasn't interested. For a young one, Singer had a pretty solid poker face.

"I didn't realize there would be rules and restrictions."

She glanced over at him, brow cocked. "*¿Qué?*"

"Us. But I figured out pretty quick you don't want anyone to know. I'm not supposed to touch you in front of other people or act like I know you better than they do. Because nobody gets close, right?"

"It comes with the territory," she said with a shrug. "I don't get a private life."

"I understand."

"*Dios*, be happy today. You did an amazing thing. Focus on that." She grinned at him and pitched her voice beneath the drums. "And so we have sex on the side. It's fun and we have a safe place to stay. Good food to eat. Isn't that what matters?"

"Yeah. Pretty lucky."

Rosa knocked back the rest of her wine and bounced to her feet. With a flash of a smile in farewell, she spun into the music and beckoned to Ex. At fiestas like this, she always danced with him and Rio, the two males she knew wouldn't entertain ideas about taking her home. Ex joined her; he was a good dancer, even with a healing wound in his shoulder. This was a social occasion, not a romantic one, and she needed to prove she was still *la jefa*, still the same. New bravo sworn in. Manuel lost. A baby born. Things would settle down soon, if Falco would just back off a bit. Otherwise she had to act.

Rosa preferred the samba, so she cued the musicians. Ex took her hand and wrapped the other around her waist. They were used to dancing together, so she executed the steps without thinking. He spun her into the turns. She loved the rhythm and the speed. On that night she didn't worry about what the bravos thought of her dancing. They had achieved Valle's greatest victory, and she wanted to celebrate.

"Good news today," Ex said.

"*Sí*, the best."

"I heard Tilly screaming all the way down in the workshop."

Rosa laughed as they twirled. "If you had to do what she did, you'd be screaming too."

"I'm glad I'm a man."

The dance ended and she called to Rio, "*Oye, mano!* Show me what you got."

It was a calculated move to determine whether he'd forgiven her for Manuel. If Rio danced with her, while wearing the black armband, none of the others could hold it against her. After a brief hesitation, the boy came to her side and they danced the cha-cha. The little *taberna* was bright and warm, and soon she needed some more wine.

Chris was gone when she looked around for him again. *He must not like to dance.*

Much later, she sought him out in the caves. He made love to her with fierce passion and aching tenderness. This time she was on top, and the pleasure was even more overwhelming.

That became their pattern. She went to him at night; they whispered and kissed and loved, but by day, he was just another bravo. That was how it had to be.

Over the course of the next month, Valle remained quiet. Everyone smiled a little wider. The fact that Tilly didn't die or develop an infection gave a lot of women courage. The bravos were distracted by the new arrivals. More than one man offered to help out in the infirmary. Rosa laughed when Viv drove them away by threatening buckshot and watered beer.

But little by little, the freed captives recovered. They were tentative and terrified at first, but soon they found places to help out, wherever they felt safe. To Rosa's amusement, Allison took refuge in Ex's workshop and would hardly let the guy out of her sight.

Such slow assimilation made Rosa happy. She knew how it felt to be treated as a possession. And in her outrage, she vowed never to let anyone hurt the women again.

Despite the apparent calm, she also sensed tension in town, bubbling below the surface. She feared the peace couldn't last. Falco still wanted his status changed, and it just wasn't going to happen.

Even before Chris showed up, I wasn't interested. And now—

Well, now she was sneaking out in the middle of the night to meet her lover. A little ridiculous, but Valle couldn't handle an internal dustup. The town needed time to recover, take stock of its position, and plan some raids. Successful ones, this time. Once Rosa increased the ammo stores and dealt with the likes of Peltz, her position would be stronger.

Maybe at some point in the future, she would feel secure enough to reveal her relationship with Chris. *Maybe*.

Slipping out of town, Rosa marveled a little at the fact that she *had* a lover. She never could have imagined seeking out a man for conversation, for physical pleasure or comfort, but things were different with Chris. She had been sure when she first met him that a guy with his hardened attitude would destroy everything she'd built. But even *la jefa* could read a man wrong. He'd slipped right into her life in the best of ways. Now she couldn't imagine being without him. In anticipation, she pulled the tie from her hair and shook it free, knowing how much he loved it.

She crept along the rocky path and into the cave, where he was waiting. The lamplight gave the space a warm, inviting air, and she dropped to his bedroll beside him. He had a book on his lap but wasn't reading. Instead he looked upset. She ran through her head all the possible troubles and came up with a list too long to do any good.

"What's wrong?" she asked, touching him on the arm.

Chris pulled away, hands folded in his lap. "I can't do this."

"Do what?"

"This. The hiding. I thought I could play along, but it turns out I don't enjoy being your dirty little secret."

"You know my reasons—"

"I know what you *say* are your reasons. Frankly I'm not sure it matters as much as you think."

"What do you want from me, Cristián?" She rubbed his shoulder lightly, trying to ease his tension.

"Cut it out."

Rosa raised a brow. *"¿Qué?"*

"You're not getting around me. Yeah, you turn me on by loosening your hair and saying my name, but it's not enough anymore. Rosa, it's been *weeks*." He paused. "I want everything."

Mierda. She didn't need this after a long day of dealing with people's fears and complaints, trying to make sure the whole world was happy. This was the one place where she could come and be herself. Now that wasn't enough for him. Rosa didn't think she had anything else to give.

Yet she didn't withdraw from him. That took some doing, given her emotional state. Instead she touched his hair, his cheek, and he turned his face against her palm.

"So let me get this straight," she said. "You decide how we're together."

"Just like you have, all along. Fair's fair. Isn't it my turn?"

"Except for not giving me a say."

"Did you give me a say in *this*?" He shook his head, seeming not angry but weary. "No. You dictated the terms and I wanted you enough to accept them."

"But you don't now." That stung. She dropped her hand from him then and curled it with the other in her lap.

Damn you, Cristián, why do this? It's good, isn't it? It's working.

"Every day I want you more. But I don't want to be the man you have to hide. I want to be the one standing by your side. Do you really think it doesn't bother me when you'll dance with anyone but me?"

That honestly surprised her. "Not true. I don't dance with Falco."

"Ex, then."

"He's not a threat. I don't think he even sees me as a woman."

"Trust me, all men do, whether they act on it or not. You're beautiful."

She smiled, though doubtless he didn't mean to praise her right then. "I think maybe you're biased, *amorcito.* You see me differently."

"None of that changes what I said."

"That you want me to stop coming to you unless I'm ready to make some big announcement? About how you're sleeping with me? It's nobody's business!"

He shrugged. "You've made all the choices so far. You can make this one too."

"So that's it, then?"

"It is if you're saying no."

"What if I'm saying 'not right now'?"

"Then I guess we can have this conversation again, whenever 'right now' finally ends. Because I'm not going to change my mind."

The hard clench of his jaw and the stiff distance in his posture told Rosa that he meant it. Their sweet interlude was over. Without speaking, she pushed to her feet and stepped out of the cave, leaving the light behind.

TWENTY-EIGHT

Oh, you've really done it up good, Welsh.

Chris flopped down on his bunk in the room above the general store. A cloud of dust puffed up from the shabby mattress, circling in a chink of sunlight. He hadn't been back to the cave since the argument with Rosa. That little hollow of rock already held too many memories.

Not that he could escape the stubborn woman. She was all over the town, of course, leading with her special blend of sex appeal, personal indebtedness, and iron dogma. Chris's path intersected with hers a dozen times a day. He made his rounds, still checking the eight new arrivals for progress regarding nutrition and a few infected cuts that had yet to clear up. And of course he visited Tilly and her seven-week-old baby girl, Esperanza.

Esperanza. Spanish for hope.

He knew Rosa was pleased with the choice—not only symbolic, but something to honor the town's distinctly Latin flavor. But would she admit as much? Even to him? Nope.

He peeled off his sweaty shirt, rolled onto his stomach,

and hugged the flat pillow, willing sleep. It was only the middle of the afternoon, but activity in Valle screeched to a halt when the sun shone so brightly as to become an enemy. Too hot to move.

Sleep wouldn't offer a reprieve from Rosa either. She followed him into the unconscious as well. After so many prophetic dreams that couldn't be explained, Chris had started believing in their power. It went against every scientific leaning, but he couldn't reconcile what had happened with any other conclusion. He had dreamed the dust pirates on foot, the girls in the truck, and then, of course, he'd shared that erotic dream with Rosa.

But now his dreams were just plain infuriating.

Night after night, there was Rosa. The familiar ones were re-creations of the hours they'd made love together— just wisps of impressions that left him gasping and hard. The ones he'd started to think of as prophetic were clearer, sharper, heartbreaking. He saw Rosa sitting on a stool in her bedroom, naked except for a lightweight cotton robe she'd left untied. She was braiding her hair over one shoulder. In another she looked about six months pregnant, and she was staring across the desert, wearing a long sundress that pressed against her swollen stomach when the wind blew. She was smiling in both.

Chris slammed a fist into his pillow with a groan. If those were prophecies, he'd eat his boots. She was as closed to him now as when he'd first arrived. Cold. Stone-faced. Completely stuck on this idea of having her sexual itches scratched while stashing him away in a cave.

He stuck to his guns. All or nothing. So they'd circled each other in a weeks-long stalemate.

After a fitful rest during which he never made it down deep enough to dream, Chris gave up on the idea of sleep. He pushed off the mattress and washed with water from a metal bucket. All the while he steeled himself for the evening to come. He'd decided, after the argument, that he would not hide. Rosa would see him every night. Walking with sixteen-gauge nails under the skin of his soles would be a more pleasant way to spend his time, but he wanted her to remember what she was missing. Comfort. Intimacy. Breathless release.

But that meant seeing her and not having her, watching as she cast her spell on the worshipful bravos. Each night she walked away, returning to her casita.

At least she went home alone.

That he'd been reduced to seeing such a thing as a victory made him surly. He dressed with staccato movements and quickly ran a comb through his hair.

Although Valle quieted down for the afternoon, everyone pushed outdoors once the sun dipped down. Chris spotted Allison and Ex closing up the forge for the night, which made him smile softly. Another odd couple. A Change specialty, which seemed to make the whole damn hell seem worthwhile. Allison offered a shy little wave.

Chris walked over to them, noticing the gentle softening in both of their postures. Closer. More relaxed. If they hadn't slept together yet, the wait would not be long.

"Evenin', Doc," Ex said. Allison added her salutation. "We're going to dinner. Join us?"

"Thanks. Appreciate it."

That odd sense of belonging stole over him again. He was becoming more than just the doctor. His responsibility had become easier to bear with so many recent successes. He was a member of the community now. He liked it. He liked it so much that the idea of leaving took on a painful edge that had nothing to do with Rosa.

Dinner at the *taberna* was noisy and boisterous as usual. He, Ex, and Allison grabbed plates of food from where Jameson was on cafeteria duty. No one particularly liked the job of cooking and serving the communal evening meal, so Viv had drafted a system of trading off weeks. Chris found it amusing to see gruff, badass bravos slopping stew. He didn't feel bad about his amusement, because they sure as hell had laughed at his piss-poor culinary disasters.

"No rest, even for the new father?" he asked Jameson.

Dark circles looped under the man's eyes, but he hadn't stopped smiling for weeks. "Viv is a vicious sergeant, *mano*. Espi was up six times last night, and still I cook."

Ex sniffed his plate of beans. "Smells . . . edible?"

"You'll eat it even if it's not." Jameson grinned, then dropped his ladle. He fished around in his vest pocket and withdrew a piece of paper. "I almost forgot, Doc. This is for you."

Chris took it. "Where in the hell did you find paper?"

"Don't ask me. It's from Tilly. Now move it. You're holding up the line."

Falco and Lem banged in through the tavern doors, their voices loud and suspiciously close to drunk. Where had they scrounged alcohol? Chris frowned but followed Ex and Allison to the table they'd picked out. He ate quickly, having realized long ago that hot food was, by far, tastier food.

Once his stomach was stuffed with really decent beans and some sort of bread made with cornmeal—an unexpected treat—he opened the letter.

Dear Chris,

My family was the traditional sort, which meant writing thank-you notes was ingrained in me since childhood. Birthday parties, Christmas gifts—we always wrote a note of thanks. My mother said it was just good manners, even in the face of chaos. That may not mean a lot to most folks now, but I think it might mean something to you.

Chris smiled. He'd become used to thinking of everyone in Valle as, essentially, well-meaning but irredeemably rough. Tilly was an obstinate reminder of the past, sometimes painfully so. Even her formal way of speaking and writing echoed a time when such things mattered.

The only problem, however, in writing this note is that no words seem adequate. How can I possibly thank you for what you did for Jameson and me?

Our Esperanza is alive and well because of you. Please don't denigrate your contribution by saying that I would've been fine without you. All I know is that I would have continued panicking without you there. Jameson, for all his strength in a fight, would have been crippled by how much he cares for me. You calmed us both. You gave us direction. For that I will always be grateful.

You asked me once, your expression slightly befuddled, how a blue blood like me wound up with a street tough like Jameson. Luck, I think. I don't see how I'd still be alive without him, and, right or wrong, needing someone can turn into love. It's been a blessing for us both, just like you are.

With eternal thanks,
Tilly

Chris inhaled tightly and looked at the ceiling, swallowing.

An elbow clipped him on the back of the head. He swiveled around, still partly lost in the letter, to find Falco standing way too close. "Sorry, Doc. Didn't see you there."

"Don't mention it," Chris said, banking his dislike.

Falco had been spoiling for a fight for months. Against Rosa. Against Chris. He was the threat to Rosa's control that scared her most consistently. For that reason alone Chris had reason to dislike the man. He also had a sneaking suspicion that Rosa wouldn't be so scared of going public with their affair if Falco weren't around.

Still, he didn't want to be the one to break the uneasy peace. Rosa might not be speaking to him, but he wasn't going to give her reason to accuse him of undermining Valle's order.

"Whatcha got there?" Lem snatched the letter, ripping its corner as he did.

Fuck politics.

Chris didn't even bother with words. He jumped up from the table and clocked Lem on the mouth. The man spun, stumbled, crashed into an empty table. Lem lay half sprawled on the floor. Blood oozed from the corner of his mouth.

With his boot on Lem's wrist, Chris retrieved Tilly's letter. "This is mine."

"You can't hit my man," Falco snarled.

"Funny," Chris said, tucking the folded paper into his back pocket. "I thought we were all bravos, yes? Rosa's men?"

"Some more than others, you son of a bitch."

The tavern went quiet. All scraping of forks on plates ceased. No one spoke; they hardly breathed. Ever since the initiation, the others had seemed to view Chris as Rosa's quiet lieutenant. He'd helped defend the town. He'd brought women and made them well. He'd delivered Tilly's baby. Any insult to Chris was, by degrees, an affront to her leadership.

Maybe he could have that fight after all. He gave himself permission to make it happen. Consequences were for another time.

He stretched his fingers, curled them into fists. "What's that supposed to mean?"

"I mean that you and Rosa are close." Falco raised his arms to those assembled. "I think we all deserve to know how close."

"Why would you think that where I put my dick is any business of yours?"

"Because she's off-limits, man. No stranger gets in line ahead of the rest of us."

Rage bubbled in Chris's veins. The image of men lining up to take a turn with Rosa was nauseating on too many levels, particularly knowing what he did about her past. He'd stick a knife in all of them before letting a single one touch her.

"A woman has the right to choose," Chris said, his voice as much a warning as his stance. "Lem learned that lesson."

"You bast—"

But Falco cut Lem off with a cold look. "You're saying she chose *you?*"

Chris put every drop of masculine arrogance into his smile. "As I said, it's none of your business."

Falco's punch came damn quick. Clutching his cheek, Chris staggered back against the table he'd just shared with Ex and Allison. They'd already retreated to a far wall. Most of the tavern's occupants had—which suited Chris fine as he returned Falco's blow. The man's jaw gave way with a satisfying crunch. Falco grunted, then bellowed his anger. He lunged, plowing into Chris with his head and shoulders.

The air whooshed out of Chris's lungs. Momentum slammed him into a countertop. Something in his vertebrae popped. Like lightning, pain shot up his spine. He hiked a knee in self-defense, at the same time slamming Falco's chest down. Knee connected with sternum. The man staggered back a step, but renewed his assault.

The rational place in Chris's mind went dark. Adrenaline flowed as powerful as whiskey, through his muscles and deep into his bones. Every action became sharper, senses on high alert.

He brought his fist down hard on Falco's ear, followed by a slam to his gut, his nose, his kidney. Cracks and grunts were the sounds of victory. When Falco managed to land a punch or two, Chris was beyond feeling pain. He registered the contact as a mistake made, nothing more. He corrected those errors and continued the beating.

Falco swore and attacked again, but his left shoulder drooped. Dislocated. Chris grabbed the wounded arm and spun, pinning his opponent against the bar. Falco's curses turned to a harsh exhale. He wasn't beaten enough to scream. Yet.

Chris grabbed a fistful of hair and slammed the man down. Face met countertop.

A gunshot fired outside the tavern. *"¡Basta!"*

Rushing back into himself, Chris felt drunk and dizzy. He looked down at his hands. Blood. Tufts of hair under his fingernails. Falco lay in a heap at his feet.

Rosa stood in the doorway, a smoking gun in hand. Her expression boiled with outrage, as much emotion as he'd seen from her in weeks. He couldn't muster the will to care. He'd just saved her ass—her precious leadership. Again.

"I don't mind brawling," she growled, her voice tight with fury. "But I will not let you kill one another. We're too few."

Chris shrugged. "I'm done if he is."

"You're done when I say you are."

"*Sí, Jefa,*" he said mockingly. "I got that one memorized."

Falco pulled up to his elbows. He was bleeding from his nose and ear. A tooth lay on the ground beside him. Chris wondered, in a weird disjointed way, if they'd be expected to play doctor and patient after everything was over.

With some effort, Falco clambered to his feet. "If he won't answer, then you should. We're loyal to you and we deserve the truth."

She stilled. Bright spots of red colored the apples of her cheeks. On a girl it would've been a blush. But Rosa looked like she might spit acid. Chris could hardly sympathize. He was too angry still, and her power games were responsible for this showdown.

She slipped the gun into its holster, all smooth frost. "Tell you what, Falco?"

Defeated only in body, Falco shot a killing look between her and Chris.

"Once and for all, are you fucking him?"

TWENTY-NINE

Moment of truth.

The whole *taberna* waited for Rosa's answer.

Quickly she ran the odds in her head. If *la jefa* didn't back Chris, the rest of the bravos would array against him. Well, Falco's cohorts, at least. She didn't have a good sense of who remained on her side. Ex and Jameson, certainly. Probably Rio. But there was no way to be sure with the others. They kept their own counsel, so long as she wasn't ordering them to do something stupid.

She'd already been leaning toward making the admission, based on logic alone. And then she saw Cristián's face. He expected her to disavow him. As if in expectation of that hurt, he braced one hand on the bar. The *taberna* was so quiet that she could hear everyone breathing, as well as scared whimpers from Maryann, one of the rescued girls. She'd only recently started venturing out of the town hall, and now this had to happen.

Perdón, pobrecita. This wasn't meant to be a place where she had to be scared. *I'll make it right.*

"You're way too interested in what I do in my private time," she said softly. "*Pero, sí,* he's my man."

Falco hauled himself to his feet. "Damn it, I've fought for respect here. This fucks with the hierarchy—"

"You're pissing me off," Jameson said, twirling a simple kitchen knife as he would one of his weapons. "And I don't get a lot of sleep these days. I'm not long on patience."

Shaking her head, Rosa held up a hand and waved Jameson off. While she appreciated his backing, she didn't need it. Not right now. "I'm not a prize that can be won. I make my own choices. If you don't like it, you can leave. The dust pirates are looking for men with no honor and no conscience. Just know if you leave Valle tonight, I *will* kill you if you come back."

"Me too." Ex stepped away from Allison, flanking Rosa. "Look, Falco, it sucks not getting the woman you want. We've all been there. But sometimes being a man means letting go. If you're *not* a man, *amigo*, then you don't belong here."

Slowly, Falco put up his hands. Everything about his posture bespoke defeat. What's more, he seemed genuinely humbled by Ex's censure. "You know that's not who I am. I give. Doc beat me in a straight-up fight. I can yield. No more problems on my end." As a sign of good faith, he offered a hand to Chris.

Eyeing it reluctantly, Chris accepted the offer of peace. Rosa wasn't sure she believed it either, but Falco gave every sign of sincerity as he sketched a salute and limped out of the *taberna*. Lem supported him with one shoulder. Rosa had never known her second to go back on his word, so if Falco said it was done, she would take it on trust . . . unless he started trouble again.

If that came to pass, there would be no more warnings. Just an execution. He had to realize that.

With the show over, the others went back to drinking and dinner. Ex patted Rosa's shoulder and returned to Allison, who was comforting Maryann. Conversations resumed and people stopped staring. Rosa let out a long sigh.

Viv nudged her, wearing a big grin. "I was going to make a play for him myself, if you didn't get your head screwed on right."

Rosa rubbed the spot between her brows. "How long have you known?"

"Weeks. You're not so good at the intrigue, and in the mornings, you walk around smiling. Though not lately."

Yeah, not lately.

As the older woman went off to refill glasses, Rosa summoned the courage to meet Chris's gaze. She might punch him in his battered, beautiful face if he gloated. She hadn't been ready to make that confession, instead had been forced into it. Yet he wasn't responsible for forcing her hand, and that was the only thing that kept Rosa from losing her temper. She didn't like being cornered.

Only anger echoed in his tawny green eyes, though whether for her or Falco, she wasn't sure. He turned and stalked out.

Some smart-ass yelled, "Go get him, Rosa!"

That sounded like a good idea. Clearly they had some talking to do. She followed him out—and watched in astonishment as he strode toward her house. No invitation. He walked in as if he owned the place. She crossed the street at a slow jog.

Rosa found him waiting in the kitchen, a trickle of dried blood on his jaw. Other bruises were forming, but unquestionably Falco had gotten the worst of the exchange. She couldn't help a flicker of pride. Chris had proven himself the toughest bastard in town. They all had to be thinking that was why she chose to sleep with him.

"You got what you wanted," she said. "It's all in the open now."

"You don't think I—"

"No, I know you didn't."

Chris took a step toward her, his knuckles cut and bruised, and touched the side of her face. "I missed you."

Not enough to relax your conditions.

But it didn't seem like the time for complaints. Besides,

she'd missed him too. So she nodded and he leaned in close. It felt strange in her home, where no man had ever touched her. But it was right. Being with Chris was right. She stretched up and twined her arms around his neck, kissing him for long, lovely moments. Her pulse kicked up a notch, her body aching for his.

"Let me get some water and clean you up."

He shrugged. "It's not that bad."

"Don't argue with me. Shirt off. You're not getting in my bed unless you're clean."

Perhaps the implied invitation shut him up. She filled a basin, got a cloth, and went to work. He hissed at the first touch, then settled in to watch her trace his body. Trickles of water rolled over tanned skin. His muscles tensed beneath her hands, responding to every little touch. Soon she was thinking not of tending his wounds, but of his reaction.

"Tell me this is foreplay," he gritted out. "Because it's been a long damn time and you're driving me crazy."

She offered a half smile. "Does it feel good?"

"God, yes."

"Pants off too, please."

"Right here? In the kitchen?"

"That might be a little shocking in your current state. Come, then." Rosa didn't wait to see if he'd follow. She carried the basin and cloth into the bedroom. "Is this better?"

"Much." Chris stripped out of his trousers as she'd asked. He was already fiercely aroused, trembling with it. Some of that might be adrenaline left over from the fight, but not all of it. He desired her with absolute ferocity.

"Lie down."

He complied with an alacrity that told her he was truly desperate, and that lightened her heart as few things could. The distance between them had hurt him too. Their forced separation hadn't just been some game to increase his status.

Quickly she finished washing his wounds and retrieved the ointment for his bruises. With great tenderness, Rosa anointed each darkening patch of skin, and again he watched her every move, hazel eyes dark with hunger. When Chris was as well tended as she could manage, she took the basin away. She returned with fresh water and a new cloth.

He groaned a little. "You're going to tease me to death."

"That's not my intention." Without explaining, she reached between his thighs for the delicious, straining erection and took great pains to wash him clean. He arched and moaned, lifting so she could do the job properly.

"What're you doing to me, Rosita?"

"I've never done this for pleasure before," she said softly. "I wanted to make sure you would taste as . . . pleasant as possible."

"Taste," he repeated, falling back onto her buckwheat hull pillows.

He made a beautiful contrast to her paler sheets, lying there with a stunned expression. Smiling, still fully clothed, she settled between his thighs. There was power in having a strong man laid out for her pleasure, open to anything she chose to do.

That gave her the courage to whisper, "Bend your knees for me."

He complied and she curled her fingers around his cock, giving a little squeeze. The throb thrilled her. Chris propped up on his elbows, his face gone dreamy with lust. Rosa slid her cheek against the hot, rigid length until he moaned. Her hair spilled over his thighs, dusting him, teasing him. He thrust into it with his fingers, mutely begging for more.

Tentatively, she touched her tongue to the swollen head, which already leaked its clear fluid—salty, but clean tasting. Nice. Rosa licked a slow circle around the tip, then focused on the sensitive skin beneath. He bucked in response, pushing for more of her mouth, but she controlled him with a little pressure.

Instead of sucking she went lower, biting at his inner thighs and nuzzling the curve of his balls. By the time Rosa finished teasing, his breath came in ragged pants and his hands twisted in her hair, tangling but not hurting. She let him pull her head up and she took his cock between her lips.

Because she didn't want to give him learned technique,

she watched his face, measured her suction and the use of her tongue against the pleasure that flared across his sharp, graceful features. Each move she offered was for him alone—what *he* liked, not what she knew from other men. He liked it soft and slow at first, with building suction and teasing sweeps of the tongue, culminating with greater pressure on the head. Her arousal grew in conjunction with his. Feeling his pulse in her mouth drove her wild.

She sucked until he began to thrust wildly. Stopping, she clamped a hand tight on his shaft to prevent the building orgasm. She didn't move until his taut longing receded. His breathing calmed. His fingers relaxed. But then she began the buildup all over again—sweet suction, teasing tongue, and a delicate hint of teeth. He whispered to her; he coaxed. And then he offered sweet little bribes. None of it changed her resolve to make him lose his mind. Four times she did that, until he was begging and incoherent, arching in long, near-climactic tension.

Only when his gaze met hers and he mouthed, *Rosita, please,* did she slide up his body. She stripped quickly.

A special position on this night, one they'd never tried before. It was for intimacy and connection, this swimmer's lovemaking. She wrapped her hand around his cock and sank down. He tensed beneath her, pushing up, even as she lay down on him, stretching fully along his body. He wrapped his arms around her, drawing her breasts tight to his chest. This position demanded tiny movements to ratchet up the intensity, putting a lovely pressure on her clitoris. Rosa rolled her hips, getting the feel of it. She had seen pictures like this, but it was nothing she'd ever done with a partner.

Dios, did he feel good.

She tightened on him. Chris growled a little, biting down on her neck. The surprising spark of pain stole her control. Orgasm startled her with its power. He rolled her over and went wild with his thrusts. Rosa's breath came in bursts as the aftershocks spiraled through her. Ten long, hard strokes later, he shook and tensed atop her, but there were no unpleasant associations this time, only the sweet pulse of Cristián's pleasure. He drove deep and held, gazing down into her face with agonized adoration.

Still calming, she stroked his back, his sides, and ran her fingers through his hair. She had never before cared if it felt good to anyone. With Chris, it mattered more than anything. For the first time she believed no other warm body would do. Maybe, just maybe, she represented something special to him. Certainly he did to her. Like Tilly and Jameson's baby, Cristián meant hope. Not just for Valle but for her lost, damaged soul.

Shaking, he eased to his side and nestled his head against hers. "Love you," he whispered into the silence. "So damn much."

THIRTY

Chris lay in the darkness, hours later. His brain felt turned inside out. There in the middle of the night, he processed thoughts as he had for thirty-nine years of life. Rationally. Steadily. But the groggy aftereffects of the previous few hours stayed with him. Bloodlust against Falco, and just-plain-lust with Rosa, had done a number on his mind. He'd operated on an unconscious level: fight, then fuck.

There was absolutely no trusting an organ that switched off for such long periods of time.

Yet how could he do otherwise with Rosita as the prize? Curling his arm more tightly around her shoulder, he kissed the top of her head. Her soft breathing altered only briefly before returning to the steady cadence of sleep. He'd take on the entire town if need be, knowing the whole time that she was the toughest opponent he'd ever face.

Maybe that was why he hadn't needed to hear her declaration of love in return. He would have a hard time believing she meant it.

But what the hell did he know about love? It just felt right. And this time it felt . . . epic. Besides, Rosa had taken a hell of a step in announcing their relationship to all of Valle—about goddamn time. They had something to build on now. That was more than enough, more than he'd ever expected.

Sleep would not come, despite his relaxed body and the lull of Rosa's breathing. He held her and relived what she'd done to him. Pure black magic. She was a sensual sorceress.

He couldn't stay with those memories, though—not without needing her again. She got so little rest.

Chris eased from the bed. He grabbed a soft throw from the back of a nearby chair and tugged it over his shoulders. The floor was cool against his soles, and the breeze sneaking in through the open bedroom window shivered across his bare skin.

Damn. That window had been open. He smiled again, but cockier now, knowing their lovemaking had been far from hidden this time. Anyone walking past her casita earlier in the night would've heard Chris begging for mercy. Quite literally.

He padded into the kitchen and poured a glass of wine. The sweetness hit him with a firm reminder of how good his life had suddenly become. An oasis in the desert.

But the wine was a simple luxury compared to finding Rosa's books. Hundreds of them. *Hundreds.* From Allende to Zola, her collection was arranged alphabetically, the Spanish thrown in with the English and French. There were even a few titles in what appeared to be Chinese and Arabic, tucked into a bottom corner of the shelves. Chris hadn't seen more than a dozen books in all his years of travel.

He was surprised to find his hands shaking when he reached out for *The Complete Sonnets of Shakespeare.* He'd always been a thriller and sci-fi guy himself, but even he was cultured enough to tip his hat to the Bard.

"I didn't hear you get up," Rosa said behind him.

The full-on sight of her standing in the bedroom doorway did away with conscious thought. *Again.* She wore a cotton wrap, done loosely at the waist—the same one he'd dreamed. Her hair, now such a sexy, tousled mess, framed her face. A strange, almost wondering smile edged her lips. Memories of what she'd done to him with that delectable mouth sent blood rushing away from his useless brain.

He cleared his throat. "Couldn't sleep."

"Anything I can help you with?"

"Your version of help, Rosita, is teasing me to an early grave."

Slinking slowly toward him, her smile growing, she seemed years younger. The burdens she carried so resolutely had been momentarily lifted. Chris felt an unimaginable sense of pride in having done that for her.

"You scared of me, *amorcito*?"

"You'd like to think that."

"I would." She nodded to the book he held. *"¿Qué tienes?"*

"Shakespeare's sonnets."

She wrinkled her nose. "It's beyond me."

"You've tried?"

"I've tried all of them." A little of her familiar defensiveness had returned, although Chris couldn't figure why. "Some of them get away from me."

"Is that why you gave me Poe?"

"No, Poe is just plain scary. I don't need that in my life."

Chris laughed, gathering her against his body and wrapping them together in the knitted throw. He nestled his chin against the top of her head. A feeling of rightness closed over them. He simply shut his eyes and exhaled, relishing such a gift.

"Are you hungry?" she asked, breath warm on his skin.

"Not for food."

She wiggled her hips slightly, nudging his rekindled erection. "You like to come across so civilized, but I know better."

"I'm perfectly civilized. Let me show you." He tugged her back toward the bedroom.

"No way. You may not be hungry, but I am. Hold on."

With the throw still his only covering, Chris leaned against the nearest wall and watched as Rosa moved through her little kitchen. She was strong and graceful, focused and efficient.

His words of love had been wrenched from his gut, pulled from him after so many hours and days and weeks of need. But a gentler emotion filled him, there in her home. He wanted this—to share a life with Rosa. Sighing, he was almost relieved to recognize the depth of his affection. This was no lark, no fling. This was something to nurture and defend. What he'd done to Falco, he would revisit it a thousand times on whoever tried to keep him from her. This was the woman he'd spent his life seeking.

"So serious," she said over her shoulder. "Read something instead of dwelling wherever you've gone."

Chris flipped open the book of sonnets to find the only one he'd ever really enjoyed, Sonnet 89. "Say that thou didst forsake me for some fault, / And I will comment upon that offence; / Speak of my lameness, and I straight will halt, / Against thy reasons making no defence."

Rosa had turned with a plate in hand, leaning against the countertop. She tipped her head to one side. "Say it again."

With a smile, Chris obliged.

"So," she said, "if I tell you you've done something wrong, you'll fix it and not complain?"

"That's just Shakespeare talking, sweetheart."

"Ha. You borrow the man's words, then ignore them. Typical."

She sauntered past, dragging the plate of snacks just beneath his nose as she passed. It was a one-two punch of primal urges, woman and food. He followed like a starving animal.

Rosa placed the offering on the edge of the bed, then pulled a little stool up beside it, as if sitting down at a dining table. She smoothed her hair over one shoulder and began to braid it. A secretive smile shaped her lips.

There in the doorway, Chris nearly crumpled under the

weight of déjà vu. That was what he'd dreamed—one of the dreams he'd been convinced would never come true.

He leaned his head against the cool doorjamb. Suspecting something and finding it confirmed were two radically different matters.

"What is it?" She'd stopped plaiting, her expression concerned.

Dizziness fogged his mind. *And let's just say it, folks—there's a good dose of fear here*. This wasn't just an inkling; it was a full-fledged premonition.

Throat tight, knees unsteady, Chris loped to the bed and stretched out on it. "I dreamed this."

"What, exactly?"

"This. You." Coming up on his elbow, he waved a hand at the sweet, erotic scene she portrayed. "You sitting on that stool, here in your bedroom. You were wearing that robe, with the tie so loose I could see the curve of your left breast."

At that, Rosa glanced down and tugged the fabric shut.

"There's no need to punish me for honesty," he said.

"Go on."

"You were braiding your hair and smiling. It was the smile I didn't believe."

"Gracias," she said with a sour expression. Finished with her braid, she tossed it over her shoulder and grabbed a slice of cheese. She regarded him steadily, almost critically, as she chewed. The way she licked her fingers afterward dragged his thoughts back to sex, but he wouldn't be deterred in this.

"Say something," he said.

"You're being honest with me? *Es importante.*"

"Jesus, I'm a trained scientist. You think I like admitting when there are things in this new world I can't explain? That *no one* can explain?" He reached across the bed and took her hand. "And I haven't lied to you, Rosita. Not ever."

"Fine. Okay, fine. You want to hear mine? Here goes. The night I left you in the cave, I came back here and finally got to sleep. And, oh, guess who I dreamed about?"

"Me?"

"*Sí, claro.* You were standing in front of my bookshelves wearing that green knitted wrap. It drooped over one shoulder so I could see your tattoo. And when you turned around, you held Shakespeare's sonnets."

Chris's lungs felt too hot. When he managed a breath, he only said, "Shit."

"Cristián, what does it mean?"

"Hell if I know. Look, things happen now. Things that can't be broken down with logic." He didn't like bringing up Jenna, knowing Rosa's opinion about the skinwalkers, but it was all he could produce by way of evidence. "A friend of mine, back where I came from—she confided that she and her partner could hear each other's thoughts."

"*¿Es la verdad?*"

"Like I said, I have no way of knowing for sure. But believe me, she wasn't one for voodoo and superstition. She seemed as freaked out by it as we are now."

Rosa ate a few more slices of cheese, her mind so obviously working. Such a clever woman. Clever and stubborn. *No wonder I can't get enough.*

"So what else have you dreamed?" she asked.

"Oh, no. I don't think we should go there."

"Why not?"

"What if it changes something? If you'd told me about finding me in front of your bookshelves, I might have stayed in bed just to prove fate wrong."

She shrugged. "But then I wouldn't have dreamed it."

Chris flopped back on the bed, elbow tossed over his brow. Which was worse? That his life suddenly contained infuriating, inexplicable elements, or that it seemed preordained? Screw free will. If all this proved true, there was no such thing.

"All right," he said, sitting up. The throw settled into his lap, but Rosa's gaze remained on his chest. She grinned when he caught her staring. "Stop that."

She arose from her stool and set the plate on it. Her next seat of choice was Chris's lap. With Rosa's arms around his neck and her lips on his temple, he had a perfect view of her cleavage. He dipped his head, kissing one luscious swell.

"Are you going to tell me or not?"

He whispered against her skin, "I dreamed of you pregnant."

"Don't joke about that."

"I'm not." He tightened his hands at her waist, his voice becoming thick with emotion. "You were wearing a sundress, which surprised me. But you were on watch, looking out across the desert. Smiling again. A breeze kicked up and outlined your belly."

"You didn't . . . you didn't pull out last night."

Damn. He'd forgotten about that.

Chris rubbed his mouth with an unsteady hand. "I'm sorry. I didn't mean—"

"Don't."

She hugged his head. Whether she was frightened or angry or pleased remained just out of sight.

"Whatever happens, I'll take care of you," he said. "I meant what I said, Rosita. I love you."

Unexpectedly she began to laugh. She pushed him back on the bed and stripped away the throw. "You'll take care of me, eh? I think you got it backward, *hombre.*"

"Fine, whatever—you know what I mean."

"*Sí*, I know what you mean." Rosa trailed a string of kisses up from his belly to his throat, where she whispered, "And I love you too."

His heart hammering, Chris framed her face in his hands, looking for the truth. He found it. Eyes the color of teak were wide and suspiciously bright. Whatever Rosa Cortez could give a man, she was offering it to him. Slowly he pulled her toward him for another kiss. They had hours until dawn.

A knock at the door startled Rosa off the bed. "What?" she called out the open window.

"Rio's on watch." It was Singer.

"What's she doing up?" Chris muttered.

Rosa waved a hand at him and went to open the door, tightening her robe as she did. "What of it, Singer?"

Singer glanced quickly at Chris, who'd only just managed to cover up. But her face was all business. "He says . . . well, he says it looks like a family."

THIRTY-ONE

"Mmm. You're distracting me." Rosa tried to get dressed, but Chris showed no sign of wanting to let her go. He kissed the nape of her neck as she tidied her braid.

"That's the plan. Send Ex to deal with it." But she felt his smile on her skin because he knew the likelihood of that happening.

How odd. This was the first time she had a private life to interrupt, and right now, she would much rather let someone else deal with the problem. She wanted to go back to bed and put her head on his chest, listening to his heart. Certainly that impulse had never taken root in her before. But that wasn't the way the town operated.

Spinning in Chris's arms, she consoled him with a long kiss. At last he released her, and she dressed quickly. If this was some ploy to test their defenses, well, they needed a reminder. No one fucked with Valle. But if it really was a family in need, she wanted to be there to welcome them home.

Rosa grabbed her rifle on the way out the door, Chris close at her heels. Anyone awake at that hour would see

him coming out of her house, but she didn't mind. The die
was cast. She'd claimed him, and he was hers. They had all
seen him walk to her casita. She needed to stop thinking of
their intimacy as strange or forbidden. *La jefa* had a man.

She jogged toward the front gate and found the refugees
waiting with Rio on guard duty. As Singer had reported, it
was a family: two parents—a rarity in this world—and a
couple of children, a boy and a girl. Rosa put their ages at
around ten and twelve. They all looked weary. Dust coated
them, and their feet were bloody from where their shoes
had worn through. They bore backpacks stuffed full of
prized possessions, a sure sign they'd been traveling a long
time.

"Who are you?" she asked.

"I'm Jacob." The man nodded at his wife and kids. "Colleen, Joseph, and Connie."

"Where do you come from?"

"California. Or what used to be, anyway."

"That's a long ways." She studied them, searching for
signs of feral behavior.

He shifted beneath the weight of her stare. "Please.
We've been walking for weeks. Can we get some food and
water? For the kids at least?"

"*Sí, claro.* This way, *por favor.*"

Once in the *taberna*, she would explain their rules. But
she would give them a meal and something to drink while
she did. After they'd eaten, that would be soon enough to
perform the test. *Which Chris says is worthless.* With some
effort, she shushed that voice and went about serving a
quick, cold meal—just bread, cheese, and sliced prickly
pear, like the snack she'd just shared with Chris. The refugees dove into the food.

She let them eat for a few minutes and said, "You're
lucky you found us. You're safe here . . . as long as you're
human."

The boy's head came up, a frown between his brows.
"What else would we be?"

"Skinwalkers. We devised a precaution," she went on.

"But I'm told it's ineffective. I've been advised that only torturing a loved one would be enough to spark an instinctive shift."

Chris put a hand on her shoulder. "What are you doing?"

"Only what you suggested."

She shook off his touch and watched the newcomers, reading their fear. But she wasn't sure if it was of her and what she might do to them, or of what she might discover *about* them.

How did a family like this come so far in a world full of raiders and monsters without a visible means of self-defense? Suspicion ratcheted up a notch. Jacob had no weapons she could see. No gun, no knives. His nails were torn—not an indictment in and of itself, but enough to make her take the hard line and hit them where they would be vulnerable.

"I'll start with the girl," she said. "Eight hours in isolation."

Connie whimpered. "Will it be dark? I don't like the dark."

The mother spoke for the first time. "I can't let you take my daughter away. I *won't*."

Even the monsters must defend their children. That wasn't proof of anything except that Colleen cared for her daughter. Rosa needed to push harder.

"You can't stop me," she said. "I don't think you understand how this works. You beg us for food and shelter. You beg for help. And yet you want to dictate terms? No. If you want to stay here, you follow our rules."

"What are you trying to prove?" Jacob asked.

"That you're not skinwalkers. This test should determine that. It will be hard for you to be separated, not knowing what might be happening to your children. I bet that stress would force a shift, if you were other than human."

Young Joseph scowled. "We're *not* monsters. If we were, we wouldn't be talking right now."

"Pardon me if I don't take your word on that. I have a town to protect." She shrugged. "Finish your food. Then you'll be split up. That's how it has to be if you want to stay."

Connie clutched her mother's hand. "I don't want to go."

"Go get four bravos to escort them," she told Chris, who wore an expression of silent fury.

"I need to talk to you," he said. "Right now."

Damn him, why was he interfering? This was still her town, and she was responsible for its safety. It fell on her head to decide who stayed. They didn't look dangerous, but why else have that old saying about wolves in sheep's clothing? He didn't get to change established policies just because he could make her come. Arrogant bastard.

With an angry nod, she let him draw her aside, behind the bar. "*¿Qué?*"

"You're not going to put these people through the ordeal you foisted on me. Just look at them. They're so exhausted they can barely sit, let alone hurt anyone."

"Or maybe that's what they want you to think." She folded her arms, eyeing him with a faint sigh. Sometimes she believed he hadn't spent enough time around people to be familiar with all the ways they could lie and betray you. "Peltz could've sent them in to murder all of us in our sleep."

"Those are *children*." The scorn in his voice raked her like hot coals. "You seriously think that's a possibility?"

"The fact that you don't only proves you know little about this world. You spent your time wandering around and not getting involved. When things got tough, you moved on, because why fight, why care, why build? *This* is why. Valle is my home and I will do whatever it takes to protect it."

"Even from nonexistent threats, apparently."

"Do you remember that baby girl you delivered? I'm not letting anything happen to her. I don't care if you think my rules are stupid. They keep us safe. What have *you* accomplished?"

Hurt flared in his eyes before he locked it down. She didn't back off, though; she couldn't. "Nothing worth mentioning, I guess," he said. "Certainly not what I thought I had."

"Now, are you getting those bravos like I asked, or do I need to choose another second?"

"This conversation's not over. We talk when I get back." He stalked from the *taberna*, the line of his back taut with fury.

She didn't care. Whatever it took to safeguard Valle, she would do it.

When she returned to the table, the family had finished their meal. Jacob held up a hand. "There is no need for tests. I admit it. We can shift. But we're peaceful folk, and we'd like nothing more than to make a home. We've been looking for safety for a long time."

That was new. She'd never had skinwalkers confess to what they were, but judging by the way Connie clutched her mother's hand, they had done so to save their children from a harrowing experience. That earned them credit in her estimation, but it didn't entitle them to stay. Nothing would.

"There has to be a sanctuary like this for your kind," she said. "But it's not here. I need you to move on. You seem normal now, but I can't take the risk that you'll lose control of your beasts and butcher us all."

"Why doesn't she like us?" Connie whispered.

"Because we're different." Her mother raised her chin. "Can you just let us sleep on the floor tonight? We'll be gone in the morning, I promise."

Reluctantly Rosa shook her head. "I'm sorry. Everyone in Valle knows the rules. If I make an exception for you, it sets a bad precedent." She hesitated. "There are some caves not far from here where you can find shelter."

She turned to find Viv at her shoulder with a basket of supplies. Though once she would have forbidden this much help, she didn't interfere when the older woman placed it in Colleen's hands. Rosa turned her back, unwilling to watch or forbid the aid being granted. No, they didn't seem like monsters. Not right now. Not until they changed and forgot they were human. Keeping folks such as these around would be akin to making love to a loaded gun.

By the time Chris returned with the bravos, the family

was gone. To the caves, she hoped, and not to perdition, but they couldn't remain in town.

"What have you done?" he demanded.

Oh, you do not take that tone with me, in front of the others. Rosa glared daggers at him and gestured for everyone to disperse. Then it was just the two of them, but she didn't kid herself that the others had granted them complete privacy. They would be lurking within earshot, waiting to see if this was when Chris tried to take her power for his own. She hadn't expected this of him. Not Cristián.

"Don't ever do that again," she bit out. "I'm still *la jefa*, even if you sleep with me."

He cast his eyes heavenward in disgust. "You think *that's* what this is about? My God." His tone said she was ridiculously stupid, which hurt nearly as much as this betrayal. "This is about your complete lack of human decency. That was a family, not a threat. You've been on the defensive so long that I don't think you can discern real danger from false alarms."

A slow burn blazed up in her chest and worked its way to her throat, giving her words a ferocious edge. "No? But you see, the skinwalkers were not monsters when we first met them, José and me. They were *people*, like this family you feel so sorry for. And in their animal forms, they tore him to bits and devoured him. Afterward they may have wept, sorry for what they did. But I didn't get to see that. Our kind is better off apart from theirs."

"That's superstitious bullshit. What you're espousing is no different from segregation. I'd think you, more than anyone, would see the wrong in what you're doing."

"Me, *more than anyone*? Why? Because I'm Guatemalan or—"

A former whore. She did not speak the words aloud but she didn't need to. He completed them with his expression, and it infuriated her.

"So I'm to have learned some great gift of generosity and humility from my former life? No, I learned to survive, and I do it well. *That's* the lesson I learned."

"Well, maybe it was the wrong one."

"Ah, so you judge me now? With your many, many degrees in a world that no longer values them? Because clearly I am ignorant, and you know everything. How foolish of me to think my experiences mean something when I have you to tell me right from wrong."

"Don't get emotional on me. I'm trying to have a rational discussion about why it's wrong to exile a family!"

"If you feel so bad for them, and it's so terrible here, then go. Join them."

THIRTY-TWO

Chris hadn't felt so angry or defenseless since Ange's death.

That Rosa could dredge up such an extreme reaction—akin to watching a dear woman die—showed just how much control she wielded over his emotions.

And, oh, he was tempted. How easy it would be just to cut ties and walk into the desert wilderness, on his own again. No responsibilities. No chance of failure.

The sparks in her eyes, however, said she expected so little from him. That hurt. And it hurt that she expected so little from the world. But right then, he was beyond being generous or understanding.

He turned on his heel and stalked out.

Perhaps it was progress that Rosa followed. "Where are you going?"

Her hushed question sounded a lot like panic, but Chris couldn't trust it. Maybe it was just that he wanted to hear she'd give a damn if he left.

"For a walk," he said.

Frustration lengthened his steps, increased his pace. He

had just reached the outside rear of the *taberna* when Rosa grabbed his arm. "I asked you a question, *bravo*."

Chris caught her wrist and her shoulder, spinning her against the stucco wall. For all her strength and stubbornness, she was still a petite woman—one he'd caught completely off guard. Her struggles didn't faze him.

"Don't move," he growled. "You'll break your arm."

"Let go of me."

He pulled her arm back until she froze. "Not until you listen."

"I'll kill you for this," she said, but her words held a tremor of fear.

"I'm taking that chance to make a point."

"About your precious skinwalkers?"

"No, about you." Softly, as he would have that morning, he kissed her temple. She kicked against him but his hold didn't budge. "Not everyone uses their strength to hurt, Rosita. I've shown you that from day one. All this time, I could've overpowered you. Used you. Worked against you. But I didn't."

"What the hell are you talking about?"

"That you still don't trust me. Worse, you expect me to hurt you. You expect me to leave at the first sign of trouble—which, believe me, is tempting right now."

He released her and stepped back, arms wide. She turned against the wall, hands pressed flat against the stucco, twisted features hurling hatred like machine-gun fire.

Chris had let her go, but he didn't relent his real assault. "Get used to it. I'm not going anywhere. You're stuck with me. And I will make a human being out of you yet."

"Human? *You* crawled out of the desert like an animal."

"You think I don't know that? I'm breathing again, Rosa. Because of this place and because of you. The fact that I'm fucking *shredded* right now proves I'm alive, probably for the first time in years."

"So what does that mean? That I'm not?"

"You live here with your rituals and rugs and homemade

wine. It's all very pretty and you've done amazing work to make it so. But you flinch at shadows and cringe away from the world. It's changed around you, but you haven't changed at all. You're still the same scared girl who sold herself—"

"Shut up!"

"And who watched her brother—"

She launched at him, all curses and shrieks. Chris caught her, but momentum threw them both to the ground. Her forehead connected with his so hard that he saw stars. Teeth sank into his forearm. He grabbed her braid and yanked. After a quick roll, he had her pinned beneath the length of his body.

"It's still early, but this is very public," he panted. "Rosa, don't do this."

"Get the fuck off me. And don't touch me."

"No problem." He rolled off her and stood, dusting his jeans. "But I'll be back. See, there's a family out there in the caves in need of medical attention. My lamp's out there too."

"You're going to give it to those skinwalkers?"

"Nope. I'm gonna trade it to Wicker for a bottle of vodka, and then I'm going to get so drunk that I can't stand up." He offered her a hand.

"Get away from me." She scrambled up, wiping a speck of red from her lip. "You said you don't use your strength against me, but you just did . . . and to teach me a lesson, no? You're not the man I thought you were, Cristián."

Her judgment stung because that hadn't been his intended lesson. Maybe once she cooled off, she'd realize that he hadn't hurt her in return—not even when she drew blood.

Despair welled in his chest. Despite their physical closeness, despite her obvious caring, she still didn't give a damn what he thought. He might have been promoted to chief consort, but when push came to shove, she still disregarded his opinions.

With a muttered curse, he stalked away. He returned to his room and grabbed his bag of medical supplies. The town was waking up, some stumbling, some blinking in the dawn. Those awake at this mad hour made way for him as he strode toward the gate.

Rio was on duty—one of Valle's most loyal foot soldiers. If Rosa told him to lock Chris out for good, Rio would do it. Was there anything the boy wouldn't do for her? And by his actions, was Chris acting the traitor she believed him to be?

But over and over, he couldn't disavow his conviction. Not every skinwalker posed a threat. Sure, he'd gone through certain wariness when Jenna first shifted, but he'd seen her goodness and sacrifice firsthand. He knew it like he knew the stretch of his own skin. In the post-Change world, he grabbed on to *any* certainty.

As dawn tinted the desert in shades of red, he also admitted that Rosa might never give in on this point. What would he do then? Stay in Valle just to prove her wrong? She'd discounted his contributions without the slightest hesitation, making him wonder if anything he did would get through to her. It was possible that no amount of steadiness—hell, no amount of love—would make this better.

He kicked a rock with a tense curse.

The caves were only a few meters away now. He'd come this far. Might as well do his damn job.

"Hello? Jacob? Are you in there?"

A bear lumbered slowly, menacingly, out from behind a shadowed dip in the rock. Chris's heart jumped into overdrive.

Well, shit.

"I'm here to help," he said, setting down the duffel. "I'm the town's doctor. Thought I'd take a look, see if you or your family needed care."

"Did she send you?" came the woman's voice. Colleen.

"No, I can't say that she did."

"Why should we believe you?"

"No reason. But I think your husband would rip me to pieces if I were here to hurt you."

Colleen stepped out of the cave, into the faint light of sunrise. "You're not afraid?"

"Hell, yeah, I am." He shrugged. "But do I fear all your

kind? Not as a rule. I had a friend who shifts into a wolf. I'm just here to help."

Indecision battled across Colleen's features. She was young, maybe thirty. Even then Chris tried to put the pieces together. Their children would've been born before the Change reached California. Could they shift? Would it be their parents or the Change that gave them such abilities?

Long ago, however, he'd quit trying to make it all work. No equipment existed to prove any theory, one way or the other. And even if it did, he doubted science would ever provide a definitive answer. There was simply too much of the unexplained in the air.

"He's not shifting back to human," she said, resolute. "Not while you're here."

"Not a problem."

"And I'm going to search you and your bag for weapons."

He nodded, taking that as permission to approach. Jacob, fully three meters tall and massive with solid muscle, growled low in his throat. A sheen of sweat spread across Chris's forehead. *Put your money where your mouth is, Welsh.*

He let himself be subjected to Colleen's search, noticing that she was both efficient and thorough. She'd done this before. They'd protected their children for nearly five years. He couldn't even imagine the terror they lived with every day. As he knew firsthand, caring for someone else was a hell of a lot harder than just surviving.

"Good," she said. "The children are sleeping. That meal really wore them out."

"I didn't have the chance to bring any more."

Colleen waved a hand. "You're doing more than we expected, frankly."

Despite his disagreement with Rosa, he felt compelled to stand up for her. She still believed she was doing the right thing. "The town has survived a lot," he said. "They've never seen anyone like you."

"Peaceful?"

"Yeah."

"That's too bad. I understand their fear, even if it pisses me off. I mean, I'd have probably done the same thing."

Chris hadn't expected her to understand both sides so readily. "I've seen groups of shifters out in the world. Why not take up with any of them?"

"A lot of them are more content as animals. They like the power." She shuddered. "That woman was right, back in town. Most can't be trusted. They use their human guise as a lure." Glancing over to the sleeping children, she said, "I have too much to protect to take that chance. So we live alone."

"Can you shift?"

Colleen nodded. "But I don't if I can help it. Bugs the crap out of me, having my brain stripped away. Besides," she said with a slight smile, "Jacob's far more imposing."

"What are you?"

"Some kind of cat. We don't know what. Maybe an ocelot?" Her laugh was tinged with a hint of mania, but Chris couldn't hold that against her. "Isn't that odd? Being something and not even knowing what it is?"

He shrugged, trying to keep the conversation light. "Think of it like your ancestry. You can only trace back so far before you don't know where you came from. We all have something other in us, probably something surprising."

"Does that work for you, Doc?"

"Whatever we can do to stay alive and sane. That's the best medicine I can prescribe."

He looked around the cave, eyeing the spare collection of rough possessions. Their backpacks were like those a college student would have used. Now their lodgings were a cave, and those meager items were all they owned in the world.

"Stay here," he said. "I'll make sure no one from town bothers you. At least you'll have shelter, and the town patrols will mean fewer potential enemies. It's not much, but hopefully you can recuperate." He paused, folding a strip of bandages that had been cut from old sheets. "I can't make any promises, but I'll see what I can do about the attitudes in Valle too."

Colleen smiled. Although she still appeared exhausted, she carried fewer tense lines around her mouth. "You've already shown more kindness than we've known for years. Thank you."

Suddenly uncomfortable with the role of lone savior, Chris fell into silence as he worked. He spent the next half hour doing what he could for their blistered, bloody feet. Even Jacob returned to the cave, human this time, and endured the cleaning and bandaging. Chris would've spent more time in their company, but the longer he stayed, the more disloyal he felt toward Rosa—even if that was irrational.

And if worse came to worst, he needed to know if they'd barred Valle to him for good. If they had, he needed to find shelter. The caves would do, of course, but food, warmth, security—all would be his to scrounge, on his own once again.

His heart hurt. God, he didn't want to go.

When he'd done all he could for the family, he wished them well and left their rocky shelter. The boy had turned into a bird of prey, perched in a high crevice. Chris could only shake his head at the dizzying wonder of it. These kids probably didn't even remember much about what life had been like in the pre-Change world.

He shouldered his satchel and eased back along the line of rock outcroppings, half delaying, half scouting the area for his means of survival—if it came to that. He was hungry and exhausted. Bruises he'd suffered at Falco's hands had popped up along his ribs. The worst, on his back, where he'd been slammed against the counter, throbbed in a steady, painful rhythm. He stopped for a moment, easing a hand along the lump at the base of his spine. Already those moments seemed years past, as did his blissful hours with Rosa.

THIRTY-THREE

When the fires started, Rosa feared the worst. "How bad is it?"

Jameson bounced on the balls of his feet. "Bad. Six houses. How many do you want me to pull off patrols?"

Shit. This was a tough decision. She would regret whichever choice she made. "Half. We can't let everything be destroyed."

Not all the structures in town were built of fire-resistant adobe. Some were ancient, dating from the Old West, and built of whatever wood fell to hand. If the blaze spread to those buildings, it could constitute a catastrophe from which they wouldn't recover. Building materials were few and far between. She wasn't even sure if anyone in Valle would know what to do if they scavenged some. Making repairs differed widely from full-fledged construction.

"I'll start teams running buckets from the well," Jameson said.

"Are Tilly and Esperanza well away from the flames?"

He gave a terse nod, but before Rosa could join the fire brigade, violence exploded in the form of gunfire. She spat a curse.

I knew it. Fucking dust pirates. That family was probably a distraction, spies reporting back on town weaknesses. And now the fires. That couldn't be coincidence.

A matter of survival now. As she'd told Chris, she had learned that lesson well. *If it's us or them, then it's us. This ends now.*

Rosa ran, rifle in hand, exchanging fire with the attacking force. Bullets sprayed the wall behind her. She dove into the general store, using the front wall as cover. Wicker was down behind the counter, shotgun in hand.

"How many?" he asked.

"Too many. No more feints. They're trying to take the town."

"How the hell did they get those fires started?"

"They must've sent somebody in while we were dealing with those skinwalkers."

A raider in ragged denim pushed in through the doorway, perhaps figuring a woman and an old man couldn't be much of a threat. It was obvious he hadn't bathed in months, his skin caked with gritty red desert dirt. Rosa aimed high, Wicker shot low, and the bastard died four steps in from the door, still bringing up his weapon. Arterial blood sprayed as he fell, slicking the floor. She listened to his dying gurgles, trying to determine if he had a partner outside.

Her caution proved prudent when, a minute later, a low voice called out. "Gil? Where you at?"

She nudged Wicker, who managed a credible imitation of a wounded man. "Here. But I'm hit."

"You don't sound good." The second stepped into her sights.

Rising just enough to target over the counter, Rosa took him through the chest. Her bullet barreled right through his heart. He fell back, a dark shape in the doorway. Clean kill, no wasted ammo. Copper scented the air, a sweet and awful smell that had become too familiar.

As angry as she'd been with Chris, as much as she disagreed with his ideas, she hoped he was somewhere safe and not among those bleeding on the wind. Fear gnawed at her; she didn't want things to end like this between them, with only hurtful words in his ears.

"How do you think our boys are doing?" the old man asked.

She heard combat on the perimeter, staccato shots and whoops of triumph, but she couldn't tell which side was winning.

One thing was sure. They'd have to kill her to take Valle.

"*No sé*. But our bravos will give it everything they've got."

"You want me on the front lines?" Wicker stood with his shotgun in hand, salt-and-pepper hair, and stooped shoulders. The determination he wore as casually as his straw cowboy hat said he was willing to fight for his home, no matter his age.

It was the people who made Valle great. Not Rosa Cortez.

She dragged knuckles across her stinging eye sockets. "No. Pick them off from behind if they come to loot the store. But don't be heroic. If you hear big numbers, go out the back and find a place to hide up on the ridge. Take the best of the town with you—medicines and seeds. They're our future. I want you alive when I return."

"Understood."

The gunfire ranged farther away from the store, now with female screams mixed in.

Mierda. They were going for the women.

Of course it made perfect sense. Out here in the waste-lands, women were a commodity like bullets or weapons. Valle was rich in that sense, but her bravos treated the new-comers as if they had minds of their own. Dust pirates didn't. These were men who had, by any definition, failed at life before the Change. This new Dark Age offered an endless playground for their perversions.

Wicker's lined face was grave. "I don't like the sound of that."

"Shoot any stranger you see," she said, vaulting over the counter.

Most of the new women preferred to stay at the town

hall, even now. Allison was the only one who had bonded with anyone, so Rosa hoped she was hiding in Ex's forge. But that left the others defenseless while the bravos fought a battle on two fronts—the hungry blaze of the flames and the vicious raider onslaught. A few of her men might hear their distress and come running, but only after they managed to kill the enemies they already fought.

Breathing hard, Rosa sprinted out the door. Her boots skidded in blood, but the dry dirt caught her. The early dawn was clear but marred by the unnatural noise, heat, and the garish orange of burning buildings.

A weighted rope twined around her ankles. She slammed down hard, chin smashing into the ground. Blood trickled from her broken lips. *Fuck me. They're treating us like cattle.* Those tactics might work on an ordinary woman, one who'd freeze in the face of pain and an attacker. Before her captor could close on her, Rosa slid her knife out of her boot and cut the bond on her legs. With no time to get into a fighting stance, she lay still, hoping he wouldn't realize that she'd freed herself.

She trusted her skills. She could take this *pendejo.*

When the man stepped within kicking distance, she aimed a vicious swipe that popped his knee out of the socket. The raider stumbled, crying out in pain. She flipped upright, striking his groin, hamstring, and instep in a flurry of brutal kicks. He swayed. Rosa aimed a final strike at the bridge of his nose and knew primal satisfaction at his crunching cartilage. She cut his throat.

In the distance, she heard the angry drone of bees—and then a raider's scream as he succumbed to the stings. Even Bee was holding her own, which gave Rosa courage. If a mute old woman could fight, so could she.

Keeping to the shadows, she stole along toward the town hall. Such screaming. Abject terror. No woman should sound like that. On the way Rosa took down another raider, her arm around his throat and a simultaneous knife thrust to the heart. She was fast and quiet; it was her greatest asset.

The wailing grew softer, dwindling to one woman's

hopeless, anguished sobs. It was Maryann, who didn't seem to believe anyone was coming to help them.

"Hang on," she whispered. "I'm almost there."

Rosa almost shot Singer as the girl careened around the corner. "What the hell are you doing out here?"

"I can't find Rio. I thought he might be trying to protect the girls."

So she did care about the kid. But this wasn't the time for declarations of affection.

"I'm sure he's fine, but he's probably fighting. You need to get someplace safe."

"And where would *that* be?"

Mierda. Good point.

"You got your gun?" In answer, Singer cocked her pistol. She wasn't the best shot but better than nothing. "Stay close to me, *nena*. This shit's gonna get ugly."

With a grim nod, Singer fell in behind her. They would defend the women Chris had rescued. The bravos were outnumbered, unprepared, and probably outgunned. Rosa's only hope lay in surprising those inside the makeshift clinic. One day soon, provided they all survived this, she'd talk to Chris about erecting a permanent place where he could see patients. It would be a peace offering, a way to show that she believed in him, even if she didn't share his crazy liberal ideas.

She and Singer crept around the corner of the adobe building, hearing cries, smashing glass, and the unmistakable thud of a fist hitting soft flesh. Rosa saw red. Gesturing Singer back, she kicked the door open and blasted the first raider she saw. Stupid assholes. If they hadn't manhandled the merchandise, she wouldn't have arrived in time.

Viv lay on the floor with a bloody face, a broken table leg beside her. Rosa guessed she had been using it as a weapon. They'd clocked her rather than kill her, maybe because she was too valuable to kill, even at her age. *We're not trade goods,* pendejos.

"Don't hurt them," Viv pleaded. "Not these girls. They've been through enough. *Please* don't hurt them."

"Rosa!" Maryann screamed.

A raider drew up his weapon and aimed at Rosa. "You killed Stan, you fucking bitch."

"And I'm gonna get the rest of you too." She took aim, knowing one of them would hit her once the firing started.

No cover. She would die. But she'd die like she did everything, with as much ferocity and fuck-you as she could muster.

Come on, then. Come. On.

"Don't kill that one." A bigger raider stayed his man's hand, aiming the gun away from Rosa. The rest of the men stilled. Rosa did too, a creeping dread choking her throat. "She looks like she's young enough to bear yet. Shoot *that* one as an example."

Everything slowed. Singer screamed. Rosa couldn't look away. Not from this.

His pistol came up, a shot rang out, and crimson flowered from Viv's forehead. The small woman fell limp, her hair spread against the pale adobe floor like black rose petals. Viv's death sparked a panic in the other women, who all tried to run. Blind with terror, they pushed for the door. Thugs beat them into submission while drinking in their sobs like fine wine. The skirmish made targeting impossible, and the big fucker who'd ordered Viv's execution laughed at the chaos he created.

He *laughed*.

Howling with utter rage, Rosa flung herself into the fight. She used her rifle as a bludgeon. A knife skated along her side, but she registered little pain. Too much other anguish already.

Not Viv. Not like this. She'd been on the ground, begging for their lives.

Rosa caved in a raider's skull with the barrel of her gun, only to be grabbed by two more. They wrestled her rifle away from her and forced her to her knees. Someone pressed the cold steel of a gun against her temple, then nuzzled his face up close. It was the big man, of course. The one who found agony entertaining.

He gestured to his men, and she heard more weeping. "Get those whores out of here. I'll deal with this slut myself."

She held herself very still, listening to the movement and a struggle outside. More gunfire and cries of pain. There could be no good reason why he wanted to get her alone. *I will not break. I will not.*

Once Rosa heard only his breathing, he yanked her head up, bringing her close to his grizzled face with its filthy beard and stained yellow teeth. "I'm thinking you're more trouble than you're worth, bitch. Give me one good reason why I shouldn't kill you now."

And she couldn't. Not a single one. Death would be preferable to what these monsters had in mind. Rosa made her peace, closed her eyes, and waited for the bullet.

THIRTY-FOUR

Chris closed the distance between the caves and Valle, but another few hundred meters remained. He ran faster than he ever thought possible. Sharp spikes of adrenaline hit him like jet fuel. He had no weapon and no idea how many dust pirates attacked. The medical duffel slapped against the back of his upper thigh, as if he were an army medic charging into the fray. Someone had forgotten to tell the world that he was just Chris Welsh, not some goddamn hero.

Lungs crawling into his throat, he barreled past the main gate, which had been opened—whether by the bravos or the raiders, he couldn't know. He didn't stop when he saw the devastation. Six, maybe eight buildings were on fire. Several men from both sides lay dead in the middle of the street. Wicker was the first he recognized, slumped against the outside of the general store.

Wanting—no, *needing*—to find Rosa, Chris was tempted to keep running. But Wicker's expression, twisted in anguish, could not be ignored. A rifle lay spent at his side.

"You're up too early, old man," Chris said.

"Glad . . . you're here."

Wicker clutched a gash along his lower ribs. He was having trouble breathing, his face ashen.

Taking the man's hand, Chris moved it aside to take a look at his injury. A knife handle still protruded from the wound. "And how does the other guy look?"

"I shot . . . his head off."

"Good man. Now hold on. This is gonna hurt like a bitch."

With a clump of bandages from his duffel at the ready, he grabbed the hilt. One hard pull, then he shoved the bandages in where the knife had been. Blood soaked the cotton red. He found another hunk of tangled bandages and layered them on top.

"Hold pressure here." Chris stood and, hands tight beneath the man's armpits, he pulled Wicker to where he couldn't be seen from the main street. "Don't move until I come back for you. I'll stitch you up then."

"Rosa . . ." the man gasped.

"Where? Wicker, where is she?"

"Town hall . . . the girls."

Chris didn't need to hear anything else. Pieces clicked in his brain as he ran. Of course they'd come for the women. And Rosa would fight to the death to protect those who'd been abused as she had.

A dead raider lay spread-eagled on the bottom step of the general store's porch. His head was half missing, felled by a rifle blast. *Nicely done, Wicker.* Chris scooped up the man's discarded weapons and checked them: a rifle with two slugs, an old-fashioned six-shooter Colt, and an impressive hunting knife. Its exact match had been responsible for rearranging Wicker's guts.

Armed now, his fury boiling into something dark and unhealthy, he charged down the main street. On the far end of town, opposite the main entrance, an explosion rattled the bloody dawn. Heat blew back across his face, even from that distance, as did the stench of some unknown chemical.

Whatever they'd used, Peltz and his men had been planning for this day.

He had time enough to shoot one attacker, who staggered when the slug took out his right thigh. As much as Chris wanted to pick off anyone else trying to escape, Rosa and the women were all that mattered now.

What had been the last thing he said to her? He could hardly remember, not wanting to, knowing it hadn't been kind or loving or in any way sufficient. Fear like he'd never known curled in the pit of his empty, clenching stomach.

Racing, he recognized bravos as they lugged buckets of water from the bathhouse to the fires. Others threw sand, their faces coated in soot. Stinging smoke fogged the back of his throat. Sparks littered down like flaming confetti. Little fires burned on the street, feeding off hunks of wooden debris. Valle had crumbled into hell.

"Doc! We need help here," shouted one of the bravos.

"I'm going after Rosa."

Within a few meters of the town hall, a raider ran into the open. Chris raised his rifle, steadied it against his shoulder, and fired. Whatever remaining qualms he'd had about shooting a man in the back died there on the street. He shouldn't have come to wreck something good and decent if he didn't want a bullet between his shoulder blades.

Female screams became the stuff of a slow-moving nightmare. Even as he flung the spent rifle aside, Chris wondered why he hadn't dreamed this. What was the use of knowing *some* of the future?

Down by the explosion, more shots rang out. He could see Brick and Rio, maybe Ex. They were being forced back by a raider perched on the defensive wall. Other attackers fled out into the desert, dragging a woman with them.

"Allison!" Ex shouted.

But the heavy fire continued. Brick grabbed Ex's shoulder and shoved him behind cover. Only after Rio took out the gunman with a clean shot did Ex rush into the desert.

A gunshot inside the town hall incited another flurry of

screams. A pair of grimy, shouting men slammed out the front door. Each held a woman to his chest. One had the balls to hold his prey by her exposed breast. Chris recognized the man's hostage as Maryann, whose face was devoid of color, expression, hope.

Although he drew his newly acquired Colt and leveled it, Chris didn't trust his aim—not with a pistol, not with so little distance between captor and human shield. Could he live with the image of Maryann's head busting open because of his missed shot? Or would that mistake be a mercy compared to being taken?

In the end he didn't get the chance to make that choice. A gun was pressed to his temple. The sound of the hammer being cocked sounded far away, as if muffled beneath a pillow. He realized that his ears weren't working. His senses were rebelling. Sight blurred, sound fogged, feeling dissolved away.

"Put the guns down, cowboy," came a savage voice.

Chris dropped his Colt.

Then his muscles snapped to action with such strength and violence that he didn't know how his opponent wound up writhing in the dirt, clutching his gut. The impact of the blow radiated up Chris's arm like an aftershock.

What the hell was that?

No time to think about it.

"Get those whores out of here. I'll deal with this slut myself."

The barked order sounded close. Dust pirates poured out of the town hall, dragging two more women.

Rage lit Chris from the inside. He charged up the two porch steps, right into another stinking, rotting piece of human filth. Bone met bone as he whipped his elbow across the raider's face. The man's jaw gave way beneath the blow. He spit teeth and blood. Chris grabbed the back of his neck and slammed his face into the doorjamb. Death claimed him in an instant, his huge, lumbering body going slack and collapsing across the threshold.

Two of the women stood just inside, their expressions matched in twisted horror. They wore blood on their clothes. No telling whose.

"Run for it," he shouted. "Find a bravo or stay hidden. Go!"

The one named Beatrice did as she was ordered, but Sara stood mute and dumb, utterly frozen. Chris wanted to help her but needed to find Rosa. She had to be here. She had to be all right.

A raider pushed past. Chris shoved him, staggering backward. The bastard's expression said he was as surprised as Chris to wind up in the dirt. But before the man could cock his weapon, Chris retrieved the hunting knife he'd scavenged. He rolled the raider onto his back, then thrust the knife upward under his sternum.

Chris jumped away from the dead man. From the porch, looking through the doorway into the town hall, he saw everything. In a blink he had every detail of that hideous scene.

Viv lay motionless on the floor, the back of her head wide open.

Rosa knelt, chin lowered, her shoulders bowed in defeat.

And a huge man stood in front of her. He held her nape with one hand and pressed the muzzle of a gun to her forehead.

"I'm thinking you're more trouble than you're worth, bitch. Give me one good reason why I shouldn't kill you now."

Pain closed over Chris's mind. He dropped to his knees, felled by a paralysis that was as agonizing as it was infuriating. Rosa. *God, help me.* She would be raped, killed. And yet his body did nothing but surge and pulse with a torturous fire.

His brain felt full but stuffed with nothing more substantial than steam. A hot-air balloon. Each mooring burst free, one at a time, until he was floating, pulling away from solid ground. And still the pain lit fire to every nerve ending.

Surely he should hear his bones breaking. Because they

were breaking. He looked down at his body as if from two stories up. His consciousness was a lookout with no power to intervene. He could only watch in horrified fascination as his limbs twitched and twisted, as his torso writhed. Staggering backward, heedless of the dead that crunched beneath his boot heels, his spine jackknifed. He collapsed onto the porch.

Chris's last conscious thought was one of confusion. *Panthera pardus pardus.* An African leopard.

Strange. I've never seen one wild in North America . . .

A fire in his mind obliterated every sense. He spiraled up on wave after wave of burning needles, jabbing under his skin and into his eyes.

Then he slammed earthward.

Meat.

He sniffed at the body beneath him. Two bodies. Fresh kills. His own odor marked both as his, but it was not time to eat. He had killed them for a reason. No reason came.

The fur along his back stood on end at the scent of fire. He should go. But he *had* killed for a reason. Sounds scratched in his ears. He pricked them back, swiveling, scanning.

Voices.

Humans.

He was drawn to them. Survival meant leaving humans be. Too dangerous. No pattern. But he turned and padded past the sprawled meat.

A cry. A *female's* cry.

Again his fur prickled, this time with recognition. He nudged forward, into the humans' shelter. That recognition bloomed and built as he assessed the vast room with a clear, steady gaze.

A human female knelt on the ground. A big male loomed over her, his posture declaring a victory he had not yet earned. The sharp musk of fear and the tang of blood obscured almost every other scent. But one came through. One that triggered a killing reflex.

Rosa.

The animal in him charged. He covered the distance in two powerful leaps. The big man fell beneath his paws. Teeth met throat. Teeth sank deep. Gurgles and screams meant nothing. There was no mercy here, only ending the danger to the woman named Rosa.

But a hard, uncaring part of him dictated these new terms. Saving her wasn't enough. He wanted this opponent, this man, this victim, to suffer. And suffer he did.

Only when the body no longer spasmed and the blood began to cool and thicken did the animal relent. He turned to the woman named Rosa. She no longer knelt. She had retreated to the far wall, her eyes never leaving his. The face he knew—it was different somehow, twisted and distant. Nothing about her posture said relief. Nothing said welcome.

She was terrified.

With the taste of blood in his mouth, the animal walked forward. He wanted to nuzzle her hand. He wanted her scent to clear the death stink from his nostrils. Again she retreated. She picked up a jagged piece of wood, held it across her body. Sounds came from her mouth. He remembered that—language. But it no longer made sense.

She stepped forward, then charged him with the club.

THIRTY-FIVE

The whole world had assumed the air of a nightmare.

Rosa watched, disbelieving, as a leopard mauled the big raider. It was a beautiful cat, as graceful as it was deadly, covered in dark rosettes with golden centers. The fur beneath was as pale as cream. This, surely, had to be one of the skinwalkers she'd driven out of town. Maybe they had joined the battle, only to find themselves unable to discern friend from foe. It wouldn't be the first time, which was why she'd sent them away.

Though she feared these monsters more than just about anything on the changed earth, she grabbed a makeshift weapon. Viv's body was lying only a meter away, as tempting to an animal as any hunk of fresh meat. Rosa didn't think she was fit enough to kill the beast, but maybe she could drive it off.

Though the cat dove away from her wild swings, it didn't pounce as it had with the raider. Instead it circled her slowly. Probably playing with its food. Her stomach roiled. If Rosa succeeded in killing it, the thing might shift back into one of those children. Her swings became halfhearted at the thought. *Dios*, there had been enough death.

To her astonishment the cat stopped and rolled over. It didn't remain on its back, but the roll was unquestionably relaxed. She could detect no hostility. A contented rumble came from its throat. That fucked with her head. Her grip on the wood faltered, the club drooping a little. She hesitated. Before Rosa could decide whether to kill it, the leopard's skin began to roil.

Backing away, she was horrified by what she saw. It was like being in the arroyo with José all over again. There she had seen people become monsters; now she would see the opposite. Only, she knew that this person would still carry the beast inside, even while wearing human skin.

The reality was so much worse. When the spasms ceased, Chris lay naked on the blood-splattered floor, his honey-green eyes dazed.

Dios, no.

For endless moments she forgot Peltz's pirates, forgot the stolen women, forgot the dead bravos and the fate of Valle as it burned. This was a crippling blow, the worst she'd ever known. Rosa staggered back against the far wall. There were no words, no tears. She could not process the depth and breadth of this betrayal.

No wonder he'd laughed at their tests and called them primitive. *All this time, Cristián, you made me believe in you, knowing you were my enemy.*

Chris pushed up on his strong forearms, as if he hadn't made this transition a hundred times before, as if his words weren't all deceit. She cringed further back, mentally scrubbing away the touch of his hands on her body. Dread spiked through her as she put a hand on her belly.

He could've given me his demon child.

That knocked every thought out of her head. Babies were rare and precious, but this one? A monster *thing*? *Dios* have mercy.

"Are you all right?" he finally rasped out.

Ridiculous question. No, she was heartbroken. She had safeguarded her emotions so well, until he came along with his promises and his lies. He must have known there could be no future for them, given his nature. The cruelty was more personal than any perpetrated by Peltz.

Rosa could hardly bear to look at him, with blood caked beneath his nails and rimming his mouth. She gazed up and over his head while he pulled to his feet. Naked. Smeared with red. She'd never seen such a savage creature up close. Her heart thumped like a wild stallion in her chest, equal parts fear and revulsion.

"No," she whispered. "Not even a little bit. How *could* you?"

"It just . . . happened. I saw him threatening you and—"

"Liar. You expect me to believe that's the first time?" She laughed, sharp and cynical. "Now I guess I understand why you were so passionate defending the skinwalkers. You belong with them."

You don't belong with me, much as I thought, maybe, finally . . .

She cut the thought. The quiet plans she'd made in her head would go no further. Now was the time to draw back and rebuild the walls that had made her strong. Nobody would get in a second time.

Chris still pretended to be the man she knew, his expression rich with confusion. "No. Even while I was . . . shifted"—he stumbled over the word as if it was strange to him—"I knew you were important to me. I recognized you. I was still *me*."

"I can't put your word ahead of other people's lives. The rules haven't changed."

"Fuck your rules." He took a step toward her and she flinched. His hands were still stained with the blood of the man he'd mauled—the man who had been ready to kill her.

She hated this world, where there were no longer simple guidelines to distinguish good from evil. Now everything was washed in shades of gray. Nothing could be trusted, not even her own heart. Stupid, traitorous thing. Of all the men who had wanted her, this one had proven every bit as disastrous as she'd dreaded.

"I need you to collect your things and go. Before the

others see you. I would rather they not know how wrong I was."

"Even now, you're concerned about your power? Your community, while it burns around us? And you'd send me away?" He stooped and grabbed a blanket one of the stolen women had used. "You're ashamed of me now, ashamed of what we shared. Aren't you?"

Memories of pleasure flashed in her head, chased by the image of him in leopard form, sleek and lethal. That was what she'd welcomed to her bed, what she'd kissed and caressed in the night. Rosa didn't answer; she couldn't.

"God, Rosita, you break my heart."

"Please don't call me that," she whispered. "Not now."

"This doesn't change anything. Not for me." His shoulders slumped as he covered his nakedness. He looked so much as he had only a few hours earlier, standing in front of her bookshelves and reading Shakespeare. "But if you can't trust me after what we've shared, then there's no convincing you."

The idea of a future without him—the human, *trustworthy* Cristián—nearly drove her to her knees. But somehow she kept on her feet until he stepped out into the gathering day.

Rosa let herself fall, sliding down the wall slowly, and wrapped her arms about her head. She sat and rocked for endless moments, agony blazing in her chest in a white-hot ball, too fierce for tears. Instead it came in a scream that tore from her depths in ululating waves, a primal song of mourning. Lost to despair, she beat her fists on the floor, sticky with blood, until her palms split on the shards of wood. Viv remained where she'd fallen, beyond all caring. Nothing but wreckage remained.

Nobody came to check on her. Valle lay in ruins. Rosa had to collect herself, put aside the pain. If she didn't round up the bravos and assess the damage, no one would. She was still *la jefa*, and it didn't matter if her heart had been torn from her chest. She would abide. The town was all she had left.

Pain surprised her when she pushed to standing. Funny her body should be wounded while her soul bled to death. She raised her shirt and found a shallow wound. Vaguely she remembered a knife skating across her side, just beneath her ribs. A better angle would have meant a puncture, which was harder to treat and could bring a slow death from infection. She'd been lucky, but she didn't feel that way. She felt almost as though Viv had gotten the better death, surcease from all pain.

She regretted the thought almost instantly. Her heart seized. What was Valle without Viv?

It was still her home. Her responsibility. She would not let anyone else down.

Rosa left the town hall with one hand pressed to her side, determined to assess the damage. She found Jameson in the town plaza, stacking bodies for a pyre. They would burn them together, too many dead for ceremony. But he'd separated the dust pirates from the townsfolk, as much proper respect as he could offer. His face showed blood and exhaustion, dirt smudges and various scratches. The knives in his belt hadn't been cleaned yet, evidence of his lethal work.

"Tilly and *la bebé*?" she asked.

"Safe. I guarded them with my life."

And that was why Tilly had chosen him, long before anything like love grew between them. Odd how such a practical decision could bring beautiful results.

"Casualties?"

"We lost five bravos," he answered, heavy with grief. "Ingrid among them."

"Falco?"

"He's already trying to assemble a strike team to hit back."

Yeah, he would be. There was a reason he'd aspired to be her man. He had determination and leadership qualities, no question.

"Ex and Rio?" Maybe it was not fair of her to care more about their fates, but they were her favorites. Her friends, more like. Or as close as she had.

"They're around. But Ex isn't . . ." He paused, apparently seeking the right word. "He isn't rational. They took Allison. He wasn't able to keep up on foot."

In his way, Ex kept himself apart from people like Rosa did. But she had seen genuine caring between him and Allison. For a man like Ex, such a bond was momentous, and he would become a force of nature until he had her safe again. Rosa almost felt sorry for the scum who'd roused his wrath.

"Have you seen Singer?"

Jameson shook his head. "I thought she was with you."

She *had* been, until everything went to hell. Cold fingers dug into her spine. Mentally she replayed Singer's cry and recognized it for what it was—the sound of a woman being taken against her will. Rosa squeezed her eyes shut.

"They get her?"

The bitterness of failure clotted Rosa's throat. "I fear so. Where's Brick?"

"Badly wounded. Jolene's with him. I don't know if he'll make it. Where's the doc?"

"I don't know."

Uncertainty gnawed at her for the first time. She had done an impractical thing, banishing medical care so fast. If she cared about Valle as much as she claimed, she needed to do what was best for the town. Brick needed a doctor.

Maybe I should look for him. Once he patches up the wounded, he can move on. I can watch him and keep his awful secret. Even if the thought made her sick.

"I'll keep an eye out for him," Jameson said quietly.

"Where's Wicker?"

In silent answer, he pointed to the pile. *Oh, no.* The old man had done precisely as she'd asked him not to—and died a hero. As had Viv. With half of the town's elders gone, Rosa felt unaccountably adrift, no longer sure of her moorings or her course. But that wasn't the way a leader thought. She couldn't show weakness in the wake of the worst disaster Valle had faced. They needed authority and a sense that someone knew what to do now, even though she wanted only to weep and mourn.

"It's a terrible morning," Jameson said.

Rosa had no rebuttal. Apart from the day her brother died, she'd never known worse.

"And the news gets worse," he went on. "Lem's missing. I can't find his body."

Qué raro. She'd never heard of dust pirates taking male captives, but she supposed some of them might like variety in their torture and mayhem. Poor Lem.

Ex strode into sight, strapped to the teeth with weapons. He bristled with guns and knives, his face tight with rage. "The living need us more than the dead. When are we going to kill these bastards?"

Rosa breathed past the hot weight in her chest. The girls would be abused, raped, maybe even tortured. She knew that. But she also knew that running off in pursuit without regrouping and a solid plan would only destroy what remained of the bravos. The line between waiting and action was sharp enough to kill.

"We're not ready," she said. "I want to raid the emergency stores, and I want our dead burned before the desert animals come for them. They deserve that much respect." She hooked a thumb toward the pile of dead raiders. "And I want those stinking corpses out of our town."

Ex snarled something fierce and riddled with pain. "What about the girls?"

Rosa's heart tightened. Even now, even in the midst of his anger, he deferred to her leadership. Only, for the first time, she wondered if that respect was warranted.

"We'll leave off until evening, with patrols to locate their camp. They couldn't have covered their tracks so well when dragging the women along too. Our cover will be better by darkness, and we can hope Peltz celebrates with strong drink." She looked Ex in the eye. "And then we'll cut every one of their goddamn throats."

THIRTY-SIX

Chris awakened in the late afternoon. He blinked in the shadows of a rock overhang but couldn't remember taking shelter there. He sat up. The taste in his mouth was rank and strong, all coppery tang. He was naked still, the blanket tangled around his feet.

The remains of a dead jackrabbit lay next to him.

"Jesus," he whispered.

He turned away from the fresh kill and tugged the blanket around his shoulders. The rock was cool against his bare skin, but his shiver had nothing to do with the elements. Some part of him was going to have to give. He could either accept what he was, or he could go mad.

But to accept that he could transform into a goddamn leopard?

Fingers clenched tightly in his hair, he rocked forward. The whole thing was just *wrong*. So wrong.

And yet even now, he knew the satisfaction of having hunted for his sustenance. His belly was full. For the moment that was enough.

He recalled that he and Jenna had once speculated about

the number of calories such a transformation would burn. Closing his eyes, he thought back to his friend. She had been radically altered by her first shift, somehow more feral, more in tune with the other side of her nature. Chris found himself caught between wanting that blissful resignation and wanting to lock the animal away forever.

A rustling sound in the distance caught his attention. A gopher, four hundred meters. And there, another one—a hawk landing on the arm of a saguaro.

There's no locking that away.

He might deny it for the rest of his days, but that wouldn't negate what he had become. The new primal surge in his blood was nothing he could ignore.

Stretching, he stood and surveyed the valley. Memories of that afternoon's hunt fused with his waking mind as he recognized where he'd taken down the jackrabbit. He concentrated, realizing that the time had not been lost. He remembered all of it. The waiting. The stillness. The final leap toward a victory that would fill his stomach. Those memories had no words and no self-awareness, just the elemental demand of the moment, propelled by instinct.

Oddly . . . freeing.

With the blanket around his shoulders, he stepped into the waning sunlight. Sight, although still useful, took a backseat to what he could hear and smell. He gave himself over to the new weapons at his disposal, realizing that he'd traveled far during his hunt. He was a long way from Valle.

What the hell is that stink?

A few minutes later he topped a high ridge that overlooked a ravine. The dust pirates in all their putrid horror had made camp down below.

Chris didn't need his sight for much longer than a few seconds, quickly assessing the camp's layout. Then he hunched close to the concealed rock face and listened. Cat met human as he paired his animal senses with mathematics and logic. Only when he identified the sounds of a woman being raped did he shake free of his trance. He was thankful he couldn't tell which of the girls was being abused. It already felt like an intrusion.

Instinct urged him to shift. He felt the gathering fuzziness and pain edging into his human consciousness. Fighting back, he held the impulse at bay. He didn't want to shift out of anger and the need for spontaneous revenge. He was just one person. And the bravos wanted their revenge too.

The sun had set when he arrived in Valle. The explosion along the defensive wall meant he could have slunk into town without being noticed, but he used the front gate. A bravo named Hector stood watch, his face bleak and his eyes sunken.

"Doc," he breathed. "Holy damn, is it good to see you. Where . . . ? Oh, man, your clothes."

"Where's Rosa?"

"*La taberna*. Making plans and trying to keep Ex and Rio sane. The raiders got Allison and Singer."

"Shit. Brick too, then, yeah?"

"No, man," Hector said, shaking his head. "Brick's a mess. Took a shotgun blast to the chest."

Chris offered nothing else as he walked through the damaged gate, but Hector touched his shoulder.

"You are going to help, right?"

A cynical smile could not be helped. "If I'm allowed."

He left Hector looking tired and quizzical. The town stank of singed, wet wood, incinerated flesh, and spent gunpowder. Chris had thought the smell strong before, but now it was nearly overpowering to his supercharged senses. He concentrated on slipping into his room above the general store and retrieving a change of clothes. After a quick wash to get the smell of death off his skin, he dressed and made his way to the tavern.

Angry voices obscured his arrival. He peered through the cracked door, waiting.

"We should've gone hours ago," Ex snarled. His pacing was twitchy and tight. "When are the patrols due back? Do you have any doubt what's happening to those girls right now?"

"I have no doubt." Rosa sat at a table by herself, an untouched plate of food at her elbow. Chris wondered briefly who'd prepared it, now that Viv was dead. "They're being used, Ex. Used like a weapon or a shirt or a tire. A commodity. But that means they have value, too."

"For how long?"

"That will protect them," Rosa said, as if she hadn't heard him.

Rio was quiet at a table next to Rosa's, his attention fixed on cleaning his rifle. His posture rippled with barely leashed anger. "She won't be a virgin anymore." When he looked up at Rosa, his features were stripped of any vestiges of youth. "Singer, I mean. She won't be."

"Maybe not," Rosa said quietly. "But she will live, and we'll make her well again."

"You can't be sure of that. You don't even know where the doc is."

Falco sat on the bar, his feet dangling over the edge, heels tapping against the metal leg of a barstool. "Yeah, and you don't seem too frantic about that, *Jefa*. Woulda thought him being missing might mean more to you."

Rosa's back looked painfully stiff. "I don't know where he is."

"Maybe he turned traitor, eh? Maybe all this time he was setting you up for a day like this. You think of that?"

"He's no traitor," she said.

That much, at least, should have given Chris some measure of satisfaction. But he couldn't muster the energy.

"I'm not convinced," Falco said.

Chris pushed the door fully open, his hands raised in preemptive surrender. "I'm here. And Rosa's right. I'm no traitor."

Falco scowled but restrained any comment. Maybe he saw this as the ultimate opportunity to let Chris be the architect of his own undoing.

"Where were you?" asked Ex.

No suspicion there. Good. Chris needed to know how many bravos could be depended upon for a counterattack.

Rosa had yet to look at him.

"I was here," Chris said. "I helped Wicker first. Did he live?" Downcast faces were his reply. A place near his heart shuddered, bursting with new grief. He exhaled and pushed it away. "I killed three men in the town hall. Then I left."

Falco laughed scornfully. "Mark of a true bravo, eh?"

"Rosa told me to go."

Incredulous voices asked questions all at once. Chris bridged the distance between the doorway and Rosa's table. He pulled up a chair and sat beside her. The scent of her was much stronger than he recalled. God, the *need* in him was stronger too. More forceful. Less . . . human.

She was still his woman.

But he would leave Valle forever if she told him to go. He couldn't stay if she wasn't his to claim, to trust, to love. No matter how much Chris wanted to stay, Rosa Cortez was his last link to humanity. He wouldn't settle again.

"Are you going to tell them," he asked under his breath, "or should I?"

"I told you to stay gone."

"That was hours ago." He leaned back in the chair. "Before I knew where Peltz is camped."

She looked at him then. Her dark eyes, stripped of their usual bright determination, held a blasted, haunted emptiness. She had lost so much. The choice would be hers as to whether she lost him too. But even as he thought it, he knew she wouldn't back down from her hatred of skinwalkers. And frankly, so disturbed by what he'd become, he could hardly blame her.

"I didn't lie to you, Rosita. I didn't know. Tell me you believe that."

"What's he talking about?" Rio asked. "We deserve to know, Rosa."

She blinked. Chris couldn't remember the last time, if ever, Rio had called her by her given name. He was always the most loyal, always the one to defer to her guidance.

She took a deep breath. "Chris is a skinwalker."

Falco pulled a gun, his expression a nonverbal *I told*

you so. Ex showed no reaction at all, his expression inscrutable.

Rio slumped in his seat. "Well . . . good. I mean—you can help us get those bastards."

"Rio," Rosa said with a warning tone. "He's leaving. He's nothing more to us than that family. People to send on their way."

"Bullshit."

"Watch your language with me," she said, pushing away from the table.

Jameson had been so quiet and still that even Chris hadn't noticed him. "You killed that big fella, didn't you?" he said softly. "The one in town hall?"

Chris nodded.

"I've never seen anything like it." The neutral tone of his voice left Chris wondering if Jameson's admiration or suspicion held more sway.

Rio appeared older as he assessed Chris. "Can you change at will? How does it work?"

"Don't know," he said with a shrug. "The impulse comes over me, like the need to sleep. I can choose to give in or fight back."

In what struck Chris as a deliberate dig, Rosa had decided to stand next to Falco at the bar. "You've shifted again, haven't you? Since leaving?"

"I was hungry," he said simply.

Rosa crossed herself.

A hollow opened up in Chris's ribs. She had never worn emotion so clearly, but the one she wore now was disgust. Silence grew like a slow, lethal infection. Every scrap of Chris's turncoat hide wanted out. He should just go. Watching her look at him like a *thing* was more than he could stand. He controlled this; he'd worked on it in the wilderness until he could.

But for the sake of what they'd shared—for the man he'd been and the dreams he'd only just started to foster—he needed to try one more time.

"Peltz and his men are in a gully to the southwest. I've

seen the camp and where the guards are stationed. I can help you plan." He stood slowly, the joints in his knees feeling soldered and stiff. "I don't know what I'll be like in battle, so I'll understand if you don't want me with you."

"You'll help us?" Ex asked.

"Whatever you need."

"With conditions, I'm sure," Falco said. "What's the catch, skinwalker? You do this for us and you get to stay?"

Chris looked at Rosa's tense face, seeing no hint of Falco's question there. She already had her answer. There would be no bargains or threats this time.

He could not let those women suffer.

"No conditions. I'll go, if that's the way of it. And I'll leave the medical supplies." Chris swallowed, his guts roiling with emotion. The meat he'd eaten was going to make him sick. "I only ask for my personal possessions. There's a book I was given that I wouldn't want to part with."

Rosa bowed her head.

"Sounds more than fair," Jameson said.

Shaking his head, Falco crossed his arms over his chest. "No way. He can't be trusted. We're better off going on our own."

"You may be willing to go in there blind," Ex said, "but I'm not. I say we take a vote."

Her brief show of emotion gone, Rosa pushed away from the bar. "A vote? Since when?"

"I say we vote too." Rio stood, a rifle cradled in his arms.

Chris wondered how much ammunition the kid still had. Valle's ammo stores were dangerously low. Perhaps they didn't have enough for a successful strike, which made his own involvement more important. Any natural skills would be an asset.

"I think you forget where we are. Valle de Bravo is still mine to lead." Rosa straightened her shoulders. She stared down every man before settling her cold gaze on Chris. "If I say this skinwalker takes a long hike into the desert and never returns, that's what happens."

Chris's insides had gone numb. "Is that what you've decided, *Jefa?*"

She held his gaze and for a moment—a moment that caused him as much pain as an outright exile—she hesitated. The woman he treasured and respected was still in there, just so hurt that she was hard to recognize.

"Let go of me, damn it!" Brick burst inside.

Jolene hauled on his arm with one hand. "You need to rest, you jackass!"

"Where is Singer? Why the hell isn't anyone giving me a straight answer?"

Prodded along by Jameson, Brick slumped into the nearest chair, which groaned under the weight of his big, strong body. He wore no shirt, but his chest was wrapped in huge swaths of fabric, all dotted through with dried blood.

"Rosa," he said, his gaze imploring, "tell me where my sister is and what you're doing to get her back."

THIRTY-SEVEN

"My plans haven't changed." Rosa found it hard as hell to say that with any semblance of authority.

The whole town was in shambles. Most bravos showed signs of doubting her leadership. And why not? Someone must have given them up to Peltz, and she hadn't seen it coming. The results of her lack of foresight broke her heart.

"What about the doc?" Ex asked.

That was the question, wasn't it? She was tired of the weight, tired of the responsibility. Mere power was no longer enough of an inducement to carry these burdens alone.

Rosa lifted her shoulders in a weary shrug. "Take your vote."

The bravos fell quiet, eyeing her with surprise, but she didn't change her mind. Falco did it quickly, when once she would have protested his leap at assuming authority. But after tonight, after everything she'd lost, she didn't care. *Mierda*, they could invite the family of skinwalkers to join them. Maybe *she* should be the one to move on. Nothing would ever be the same in Valle again. She had suspected it from the first, that Chris Welsh would break everything she'd built. Just not in the way she'd expected.

The numbers came out with a three-vote majority in favor of his participation. They didn't all hate and fear skin-walkers as she did. Maybe they were right. There was no question she was biased, but she'd had good, sound reasons for her beliefs.

Now Rosa wasn't sure of anything.

She glanced at Ex. "There's your answer. Talk strategy with him, based on the location and terrain, then get ready to roll out at midnight. I want to give them a chance to get good and drunk, celebrating their victory."

"You don't think they'll move camp?" Falco asked.

"If they do, then we'll find it." She felt half sick standing there. *Dios*, she needed to get away. "You can use him to track if necessary."

"I'm not a bloodhound," Chris said, his tone bleak with pain.

Rosa ignored him. There was just no way she could deal with him along with everything else. She needed to chop the heartbreak into tiny, digestible pieces and process the loss a little bit at a time. Otherwise she wouldn't be able to function.

While the men talked, she stepped outside into the evening quiet. The burned buildings filled the air with the scent of cinders and hot ash, and the stacks of bravo dead made a mockery of their rituals. There had been no respectful gathering for Viv, Wicker, and Ingrid, nobody to speak thoughtful words over their passing. It was meaningless anyway; in this world, it was hopeless trying to carve out a corner where people respected rules. This wasteland knew neither mercy nor justice. She had been a fool to suppose otherwise.

The wound in her side burned, but at least it gave her a distraction from emotional distress. She strode away from the *taberna* toward the watchtower, slowly climbing up to relieve the young bravo on duty. He eyed her with a question in his gaze, and she shrugged.

"They're planning the raid to get our women back. I thought you'd want to sit in."

His fierce expression said he did, and he clambered down quickly. Rosa was alone with the desert until Ex came to join her. By lantern light his features were fiercely drawn, as if he choked back terrible emotion through sheer force of will. She knew all about that.

"Are you ever going to forgive him?" he asked.

No point in pretending to misunderstand. That would do a disservice to their friendship. "I don't know if I can."

"He's pretty wrecked, Rosa. The ground's been cut from under him too."

"So you believe he didn't lie when he came to us, claiming to be human?"

Ex faced her, arms folded. "He's still human. He's just something else on top of it. And if you want the truth, so am I."

There should have been shock and betrayal, but she'd felt too much of that recently. Now she felt only numb astonishment. So Chris had been right. The test *didn't* work.

"I've never seen you shift."

Looking at Ex, she realized this explained a lot about him: his silence, his reticence, his slight distance from the rest of the town. There was no reason to tell her now, if he had managed to keep his secret for so long.

"I control it," he said quietly. "Not the other way around."

"Even when you're—"

"An animal? Yes."

"Did you change last night?"

"No. I was afraid I'd catch friendly fire."

He probably would have. Chris was lucky as hell he hadn't been shot in the confusion. She felt queer and sick, imagining him as a bloody heap on the ground. Hell, maybe she'd saved his life by running him out of town.

"What are you?" Odd as hell, but that seemed like a reasonable question.

"A wolverine."

Rosa rubbed her eyes. Ex had to know that in confessing, she had the right to exile him too. But he didn't look worried. Instead he folded his arms and steadily regarded her. Nothing about him was any different. He hadn't assumed a satanic cast or suddenly sprouted horns from his forehead. He was still Ex. Perhaps their long friendship explained her lack of fear. She found it easier to believe his ability to control his affliction.

Or maybe that was the wrong word. Maybe it was an *ability*, like being able to shoot or sew.

Maybe.

She simply couldn't look at him and see a monster. It helped that she'd never seen his altered form, never watched him rip out a man's throat. This new knowledge was just an idea she needed to wrap her head around in the abstract—no violent, incontrovertible proof.

"When did it first happen?" In asking about the past, she was violating the first rule of Valle.

"Not long after the Change. I . . . lost my wife and son. Do you remember the failed shifts, early on?"

Rosa gave a jerky nod. Those months had been a nightmare of twisted bodies and half-animal corpses. She'd lived in fear that could happen to her brother. So many failed skinwalkers lay dead in the streets, their anatomy ripped apart by the sudden flow of magic across the world. At the time she'd pitied them, but José's fate had changed her beliefs.

"*Sí.* I remember."

"I succeeded in shifting. They both died, trying to—" He broke off and turned away, gazing out over the desert. The terrain rose and fell in rough waves. Tiny patches of shadow from the saguaro broke up the nighttime landscape.

Instinct urged her to touch him on the arm in comfort. He was still human. Ex spoke and thought and hurt. If she accepted that what he could do didn't alter the fundamental human core of him—that he hadn't *let* it—then she had been wrong. So wrong.

"I'm sorry." Inadequate words, but they were all she had.

"After that, I traveled. It wasn't until I found Valle that I even considered staying in one place. I was trying to outrun the memories."

That she understood. With a nod, she encouraged him to go on, sensing he needed to lighten his load. She had played mother confessor before, but never for Ex.

"But I wasn't sure I *should* stay," he said.

"Because of our policy on skinwalkers." *My policy.* There was no getting around that. She'd made the rules and the others went along.

"Yeah. But I figured if I kept to myself, I should be able to hide it, as long as I wanted to stay. And then . . ." He shrugged. "Eventually I didn't want to leave anymore."

"Why are you telling me this now?"

"Because I see a lot of myself in you. I tried like hell not to care about Valle because loss hurts so fucking much. Sometimes it feels better to shut yourself off, but Allison . . ." His voice tightened to the point of silence. Ex looked out on the desert. The silhouette of his Adam's apple bobbed in the shadows. "She still smiles. She taught me that I haven't been living, just going through the motions."

So this confession wasn't for him, after all. It was for her benefit. "A lesson for me to learn here, *amigo?*"

Ex shook his head, sharp features still twisted with pain. "After what she's been through, she still had the courage to reach out to me. To try and make a connection. I didn't want to give a damn about her, but she was relentless. So now I . . . care, and she's gone."

"And you don't want to see that happen to me and Chris?"

To her surprise, he laughed. "Fuck, Rosa, you really think I'd meddle in that? No. I'm telling you this because I'm done hiding. I'm done cowering and trying to pretend I'll never get hurt again. So if you want to banish me, you go right ahead. It comes down to trust, doesn't it? Either you know me as the man who's stood by you all these years, or you don't. That either means something or it doesn't."

Ex was her friend. She cared for him, but without the

blinding intensity of her need for Chris. Maybe that distance made Ex's decisions seem less like a betrayal.

"You're welcome in Valle, *compadre*. You always will be. And we'll get Allison back, I promise."

If that was true for Ex, who laid a claim only to her deepest friendship, then she owed far more to the man she'd professed to love. She didn't know much about love, akin to struggling over rocky ground blindfolded with her hands bound behind her back. In such circumstances, she was destined to fall down repeatedly and bloody her face. Such a challenge had never stopped her from getting back up again. Not once. And she wasn't about to start now.

Though Ex wouldn't admit as much, Rosa knew why he'd opened up. They had been emotionally crippled in the same way, curled into themselves like hermit crabs. They'd both needed someone a little braver and more determined to get them to open up. Maybe that explained why they hadn't become lovers. Without that external courage and resolve, they would still be shrinking from the light.

In that way Chris and Allison were stronger—fearless, willing to reach out no matter how much it hurt. *Dios*, she'd run him off in terror and revulsion, but still he'd come back. That spoke volumes.

She'd make it right. She'd beg his forgiveness. Hope kindled inside her for the first time since the attack. Yes, they'd lost loved ones, but if they didn't fight, it was over. Valle would be doomed, with nothing beautiful left in the post-Change world.

Rosa wouldn't let that happen.

But she couldn't carry it all anymore, nor did she want to. For the first time she realized that being fallible didn't mean she would automatically lose everyone's regard. She could laugh and cry. She could be *wrong*, as people often were. And even so, she would still be worthy of respect.

If—no, *when* they rebuilt, she would propose a town council. No longer would it be *la jefa* and her bravos. Issues would be put to a vote, just as they had been in the *taberna*.

This wasn't her feudal kingdom, run by a tyrant with an iron fist, but a community where bonds of concern and affection kept everyone working hard and doing the right things. She had made Valle a strong, safe place where people wanted to stay, but it was time to open her hands.

Ex watched her, his gunmetal eyes heavy with anticipated heartbreak. He had already lost so much to the Change. They all had. And she had been so judgmental, condemning her lover because he didn't meet her expectations. If she trusted Ex, then she could offer no less to Cristián.

"I need to talk to Chris," she said softly.

"I thought you might."

THIRTY-EIGHT

Chris held still, assessing the new data his senses so relent-lessly provided. Rosa was standing right behind him. How exactly had he known? Her respiration was agitated, yet calm enough that she still breathed through her nose. Her scent, that particular mix of desert and a woman's salty sweetness, swept over him in a torrent of want.

He tried to push it away, hold *her* away, but there was no changing what he was.

Steeling himself for another face-to-face encounter with Rosa's disgust, he turned slowly away from the desert night.

At least his amplified senses permitted him some mea-sure of surprise. Her expression, for example—he never would have guessed before seeing it himself. She looked devastated, almost childlike in her pain.

The impulse to drag her close and hold her was so strong. He crossed his arms over his chest in what felt like a shield. But physical strength—never something he'd placed much stock in before the Change—would do little to protect his heart.

"What can you see?" she asked softly, moving to stand by his side.

He'd been practicing all evening, but not in a way he could ever explain. The information was there. His practice had been in trusting instincts that provided answers he couldn't possibly know. Not as a human, anyway.

"About two hundred meters out, there's a fox scratching under a creosote bush."

"You see it?"

"Some. The shadow moving. But I can hear the scratching. I can smell its musk and know it's a lone male."

Rosa let out a shaky sigh. "You saved my life. I wanted to thank you."

The moments before Chris's life-altering change swarmed in tight. Rosa on her knees. A gun to her forehead. Even now, hours on from that trigger, he crossed his arms more tightly. That remembered threat to her sparked the impulse to shift; it hung *right there* under his skin. He tipped his face to the sky and focused, really focused, on a single star until the urge passed.

For the first time, he wondered if he could change at will. Jenna had always said it took moments of panic or anger, but he hadn't seen her in years. Maybe it became easier in time—giving over to the animal, then reclaiming one's humanity.

"No matter what you think of me now," he said, "remember me as we were last night. Could I have let you be killed? Hell, no. Not when I could do something about it. He may as well have shot me too." Forcing more and more calm into his body, Chris let his tense arms drop. "So I attacked."

"You really didn't know, did you?"

"No."

"And it's important to you that I believe that."

Daring a glance down at her face, he bit his back teeth together. She stared out into the desert, as if she might see what he did. Her breath came quicker; the shallow rhythm lifted her breasts. But it wasn't fear or revulsion. Rosa seemed . . . nervous. Not a word he would have associated with her before.

"Yes," he said. "No matter what happens, I can't have you thinking I deceived you. I never have."

"So when you . . . shifted . . . you were just as scared and confused as me." She faced him. Surprising tears shimmered beneath the pale moonlight. "And I sent you away."

Chris could only swallow.

"I'm sorry," she whispered. "I said I was protecting Valle, but I don't think I was. Not right then. I was in shock. Everything was burning, and Viv . . ."

Her voice cracked. Chris could no longer maintain the protective wall between them. He folded her against his chest as agonized sobs tore her apart. Her shuddering grief sank into his heart. He wrapped his arms around her, relishing the feel of her, even as she mourned.

Salt stung his eyes. His pain was grief too—the grief of saying good-bye. If this was all he got, all that was left of him and Rosa, he would soak up every precious detail.

The last of her sobs quieted. She slowly lifted her face, wiping tears away with surreptitious movements. Red rimmed her lids. She sniffed. But she didn't pull away.

Chris knew it wouldn't last. Soon she would realize who she held—*what* she held.

"I'm sorry," she whispered again. "I haven't cried . . ."

"It's okay."

He steeled himself and did what he needed to do, taking the step so she wouldn't have to. He pushed her gently away from his chest, then eased the blunt action by rubbing her upper arms before letting go.

"Are all the plans in place?" she asked. "The bravos know what to do?"

And she was back. Chris was glad. At least he knew where he stood with *la jefa*.

"Yeah, they're good to go. We're low on ammo and gas, but going in on foot will solve that. It'll be grim. Knife fighting. Hand-to-hand. But frankly, I think most of the boys want it. This is a grudge match as much as a rescue."

"How long by foot?"

"We can get to the border of Valle territory in the pickup.

Then about five kilometers beyond that. Maybe an hour?" He shrugged. "If they're as drunk and stupid as we hope, we should take them by surprise. Unless . . ."

"Unless?"

"Unless they have a shifter too. If there's anyone in that camp with senses like mine, we're done."

Rosa tipped her chin up, meeting his gaze. "You want something from me. What is it?"

"Two things. But know that I don't ask them for myself."

"*¿Qué?*"

"Once we're nearby, I'll want to go on ahead, scout the area and make sure we can attack without warning."

"Fine. And?"

"I need you with me on this. On all of it." He rubbed the back of his neck, as if the eyes of all of Valle bored into him. He'd never felt more conspicuous as when the bravos had taken that vote, but he knew it couldn't have been any easier for Rosa. "The result was only three in favor of having me along. Together, though, we need to get everyone in the right frame of mind for fighting. To work as a team."

She was quiet for a long time, simply staring at his sternum. Plans and fights and things left unsaid flittered across features that were both soft and tough. Then she squared her shoulders and nodded. "It's actually four in favor of having you along. No one bothered to ask my vote."

Chris frowned. *I'm not hearing her right.*

"Maybe that's my own fault," she said with a wobbling smile. "Being *la jefa* for so long, they probably just thought I'd overrule any outcome I didn't like."

She'd needed to offer her thanks and her apology. She'd needed a shoulder to cry on. And now she needed the best tool for the job. All of it was more than he'd hoped. But no matter how much her grudging acceptance lightened his heart, Chris knew that things weren't back to the way they were.

He exhaled heavily. "Good. Thank you."

"But I ask that you take Ex with you when you do your recon."

"Rosa, I'm going to try and do it as . . ."

"As the cat. I know. Believe me, Ex can help." She tipped her head. "Just what are you, exactly? Some sort of leopard?"

Another frown from Chris.

"I want to know what we're dealing with," she said. "Strengths and weaknesses."

"Right." Information. Leadership. That was all. "Yes, a leopard," he said at last. "An African leopard, actually. They're opportunistic hunters, stealthy and strong. Very adaptable to terrains from jungle to desert. Great at climbing trees and dragging up prey. And they're relatively fast, about fifty-five kilometers an hour."

"They," she said softly, her fingers brushing his forearm. His hairs prickled at the touch. "You used to study them. And now . . ."

"Now I am one. Yeah, don't mention that too often. I don't think I can handle it."

The tension between them spiked again. Chris wouldn't trust any of it, not on the verge of such violence. They would fight like hell to do their jobs, to come back alive. Then, if they had any future at all, they'd figure out how it looked.

The truck fired to life. A whoop of male voices followed. Chris couldn't help but smile. There would be death and there would likely be more heartache, but the thrill of the hunt was something he was quickly learning to indulge.

"Showtime," he said, grinning.

"They deserve everything that's coming to them."

"Damn straight."

Rosa threw him a cocky, hard-edged smile. Wrapped in moonlight, her features still slightly exaggerated after crying, she was the strongest, most erotic creature he'd ever seen. Chris threw away his caution and the last of his shame. He was what he was. And he was still a man in love.

He framed her face with his hands, swooping in for a hard kiss. Mouth met mouth. She was warm, smooth, so damn sweet. It seemed a lifetime had passed since he'd last tasted her. The blood in his ears became a crashing tide.

Rather than shove him away, Rosa looped her arms around his neck. Her tongue slipped between his lips. Roughly, her body shaking, she kissed him back with a fervor to match his own. Soon it wasn't enough. Kissing her was beautiful and utterly overwhelming, but it would never be enough.

It was nearly midnight. They had work to do.

"Ah, Rosita," he whispered. *"Buena suerte."*

"Tú también." She eased out of his arms, pushing a tangle of black hair behind her ears. "We'll talk, Cristián. When we get back."

He nodded. "When we get back."

The words felt like a promise. It was all he needed.

They rejoined the bravos, many of whom were decked with armaments he didn't recognize. He glanced at Rosa. "Where the hell did all that come from?"

"We kept a secret store of weapons, buried out by the scrap yard. Emergencies only." Rio and Falco flanked her, offering ordnance. She took a machine pistol and a serrated blade from her men. "Invasion was always a possibility, but we made sure that retaliation would be possible too."

Rio stowed his rifle in a holster across his back. "Might as well go down fighting."

Rosa climbed atop the truck. She stood like a goddess on a mountaintop, demanding their attention.

"Mis bravos, dawn is a long way off. Darkness and death wait between now and morning. But you all wear a tattoo in the shape of the shadows leaving this valley when the sun rises. That's what I saw when I first came to Valle. It's what we'll see when we return victorious."

A shout came up from the armed men. Chris couldn't turn his attention away from Rosa. His woman. She would be his again. That kiss, that thawing of fear and pride—they could start again. In the meantime he simply indulged in the fierce, stunning sight of her shaded in darkness, eyes flashing pain and rage. She had forged both into an arsenal that would see her through.

He had to believe that.

"The dust pirates, those filthy *hijos de putas*, have taken women from our town. Free women who deserve happiness and security." She paused, every bravo in the palm of her hand. "Tonight, we take them back and we end that threat for good."

Green light.

The men channeled their shouts into action. Someone gunned the truck, which was soon packed with eager bravos.

Chris found himself next to Falco. He turned and offered his hand. "Take care, Falco."

Despite the differences between them, Falco seemed to share the moment of unity. He shook Chris's hand. "You too, you crazy son of a bitch."

Then he was gone.

Jameson joined the bravos in the middle of the street. Tilly, her cheeks wet, held Esperanza on the porch of the general store. She blew her partner a kiss.

"You don't have to go," Chris said to him.

"I'm a bravo. The town means more than any one of us." He hooked a thumb back toward the store, where Brick had taken up position next to Tilly. The big man held a semiautomatic rifle, one arm around Jolene. "But it's not like I'm leaving them alone. I do this for Singer, just as he watches Tilly for me. That's how it should be."

Ex skidded a motorcycle to a stop next to Chris. "Climb on, brother."

He did as the quiet man commanded, while watching their one-truck army drive out of town.

Glancing over his shoulder, Ex raised his eyebrow in question. "Hey, Doc?"

"Yeah?"

"Do leopards hunt wolverines?"

Ah, so that's what Rosa meant.

Chris offered a tight grin. "Not if they're sane, they don't."

THIRTY-NINE

A chill wind swept down from the mountains, stirring the ragweed and snake brush, but gas and motor oil nearly overpowered those natural desert smells. The truck jounced because they'd gone off-road in a big way. Rosa sat next to Falco in the cab. He was still Valle's best driver—the one she trusted not to steer them into a ravine.

The bravos stuffed in the back joked and made promises. How fast the fight would be. Who would take the most lives. All bravado, of course. So many things could go wrong. Despite her rousing speech, Rosa knew triumph was far from certain. The plan hinged on an insane number of variables.

"I'm sorry," Falco said over the rattling engine.

She knew what he was apologizing for, and why now of all times. Before a battle, it was best to tie up loose ends and erase the regrets. That could be their town motto, in fact.

"No te preocupes. Está bien."

And that was all she needed to say. The air cleared between them, clean for the first time in ages, devoid of silent resentment. She permitted a tight smile then leaned away from his shoulder, judging the weather. Heavy cloud cover kept the night dark, hiding their approach.

Falco parked. Bravos grabbed their weapons in practiced motions; the aged truck bounced with the men disembarking. Rosa focused on her breathing, not the chaos that would come later.

This is for Viv and Wicker.

Though she mourned Ingrid and the other fallen bravos, she made a distinction in her mind. They'd signed on to fight. Viv and Wicker had never been intended to defend the town—and yet they had, with their last breaths. Anger and grief tightened her mouth into a hard line.

As the others checked their gear, Cristián drew her to one side. He cupped her face in his hands. "Promise me you'll be careful?"

"I will be."

Other than that one request, he didn't try to talk her into staying behind. She appreciated how well he understood her nature. She thought he might kiss her as he had in town, but he fell back. He knew the importance of the mission at hand, never imposing limits or distracting from her duty. He would never laugh at the idea that her leadership mattered. Instead of a kiss, they shared a long, level look, and for a moment, her worry faded.

Falco cleared his throat. "Should we send a scouting party first?"

That might have been the only time he asked for input without trying to take charge. Apparently he was trying to change too. More of Rosa's fear scaled back. Not all, of course, because it wouldn't be an easy fight. They were about to take on the worst murderers in the wasteland. But she had the best.

"I'll take Ex and Chris with me," she said. "They can move in ahead quietly, if need be. Listen for my signal."

"Elf owl?" Falco asked.

"That's right."

She was best at those sounds, like quiet, mocking laugh-

ter. Maybe the calls would be interpreted that way. Spook-
ing the drunken, trigger-happy bastards might help waste
their ammo. No one had unlimited supplies, especially
considering how well her people patrolled the local roads.
She hoped they could salvage some rounds after the battle.
If they cleared out Peltz's men, circumstances would become more stable. Nobody else had ever dared set up camp
in her territory. She wanted this confrontation so brutal that
no one ever would again.

Rosa, Chris, and Ex moved out in silence as Falco and
the others fanned out behind. Even the smallest sounds carried, so she stepped carefully, taking no chances. She was
conscious of the loose rock beneath her feet and the two
men at her back.

*How funny that I should lead two skinwalkers into bat-
tle. The universe has a sense of humor.*

Midway into their mission, Ex stilled, his head lifted as
if scenting the air. He turned to Chris. "You smell that?"

"God, they stink. Raider to the northeast."

She tilted her head, trying to detect what they did, but
her senses just weren't equal to the task. "How far?"

"A hundred meters," Chris said.

They needed to take out that sentry, so Rosa spoke in a
nearly noiseless whisper. "Shift now or later?"

Ex considered. "Now. You up for it?" he asked Chris.

Grim lines added gravity to Cristián's features. He was a
thinking man volunteering for animal instinct. For the first
time she realized how much it must cost him. But he nodded, his expression determined. He was willing to go leopard because she needed a silent kill. He would do it for her
and for Valle. Her heart went tender at the implicit sacrifice.

Rosa took a step back, bracing for the transformation.
An odd aura surrounded both men—not quite light, but an
otherworldly shimmer that filled her with wonder. Her
pulse quickened as their skin rippled and their bodies . . .
twisted, lengthening in some places, shrinking in others.
Clothes dropped away and animals stepped out of them.

Quickly she grabbed their garments and stuffed them in her pack.

Trying to steady her respiration, she drew a deep, harsh breath. Despite her faith in both men, Rosa still feared them a little—or rather, the unknown element of that power.

Chris, in the body of a sleek, powerful leopard, drew close and twined around her legs. Her hand trembled as she reached out to run her palm over lush fur. Rosa traced a line down the middle of his head, along his back to his lashing tail. He was strong, fierce, terrifying, and . . . beautiful. Unexpectedly beautiful. Later, she would tell him so.

His weight solid against her thigh, he stared up at her with soulful hazel eyes that were somehow the same. She saw his patience and kindness and everything that made him Chris. He cocked his head, ears flickering at whatever he heard with his cat senses, but his expression never changed. How odd that an animal could look so intent. And not in a hungry way.

It's true. He's in there.

Ex didn't invite contact, demonstrating the same quiet reserve he wore as a human, so Rosa kept her distance. In his wolverine form he was compact, probably thirty kilos, but had ferocious teeth. She wouldn't want to tangle with either of them. As a team, they would become her stealthy wrecking crew.

Crouching, she gave her signal. They moved as one toward the sentry. She gave them a significant head start before following on silent feet. Even from such a distance, she could see how smoothly they worked to take down the guard, human minds directing animal grace. But—*gracias a Dios*—they didn't feed on or maul the body. Once the man died, they withdrew, flanking her once more.

They slid through the darkness toward the camp, stopping behind an outcropping of rocks. Before them lay Peltz's dust pirates. No wonder they could pick up and move so fast. They owned nothing permanent: no houses, no farm animals, no patches where they coaxed life from the thin, rocky soil. Raiders didn't plant or build. Like locusts, they consumed and departed. On that starry night, Rosa stared down at their shantytown of tents and rusty vehicles and mentally executed them all.

Even from such a distance, the camp was worse than she'd imagined. The smell made her sick, a putrid blend of blood, shit, urine, and rotten meat. It was wrong for human beings to live like this. If Peltz had his way, he'd bring that filth to Valle, polluting everything Rosa had spent years building.

The human animals had been whooping it up. Those remaining even half awake were singing in drunken revelry. Of all things, they belted out "Ole Ole" like football hooligans celebrating a win. The repetitive chant came from the largest tent. In the air hung a liquor-tinged pall. The bastards had left only one other man on watch, and by his expression it was clear he was drunk and distracted by something going on nearby.

Rosa narrowed her attention, working against the heavy darkness. She held motionless with horror. The abducted women sat chained like animals to a post in the center of camp. Some were obviously injured, showing the marks of a man's fist. But she didn't see Singer.

Oh, no.

It would kill Brick if they didn't bring Singer back safe. Rio wouldn't fare much better, after having recently lost Manuel. With a mute head shake, she glanced at Chris and Ex. Even in animal form they seemed to read her questioning look. Their coiled postures were clear answers of readiness.

How astonishing.

She hooted her owl call, giving the rest of the bravos their cue. The call echoed across the ravine. The drunken sentry startled, gazing around into the darkness.

He clutched his weapon and muttered, "Fucking owls."

Rosa's stomach roiled. She waited in silence with Chris and Ex, now and then checking over her shoulder. The time that passed probably wasn't as long as it felt, crouching there in the dark, but the waiting needled under her skin.

As Falco arrived with the others, motion in the camp drew her eye to a familiar young man. He looked like the kid she'd sent back to camp with a warning, but he didn't stagger. His movements quick and stealthy, he turned his head as if scanning for possible witnesses. The guard wasn't paying him any mind. The boy crept up to an ancient pickup truck and clambered up quietly. He did something in the shadows, moving beyond Rosa's range of vision.

"Can you see?" she whispered to Chris.

The leopard cocked his head in apparent amusement. *Claro*, he could see. He just couldn't answer.

Falco pulled up behind her. He glanced at the leopard and wolverine, momentarily dazed before shaking out of his trance. "We're in position."

After a clank like a cage door opening, the boy led Singer to the edge of the truck bed and helped her down.

"They separated her from the others," she whispered.

Falco answered with a grim twist of his mouth. "She's young and innocent—not for the likes of these boys. The O'Malley will pay big for a girl like her."

Guaranteed pure and disease-free. What was it the big brute had said about Rosa? *She looks like she's young enough to bear.* There couldn't be many like Singer remaining in the post-Change world, but the girl was priceless for other reasons—the only reasons Rosa put stock in. She was like a younger sister, much as Rio had crept into her heart after losing José.

Rosa drew her Stechkin, which she'd discovered when cleaning out a private gun collection during an early raid. The pistol was her favorite weapon, too nice for anything but the most dire of situations—which was why she carried it now. She could use the automatic to fire one-handed. If she didn't drop an assailant with the burst, she held a blade ready.

A scream rang out, then softened to a long, drawn-out moan. A raider had pushed one of the women down. Rosa knew exactly what came next. Rage roared through her like an erupting volcano. She twirled her fingers at the rest of the bravos. Time to hit hard.

"Keep it quiet. No guns until we get the women clear."

Moving in a crouch toward the drunken guard, she noted the progress made by Singer and her rescuer. The two kids sneaked along the ravine's edge, keeping to the shadows and making their way to where the women were chained. Grunting sounds and a girl's cries turned Rosa's fury to ice.

She cued Jameson to take out the sentry. He performed the execution in complete silence. Another raider staggered from the tent. He raised his head, peering around in the dark, but he was too drunk to check the whole perimeter. He took a couple of steps and fell. Rosa waved everyone else in, drawing her finger across her throat. No warnings, no prisoners.

A startled breath escaped her when Chris, still in leopard form, slid alongside her leg. Heart in her throat, she fought down the instinctive panic. Just as well, because soon enough a wolverine arrived on her other side. Unnerving as hell. But she could deal with the residual uneasiness. They weren't her enemies, and she trusted them both.

"Go now," she said. "Give them hell."

Combat started in earnest, with bravos working in silent, deadly pulses. Singer and the boy had returned to unlock all the manacles. The women struggled upright.

Rosa's finger tightened reflexively on the trigger of her pistol. *Just as soon as they get out of there . . .*

Avoiding the men fighting in a melee all around her, she dodged a raider who lurched up in her path. Ex slipped past her and sank needle-sharp fangs into the man's Achilles' heel. Chris pounced when the raider screamed and fell, silencing him. A shiver of pleasure shot through Rosa. She found an odd satisfaction in seeing them kill for Valle. But the attack roused more sleeping guards. The unmistakable sound of weapons being cocked echoed through the canyon. Rosa cut a quick path toward the hostages, toward Singer and her savior.

There was no point in stealth and silence now, as staggering men poured out of the big tent. Rosa got her first glimpse of Peltz, who shouted orders to his men. The boss wasn't as big as she'd expected. He had a clever face with oversized front teeth. In fact he looked more like a weasel than a dangerous sociopath, but the Uzi in his hands spoke louder than his appearance. He scanned the area, focused on the escaping prisoners, and went full auto with his weapon.

Rosa dove wide, scrambling behind a truck. The freed hostages followed. One girl cried out, but there was no telling who'd been hit.

Any fool looked impressive wasting ammo that way, but he wouldn't hit much. Of course, it did serve one purpose—pinning them down. Rosa crouched low behind a tire.

When the weapon went briefly silent, she leaned out and returned fire, but she only had one clip. The battle raged beyond her line of sight, grunting and scuffling in the desert dirt. Men screamed and moaned. A leopard roared with rage.

Eat them alive, Cristián.

The women huddled around her as more bullets pinged the metal. But Peltz's one-man assault didn't continue as she'd expected. Though she hoped he'd run out of ammo, she didn't trust the lull. She just needed to hold out a little longer and save the women. Her bravos would do the rest.

"I want the girls out of here," she told Singer. "I'll keep them pinned down. You get them out of camp and circle around to Valle."

"We're not going anywhere," Allison said fiercely.

Ex would be amazed at her bravery, this California blonde, as she gripped an opened manacle and chain like it was an old-fashioned mace. In the darkness she radiated determination and steely resolve. The clouds swept over on a cold wind, and in the scant light of an eerie, overcast night, the women looked like avenging furies. Keeping out of weapon range, they'd all armed themselves with whatever they could find: rocks, broken wood, scrap metal.

Instead of running, they intended to retaliate. Rosa had

never been prouder—or more terrified. Though the girls couldn't win in hand-to-hand, they'd committed their fierce spirits to the fight. That was the heart of Valle. Even if they died tonight, it would be well.

Peltz opened fire again, and a rain of bullets sprayed all around them.

FORTY

Fear had a scent. So did rage. The leopard could smell both, even with blood in his mouth. Words began to filter back into his animal brain. He concentrated. They came slowly, one at a time.

Stalk.

Fight.

Bullets.

Muscles pulled in his lithe body. He leaped, landing on a thin man who stank of evil things. That face contorted in agony as claws gouged his gut. There was no meat to be had on such a kill. Only disease.

The leopard shook his head, his ears so sensitive that the gunfire hurt. Rosa was behind that truck. He'd left his woman. But that was the plan. She was strong. She was well.

Crouching, he slunk low along the ground. Muscles coiled. So strong and ready.

A man called out, his voice raw with pain.

Bravo.

The closer the leopard got, the more clearly the fight took shape in his quick, reflexive mind. There, within pouncing distance, a raider felled a bravo.

Enemy.

The cat pushed back onto his haunches. Strength made him confident. He judged the angle of attack before springing. Instinct made it easy and right. The ferocious leap was not wild but completely focused on his target. His paws landed hard on the raider's chest. Bone cracked. They landed back in the dirt. A quick bite, a scream, a gurgle. Then stillness.

He returned to the downed bravo. But there was no movement. No breath or sounds.

Death.

The fur on his back tingled and itched, standing on end. Death had a smell too. He nudged the bravo's slack face.

Good-bye.

Another scent caught his attention. From a nearby tent, its white walls filthy, came a woman's cries. The scent was sex. He thought of Rosa, but that wasn't right. His thoughts jumped too fast to catch.

Creeping low on his paws, slinking forward, he waited for a man to emerge. He knew there would be a man. An enemy. Others fought, but this man hid and made a woman cry. The cat shivered with a revolted hatred, part animal, part human.

A swish of noise at his back made him turn. A familiar face. Falco.

There was no word for Falco, neither enemy nor friend. His posture said aggression, suspicion, even fear. But he was still a bravo.

The cat waited, watching. He concentrated.

"You flush him out," Falco said.

The words made sense. It was easier now. Rosa. He'd understood Rosa too.

Unwinding from his tense crouch, the cat eased forward. Sensitive whiskers brushed the flap of stiff, stinking canvas. Piss. And rot. Inside was another familiar face. The human male buckled his belt, standing over a naked woman. Maryann. Her clothes were shredded. She bled. She cried softly.

A growl bubbled in the cat's throat. Revulsion mixed with the outrage of betrayal. He leaped.

The man screamed. Paws pinned his shoulders to the ground. His neck was bare, offering a quick death. The cat was feeling none so generous.

"Lem!" Falco called, his voice revealing shock. "Shit, *hombre*. What have you done?"

"Shut up and get this thing off me!"

Rosa pushed into the tent. "Falco?" The cat growled deep in his throat, wanting to go to her. But trash wiggled beneath him. He flexed his claws. "What the hell is going on?"

"I found him in here," Falco said. "Over her."

"Dios, no." Rosa dropped to her knees, holding Maryann. "Did you sell us out?"

"Fuck you, *Jefa*."

The cat bristled, understanding that word even as he read fear on the man's face. Tightening his claws again, he dug hard and deep into soft human flesh. He growled to Rosa, a question. She petted the damp hair back from Maryann's anguished face. Rosa's eyes narrowed. Anger had a scent like fire or blood—hard smells.

"Do it, Cristián."

He always enjoyed when she gave him permission. Using his strong back muscles to power his claws, he ripped open the traitor's middle. Lem cringed and screamed, dying as he'd lived.

Coward.

Rosa snapped her fingers. The cat left his victim, tasting the blood of victory. He led the humans back into the dark, with Falco supporting Maryann. He sniffed. He growled.

"What is it?" Falco asked. The abused woman leaned heavily against his side.

The air wasn't right. It was oily. Fermented. The cat growled again, hating that the word wouldn't come. Then knowledge burst over him, as strong as pain.

Gasoline. And fire.

He took off at a run. Rosa would follow.

The big tent was empty. Men had scattered, their rotten stink like a glow in their wake. Some lived, but not many. They scratched on the rock and in the dirt, every noise bright and clear in the cat's ears. He stilled, listening deeper into the night.

Wolverine.

Ex.

The remaining raiders would not last long. They had company in the darkness.

But the gasoline remained. He ran to the truck, where humans waited. Human women. Rocks and sticks lifted, with the cat as the target. He hesitated.

"Don't hurt him!" Rosa ordered.

She joined him at the truck, her body shielding his. The cat bumped the backs of her knees. He took her pant cuff in his teeth, pulling, tugging.

Rosa looked down, her face full of questions. Another tug. Another low growl.

"Chris, please, I—" She stopped too. She sniffed the air. "Damn. It's gasoline. Everybody move, now!"

The cat led the way away from the busted truck. His spiking fur wouldn't lie down. They needed to move faster, go farther. But the women were still injured and fearful. Though strong for human beings, they needed care.

Bravos emerged from the shadows. Some wore blood, their own and that of their enemies. Some carried boxes. The cat's mind couldn't find the words and names fast enough. Purpose drove him, sinking language into a far corner of his mind. He snarled again.

Come now. Faster.

Rosa stopped to help one of the girls; she lifted the woman, pushed her on ahead. The cat doubled back. He would not lose his mate. They took up the rear of the straggling line, escaping the stink of gasoline. An explosion flared over the ravine floor. He pounced on her, human and animal huddled low and silent. Flames shot skyward, then swirled down from the canyon's steep walls. Heat spiked across his pelt, followed by chunks of metal. He cringed beneath the pain. A whimper escaped his throat.

"Chris?"

Rosa tried to push free, but he held her still. Not until the worst was over.

When the explosion had ceased, when fire was all that remained of Peltz's truck, the cat eased off the woman and crouched in the dirt. His tail flicked.

Chris's mind shut down as pain flamed over his pelt. His body realigned, shaking, trembling under the shock of so much change. Fur shrank to the hair on a human male. Dizzy, Chris crashed back into himself, lying flat on his stomach. His throat felt parched and dry, the air suddenly colder on his bare skin. Lying there, he realized Ex was missing. Each individual scent lined up in his mind in a list, mingling feline and human knowledge. Some were dead. Some lived, fleeing the camp and its stench.

The habits left behind by his feline self meant his first reaction was to nudge and touch and rub, checking her for injuries. Instead he forced his tongue to form words. "You okay?"

"Claro." She sat up and touched his naked back. Her fingers came away bloody. "Damn you. Stubborn no matter what you look like."

Chris grabbed her backpack and retrieved his pair of jeans, quickly kicking into them. "Let's go."

It was a short way to the truck, but it required picking a careful path through a narrow canyon, up loose sliding rocks and onto level ground. Chris scanned the terrain as they ran to catch up with the others, cocking his head to scent the night air.

Blood. Death. Distant fires.

Ex was somewhere nearby, injured, he thought, but not fatally so. A darker stink filled his nose, and he sneezed as Falco led the way through a narrow crease in the rock,

Maryann still cradled in his arms. Her head lolled against the bravo's shoulder, and Chris felt sick at what she'd suffered before—what had been done to her tonight.

The path had a blind spot, but before he could call out a warning came the unmistakable sound of a rifle being cocked. He jerked his gaze up to find Peltz on the high ground, weapon trained on Falco and the woman he carried.

"No one moves," the dust pirate ordered. "Or they both die."

Rosa obeyed, but Chris saw how she calculated the distance and angle, the likely speed of her enemy's reaction time versus the wind speed. And he saw her conclude that someone *would* die before she could get her weapon up. *Damn it. We were so close.*

"What do you want, Peltz?"

"Safe passage, of course."

"You fucking coward," Rosa spat out. "You ran when your weapon emptied, abandoning your men. What kind of leader are you?"

"One who'll see the next morning, if you care about your people as much as you claim. I know you don't want to watch this pretty thing die tonight. Hasn't she suffered enough?"

In response, Maryann whimpered and turned her face against Falco's shoulder. Chris noticed how the bravo's fingers flexed at his side; like Rosa, he was wondering if he could get a shot off before taking one in the face. He stilled, evidently realizing that the woman would be caught in the crossfire. Even as he died, Peltz could still nail her, curved as she was across Falco's chest.

Rosa let out a slow, agonized breath. "Don't hurt her. I'm listening."

The raider boss nodded, as if he'd expected them to cave to his demands. Chris wished he could shift instantly. He'd love to disembowel this son of a bitch.

"I can do the math. My men are gone, and the minute I take a shot, I'm a dead man." Peltz lowered his rifle a fraction. "But we have supplies buried all over. See, we put by a little something at each new campsite. We can make a deal, if you're willing to do business."

The need for ammo had been foremost on Rosa's mind for months, but her face remained stony. Chris couldn't imagine two more different leaders. There was no way she'd go for this. Not in a million years.

"What do you say, *Jefa*? Do we have a deal?"

As she pretended to consider, no doubt stalling, Falco spun, swinging Maryann away from danger. Peltz's rifle sparked at the same time as Falco's Colt. The scumbag toppled from the ridge, slamming onto the rocks below while the bravo dropped his pistol and clung to the rock wall, trying to break his own fall. Somehow he still tucked Maryann safely against his side.

"Falco!" Rosa raced to him, where he bled from his mouth and from a massive hole in his back. "*Dios*, he's bad."

Singer pushed past, urging the women to move. "Rosa, we're getting the truck. I'll bring it as close as I can."

Chris knelt, stripping Falco's shirt, and covered the wound with wadded cloth. Blood spilled out like a fountain, staining the fabric. "I don't know what else I can do."

In truth, it was a kill shot, severing his spine. The bullet was probably lodged in one of his internal organs. Even before the Change, it would have taken a blood transfusion and hours in surgery—and he still might not walk again. Now, Chris could only try to make him comfortable.

Rosa choked on a sob. "Don't die. We just figured things out, you and me."

Above them, the horn blared, skidding to a stop some twenty meters away on the ridge above. With help from the uninjured women, bravos loaded their stolen provisions into the back of the truck. They hadn't found all of the caches yet, but there would be time for exploration. He and Ex could check things out, once this hellish night ended. Chris watched the movement, one hand still applying pressure to Falco's wound. Everyone fit inside, with a sickening amount of room to spare. They'd lost so many.

At Singer's orders, Rio jogged over to help get Falco up

to the truck. Chris and Rio made a chair of their arms and carried the man as best they could. Falco bore the motion with gritted teeth, though it had to be agonizing. As they reached the vehicle, a wolverine, its muzzle coated with the scarlet of his kills, emerged from the shadows.

With Rio's help, Chris settled Falco into the passenger seat.

"Mount up," Rosa called.

Ex shifted. Chris tried not to stare, but it never lost that unnerving quality, even though he'd lived through the process. Then he was looking at a naked man, who had a slash in his shoulder. The wound had already scabbed over. Chris remembered Jenna's uncanny healing powers after she'd first shifted and wondered if that useful trait applied to all skinwalkers. He'd like that to be true, if only for the sake of his own singed back.

"You with us, man?"

Ex grunted. "Where's Allison?"

His woman called his name and ran to him, still wielding a machete she must have grabbed off a raider. They hugged, and Chris leaned in to check on Falco, fingers against his wrist. *Pulse thready. This is* not *good.*

"I don't mean to impose," Ex said, "but I could use some pants."

Chris handed him the backpack, urgency firing in his veins. "We gotta move."

Rosa leaned out from the cab, where she sat with one arm supporting Falco, the other on his wound. "Ex, can you ride?"

"Sure thing."

"Circle the camp. Kill anybody still moving, then come home."

Home, Chris thought. *Soon.*

His gaze sharp on every night shadow, Chris put his hands on the rear lift. "Someone find me a lantern. Anything. I'll need it for Falco as soon as we're back in Valle. And I want to know injuries, so look yourselves over and assess the worst." He shut the lift and raced to the driver's seat. "Everyone hold on! We're going!"

The pickup surged into motion. He fought the steering wheel across every bump, every pit, every rough desert bush.

"He's dying," Rosa whispered.

Chris gunned the engine. The headlamps did little to combat the pitch-black emptiness. Only his animal sense of direction told him where to go. They were halfway back to Valle when Falco seized, his whole body trembling.

"I'm stopping," Chris said.

Brakes squealed as he fought to slow down, conscious of the men in back. The vehicle bucked like a wild horse, and Chris's chest slammed into the steering wheel. He groaned. But adrenaline still burned, keeping him moving. One of the women handed him a pocket flashlight before he even asked.

"Falco," he said, circling the light. Though he'd once been a rival and a pain in the ass, now he was a bravo on the brink of death. Light didn't matter. There was nothing he could do.

Falco's eyes closed. "Shut up, *hombre*. Rosa was singing to me."

Easing back toward the driver's side, Rosa cradled the bravo's head in her lap. "Falco, look at me, damn it."

She wept, tears streaming, her face beatific. She smoothed Falco's hair while singing a low Spanish lullaby. Deciding to give them some privacy, Chris opened the driver's side door, but she clasped his hand, keeping him nearby.

"Stay." Her expression said she didn't want to do this alone.

The fallen bravo's breath came in shallow rasps that carried a watery gurgle. He gazed up into Rosa's face as she whispered an unfamiliar prayer. Chris saw that, whatever his faults, Falco had loved her. He'd loved Valle too, never pushing the fragile town past its breaking point. He'd backed down rather than fragment what they'd built, and he'd kept his word when he promised no more trouble.

Falco gazed over Rosa's shoulder, his blue eyes filming with gray. "Take care of her, Doc."

Through her tears, Rosa smiled. "We'll take care of each other. Keep a light on for us, *mano*. We'll see you again someday."

"Count on it." And he closed his eyes forever.

FORTY-ONE

By the time Valle came into view, fingers of light plucked at the far horizon. They crept over the mountains with seeming reluctance, as if the sun shouldn't shine on this night's work. Rosa felt the same way. She drove the truck, giving her hands and her mind something to do.

Yet, despite their losses, gratitude shimmered in her veins. She'd survived. So had Cristián.

Exhaustion weighed on the faces of those spilling out of the pickup. Some were injured, others spattered with the enemy's blood. Everyone was filthy. No surprises there. But Rosa hadn't expected to find a young raider crawling out of the back. In the confusion and darkness he must have slipped in, but she wondered why the hell he'd waited so long to act.

Rosa drew her weapon and pinned him with a look. "What are you doing?"

"Don't," Singer said, stepping between them. "He saved me. Helped me unlock the chains."

"So you brought him with us?"

"He's not like the others. When his dad died, he didn't know where to go, and he ran into one of their patrols—"

"*Sí, pobrecito*, he has a sad story. I get it."

If one of their own could turn traitor, then maybe a dust pirate could become a man of honor. The world she'd known, where all skinwalkers were the enemy, had ended. Time to build something new.

She turned to the young raider. "What's your name?"

"Kyle."

"Well, Kyle, we have rules here. Women are treated with respect. There's no fighting or stealing. And *everyone* works. Can you live like that?"

"It sounds like heaven," he said quietly.

So young. A boy saved from the darkness.

"*Bueno.* Singer, you get him settled."

Rio, she noticed, looked none too pleased, but the kids could sort it out.

Though Rosa's eyes burned with exhaustion, much work remained. Falco went, like Manuel, with a quiet ceremony on the edge of town. They hadn't been able to recover all of the fallen, so they honored him in their stead.

The numbers between men and women were now far more equal. That too would be different. She needed to find someone to take over the *taberna* and the general store. Such concerns could wait until they restored order.

The day dragged, and Rosa didn't see much of Chris as he tended the wounded. After bathing, she caught a few hours of sleep in the hottest part of the day. Then she called the survivors, battered but better for the rest.

Once they assembled in the *taberna*, she climbed up onto a table. "This is the biggest victory we've ever known. Our territory is free from fear. We can rebuild and prosper, as we deserve. I think it fitting we celebrate with a proper Burning Night. Our lost ones would appreciate a celebration in their honor."

Ragged cheers followed her announcement. Though tired and grieving, her people counted their blessings and rejoiced in their lives. That was Valle.

Allison sought her out afterward. "What can I do to help?"

"Can you cook?"

"Well enough."

"Would you consider taking Viv's place in the *taberna*?"

Allison gave a soft little sigh. "It would feel good to have a purpose again."

Ex smiled, quiet pride suffusing his features, and Allison beckoned to Maryann, whom everyone had judged broken beyond all mending. The woman pushed to her feet and nodded her agreement.

Rosa stayed her with a gesture. "Are you sure you're up to it?"

"Falco wanted me to survive," Maryann answered fiercely. "He granted me this chance. I won't waste it . . . or shame him by cowering."

He would like this, Rosa thought. *Being the hero who gave the girl a reason to live.*

Hours later, at sundown, the lamps were lit and the stars came out. They devoured the usual refreshments, plenty of agave wine. The new boy, Kyle, showed some skill on the shopkeeper's fiddle. His father had played, he said with a sad smile. Rosa enjoyed the music, even as she mourned Wicker.

The citizens of Valle filled the plaza, where a modest bonfire lit the sky—so unlike the terror of her town set alight. The mood was restrained at first because the loss remained fresh. But soon the melody got to them, as did the wine. Jolene sat beside Brick where he lay on a makeshift pallet, his chest still bound. She tapped her feet, and when other bravos requested her company, she simply smiled and shook her head. Singer only had eyes for Rio, apparently having convinced him Kyle wasn't a threat.

For long moments Rosa merely watched: Tilly with Jameson and their baby, Ex with Allison. Others paired off for the night, though some of the women, like Maryann, sat stiffly near the warming bonfire while enjoying the music. It was enough. It was a start.

Things weren't the same, of course. There weren't enough bravos to assemble as they'd once done, dancing with the hope of attracting a female for the night. But customs could change. Valle would adapt and become stronger for it.

If Falco were there, he would have tried to drag her into the revelries. But he was gone, and the man she wanted hadn't yet put in an appearance. For all she knew, Chris might be sleeping; she had no idea if he'd also snatched a siesta. With a half shrug at her thoughts, she took the food and drink tray from Singer and offered it around. The girl had no cause to be serving drinks when Rio waited for her to dance. Brick glowered a little because everyone knew what it meant, but the girl was old enough to make her own choices. The young couple kissed softly, tenderly, with Rio's hands on her waist. Rosa's heart surged at another beginning.

Tonight, Valle had hope for the future, and it sparkled like pyrite.

She felt someone's gaze, her skin tingling with heat. Even before she turned, she knew. Cristián stood silhouetted in the darkness. That was all she needed to make the night perfect.

Mi corazón, she mouthed.

Quite deliberately, she set down her tray. *Let people serve themselves.* As the music played, she undulated her hips with sensuous intent, arms up, back arched. Up and down, that slow, suggestive shimmy drew him. He showed no hesitation. Cutting through the revelers, his face colored by twisting flames and night shadows, he took his place with her. As it should be. Rosa danced for him, only him, her body telling him everything she had yet to say in words.

He pulled her close, a flattering tremor to his hands. "You're dancing with me."

He'd once complained that she would do so with anyone except him, but from that night forward, all of her dances belonged to Cristián. She smiled up at him, heart in her eyes.

"It means I plan to take you home with me, *amorcito*."

"When?"

"When we're done dancing."

His hands splayed across her hips, pressing her closer still, so hard and hot against her stomach. "I'm ready now."

"So I see." She wrapped her arms around his neck as the music slowed.

"Are you *teasing* me? After everything you've put me through?"

"Do you feel teased?"

"God, yes."

"I don't think that's entirely a bad thing."

Rosa made him dance through five songs. Each one jacked the tension between them to a new level. Each movement, each caress, each sway of her hips and brush of her breasts drove him mad. She glimpsed the feral part of him snarling in his animal gaze, and he lowered his head to nuzzle her neck.

"Espera, por favor."

He lifted his face from her throat, seeming dazed. "What?"

Rosa knew she could only push him so far. That limit was very close. But with a smile, she slipped out of his arms. "I'll be back. Don't go anywhere."

"You're not leaving me for Valle business—" he began, but she darted away before he could finish the objection.

This surprise would be worth the wait. She went at a run, taking less care than usual on the rocky paths, and prayed it wasn't too late. Out of breath, she approached the cave.

The woman, Colleen, came out to meet her, with the rest of the family at her back. She cocked a weapon. "What do you want now? We've stayed away from town."

"I know, and I'm so sorry for the way I treated you. I'm issuing an invitation to live in Valle, if you want it." In the face of the family's still blankness, Rosa couldn't read how they received her words. She stumbled on, both because it was right and because it would be a tangible gesture of remorse for Cristián. "There's a party tonight . . . because we ended the raider threat. And I want you to know you're welcome with us. No tests."

"A party?" the little girl asked.

Rosa's heart twisted. Cristián had been right. This was a child, one who'd never known such simple pleasures. Her clearest memories would be full of pain, no sense of belonging or community—except what came from her family.

"There's food and music," her father answered roughly. "Dancing."

"Will you come? We have houses." Sudden inspiration made her add, "And we need someone to run the store. Take inventory, keep track of supplies. Does that interest you at all?"

"It does," Colleen said slowly, as if she couldn't credit the change of heart.

"Thank you," Joseph said. Though the kid hadn't lost his wary edge, he was almost smiling now.

Jacob nodded, apparently making a decision. "Let us pack our things."

She waited, knowing Chris had to be out of his mind with impatience. Half an hour later, she led them back along the rocky path to the lights of Valle. Her Cristián had waited for her. He perched with sizzling impatience on the railing outside the *taberna*, where cowboys might once have tethered horses. Catching sight of the new arrivals, he strode toward her with a gradually burgeoning smile that started in his sharp eyes and spread to his mouth.

"*This* was your business?"

"They should be here," she said. "They need a home."

It took time to show them to their new house. Then they returned to the outdoor celebration so Connie could enjoy the fun as any girl deserved. Both children's faces reflected such sweet wonder. Jacob led his wife into the dance.

Chris took Rosa's hand and pressed a kiss to her palm. "Tell me we can go home now."

"There is nothing I want more," she said as they strolled,

hand in hand, toward her casita. "You understand why I did this?"

"To show me you've really changed."

"*Sí*. In heart and mind. If you will forgive me, *mi corazón*, then I am yours."

"You're everything I ever wanted. I just don't think I knew it."

In a movement so fast he surprised her, Cristián swept her into his arms and jogged the remaining distance. Instead of fighting as she might once have done, she twined her arms about his neck and let him prove his strength.

Once wrapped in the privacy of Rosa's bedroom, he tore at her blouse, shaking with need. But she felt it too, this soul-deep passion. She reached for him in turn, desperate to have his skin against hers. The time for teasing was done, as was the time for foreplay. The dancing had stirred her as much as him, but she needed his kisses. He'd taught her to like them, to crave the dark, hot feel of his tongue sliding into her mouth.

"*Mi amor*, I am yours."

The words spurred him into a growling kiss, his lips slanting over hers with delicious heat. His tongue stroked, and Rosa rocked against him. He pulled his thigh up, adding pressure. *Ay, Dios, sí*. Sucking and biting with tender nips, he put his mark on the side of her throat. She arched for him, wanting it, wanting to be his.

He was rougher than he'd ever been, but she had no fear. Her arousal spiked, fierce and desperate. Even the little bites on her throat felt divine. Nothing but love and desire here.

Rosa shifted, wrapping a calf around his hip. Chris groaned. He plunged his tongue in and out of her mouth, and she tasted sweet agave wine. His shirt was long gone, but his jeans took moments to remove because they both were so unwilling to stop kissing. The shocking delight of coming skin to skin stole her breath.

She cupped his ass in her hands to draw him toward the bed. He needed no urging.

"Want you," he growled.

She fell back under his tender onslaught. When he came up over her this time, she didn't freeze. There was only Cristián above her, burning and beautiful. He shaped her breasts with reverent hands. His mouth was hot and hungry as he sucked one rosy tip into his mouth. Her hands cradling his head, Rosa cried out and arched her hips, urging him closer.

His lips, his teeth, his tongue were everywhere, first at her breasts, then her belly and thighs, nibbling until she could only close her eyes. With anyone else, she would have feared the beast she'd roused, but there was no fright—only a hunger that matched the leopard in him. If he devoured her, so be it.

Growling a little, he nuzzled his way down her body, pressing kisses against her hot skin. He pushed his face between her thighs. His tongue lashed her clitoris. Circled. Skated away to tease her thighs. Rosa writhed, willing to give him *anything*. She sank her hands into his hair.

"Tell me you like it."

"I love it," she gasped. *"Ay, sí."*

He slid a finger inside, hooking it to provide the most pleasure. She came for him in long, tense waves. As she lay replete and he glided up her body, she wrapped her arms around him, legs about his hips. No fear. No memories. Only silken welcome and wholehearted trust for Cristián.

"Please," she whispered.

"Mine." His voice sounded so guttural she hardly recognized it.

Siempre. Always. She sang the words into his ear, threading through his hair.

With a groan of satisfaction, he drove inside. She gloried in his length and his heat, the rich fusion of his weight and steady thrusts, the wicked slide of his body deep inside her. She matched his thrusts with equal vigor, exulting in their primal sounds.

His beautiful eyes opened, all reason gone. Cristián gathered her to him, hammering them together with a rhythm desperate and fierce.

"Rosa," he whispered, his voice awed.

She kissed him, working his hips to drive the pleasure. At first she didn't think she could come again, but, despite his obvious need, he kept pushing her higher until she broke open and screamed. Her hands dug into his back. He pushed deep and held there, with long pulses as he poured into her.

In the quiet aftermath, she whispered, "I love you. You are my heart, my conscience, and my courage."

Exhausted, he cuddled her against his chest. "Love you."

She listened to his heart, proof that this was real. That she'd arrived—at great cost—to her own happy ending. Rosa had no memory of sleeping, but she must have done. And she woke to find him still in her bed.

It will be like this forever. He loves me, no matter what I've been or what I do. The surety of that love humbled her.

Hunger stirred, so she went to fix some food, careful not to wake him. When she returned with the bread and cheese, she found him propped on one elbow, the sheet teasing her with glimpses of his tanned, taut abdomen. The words were inevitable, for she recognized this moment, this long-ago dream. It felt to her like a promise kept.

"You are so beautiful," Rosa said, and déjà vu hit hard.

Like a golden cat, he sprawled on her sisal mattress, her handwoven blanket covering one lean hip. His belly made her want to trace each ripped muscle with her tongue. God, he was gorgeous. He had the scruffy wildness of a man who knew how to take care of himself.

She started toward him with a sultry smile. After all, she knew what came next, and it was magnificent.

EPILOGUE

The sun was warm on his back, the flinty soil hot against the pads of his paws. Chris trotted across a never-ending expanse. His thoughts and his animal body worked in concert now. He remembered who he was, where he belonged, and he returned unerringly with a fresh kill in his jaws. Though he loved Valle, it was Rosa to whom he returned, time and again. Real leopards might not mate for life, but he wasn't wholly feline, and she held his heart. Forever.

Town life always startled him after the strong silence of the desert. A hammer in Ex's forge rang out against metal, strike after strike. Singing from Tilly's little kitchenette. Haggling and the chatter of children in the general store.

Chris reacquainted himself with these sounds, slowly emerging from his solitary frame of mind.

He padded over to the tavern. After nudging the door open, he passed the tables and chairs where bravos sat playing cards or having a quiet drink. The sun was setting, which meant these same men would be on patrol shortly. The pattern of their lives had become good and steady again.

They greeted him with affectionate nicknames no one

dared use when he was human. Their fear had receded, their suspicion too. He stalked past to where Allison and Maryann worked. Maryann, so quiet and reserved, scratched him between the ears, then retrieved the two dead quail from his jaws.

His duty discharged, he moved into the back pantry, where he and the other skinwalkers kept spare clothes and toothbrushes. Shifting was no more pleasant than it had been months earlier, but he knew better how to ride the waves of pain. Fresh game had been a scarcity in Valle. He, Ex, and Jacob changed all that. So he weathered brief agony for the luxury of meat.

Dressed again, his mouth rinsed, he grabbed a hunk of buttered bread. Maryann always had one ready after he hunted, knowing how famished he and the others were following a shift. She never showed a scrap of fear around them, whether in human or animal form. Perhaps that was because, out of all the men in Valle, the three skinwalkers were among the most prominently spoken for.

"Thanks, sweetheart," he said, dropping a kiss on the back of her hand.

She blushed and, per usual, didn't say a word. She just smiled and went back to preparing the evening meal, Allison singing softly beside her.

Chris slipped out the back door and inhaled. Rosa was nearby. Her body chemistry had altered slightly, but she was still unmistakable. His respiration picking up speed, he rounded the corner and pulled up short.

Rosa stood in the open front gate, which had been repaired with materials from the fire-ravaged buildings and salvaged semis. Jameson and another bravo flanked her up on the wall, but she stood alone. The sundress Singer had made molded against her rounded belly when the wind kicked up. She raised a hand to her brow as shade. A smile shaped her mouth.

Like all the other dreams, this one had come true too.

Thighs tingling and slightly numb, he joined her at the gate. Silently she folded into his arms, welcoming him with an openmouthed kiss. She was soft, strong, always able to turn him on with the slightest nudge. But this wasn't a nudge. This was Rosa, and she wanted him.

"Well, hello to you too," he said.

"Anything good?"

"Quail."

"Now there's a good boy." She teased him by scratching behind his ear.

He flinched away, laughing, then noticed figures in the distance. "Hey, is that Beatrice? Walking away?"

Rosa sobered a little. She nodded. "And Hector and Louie too. I guess they figured two-to-one odds were better going with her."

"Sure, but . . . she's leaving?"

"She confided that she'd been on her way to someplace in the Everglades when flesh traders picked her up. Now she's healthy again and ready to move on."

"The Everglades? Did you ask why?"

"You know I wouldn't," she said with an indulgent look.

"You're better at that than I am." He touched her lips, tracing that soft fullness with his thumb. "Then why were you smiling? Valle just lost three citizens."

"We saved her life. We helped her heal. Then we gave her what Peltz never did—a choice. I'm proud of that."

"As you should be." He pulled her against his chest, indulging in the sweet, warm comfort of her body, firm along his. "All of this, Rosa. You made your territory into something wonderful."

She looked up at him. "*Our* territory."

Such amazing eyes, dark with mystery but more expressive now. They shone with a love that humbled and inspired him.

"No, that's where I beg to differ. This is yours." He waved a hand at Valle, at the expanse of desert beyond. The homes, the lives, the hope in this foreboding place—they owed their existence to the determination of one woman. Then he settled his wide palm over her womb, where his child grew. "This is the only territory I claim," he said against her temple. "You and this baby of ours. I don't want anything else."

With a laugh, she nuzzled his neck. "Good thing I have bigger ambitions for her."

Chris stilled. The thump of his heartbeat faltered. *"Her?"*

"You haven't dreamed of her yet?"

He swallowed. *Sweet Jesus, a little girl.* He'd never even imagined being a father, not once in the long years before Rosa, but she made it a beautiful privilege.

"No," he said then. "No, I haven't."

"Ah, you will. Or you can wait to meet her." Rosa smiled even as a shimmer of moisture brightened her eyes. "Either way, *amorcito*, you won't be disappointed."

He exhaled. The prospect was still too much to face head-on. He had another few months to get past these jitters.

Rosa seemed to read that in him, returning her hands and her mouth to more overtly sexual pursuits. She kissed his jaw, his chin, and up to his mouth. Feather-light fingers tickled down his ribs until she found the waistband of his jeans. She gave a suggestive tug.

He grinned. "Lately my dreams have had a one-track mind."

"So no different than your waking mind."

"No different at all."

"Then take me to bed, Cristián."

He glanced around. The town pulsed with the regular activity of a day winding down toward night. There was the changing of the guard to come, and dinner to be served, and night patrols to supervise.

In other words, there was all of Valle to run.

But Rosa's hands became more eager. She threaded her fingers into the tight curl of hair at his nape. Chris's blood fired to life. His heart beat with the thrill of yet another hunt, this time for pleasure. It was a talent they were so damn good at sharing.

From up on one of the gate's watch posts, Jameson cleared his throat. "Get a room, you two. I don't get to go home for another hour."

"I think that's a good idea," Chris whispered against her lips. "Don't you?"

"Absolutely. Valle will be here in the morning."

"That it will."

She tilted her head, thoughtful. "Bee predicted all of it, you know. 'Valle burns. The world is born again in fire.' I wish we could get her to tell us what else is to come."

"We've seen enough, I think."

Chris put his arm around her shoulders. The pride of that moment hit hard against his heart. His woman was strong, strong enough that she could let go. She trusted. She shared the burdens. With one hand cradling the shape of their unborn child, she walked through the town she'd wrested from nothing.

More miraculous, she'd pulled him out of the wilderness and made Valle his home too—a home he would never need to leave, a home he'd always fight to protect. For the first time in his life, his love and his work came together in a single satisfying passion.

"I love you, Rosita."

She led him into the casita they shared. "Come show me how much."

Chris closed the door behind them, happy as he never would have dreamed possible at the start of this Dark Age, but with Rosa in his bed, midnight was the sweetest hour of all.